Ari was all business, getting the two passengers in and settled. Then he came up out of the lifeboat and spied Ming's pistol. "What's that for, Doll?"

"Long story. Anybody missing?"

"No, we're as good as we're gonna get. Come on!"

Angel reached the hatch, looked in, then turned and frowned. "Where's Tann Nakitt?"

"Long story," he responded, bringing up his own pistol and firing on Angel. Her body was bathed in a sudden glow, and then she collapsed, unconscious, to the deck.

The action was so automatic it caught Ming by surprise, but she brought her pistol around on her old friend immediately. That was the problem—he *was* an old friend, and onetime lover. You don't pull the trigger that fast on somebody like him when your pistol is set to kill.

That allowed two stun blasts from the Wallinchky women behind her to strike her and knock her as instantly out-to-the-world as Angel.

Ari looked down at them. "Take them to the lounge. Any barriers, start shooting up the electrical plates. *Move!*"

By Jack L. Chalker
Published by Ballantine Books:

AND THE DEVIL WILL DRAG YOU UNDER
DANCE BAND ON THE *TITANIC*
DANCERS IN THE AFTERGLOW
A JUNGLE OF STARS
THE WEB OF THE CHOZEN

THE SAGA OF THE WELL WORLD
Volume 1: *Midnight at the Well of Souls*
Volume 2: *Exiles at the Well of Souls*
Volume 3: *Quest for the Well of Souls*
Volume 4: *The Return of Nathan Brazil*
Volume 5: *Twilight at the Well of Souls:*
                  The Legacy of Nathan Brazil
Volume 6: *The Sea Is Full of Stars*

THE FOUR LORDS OF THE DIAMOND
Book One: *Lilith: A Snake in the Grass*
Book Two: *Cerberus: A Wolf in the Fold*
Book Three: *Charon: A Dragon at the Gate*
Book Four: *Medusa: A Tiger by the Tail*

THE DANCING GODS
Book One: *The River of Dancing Gods*
Book Two: *Demons of the Dancing Gods*
Book Three: *Vengeance of the Dancing Gods*
Book Four: *Songs of the Dancing Gods*
Book Five: *Horrors of the Dancing Gods*

THE RINGS OF THE MASTER
Book One: *Lords of the Middle Dark*
Book Two: *Pirates of the Thunder*
Book Three: *Warriors of the Storm*
Book Four: *Masks of the Martyrs*

THE WATCHERS AT THE WELL
Book One: *Echoes of the Well of Souls*
Book Two: *Shadow of the Well of Souls*
Book Three: *Gods of the Well of Souls*

THE WONDERLAND GAMBIT
Book One: The Cybernetic Walrus
Book Two: The March Hare Network
Book Three: The Hot-Wired Dodo

THE SEA
IS FULL
OF STARS

Jack L. Chalker

A Del Rey® Book
THE BALLANTINE PUBLISHING GROUP • NEW YORK

A Del Rey® Book
Published by The Ballantine Publishing Group
Copyright © 1999 by Jack L. Chalker

All rights reserved under International and Pan-American Copyright Conventions. Published in the United States by The Ballantine Publishing Group, a division of Random House, Inc., New York, and simultaneously in Canada by Random House of Canada Limited, Toronto.

Del Rey is a registered trademark and the Del Rey colophon is a trademark of Random House, Inc.

www.randomhouse.com/delrey/

ISBN 0-345-39486-0

Manufactured in the United States of America

First Edition: November 1999

10 9 8 7 6 5 4 3 2

This has to be for Marg and Joe Brazil
and their son, Nathan,
who didn't know about me until *after* they named him,
but who prove that all those folks
who said years ago that "Nathan Brazil" was
such an implausible name.

Now we know that Nathan Brazil is a Canadian.

That's a fact. A *Canadian* fact.

Sorry Nathan's not in the book, but . . .

Now, then, any Mavra Changs out there?

Foreword: Slightly Different

IN 1976, I WROTE A BOOK CALLED *MIDNIGHT AT THE WELL OF Souls*, (which Del Rey books published in mass market paperback.) The book seems to have struck a near universal chord; it has sold an incredible number of copies in North America and continues to do so; it was a Penguin book in the U.K. and Commonwealth, and it has since been sold to twenty-seven nations and has appeared in German, Hebrew, Italian, Russian—well, *lots* of languages.

Being poor and just starting out in the business, I was suddenly faced with my second novel being a kind of best-seller for the new line, and thus I was urged to do a sequel. I hadn't really thought about it, but they were offering a *lot* of money for me at the time (about the equivalent of what I'm being paid for a small nation reprint these days, but I was poor then), and I had a vast canvas and I was also able to write and sell other books, including nonseries ones, so I proceeded, introducing Mavra Chang and creating what became a five book saga. Then I stopped, and did other things, and had no plans to return in spite of entreaties by readers and publisher alike to do so.

Then, ten years later, I got an offer I couldn't refuse at a time when I was riding high, and I discovered that it was kind of fun to revisit after all that time. Thus the three volume *Watchers at the Well* set arrived, and was very well received, including by a lot of folks who never even suspected that prior books existed.

When I went back to the Well, so to speak, I wanted to do something different. For one thing, I wanted to visit some of the underwater hexes. I also wanted to return to the Northern Hemisphere with its bizarrely different creations.

Unfortunately, the plot and the requirements that my two principal characters remain "human" really killed the deal. To divert them would be to lengthen an already long book.

If I were to do that, then I'd have to create a book that had no previous characters in it and was not, strictly speaking, directly part of the Canon.

Nathan and Mavra are not here. Do not look for them. They are not hiding, they will not show up in the end. In fact, much of the book takes place to the *east* of the eastern edge of that skimpy map, which, as anyone who noted that there are 1560 hexes on the Well World knows, shows barely a quarter of the surface of the Well World. Our creatures are new, our landscapes are new, and our characters are new. The Well, of course, remains.

Originally I was going to do two different books, which gave me the idea to call the set *Tales of the Well World*. It didn't work out that way, and wound up being a two volume saga on its own. It is not really about the Well World, although it's kind of fun to imagine what the Well might make *you*. It's about Something Else, as you will discover.

This book will take you first to a whole new interstellar civilization, and from that point to the Well, but, again, with things going very wrong. Why aren't Nathan and Mavra called? Well, you decide for now. Maybe I'll tell you before this two-book, rather different adventure is done.

These are the last two Well World books for which I have any sort of notes or outline, so it is hard to say if this is the last or the latest Well World saga. You, to a large extent, will determine the answer, although I have other work to do. This one came out darker but more interesting than any of the others, and I'm content with it. I hope you will like it, too.

In the meantime, visit me anytime at http://people. delphi.com/jchalker/, and check on the sometimes active Well World newsgroup alt.fan.nathan.brazil.

Jack L. Chalker
Uniontown, Maryland U.S.A.
November 18, 1996

Asswam Junction,
Near the Crab Nebula

MONSTERS ARE NOT ALWAYS SO EASY TO SPOT, AND WHEN they walk among you they often do so with a smile, and when they become what they are underneath the glare, you don't really know what's happened. And when a monster has friends and followers and sometimes even worshipers, it can become far more than a single dark blot of evil on the fabric of time; then it has the capacity to suddenly rear off and carry even the most innocent straight to Hell, or to do even worse and take your own existence and extend Hell to that as well. This is a story of monsters and maidens and the walking dead. The fact that it begins on a starship only drives home the point . . .

He had the smell of death and the look of the grave in him. Everyone could sense it, almost as if he were somehow broadcasting the cold chill that those of any race who encountered him instantly felt.

He'd been handsome once, but long ago. Now his face was badly weathered, wrinkled, and pockmarked, and there was a scar on one cheek that didn't look to be the result of a slip in some friendly fencing match. His eyes were deep, sunken, cold, and empty, his hair thick but silver, worn long and looking something like a mane.

It was eerie when he walked past the small group of passengers in the waiting lounge; they were of perhaps a half-dozen races, some inscrutable to others and tending to hold far different views of the universe and all that was in it, yet when he passed, every one of them reacted, some turning to look, some turning away, and some edging back as if the mere touch of his garment would bring instant death.

A Rithian watched him walk down the hall toward the

vendor hall, its snakelike head and burning orange eyes
almost hypnotized by the figure now going farther away. "I
had not believed that he could draw so much more of the
nether regions than he already had long ago," it muttered,
almost to itself.

The Terran woman shook off a final chill, turned and
looked at the creature who'd made the comment. "You know
him?" she asked.

"I *knew* him," the Rithian answered, finally bringing its
face back down to normal by distending its long serpentine
neck and looking over at the woman instead. "At least, I
have seen him before, long ago, and I know who he is. I am
surprised that you do not, he being of your kind. He is certainly a legend, and, someday, he will be a part of your
mythology I suspect. I hope he is not on our liner."

She shook her head, trying to get a grip on herself. "I—I
don't think I ever felt anyone so—so *evil*." She actually
started to say "inhuman" but realized how inappropriate that
would be in present company.

"Evil? Perhaps. It is impossible to know what he has
become inside, and to what he's sold his soul. But he is not
precisely evil. In fact, he seeks an evil, and until he finds it
and faces it and either kills it or it kills him, he cannot rest
or ever find peace. He is Jeremiah Wong Kincaid. Does that
name mean nothing to you?"

She thought hard. "Should it?"

"Then what about the scouring of Magan Thune?"

It was history to her, ancient history from the time of her
parents at least, and thus the kind of thing you didn't tend to
dwell on later in life unless you liked to wallow in the sick
and violent history of humanity. She only vaguely recalled it
even now. "Something about igniting the atmosphere of a
planet, wasn't it? So long ago . . ."

"The atmosphere of a planet with six billion souls upon
it, yes. Six billion souls who had been infected with a most
horrible parasite by a megalomaniac would-be conqueror of
the Realm, Josich the Emperor Hadun. A Ghoma, you might
recall. A creature of the water, really. He'd found a way, the
only known way, to conquer whole worlds composed of
various races alien to him, and to even control environments
he could not himself exist in without an environment suit.

Tiny little quasiorganic machines, like viruses, transmitted like viruses as well, who could remake and tailor themselves for any bioorganism, any place, anywhere, and turn whole populations into slaves. There was no way to cure them; the things were more communicable than air and water. Isolate them, and they killed the hosts, horribly. Let them go, and a whole planet would be devoted to infecting everyone and everything else. It was the greatest horror our common histories ever produced."

She shivered, remembering now why she'd not liked that kind of history. "And this Kincaid—he was a part of this?"

"A liner was intercepted and boarded. Everyone on it was infected. It was only because of security systems that it only reached Magan Thune before being discovered and dealt with. There are such horrible distances in space for even messages and warnings to cover, and you cannot station naval ships with great firepower at every one. We—all our races—breed a bit too much for *that*. Kincaid was commander of a small frigate, an escort naval vessel used in frontier areas. He'd come to the sector to meet his mate and children, and have some leave on some resort world. He wasn't supposed to come to Magan Thune at all, but went to check when the liner was late making its next port of call."

She was suddenly appalled. "He was the one who ignited the atmosphere?"

"No. He was spared that. Much too junior for such a thing. That took a task force. All he could do, upon discovering what was taking place, was to deal with any spacefaring craft, to ensure none got away. That, of course, included the liner . . ."

She sat down, not wanting to think about it anymore but forced to do so anyway by the sheer magnitude of the tragedy the Rithian was relating and the knowledge that it was true.

He'd had to wipe out his whole family. Almost certainly he'd done more than give the order. He would have been human; he couldn't have allowed anyone else to do it for him while he watched.

"Only months after, they figured out how it all worked," the Rithian continued. "They discovered the shifting band of frequencies by which the things communicated with each other, with others in other bodies, and with the command. Block them, work out the basics of what had to be a fairly simple code to be so universal and require so little bandwidth, and then order them to turn themselves off after restoring normalcy to their hosts. There were recriminations, trials, insistence on affixing blame. Nobody blows up a liner, let alone a planet, without the highest orders, but the public wanted heads. They second-guessed from screeching journalism, demanded to know why containment wasn't an option, and so on. Never mind that one major industry of Magan Thune was the construction of deep space engines. That's why the Conqueror had wanted it. And a hundred planets within days of there with possibly half a trillion souls."

She tried to put the vision out of her mind. Thank God she never had to make those kind of choices! "And he's been like that ever since?"

"That and more."

"I'm not sure I wouldn't have killed myself after that," she mused.

"He might have," the Rithian responded, "and some say he all but did anyway. You saw him, *felt* him, as did I, and I do not believe we have a great deal physiologically in common, and perhaps culturally even less. There are things that are universal. But he will not die. He will not permit himself to die. I believe he has been through a rejuve or two. He has unfinished business. He cannot leave until it is completed."

"Huh? What—What kind of business could he still have?"

"They never caught Josich the Emperor Hadun, you know. He is deposed for a great amount of time, and some say he is dead, although if Kincaid is not dead, then neither is Josich. One will not go without the other. Many say instead that Josich has become the emperor of the criminal underground, and that he is the source of much of the evil on countless worlds even now. Sixty years and Kincaid still hunts. That is why I hope he is not going on the same ship as we. If Kincaid could but guarantee the death of Josich, he would willingly take all of us with him. I would prefer he walk a different path than myself."

But Kincaid was already returning to the departure lounge, and it was clear this was going to be an interesting trip.

* * *

The tale of the haunted man involved what the Rithian had called a "liner," but even in those days that designation was for the rich and powerful only. Transport, then and now, was more complex than that for most travelers, and even now it was someone very rare who'd been off his or her own native world, and even fewer who had ever left their solar system. Travel was expensive, often long, and, in most people's cases, unnecessary. And with more than forty races in the Realm and perhaps two dozen others that interacted with it, it wasn't all that easy to support them in ecofriendly quarters for the weeks or months a trip might involve. Even with such as the Rithians and Terrans, who comfortably breathed each other's air and could in fact eat each other's foods, there were sufficient dramatic differences in their physical requirements to make things very complex.

The money in deep space travel was where it had been in ocean travel and river travel and rail travel in ancient times. The money was in freight. The money was always in freight. That was why ships that went between the stars resembled less the fabled passenger liners of oceanic days than trains, with powerful engine modules and an elaborate bridge that could oversee the largely automated operation, and then, forward of this, were coupled the mods of freight and then the passenger modules designed for various life-form requirements. Robotics and a central life-support computer catered to them; for a considerable fee one could have a real live concierge assigned, but this was mostly for status.

The larger races, the ones that, in the Rithian's terms, bred fastest, almost always would have an entire dedicated module for their comfort, often with amenities and social interaction between passengers. Some were split modules, with common lounges and services, for those like the Terrans and Rithians, who could be comfortable together and didn't have a long history of mistrust. Those who traveled pretty much alone, the one-of-a-kinds and small groups who also had special needs, had it worst of all. They were pretty well confined to their cabins, isolated save for the computer and communications links.

The ships never came to a planet. They would dock in orbit around the various worlds, and then the modules due for unloading, freight and people, would be separated and mated to specific offloading ports. Automated ferries would take the people from the floating spaceports down to various destinations on the planet below; tugs would remove the specialized containers from the modules of freight, where customs would inspect them and approve them, and then they would be taken down to where they were needed and replaced with ones from the planet's surface.

Some spaceports weren't around planets at all, and were in fact in deep space, floating artificial worlds, sometimes many kilometers in size, composed of similar customized modules around a central core. These were transfer points, the equivalent of the old railroad junctions and yards, where passengers would "change trains," as it were, and freight would be redirected. These had their own centralized governing authorities, their own offices, shops, stores, hotel accommodations for all known races, emergency hospital services for all of those races as well, and much more.

The one they were now on was called Asswam Junction. It wasn't as huge as some of the others, being a bit off the busiest shipping lanes, but it was plenty big enough, with all the services and amenities. Many in the passenger lounge had been there for days or even weeks, waiting for their connections, which might well only take them to another junction.

There were perhaps twenty in the departure lounge, of which a dozen were Terrans. This was basically a transfer point along the Terran Arm of the Milky Way, and it was only natural that they would be the majority. Another four were Rithians, who inhabited the same region; three were Mallegestors, a mottled, tan-and-white elephantine race with enormously thick skin and a series of mean looking horns, who, nonetheless, also could share the same atmosphere and general requirements of Terrans and Rithians; and one was Geldorian, a small, lithe, furry weasel-like race, that looked more like an escapee from a pet store than a sentient being, save for the fact that it tended to smoke some odd substance in what seemed to be an oversized calabash pipe, and had a bulky purse over one shoulder.

Neither the Mallegestors nor the Geldorian were anything like local; how they'd wound up over in this sector of space only they could know. Still, a single module with common areas would do for all of them.

Below, at other gates, there could be others boarding this liner as well, and they might not ever know it. At least a dozen races within the region were water breathers, and several more breathed really unpleasant stuff like methane. They might well travel the same way on the same composite ship, but they were not the sort of folks you'd ever actually meet, or, in some cases, want to meet.

There was a Terran purser at the gate with maps and instructions. The gate could have been automated, of course, and in most cases was, but it had been found over long experience that when boarding and getting off, people wanted somebody to ask questions of and talk to someone who had some expertise and authority, even if it wasn't really necessary.

The purser, in fact, was really nothing more than a gate attendant. He would not even be going along with them, and would probably do this two or three times during the day for different departures.

Still, there he was at the boarding ramp, behind a small desk, smiling and checking out things on a computer screen. Something flashed on the board in front of him, and abruptly he was all business. They all put in what resembled little hearing aid devices, having no need to look at the cartoon graphic showing how to do it for all the races present that ran on the screen above the purser. After observing them, the purser picked up a small headset, put it on, and then punched in a code on the control board in front of him.

"Citizens of the Realm, I welcome you to Flight A3744X5. This is a nonstop to Crella Six spaceport, then on to Hasimoto Junction. The time to Crella Six is eleven days six hours, and there will be a twelve hour layover there before proceeding for sixteen days ten hours to Hasimoto Junction. Those disembarking at Crella Six should have their passports and other travel documents in order and on their person, as they must be submitted to immigration authority here before you can board. Those going on to Hasimoto Junction will require only their through ticket, as the automated systems will not permit you to disembark at Crella Six."

The voice was pleasant, professional, friendly. It was

being delivered in Asparant, the language of interstellar commerce and trade that was the standard on all the Junctions and spaceports. There it went to a computer, which translated it and sent it to each of the earpieces in the language and dialect of the individual wearer.

"Once you submit your travel documents and/or ticket, and it is validated and approved," the purser continued, "you will receive your cabin assignments and master keys, one for each person. These keys will operate only your cabin entrance, and after being used the first time, can be used only by the bearer. A map showing where your cabin is and how to get to it will be furnished with the key. Once you are approved, please collect key, map, and documents and proceed on board and to your cabin. All luggage should have been delivered there by now, so please check, and if anything is missing report it immediately via the ship's phone. Once you leave, there is no telling how long it might be before we could get anything left behind to you!"

The speech was stock and they'd all heard it before, but it was welcome nonetheless because it said that they were on their way.

Angel Kobe looked over at the Rithian, who was shuffling through his document pouch and checking with the rest of his party, then she looked around for Kincaid. He was there, paying no heed to the purser—he hadn't even inserted his little earpiece—and with ticket in hand, he also appeared to have little interest in his fellow travelers. Whatever he was doing on this run, it clearly had nothing to do with anybody else here.

She couldn't help but wonder if he thought of them at all, except as objects, perhaps. There were eight non-Terrans in the lounge, but the only really alien life-form was standing right there looking like a Terran man.

What was he doing here? What was he doing, period? Was he pensioned and spending all his time hunting this monster, who must be well-hidden and well-protected and in a biome the hunter couldn't ever really pierce? What would be the result if this creature was discovered living the good life down deep in some planetary ocean and giving orders to its minions? Kincaid would have to go down in an environment suit just for starters, and he'd be in unfamiliar territory against a probably well-guarded foe who felt completely at home there. Blow up the whole planet, perhaps? But then how would the hunter ever really know if the quarry was dead, or sheltered and ready to depart once conditions allowed, or, worse, had already left before the attack? She considered this while waiting not two people behind him in the queue for validation and boarding, and felt both curious and a bit sorry for the man. He was hunting Moby Dick and he didn't even have a harpoon or a ship.

She reached ticketing, inserted her documents, then placed her hand in a cavity inside the console. A slight tingling sensation resulted, and then she felt a swipe of something across her thumb as the boarding computer took some dead cells from the surface of her skin and compared the generic code to that registered on the documents. It took only a few seconds, and she received a green boarding arrow and her documents back, along with a map of the module and a small book with descriptions of the facilities available, the services, and the numbers to contact for any of her needs, with her own cabin number printed on the front.

The boarding process was more than just a validation, though; it was also the cue to the documents and terminal computer to upload all the information it had on the passenger to the local computer governing the module itself. The computer would know who was who, what their requirements and preferences were, medical needs, everything, even the language and translation routines required. She would be automatically given access to her own cabin and to the corridors and public areas; she would be prevented from entering any area that might not be good for her health or the ship's routines. In a sense, you were back in a sort of womb, and Mama was always around whether you wanted her there or not.

For a mixed race module, it was nicely full service. You could have your meals in your room, or go to a pleasant, intimate little café where no race would be visible to you eating something that would make you lose your lunch. There was a bar and lounge, a small gymnasium with equipment for every physiology, and a holographic staff that couldn't really do much but would provide company and conversation if need be.

The cabin was quite spacious. She'd arrived on a more local type of vessel where passengers weren't always the rule, and the quarters and amenities had been extremely cramped and limited in most ways. This was almost like a luxury hotel suite, with a sitting room, bedroom, full bath and shower, in-room entertainment, a direct virtual reality link for really going where you otherwise couldn't and experiencing things you might not otherwise experience, and all the rest. There was even an octagonal window showing the immediate complex, although the window was really a wall screen that connected to external ports. For most of the trip it would be a mirror, and more useful for it.

The bottom line was, passenger travel in the age of interstellar civilizations did what passenger services always did in times past: it provided as many ways as economy and technology permitted to kill time and give you the illusion that you weren't just sitting around bored.

Angel looked back at the cabin door and saw a display over it. Right now it was counting down toward 00:00:00, the time of departure, after which it would reset to the days, hours, and minutes until docking at the next stop.

It was all so new to her, and so wonderful. She'd seen most of the technology, of course, but she'd never dreamed of this level of luxury travel. She only wished that some friends or family were here to enjoy it with her. That, however, couldn't be, and was the one real drag on an otherwise wondrous journey that she nonetheless knew she'd remember the rest of her life.

There was still almost an hour until departure. She decided to shower and freshen up and put on something light-weight and comfortable, then explore the module. It was, after all, going to be home for quite a while.

She saw a glowing red light on her desk console, and, realizing it was a message alert, pressed it.

"Captain Melak Dukodny of the *City of Modar* speaking to all guests," came a pleasant if slightly stiff voice. "I welcome everyone who is joining us on this leg of our journey and invite you all to a reception in the main lounge. The reception will begin fifteen minutes before departure, but you may come down at any time after that, and I will join you shortly after we make the jump into null-space. Since this is a Junction board, none of you will be experiencing this for the first time, and I anticipate nothing you haven't seen, heard, or felt before. Dinner will be served beginning one hour after jump, although, of course, you may order anything at any time from room service. At 2200 ship's time tonight there will be a general talk in the lounge of all of the features available in your module, as well as information in case of emergencies. All passengers who have not attended a briefing aboard this ship are required to attend. Thank you, have a pleasant trip, and I hope to greet each and every one of you later this evening."

The red light went out.

It sounded like a full evening. Well, if she was going to shower and change and still go through it all, she'd better get started, she decided.

She was startled to see that all of her clothing and toiletries had been unpacked and placed in drawers, closets, and the like. On the *Queen of Tyre* they'd just dumped the bags outside the door. There was even a ship's clothing dispenser where you could get a basic utilitarian throwaway, loosely fitted, in case you didn't want to mess anything up, but for social nights that was unthinkable.

It hadn't occurred to her that this module had come in with the ship from someplace else and that there might be continuing passengers. So it might well mean more people, and even more races. She wondered just how many were aboard.

The lounge was more crowded than she'd anticipated. It was a very pleasant rounded and sunken space in the center of the mod, and with a nicely done but somewhat schizophrenic layout providing comfortable seats for all the races aboard, and indented areas along the curved walls offering various hors d'oeuvres carefully selected as delicacies for various races while being inoffensive-looking to others. The latter wasn't always possible, but this company clearly knew its business.

Likewise, there were different drinks tailored to the racial makeups, and in the correct proportions and containers. It wasn't that hard; all food and drink aboard was actually created by small energy-to-matter converters using various authentic programs supplied by chefs of the various races. In fact, all of them were really eating and drinking the garbage, but it had been nicely reprocessed and one just didn't think of *that*.

Angel Kobe had been born and raised on a vast farm that used none of this technology, and its farmers only feared the widespread discovery of cheap and easy ways to do the synthesizing on a mass scale. Fortunately, it was expensive and high maintenance, and was only possible on spacecraft as a by-product of the life support and propulsion systems.

Although she was in her fanciest evening clothes, she felt much the ugly duckling among the Terrans present. Her feeling of glamour when she'd dressed and made up in the cabin and examined herself in the mirror completely faded when she saw the competition. She would have been the belle of the ball back home, but in *this* company she was the rube at the prince's ball. These people wore elegance like a comfortable pair of shoes.

Worse, she felt conspicuously . . . well, *alone*. Most of the others seemed to be in pairs or small groups. It seemed she was the only single person on the ship.

No, that wasn't true, but the other one hadn't shown up yet. Oddly, she almost wished that Jeremiah Kincaid *would* show up. Once he entered the room, nobody but *nobody*, would even remember that she existed.

What had begun as an exciting taste of unaccustomed luxury had already turned into a miserable and lonely time, and she knew there was a long time to go yet.

There was a countdown clock in almost every public area, and, as if tuned into her thoughts, it reached all zeros. Almost immediately a vibration ran through the entire module, and she felt momentary dizziness caused by the switch to internal power and ship's versus station gravity. At the same time, the circular ceiling became a viewing screen showing the disengagement from the large space station. Angel took a glass of juice, sat down on one of the comfortable recliner chairs, and settled back to watch it. If she was going to be the rube anyway, she decided, she might as well do what she felt like doing.

The grand, kilometers-long space station and freight yard looked utilitarian and not at all glamorous from the outside.

It *was* big, though; a lot bigger than even she had thought. The freighter she'd come in on hadn't had this kind of view. She was surprised to see, for instance, that the module was not actually part of the ship, and that the actual *City of Modar* wasn't docked at all. It sat in a parking orbit off the station, along with a number of other ships, and was mostly engine and fuel containers. It looked like nothing anyone without knowledge of the system would expect; a gigantic cylindrical mass with huge ramjetlike scoops flanking it all around except right on "top," where there was a large whale-shaped bulge and rows of lights around it. The rear area had a series of large steering jets arranged around a central yellowish core that seemed to pulse regularly. Forward, a seemingly endless row of modules almost the size of the ship itself were connected one to the other like children's building blocks. All of them were basically contoured octagons, but the eight surfaces surrounded a cylindrical core. How long the train of modules went on, she couldn't guess; it was longer than the vast space station she'd just left, that was for sure.

The train wasn't yet connected to the engines, but was held there by a couple of small ships using tractor beams. They were so tiny compared to the modules that they could only be seen by their anticollision lights blinking on and off.

The tugs were basically used for maneuvering; out here, a ten-kilometer train of even the heaviest raw materials or finished goods weighed the same as a feather. The longer it was, however, the harder to manage, and there were surely other tugs well along the train to keep it in line.

Their own module was certainly being carried by one or more similar tugs, although they were not visible on the screen.

"You'd best look away if you get the least bit dizzy, until this docking is over," a pleasant baritone voice commented.

"Huh?" She looked away reluctantly and saw a man in shining brown formal wear with what looked to be a fortune in jewelry on him.

"Sorry. I just saw you fascinated, and wanted to warn you. If you look up when they tilt the module, you'll be disoriented. It catches many by surprise."

She was undecided whether to follow up this obvious

opening right now or look back at the docking. "Thanks. I guess I can look away if it gets me. I've been pretty good about balance."

She stared back up, and almost immediately the module began to turn from camera angle, facing the gap between ship and train and the docking mechanism on the ship itself. It was slow, easy, but took up most of the field of view. Even though the gravity inside was artificial and constant, Angel suddenly felt as if she was falling off the chair onto the floor, and in an instant, that's where she found herself.

Several people turned and chuckled, infuriating and embarrassing her. The strange man, who looked to be middle-aged, with thick black hair and a very stylish goatee, tried not to say "I told you so" and instead offered his hand to her.

"Don't feel too badly," he consoled. "I think we all did that the first time."

Still, she was mortified by what had happened to her, and *only* to her, and also because she'd spilled half the juice on her best suit. "Thank you," she managed as best she could, only wanting to get out of there. "I think I'll have to run back to my cabin and change."

Angel walked out of the lounge, but almost began running once out of sight of the crowd. She didn't know how she could face them again. As she reached the emotional safety of her cabin, there was a shudder and an awkward jerking motion that almost dropped her to the deck. Bells and alarms were sounding somewhere, and for a moment she wondered if they'd collided with something or maybe cracked up against the ship. She almost hoped so.

There was a second thump and another jerking motion, another set of alarms, and then, abruptly, it was quiet and stable once more.

The module had docked with the ship just forward of the bridge, and then the train had been docked to it. Now, stabilizing devices, connectors, and long energy rods held it firm and straight, making the massive vessel less a collection of independent devices than a kind of mechanical organism, a whole greater than the sum of its parts.

For a while there was nothing but the vibration and a sense of being so still it felt to Angel as if she were sunk in concrete. Then, when the bridge computer contacted and networked with the computers for each module, passenger and freight, and had checked all safety and stability items and passed everything off, a kind of unanimous vote was sent to the bridge stating that the ship was ready to move. It was the one thing the vessel's Master did on a nonemergency basis. Only he could give the order to move out.

Angel slipped out of her wet clothes and looked at herself in the mirror. She sighed, and removed the brown wig and put it back in its container, revealing a head that was perfectly shaped but now totally hairless. Lucky the wig didn't come off, too, she reflected dourly, but though she had no problems with the way she looked, she was pleased deep down to have been spared that one little embarrassment. It was just God's punishment, she thought, for her trying to pretend she was something that she was not.

She rinsed off, reflecting that this was the second shower she'd had in three hours, but also only the second in many months. Afterward, she wiped off what makeup remained, removed the fake gold earrings and replaced them with the simple copper alloy ones she normally wore—a cross with curved wings set upon a hexagonal base, the same design as on the medallion she always wore around her neck, which had been concealed by the suit. The simple ring, also forged with the same design, went back on her ring finger. No more pretenses, she decided. She would be herself, and if they didn't like it, well, how much worse off socially could she be?

She took out a simple off-white cotton cassock and put it on, leaving the hood down, and looked at herself once more. The loose-fitting cassock disguised her thin figure, although it couldn't disguise what was to her an overly-large nose and brown eyes too small for her face. She was reconciled to not being a beauty, and this felt almost normal and natural.

A speaker came to life, startling her. "Your attention, please. We have cleared the traffic yard and will be punching into null-space in one minute. It is suggested for your own safety that everyone please take a seat or become still on the floor. Anyone experiencing discomfort beyond the all clear should signal for some mild medication. Thank you."

She shrugged and took a seat against the bulkhead. *This* she'd done more than once before. Even so, it wasn't totally pleasant.

Three bells sounded, followed by a pause, after which it suddenly felt as if she wasn't holding on to anything at all but falling without physical reference points. The first time she'd experienced this, she almost lost her lunch, but now it was no big deal. There was a roaring, and then a flash. The lighting seemed to go out and then come right back on again. And that was it. Three bells sounded once more to indicate the all clear.

For the next two weeks it would generally feel like they were standing still inside a building on the planet's surface. From this point on, until they returned to normal space, it was all automatic.

Angel decided to reemerge as herself and perhaps get some dinner in the public dining room before the mandatory ship's briefing. Heads turned from the still milling group of passengers in their formal wear as she reentered the lounge, but it didn't bother her. The odds were that few if any of the Terrans, at least, would even recognize her as the same woman who'd been there before.

They weren't snickering, anyway. The one thing about anyone wearing clerical garb in a crowd of strangers, no matter what the various religions were, was that the cleric usually left the others feeling uncomfortable.

She bypassed onlookers and made for the small café entrance. A man and a woman were standing just inside, looking the café over, and both turned and gave her the usual facial reaction she got from strangers. She returned a professional smile, and felt very much more at ease with herself. "Please relax," she told them. "I only try to convert people during business hours. I'm Sister Angel then. Now I'm just Angel Kobe, going to dinner."

The ice was broken. "I am Ari Martinez," the man responded in a pleasant voice, and looked at his companion, whom his gesture indicated was not his wife, or probably paramour, either. She was, however, quite a looker, Angel thought, one of those people with all the exotic features of a dozen races and colors and no dominant single one.

"I am Ming Dawn Palavri," she introduced herself, smiling more nervously than the darkly handsome Martinez. "Please—won't you join us? I do not think there are many in here at the moment and we'll be shipmates for quite some time."

"I . . ." Angel looked at Martinez, who betrayed no signals. "I shouldn't like to impose or interrupt . . ."

"Not a problem," Martinez assured her at last. "Ming and I are sort of in the same business." He turned, and Angel was startled to see a formally dressed and quite officious-looking maitre d'. "There will be three for dinner now," he told the majordomo.

"Very well. Please come this way," the maitre d' said in a thin, upper-crust voice, and led them to a quiet table, pulling out the chairs for each of them and lighting the atmospheric period lamp. He then put down three old-fashioned *printed* menus. "Your waiter will be with you shortly," he told them, and left.

Angel was startled. "*People* just to *seat* you in a *restaurant*? Am I showing how primitive I've been living, or is this truly unusual?"

Ming laughed. "Not really. There *are* a number of worlds where it's still the norm, but most of the expensive and classy places, and pretend classy places, are more like this. It's actually all holographic. You could walk right through him if you really wanted to. It's kind of pretend service over the usual automation."

"I see," she responded, somewhat disappointed. Not that she hadn't had a lot of human table service, but it had usually been in dumps and in backwater situations where automation of this level, when available, was usually five years out of whack and in bad need of repair. Well, much of what was fun in this life was in the imagination.

The menus certainly *felt* real, and looked real. Hers seemed tailor-made for her own likes, dislikes, prohibitions, and requirements. No animal matter of any kind, synthetic or not, and a wide variety of veggie, rice, and sauce-heavy dishes including curries, with juices and herbal teas. Ari Martinez's menu, while apparently identical, appeared from his ruminations aloud to be heavy on steaks and fine wines, while Ming's seemed to have a lot of egg and seafood dishes and elaborate salads. Out of curiosity, after all three had put down their menus, Angel reached over, picked up Ming's menu and looked through it.

It listed the same dishes as her menu had.

"Caught them in their little trick, huh?" Ming chuckled.

So even the menus were careful illusions. "In this kind of controlled atmosphere, it's going to be next to impossible to figure out just who and what's really there," she responded.

"But that's the trick," Ari commented. "Magic shows are far more fun when they are so well done you cannot catch them working the show. The best way is to simply take everything at face value in an environment like this and just enjoy it. We'll be back in the real universe soon enough."

A waiter out of a classic movie took their orders, almost certainly a hologram as well, but as Ari had said, it didn't matter.

"I can't help noticing the winged cross on the hexagon," Ming said to her, curious. "I am not familiar with this symbol. Might I ask the order?"

"I am of the Tannonites," she told them. "It is a very Old Order denomination but it is not well known. It does not go back like so many to old Earth times, but evolved on Katenea, one of the early colonies. It is basically Christian, but there are elements of many ancient faiths in it as well, including some that are from other races. Our goal is to synthesize the One Truth out of the Many, and to do that we no longer have a home, as it were."

"Sounds like you travel as much as we do," Ari replied. "We're management consultants. Not, I might add, from the same company, but we do basically the same thing. We go to the various enterprises our companies run that are having problems, and we try and determine what the cause of those problems might be and to find fixes for them. Nine out of ten times it winds up that we have to discover and weed out an incompetent or nest of incompetents somewhere in management."

"Ninety out of a hundred," Ming added. "And all but a tiny speck of the rest turn out to be downright crookedness. It's quite a fascinating business, really. Sort of like being a detective, only the solution may be far different than simply discovering that it was the butler with the knife in the living room."

"I should think it would be fascinating," Angel responded.

"And not nearly so dangerous as tracking down genuine nasties."

"Oh, we've had our share of nasties," Ari assured her. "I would say that someone's tried to push me off a balcony or crack me up or some such, oh, maybe on the average of once a year since I started. I think Ming's average is similar."

"About that," she agreed. "The thing that saves you most times is that it always has to look like the perfect accident. Otherwise you'll just get the *real* cops plus a lot more people like us showing up, and they'll find the same thing and generally run down the bad guys. But, it is true, the *real* challenge is that they are often quite clever and will try and lead you to the wrong person or group or around in circles. Still, it beats sitting in an office somewhere."

Maybe it did, but they sounded to Angel like two private detectives doing their job for money and the good life rather than out of a sense of service. Still, she wasn't going to judge them. At least what they did resulted in good; mercenaries could have their uses.

As the food started to come, the conversation turned back to her.

"You say that your denomination has no home?" Ari asked, curious.

"Not anymore," she told them. "We grew inward on our home world over the years, and very insular, cut off from the rest of society. That was not why God caused us to exist, and it did us very little good except to breed a kind of local colony that was in danger of straying or atrophying. God had no other way to kick us in the backside and get us into action on our true mission, so He caused our sun to go nova."

That was a meal stopper. "I beg your pardon?" Ming and Ari almost said as one.

"Oh, there were enough warning signs that we knew it was coming. The whole planet had to be evacuated. In a way, it was a shame, since it was quite rich and quite beautiful, but we would never have gone otherwise. This was long ago, you understand. Centuries. I have only seen the pictures, which are kept by the Elders. It was the Patriarch and Elders of that time who received from God the divine commission, and since then we have had no home. Wherever we are is our home, and we take with us that which we need. I was born on a far-off world inhabited by a race not unlike the Rithians, which is why I think I get along with them so well. When I was eight my birthmother sent me to the nearest convent for formal education. These are small affairs that are actually attached to space stations like the one we were just on. In fact, I just visited the Asswam sisterhood. That's where I stayed until this ship arrived."

"Funny. I'm in and out of space stations all the time, and I don't remember ever seeing or hearing about one," Ming commented.

"That is deliberate. We do not wish the convents to be known. They are primarily shut away from all other parts of the station, in strict seclusion. Only the Elder in charge and the Mother Supervisor deal with the station and maintain commerce and communication, as well as, of course, ones like me who pass through, and I cannot really interact with them, as anyone of the faith just visiting must take a vow of silence while inside to preserve the cloistered atmosphere for the students and permanent staff. I realize this must seem odd to you, but it is our way."

"I hope you are not offended, but *all* religions seem odd to me," Ming commented. "The more you see of the universe, the less you believe that there is anything but randomness out here."

"You see no pattern? No wonder in its many forms and variations, its sheer complexities?"

"Pattern? No, I don't think so. Galaxies spin away and crash into one another, stars go nova and wipe out whole worlds, and the range of creatures both sentient and not that could use a *much* better engineering design, including us, are legion. I live for the here and now, expecting nothing beyond. If I thought there was *justice* even, I might waver a bit, but I work for too many scoundrels as it is. Did you see that walking zombie Kincaid?"

Angel nodded. "Yes. A very tragic man. He hunts an ancient evil in the guise of a fellow creature, but because it is from vengeance, he usurps God's role. What about you, Ari?"

The man gave a weak smile and shrugged. "I don't know. I was raised Catholic, and, I suppose, I remain so, although not exactly in the best of graces. I keep wondering about some things, all those ancient dead worlds of long vanished civilizations we keep stumbling over. Who were they? Where did they go? Why and how did races that traveled through space millions or perhaps a billion years before anybody *we* know vanish so completely and so abruptly? I was talking with an archaeologist, and he said that the primary mystery civilization had been found across the entire galaxy at the least. We haven't gone anywhere that we haven't found their colonies, nor met a new race that didn't already know them, if no better than we. My old Bible study teacher always was fond of noting that the book of Jeremiah, among others, talks of ancient civilizations and spacefaring angels that existed long before Adam was made. I am not so sure of the faith of my ancestors in a word-for-word fashion, I admit, but I am well aware that there are things of vast cosmic significance about which we know nothing. I lost my father a couple of years ago, and I like to think that he is still somewhere, beyond this sort of life. Call me someone reserving judgment, but with an open mind."

The meal continued that way, quite pleasant from Angel's point of view in spite of the lack of spirituality of her companions. There was some hope for Ari, no matter how material his life and attitudes were. Ming, well—none saw God unless they were called to do so, and like most people, Ming was spiritually deaf. Angel knew it was not her job to convert such people, only to find those who heard the call but had no clear idea which direction it was coming from. Converting the deaf ones was not only fruitless, it was, to her people, blasphemous. If God had wanted them, He would have called.

They finished dessert and got up to go to the Captain's reception and briefing, but they continued trying to get to know one another. The fact that Angel had made no effort to thump a Bible or preach to them made her acceptable as a fellow traveler. Ari had been aboard and thus wasn't required to attend, but he hadn't much else to do.

"So where are you heading?" he asked the nun. "If it's not too personal, that is. You say you have no home, and you're far too young to have both education and lots of experience."

"It's not too personal, no. Actually, you are right. I've just come from a two year assignment assisting a mission on a rather primitive world. It was very basic stuff—digging wells, showing how to create and plant and harvest rice in the old ways, that kind of thing. Our tradition is to get right into the mud and teach by example. Of course, I was also being tutored by the Holy Sisters at the mission, and evaluated for personality, aptitude, you name it. They decided that I *did* have the calling to mission work and that I should be sent to university. I have decided that I have a talent for growing things that experts say can't grow where I put them, so I will be taking a degree in plant exobiology."

"Really? And that's where you are heading now?"

She laughed. "Not directly. Actually, I'm on my way to be married."

"Married! But I thought—"

"I understand. You were raised Catholic and you probably also have run into Buddhist nuns and that's what you think when you see me. We're not celibate. If we were, we wouldn't last another generation. God commanded us to be fruitful and multiply, and that's part of it. It would be unthinkable for any of us to go outside of our own people, such as to university, without first the joining of a family and the sacraments of marriage to impose discipline and also liberate us from the usual romantic tugs such places are known for."

He frowned. "Hmm . . . That was the best part of going to university, frankly. Oh, well, we each follow our own paths, eh? Have you known your fiancé long?"

"Actually, I've never met him, only seen a video of him. But I've met three of his other wives and they've given me a good idea of what he's like."

Ari Martinez decided to leave that part alone. He'd been around enough not to be shocked or even surprised at the various cults and cultural systems human beings had devised over the centuries, some of which made totally alien life-forms seem ordinary by comparison. Instead, he decided to keep it casual.

"I don't remember seeing others like you, and I travel a lot," he told her. "If your group is large enough to exist on Junctions all over the Realm, I'd think I'd have run into someone else before."

"You probably have," she told him. "We don't travel in

uniform, as it were. Not usually, anyway. I carry a modest wardrobe with me, including wigs and such."

"But you're not in disguise now."

"I was, for a little while, but it was too embarrassing, not to say *messy*. I think in this case I'm better off the way I am."

He stared. "You're the girl who took the tumble when we docked! Well I'll be d—" He stopped himself.

"Damned? I doubt it. *That's* the kind of reason we don't travel as ourselves. People seem to think that if you're with a mission, you have to be sheltered from bad language and dirty jokes and all the rest. Believe me, there's very little I haven't heard already. It's not *what* you say, it's what you *mean* that counts."

They went back to the lounge, where the newcomers and most of the rest of the passengers had gathered. Other than returning to the cabin, there really wasn't much else to do.

There was some milling around and general impatience as the appointed time for the briefing came and went without any announcement, not even that the Captain would be late. Angel looked around and saw Jeremiah Kincaid sitting by himself, nursing a drink. He was hard to miss; everyone who walked into the lounge got an icy stare and a thorough scrutiny from head to foot from the eerie man, as if he were looking for someone who might not want to be recognized.

Ming had departed for her cabin, but apparently had done whatever she had to do and now reappeared, emerging from a passageway. She saw her two dinner companions and started over, Kincaid giving her the remote third degree.

"You know, I'd swear that bastard had X-ray eyes and was telepathic to boot," she whispered to them. "It felt like he looked right *through* me! I don't know what he thinks he's looking for here. I mean, everybody knows that the monster he's looking for is a water breather. He should be on the other side, with a breathing apparatus that didn't work right."

"You're not that sympathetic," Angel noted.

She shrugged. "Hey, I'm as much a bleeding heart as anybody, but it's not my war, not my fight, and all I want is him to be somewhere I'm not. If he thinks he's going to spot water breathers here, then he's gone completely over the edge. Of course, considering how many decades he's been chasing his demon without success, it's not surprising."

Ari seemed uncomfortable, but not with the sentiment. "What do you mean, he should be on the other side? There are water breathers aboard?"

"Sure. In this module. About a third, or two pie sections. Happens all the time. That's why you'll eventually hit a wall if you try a complete circuit. You can call them, or use the virtual bar and lounge to interact. I've got to talk to a couple of 'em here on business, in fact." She looked at Angel. "See, it's pretty awkward for me to go to *their* element, and unlikely I can do much anyway. Same goes in reverse. So we swap information, research, and such as a professional courtesy."

Ari nodded. "Yes, it's done all the time. I'm pretty much between assignments, but if any of them who know me rang me up in my cabin and asked me to run down something, I'd probably help if it didn't go against somebody I'm likely to be working for or have worked for in the past." He looked around at the gathering group. "Funny. I always know some of the people on a trip, because those of us who have to actually move from system to system are a fairly small number within a sector, but I know *most* of these. Not necessarily well, or as friends, but I know them."

Ming nodded. "I noticed the same thing. The Rithians are all from the Ha'jiz Nesting, for example. And the middle-aged man with the good looks and silver hair and the woman in the sparkling scarlet are the Kharkovs. Gem cutters and master jewelers. That's no coincidence."

"I agree," Ari replied. "And there are others here who are even a bit darker. That Geldorian, for example, is Tann Nakitt. He's a go-between for various factions, whether it be companies or criminal groups or whatever. Not a bad sort, really, unless you're opposed to him, but he's also not cheap. I don't know the Mallegestors, nor much about them as a race or culture, but it's curious to see them this far afield. Assuming we can discount Mom and Dad and the two kids there, the distinguished-looking fellow with the goatee and the two overbuilt young ladies is Jules Wallinchky, a man who makes a lot of money providing goods and services to folks who want things they can't legally have. I assume that the two with him are either recent acquisitions or kept because of their looks and attitude, although you never know.

Makes for an interesting mostly rogue's gallery, though, doesn't it?"

Angel recognized the man identified as the gangster as the one who had tried coming on to her until she did her ungainly spill. I sure attract the odd ones, she thought sourly, although she wondered what interest he might have in the likes of her, with two superior warm bodies like *those* hanging on his every word and gesture. On the other hand, maybe he was looking for a woman who wouldn't pass a light beam in one ear and out the other. She'd never seen women like this, and only heard of them in stories and warnings; she did not understand why they would put themselves in that kind of situation, as little more than, well, *property*. She knew some faiths had women subordinated because of Eve's corruption, but this had nothing to do with religion or true culture. To Angel Kobe, it was as inexplicable as the bipedal hippos over there, the Mallegestors.

"Well, I don't care *what* the rules are," Wallinchky said loud enough for all to hear. "If the Captain's gonna stand us all up without so much as a word, he can damned well come find me when he wants to talk. I'll give him five minutes and that's *it*. Then *we're* goin' to the cabin!"

Tough guy or not, this sentiment was pretty much universal for the assembled passengers.

Jeremiah Kincaid arose, his huge form towering over the Terrans and Rithians, and made his way silently through the increasingly impatient throng to the restaurant. As soon as he stepped inside, the maitre d' appeared.

"The Captain has allowed the passengers to wait without sending any word for more than a half hour," Kincaid told the hologram in his deep baritone. "Please check and see if there is anything wrong."

The maitre d' seemed to freeze, but Kincaid's words went through the generated character to the central module computer and from there to the master computer. Suddenly the hologram came to life once more, looking concerned. "We do not have a clear fix on Captain Dukodny. This is unprecedented. Validate that you are Jeremiah Wong Kincaid, passenger?"

"Yes, I am Kincaid."

"Do you still hold captain's papers?"

"Yes, although I couldn't legally take command without going through a recertification. It has been a long time since I was master of anything large and complex, and technology has gone on."

"Captain, you are the most qualified individual other than Captain Dukodny aboard. We would like you to go up to the bridge and see if there has been some kind of problem we cannot monitor."

Kincaid nodded. "That is what I had in mind. What do your sensors see on the bridge?"

"Normal operation is reported, although there is some sort of weight imbalance we can not properly categorize."

Kincaid frowned. "Weight imbalance? You mean at the bridge?"

"Yes, sir."

"Wait here a moment. Then we will go up there."

Kincaid turned and walked back to the people in the lounge, most of whom reacted nervously or recoiled from his powerful and mysterious visage.

"Citizens of the Realm, there might be a problem here," he announced as loudly as possible. "I would not feel bound to wait around here any longer. On the other hand, I should like a couple of volunteers to accompany me to the bridge to check on the Captain. I fear he may be ill or worse."

That got a lot of them agitated, and he moved to calm them down. "Please! This ship runs without live intervention. The ship's Master is the boss, but doesn't run the day-to-day operations. I am rated as captain and could do what little is necessary in a pinch, but this ship not only can do everything by itself, it has three to five levels of redundancy. There is no danger to us from that quarter. Still, something is amiss. Would anyone like to accompany me? *Anyone?*"

He wasn't exactly the kind you willingly jumped up and volunteered to go off with into the internal bowels of a strange ship. Most of them would have preferred if he sat in a different room. Still, curiosity overcame a few of the courageous.

"I'll go up with you," said a Rithian, perhaps the one, Angel thought, she had talked to about Kincaid. The cobra-faced quadruped was welcome, because Rithians were so supple they could twist and bend as if they had no bones and get in and out of tight places.

"Fine. And one more?"

"I'll come with you," Angel heard herself saying. Was she the same person who had not long before been terrified at the very sight of this man? Perhaps being herself was always best; that way she could place herself in God's hands.

Kincaid wasn't too thrilled with her, but he didn't want to wait much longer. "All right. You two come with me. Everybody else, stay or go as you please. We'll report as soon as we know anything."

They walked back over to the restaurant. The maitre d' was nowhere in sight. Instead they were met by a tall, tough-looking man in a utility jumpsuit. This was crewman mode, and meant that this particular hologram wasn't from the module computer but from the *City of Modar* itself.

In addition to curiosity, Angel had volunteered because it looked to be a chance to see the parts of the ship otherwise barred to passengers.

They walked back along utilitarian service corridors that had no mystery in them at all except perhaps where they went, and finally the trio reached a stair that descended from the ceiling as they approached. Without the computer authorizing things, nobody could have gotten up there or even noticed that the stairway existed. This was Officer Country, even though there was only one officer on the whole massive structure.

They went up it, the holographic crewman and Kincaid in the lead, then the Rithian, with Angel bringing up the rear. They came to an airlock with its warning lights flashing red.

"That's odd," the crewman commented. "Our sensors indicate that the external corridor is fully pressurized."

Kincaid looked around. "Any emergency gear here?"

"In the compartment there. Just use the floor ring and lift up."

Inside were several safety harnesses, two environment suits, and a number of autofit breathing masks.

"There is no suit that would handle my form," the Rithian noted. "I shall be all right with the breather and safety line."

"That should be all right for all of us," Kincaid replied. "If it's a vacuum, the airlock will either refuse to open or be shut again by the pressure here. I doubt if there are any lines for toxic gases in there. Everybody get on a safety harness and hook to the railing here. Then pull up a breather and hold it. Okay, good. Check your masks."

Angel had never had one on, but it seemed simple enough to do, and the mask over her nose and mouth fitted itself to the contours of her face and fed oxygen-rich air. The Rithian also hooked up, and the mask contoured even to its snakelike face. Kincaid nodded to the crewman and said, "Open it."

Warning bells sounded as the airlock was opened while still in a red condition, but the rounded airlock twisted like a spiral lens and opened onto the nearly kilometer-long tunnel that linked the passenger module to the bridge on the main ship.

Water gushed out in an enormous rush and washed over them, knocking all three of them down. The harnesses, clipped to the railings, held them in place for what seemed like eternity but was actually no more than a minute or two. The water itself was salty and mineral-rich, but it wasn't the main problem, as it was vented and recaptured by the ship's systems and slowly went down to a trickle.

It was so unexpected that Angel had been completely bowled over, and she knew that it had been sufficient to probably cause some bruises.

"Everybody all right?" Kincaid shouted, picking himself up.

Only the crewman stood there, looking totally confused. "We are shifting the water out through vents to the main tanks," he assured them. "Restoring normal operation should happen in a matter of minutes. It is, however, very confusing. This is impossible. It cannot happen."

"Your sensor systems were bypassed," Kincaid told the crewman. "It was probably done outside, while we were in station-keeping. Was any maintenance done on your overall systems?"

"Just the usual preventive maintenance and refreshing of systems. Nothing major."

"But somebody or some maintenance robot had access to the computer memory section or comm interfaces?"

"Well, that is not unheard of, but any shutdowns or modifications would be logged."

"Is there any way to pump this amount of water under

pressure into the catwalk from either this module or the main ship's module?"

"No. It would have to have been done externally."

Angel managed to stand up, then removed her mask and tried to get her bearings. Her eyes hurt from the mineral salts, and her robe felt like a soaking wet blanket.

She looked around, appalled at the implications. "So where's the Captain?" she asked them, shaking her head.

"Where indeed?" echoed Kincaid.

On the Freighter *City of Modar*

"YOUR SENSORS WERE OBVIOUSLY DISABLED ON THE CAT-walk," Jeremiah Kincaid said to the holographic crewman. "And your view of the bridge is obviously also false, probably a looped recording. Assuming that this is true for the sake of argument, is there any way you can *physically* determine the actual contents of the bridge void?"

"I have already gone to work on that," the crewman replied. "A routine air-cleaning robot was dispatched into the ducting and reports the ducts on the deck level are flooded to the emergency lock stop; the ones on the top are clear, but it is likely the void is predominantly the same fluid as was in the catwalk. That is most unfortunate since the salts and minerals in the water are somewhat caustic and can cause damage."

"Can you pump it out?"

"I could vent it to space, but it would be irrecoverable."

"The hell with recovery! It's obvious that it's not part of the main system anyway. Probably pumped in during the master refueling. It would do as fuel for the engines just as well as the normal gel. That's probably why you have such a weight imbalance in the gravity enabled sections. The water is shifting with the engine pulses rather than having a steady ooze as with the gel."

"Most certainly a good hypothesis," the crewman responded. "It will also mean that we will be short on fuel."

"I suspect that's partly the idea. We'll hold off on going further in that direction until we get the rest of the picture. Vent the water from the bridge and reintroduce the gas atmosphere that should be in there." He turned to the pair he'd brought with him, who now were simply trying to dry out.

30

"You two want to go back? I apologize for bringing you along just to get a dunking, but I couldn't know what we'd find here and I believed I might have needed extra hands or backups or even witnesses. Now I see that the perpetrators are long gone."

"I could use a fluffy towel and a dry cassock, but I'm game to see this through," Angel told him. "I think I paid the price to see what's at the end."

"I, too, should like to see it through," the Rithian told him. "I do not like the implications of this, and I would rather have knowledge than allow my imagination to flow as freely as the water."

Kincaid nodded, seeming pleased. "All right, then. If there *was* anybody left in there, I suspect they are even now drowning in a nice nitrogen-oxygen mix. I certainly hope so."

"You may go ahead," the crewman told them. "I will meet you at the other end. I cannot restore things until you can get inside, since I will need to extend this probe to see what is actually there."

Kincaid unhooked but did not remove the safety harness. Angel and the Rithian had both already discarded theirs, and neither felt like putting it back on unless they had to. Kincaid seemed to read their thoughts.

"I doubt if the harness will be necessary. It's up to you."

"You two go on," Angel told them. "I will catch up to you in a few minutes."

Kincaid frowned. "Be careful rushing on the catwalk. You are out of a full gravity field there."

"I'll be careful," she promised him, and first Kincaid and then the Rithian went through the lock.

Angel needed a few moments to slip off the cassock, which was all she had on, and roll it up. Then, by standing on it, kneading it with her feet and twisting with her hands, she squeezed an amazing amount of water out. It wasn't dry when she put it back on, but it wasn't heavy and sopping wet, either. It was, however, cold.

There was an odor in the air, of salt and some fairly unpleasant substances that reminded her of spray cleaners or insecticides. That water was *foul*.

She walked up to the lock, which opened for her in that

curious lenslike fashion and gave green lights. She stepped
out onto the catwalk, and the lock closed behind her.

The catwalk was another world, almost—a metallic grat-
ing for a floor, and two thin handrails, one on each side, the
walkway not large enough for two of her to walk abreast. It
was in fact nothing more than a great transparent tube with
its own emanating light around it, and it seemed to go on
and on.

Angel weighed about sixty-three kilos in gravity norm,
and was used to slightly more in the heavier gravity of the
world where she'd been working, but now she bounced along
as if she weighed almost nothing. It wasn't quite as dramatic as it felt, she realized, but not only was gravity well
down in the tube, as Kincaid had warned her, it also varied,
sometimes significantly, as you went along. It was disori-
enting enough that she found herself grasping the handrail
and going nice and slow.

Kincaid certainly had been a godsend in this emergency,
she reflected. If he hadn't been aboard, what might have
happened to all of them? Not that they were out of the
woods yet, but what had seemed icy, alienlike distance and
fearsome hatred had been transformed by circumstances
into just the kind of confident authority she and probably
most of the other passengers would need.

. . . godsend in this emergency . . .

This *wasn't* an emergency! she realized with a start. Somehow, Kincaid had known, or at least suspected, that something
bad was going to happen. That was why he was aboard. And
if he'd devoted his entire existence to hunting down and
destroying one of the legendary evils of history, then . . .

Didn't that Rithian say the would-be Conqueror of the
Universe was a water breather?

She didn't catch up with the two, but did have them in
sight, tiny figures in the distance whom she made out mostly
by the fact that they moved.

Angel quickly discovered that to walk without getting
dizzy and sick along this passage, she had to keep her eyes
steadily on that vanishing point ahead. The tube was transparent; in null-space there was a Great Void, a nothingness
that the brain interpreted as jet-black because it had no other
way to depict it. Otherwise, there was only the ship, bathed

in an energy glow that kept it insulated from the Great Void beyond.

She didn't think she was going to make it, but eventually she did. Out of breath, disoriented, with some nausea to boot, she finally reached the end and a solid section with a double airlock. She stepped inside the one, heard it close behind her, and felt gravity of almost ship's normal return. When the aft lock was closed, the forward one opened, and she walked into one huge wretched-looking mess.

There was the smell of electricity in the air, and a lot of the instrumentation on the big semicircular control panel was blinking red or simply shorted out. The whole place seemed covered with rusty reds and bleach-white and granular yellow scum, the undoubted residue of what was in the water. A computer pad, some papers, and a few customized real printed books—rare in this day and age, but common, she knew, among starship captains—were waterlogged, twisted, and ruined.

The whole place smelled like it had just been fumigated and not properly aired.

"Don't mind the smell!" Kincaid called to her from a slightly elevated platform in the rear of the bridge. "I'm afraid it'll get worse before it gets better, but the computer probe assures me that it won't really damage any of us, just annoy the hell out of our lungs."

She saw the big, padded command chair in front of the bridge, definitely the seat of authority, its high back blocking the view of anyone who might occupy it. It had controls and circuitry in the arms, and a set of modules on arms that could be brought in front or to one side. A series of monitors, six of them, were directly in front, although only a couple were working. She had the sudden, uneasy feeling that somebody was in that chair. Without saying a word, she walked toward it, slowly, almost as if expecting some monster to leap out from it at her throat, and for some reason she couldn't explain, she began reciting the prayer of comfort to the Blessed Virgin over and over again. Still, she was drawn to the command chair.

Kincaid looked up, saw her and shouted, "I think you'd better not!"

But it was too late, nor could she have stopped if she

wanted to. She came around the side of the chair, saw the occupant, stifled a scream, and looked away. She felt like throwing up, and couldn't stop it. That nice dinner mixed with the mess and ooze on the deck.

The occupant of the chair was quite dead, and was almost certainly the late and heretofore missing Captain Dukodny. At least he hadn't drowned, for all the good that meant. Clearly, whoever had done it hadn't wanted the ship's Master to have any idea of what was going on, nor any opportunity to stop it. They'd blown an airlock, probably from the tug, once they'd bypassed the ship's computer, and Captain Dukodny had essentially imploded.

Captain Kincaid was by her side in a moment. "Are you all right? I tried to stop you—"

"No, no, I'm okay," she assured him. "It was just—I hadn't ever seen anybody dead like *that*. I'm all right now."

"Hmm . . . I don't know . . . Great Scott! Are you *barefoot*?" he exclaimed, looking at the prints in the sludge.

It hadn't occurred to her. "Yes, I—I just didn't think I needed anything when I came to the lounge to have dinner and get the briefing."

"It never occurred to me that anybody would walk barefoot around this crud."

"Is it toxic?"

"Probably not, but I'd wash it all off as quickly as possible when I could get to some plain water, and watch for any reactions just in case. Not toxic doesn't mean that it might not be caustic. If it starts to burn or feel inflamed, get to the medical station."

"It feels all right. I admit to feeling foolish now at not thinking of it myself, but things happened so fast . . ."

He nodded. "Good girl. You are some kind of priest or nun?"

"Some kind, yes. I am Angel Kobe. You could call me Sister Kobe if you would feel more comfortable doing so, but Angel is fine."

"Okay—Sister. You got guts or faith or maybe both, and that's a handy set of attributes to have right now."

"I'm afraid I'm beginning to think you may need a naval escort instead of a woman of God," she commented. "Or am I wrong in what I am thinking here?"

He lowered his voice to a whisper. "I wish you were. And I'm afraid we haven't any idea how many of our fellow passengers know all about this as well. Our Rithian friend seemed less surprised by the condition of the bridge or the Captain, for example, than in checking out how much damage might have been done."

She got the hint. "Where is he now?"

"Teynal is helping the main computer by running temporary lines back in here independent of the usual systems. He can move through those ducts rather handily. We'll need to get this up and running and also run down the taps and bypasses that allowed them to do all this right in plain sight. The computer thinks it's got most of them now, but we'll see."

She looked over at the chair. "What will you do with—" She nodded toward the body.

"It is a tradition that if you die in the line of duty, you are given to space. We'll pass him through to the fuel chambers, where his mortal remains will be consumed and then output as exhaust gasses that will join with and return to the universe. One day some tiny fragment of him may become part of a new star, a new world, or who knows what? It's what he would have wanted."

"I know nothing of him or his faith, if he had one, but I should like to perform a basic funeral rite and prayer for him as this is done."

"It's not necessary."

She looked into those hollow eyes. "Yes it is. His place in the universe was as Master of this ship. My place is to perform what God has made me to perform."

He sighed and nodded. "All right, then, Sister. It won't do any harm. Now, though, you should go back if you can and see to those feet, and then you can do best in this circumstance by calming and informing the others. Don't give too much away, but give them enough."

"I cannot lie," she told him.

"But you can playact. I saw you with the gown and the wig earlier. I assume you were just trying to mix without having the usual reaction to clerics kick in, but if it wasn't a lie, it was at least not bringing up an important fact. There are two important facts here that we should keep quiet about, at least for a while: say nothing about this being a deliberate act, and nothing about the possible fuel shortage."

"Is that really a problem? I thought the scoops brought in enough."

"No, that's only true in normal space. Propulsion here is from carried fuel. However, it's not as bleak as all that. The purpose clearly was to have us not know what went on here, and run dry at a predetermined point. They didn't count on me being aboard. Once we get this bridge back to some sort of normalcy, if need be I can use some of the cargo ahead. Almost anything works. It's just not as efficient as the real stuff. Back in the age of steamships on oceans, on old Earth, there would be emergencies, they'd run out of wood or coal, and wind up cannibalizing the ships, which tended to be wood, and any cargo that would burn. That's what we can do, and we have a *tremendous* amount of cargo stretching out in front of us. In fact, I'd like to find out what's really *in* some of those container modules. I'll bet you it isn't all just what's on the manifest." He paused a moment, licking his lips. "And then we'll look over the passenger manifest as well. Particularly the one for the two water modules . . ."

"You'll be all right here? I mean—you're going to be the target next if half of what you suspect is true, and you are a long way from friends and help if I leave," she said, concerned.

"Well, bless you for the thought, but go ahead, I'll be all right," he responded, seeming genuinely touched by her concern. She wondered just how long it had been since anybody had treated him as a real human being. "I'm not as helpless and vulnerable as you think. In fact, I daresay I may be the only person anywhere who these people genuinely fear."

Most of the people who had been milling around were gone by the time she got back, which was fine with her. She went immediately to her cabin, took a full shower and washed all the crud off her feet, found some sandals with thick soles in case she had to get back up there again, and felt a little better clean and dry. She was concerned about Kincaid even if he wasn't worried about himself. It was odd how an object of fear and pity had turned so quickly to friend and ally, but she had taken a liking to the man, who had proven not as grim as his outward persona nor as unfeeling in his hate as his reputation suggested. Not that he didn't hate. She could sense that, and the fact that he cared little about his own personal safety and well-being. He did, however, care about the safety and well-being of others, and that was what she found so likable in him. She had much the same attitude herself.

Angel decided to see if she could get a lighter and calmer fare for her now-empty stomach and then pretty much sit and wait. If any of the others came by and asked, she would give them a limited amount of information. Mostly, she wanted to see Kincaid again and be reassured that he was okay.

A ship's clock with a standard time setting was maintained aboard so that guests wouldn't get thrown completely off and some routine cleaning and maintenance by the module computer was possible. By that clock, it was now past two in the "morning," so she wasn't at all surprised to find the lounge empty. She was able to use the restaurant automation to order a light room service breakfast—some toast, jellies, and herbal tea—that made her feel much better. Still, as nobody else showed up, she was tempted to make the long walk back to the bridge. The restaurant holographic host, however, advised against it.

"Captain Kincaid is all right," the maitre d' assured her. "I have conveyed your concerns to the ship's computer and on to him, and he states that you are to get some sleep and be prepared to brief passengers in the morning. He also states that you should be prepared to do your service for Captain Dukodny at 1000 hours, if that is convenient for you."

She nodded. "Send him my thanks. I suppose he's correct, but it will be difficult getting to sleep after all this."

And yet, oddly enough, it *wasn't* that hard getting to sleep. It had been a long, tense, and tiring day, and the future was even more questionable, but for some reason, she was out as soon as her head hit the pillow.

Angel had never needed a lot of sleep, and she'd left a wake-up call for 0800, enough time to get composed and dressed, talk to people, and then make it up to the bridge. She was still concerned about Kincaid, alone in a possibly compromised bridge with a computer that might be compromised as well, and with a Rithian he felt might be part of it. But she had the strong feeling that Kincaid knew what he was doing and was used to being alone. That, in fact, was his true tragedy—that he lived his life isolated and alone.

Some of the passengers were up and about when she got to the lounge the next "morning," but she checked first with the computer connection inside the restaurant in the guise of a maitre d'.

"Good morning, madam," he said in his usual stuffy tones.

"Is Captain Kincaid still up there?"

"No, madam. He and his companion returned about two hours ago. It was necessary for the area to be sealed before it could be sanitized. He said you should meet him here at 1000 hours."

She thought a moment. "He can't have had any sleep. Do you think he will be awake then?"

"I have instructions to ensure this. He shows evidence of using tricaps in the past, perhaps too much. I believe he has a more difficult time sleeping than staying awake."

Angel didn't like the sound of that. Using that level of stimulant at all was wrong, but using it enough to develop the characteristic pallor and lines and raised blood vessels in the eye said that it was dangerous. It certainly explained his hollow, almost corpselike appearance.

Even if she could override his instructions, which she couldn't, she still wouldn't order him to bed now, though. As much as Kincaid needed sleep, and as much as he'd need it even more later on, if he slept, he would be vulnerable, and she saw the problem with that.

She'd been relieved that her feet and ankles weren't burned or peeling when she'd awakened, but the mixture of rust and yellow had dyed them a striking random pattern. She wondered if it wasn't mostly the toughness of her skin and the callused soles and sides that had saved her. Save for the times out in the Junction and the little time of masquerading here, she hadn't worn shoes in two years.

Angel took a light pastry and herbal tea breakfast and let the curious come over to her.

"Well, good morning, Sister Angel," Ari Martinez said, approaching her small table still carrying a mug of coffee. "So, what was the big mystery and where did everyone go?"

She nodded but didn't smile. "It wasn't a very pleasant thing. We found the captain dead and the bridge flooded."

There was always a slight murmur, an undercurrent of collective conversation, in almost any restaurant or café setting. It suddenly ceased, as if somebody had turned the volume down.

Martinez seemed genuinely shocked. "Dead! How?"

"We don't know. It looks like some foul play back at the Junction. All of this is essentially handled by the various computers, you know. It *did* appear that it was quick. Then they filled the bridge with pressurized water to keep anyone from coming in until, I suppose, we were in null-space and far beyond any legal jurisdiction."

"Then we're running without a captain?"

"No, Kincaid's a certified captain. A little out of practice, but he can do what little has to be done. At least the ship's computer thinks he can, and that's good enough for me. It's not like we have a choice, is it?"

"Um, no. But—*murder* you say? And water? Why would anyone do this? *How* could they do this?"

"When we find out, you'll be among the first to know," she assured him.

In the time after the initial breaking of the news, Angel discovered that she'd become quite popular. Some seemed to be pumping her for details; others just wanted confirmation or merely reassurance that the ship was still going to get where it was going.

What she found most interesting were the various people who *didn't* question her. She could understand why the Rithians didn't—Teynal certainly gave them the gory details—but when she thought back on it, neither Wallinchky nor the Kharkovs came near her, nor did that little weasel Tann Nakitt the Geldorian.

And then there was Ming Dawn Palavri. She came over, all right, as friendly and casual as the night before, but the kind of questions she asked had less to do with the crime than with wanting exact details about it. Angel had the impression she was being interrogated, and she didn't like it.

"I am not going into any more detail right now," she told the businesswoman. "Sorry. Why do you want to know every little thing, anyway?"

"Just curious. Maybe curious as to why somebody would do this, and looking for some clues." Ming sighed and smiled and patted Angel on the shoulder. "Sorry. I should know better. Force of habit. Still friends?"

Angel frowned and looked up at the other woman, feeling both patronized and lied to at the same time. Still, she answered, "Yes, of course. It was a very tiring day and I am short on sleep."

Afterward, Angel wondered about her own reactions. Ming and Ari *were* kind of private detectives, after all. Was she getting as paranoid as Kincaid? But then, Ari hadn't pressed her as Ming had. Why would Ming give her the third degree? Unless . . . unless she wanted to find out how much she and Kincaid really knew and what they might have in mind to do about it. That possibility annoyed Angel. She didn't like the notion of being reduced to a pawn.

Promptly at 1000 hours, Jeremiah Kincaid showed up. He was dressed in utilitarian work clothes and boots, but he'd obviously had a shower and cleaned himself up, and he looked in remarkably good shape.

He seemed genuinely happy to see her. "How's your feet?"

"Colorful, but otherwise no problem," Angel assured him. "They are pretty tough."

"Are you ready to go on back up?"

She nodded. "Lead on."

They went back through the café and out the rear once more, into the bowels of the module. This time, however, Kincaid stopped her short of the ladder.

"That's a storeroom with light over there," he told her. "I think the pragmatic thing to do is to get you into general disposable work clothes. I took the liberty of having some made up by the computer. I think things will be warmer and generally better suited to this sort of area."

She wanted to object and point out that the robe was okay with her, but she saw his point. The stretch jumpsuit was the same bright orange he was wearing. It fit like a glove and adhered to her body. The ankle-top sneakers grabbed where they met the deck, and she had to admit that the outfit was far more utilitarian.

She walked out and struck a pose. "Better?"

"Somehow I hadn't expected you to have quite that good a figure. But, yes, it'll serve. For one thing, it breathes but can also be a good insulator if need be, and the bright color allows you to be seen at a distance, which can be imperative inside the bowels of a ship this size. If you are satisfied, the computer can deliver a dozen more to your cabin. When you are done with this one, simply dispose of it as trash. Now— you aren't bringing a Bible or something?"

"I don't need one," she assured him. "It is a simple affair."

They went topside and then down the long tubular corridor to the main ship and bridge. Kincaid had been right about the work suit and shoes—there were few drafts and it was quite comfortable and flexible; and the sneakers, while feeling odd to her after not wearing shoes for so long, hugged the deck and gave her confident footing through the varying gravity field.

The bridge was almost unrecognizable. It gleamed, and everything seemed to be on and work. It looked brand new, as if nothing at all had happened. Only the body in the area behind the command chair reminded her of what had happened here only the day before.

The computer maintenance robots had prepared the dead captain's body after running a full pathological study, then placed it in a gel-filled container. It was impossible to make the body look presentable, but at least there was a discernible human form inside and the gory parts were not obvious to the onlookers. Four small cleaner robots floating a hair above the deck by magnetic levitation held the makeshift sarcophagus.

"Would you like to say something?" Angel asked Kincaid. "Even if you did not know him, you knew his kind."

He nodded. "Masters of spacefaring ships are the most lonely of people," Kincaid began solemnly, "often cut off from friends and family by the time differential wherein we in space age at a rate far slower than those who never move. His family is his ship; his friends are whoever books passage from point to point. He doesn't do it for the money, but because this is what he loves doing, what he is born to do. Captain Melak Dukodny died at his post, in his chair, doing what he loved. He certainly would have preferred it to go on longer, but he would not be sorry as to the place of his dying, nor the manner of disposition of these, his last mortal remains. I accept the temporary assignment of his commission, and bid him farewell." Kincaid stood ramrod straight, faced the body, and saluted.

Angel began the Prayer for the Dead and the Commission of the Souls. It was a mantra less biblical than traditional, out of the sect's book of common prayers.

"May he pass on, his soul joining the Universe of Eons, the Plane of Angels, cleansing him of all that is mortal and all that is sinful, and present himself to God bathed in the Ultimate Light. May he touch the six points of ultimate truth, and have everlasting life in the bosom of the Lord. That which cannot pass we commend to the deep, as the ashes of a fire long burning that now has passed beyond mortal ken, leaving only husks. Ashes to ashes, dust to dust, we return him to the stars from which all came. Amen."

She bowed her head in silent prayer, did the sacred signs of the Hidden Truths, touching the six points and then making the cross within, then looked up. "Convey the Captain's remains to their final destination," she said, looking up.

The robots began to move it across the bridge, into a compartment in the rear, which then closed behind it. There was the sound of hissing as a seal was made, and then a roar, and it was over.

"Interesting ritual," Kincaid noted. "I hadn't ever seen that one before, although some of it is the same."

"We have many levels to our faith. It is not as simple as most people believe faiths should be. Why should God be simple and create such complexity?"

He sighed. "Why indeed?"

"You have checked out the water breathing passengers?"

He nodded. "There are some bad sorts, and it's clearly somebody or maybe most of them there, but the one I expected isn't among them. I'm still having a physical inventory of all the barges ahead of us done, and that will take some time. We can't trust anything except a true examination and analysis, and there are 311 cargo modules, including the passenger one. If something illicit in the cargo is the reason for this, it may be fairly small and be in a false compartment in just one of those. It will take a great deal of time for the probes to do their work. Days perhaps. Anybody in our area not surprised by the news?"

"It is more remarkable how really unconcerned they all were," Angel told him, running down those who had something of a normal reaction, like Ari, and those who were unnaturally curious or equally unnaturally *not* curious.

He listened carefully until she was done, then said, "It may be worse than I thought. You see, of course, what the link is to many of those aboard?"

"Not exactly."

"Jewels. Gems. The Rithians are all from the Ha'jiz Nesting, and that family's entirely involved in the gem trade. The Kharkovs are gem cutters and also specialists in fine settings. Wallinchky is a man who likes the universality of gems both as collectibles and as commodities, and he doesn't care about the source. I would suspect that, somewhere in that vast train in front of us, we have some very, very hot gems that are changing hands here. There is no particular reason for Wallinchky to be selling, so let's assume he's the buyer and that he's brought the Kharkovs along to render the loot into something customs won't recognize without devaluing them. The Rithians are the go-betweens who are guarantors of the deal. They will certify the transfer and ensure payment. I strongly suspect that the payment isn't money. So what is it? What could be of such importance that this kind of crime, the murder of a starship captain, the sabotage of a ship, and the almost certain intent to do in the uninvolved passengers, would be warranted?"

She gasped. "They mean to murder us?"

"Perhaps. Perhaps not in the way you think. Wallinchky, for example, has more money than any human can spend in a thousand lifetimes. He's not really interested in that except as a means to power. Power is what drives his type. Power over just about everyone and everything. Those two women he flaunts as his companions—they are treated like property. He has them in his grip and he enjoys showing it. It could be drugs, some kind of mind control, hard to say, but he owns them."

"Why would anybody want slaves when he could have robots do anything by snapping his fingers?"

"Robots are no fun at all to him." He stared at her, grimly amused at her questions. "You really can't understand that kind of thinking, can you?"

She shook her head. "No, I can't. I can understand how this happened in the past, but not in this day and age. There is no *reason* for it. No logic."

"The universe is neither reasoning nor logical nor even moral," he said grimly.

"You do not believe in God?"

"I've found little evidence of Him, and I've looked. Believe me, I've looked. But I believe in the devil. I've actually *spoken* with him. And I can hardly avoid his handiwork. If you cannot understand the way these people think, then at least believe in evil. It's out there. It may be the only pure thing in all creation. Call upon your God in crisis if you wish. They will still burn you at the stake, but it may make you feel better when they do. But believe in evil. It's all around us. It's traveling with us, and we have to figure out a way to deal with it."

She looked at him. "I am prepared to die battling such evil if that is God's will, but I do not believe in suicide. Is there some way we can regain full control of the ship and keep them away from us?"

"We could. I have pretty full control of the ship, and I know what to watch for if they make a move to take it back or take something offline. Captain Dukodny could have blocked all this if he'd had the slightest suspicion something was up, but they counted on him considering everything routine, and that's what happened. At best, I suspect we're no more than fifty-fifty between friends and enemies. Operations like this travel with large entourages and lots of agents and hidden guards. That's why the likes of Wallinchky can travel so openly and comfortably even though a man like him has ten thousand mortal enemies. And of the ones on our side, many will be frightened and neutral, hoping to make a deal and escape with their lives, or else put themselves into denial, and the rest probably would be lambs to the slaughter of these killers."

"I can't believe it's as bad as all that," Angel said. "Still, why not simply withdraw the tunnel here and isolate yourself?"

"It may come to that, but it wouldn't stop them from calling me, and from executing a few people—like one of the children, or someone equally helpless—if I didn't let them in or didn't come down. I had to make that decision once. It is the most horrible decision a ship's Master can make. It's why I've spent most of my time since then getting close to no one, having no friends or relatives, keeping my relationships anonymous. Even then, I should not like to have to make that decision again. Once in a lifetime is too many times."

She decided not to argue with him, knowing they'd reached a point in their relationship where the walls would be too thick to bridge even under perfect conditions in the time they had remaining aboard, and these were not perfect conditions. She decided to turn things back to the issues at hand.

"It seems so particularly awful that all this should happen over something as base as who owns some gems," she commented.

"Oh, it's far more than that afoot here," he assured her. "I told you that this was the devil's work, and that means we must look not just at who is buying whatever it is, but who the seller is, and why he is selling them. This took a lot of money and influence to set up; money, then, is the tool here, not the object. In fact, I would be surprised if this wasn't some sort of barter. A weapon, perhaps, or something along those lines."

She stared at him. "You mean that your enemy is going to try once more to overthrow and rule the Realm?"

"He has always thought that way. He cannot abide that which he cannot rule. The odd thing is, if he ever *did* rule the known galaxy, he'd probably tire of it quickly and find some new things to step on. His pride was hurt that time so long ago. It's his pride, and his ability to hold a grudge almost to infinity, that moves him now."

"What does the devil look like?" she asked. When he smiled, she added, "No, I'm serious."

"No horns, no cloven hoofs, but it's an ugly little thing. Like a lump of raw undulating meat, really, with two very mean-looking eyes protruding from the rise in the middle. *Lots* of tentacles beneath, making it sometimes look as if it was sitting on a nest of hair. They're quite small, really, and can flatten out even smaller. They're parasites in spite of the eyes; those hairs are like needles, injecting into a host and then extending within until it controls all motor and nervous system functions. But since it does have eyes, and a kind of sonar common to water creatures, and since it can extract oxygen from water through rudimentary gills, it can detach and move from host to host. What it *can't* do on its own is eat. It draws what it needs from the host, and when the host gets used up, it moves on. But it has a mind that's surprisingly close to ours, and maybe smarter. *That* still remains to be seen."

"A surprising number of races are parasites, or at least symbiotic," she noted. "Evolution almost favors it. Otherwise you get races like ours, which tend to rape landscapes and then move on until they either find an infinite supply of new resources to destroy or cause their own demise. A smart parasite knows how important it is to keep things in balance."

"But it does tend to color the smartest ones' views of other races," Kincaid pointed out. "It has a vision of operating and sucking dry whole worlds."

"Are there any Ghomas riding with us this trip?" she asked him. "It would seem logical."

"None show up, and I'm sure I have the computers back online and all the bypasses and plants removed. They couldn't do an in-depth job on them without jeopardizing the ship itself. Still, there are at least two races breathing pretty much the same muck—those salts are a dead giveaway, since Ghomas need to ingest them when free of the host and forced to breathe the water. The fact that it's a near optimal Ghoma mix says to me that either they expect Ghomas to show up or, equally likely, those people in that atmosphere are used to the Ghoma mix. I think we can safely say that they probably either had a hand in this or directed it. Not a one boarded at Asswam Junction, but they boarded at three different stops before it."

She looked around at the vast bridge, which seemed so cold and complex. "So what will you do now?"

Kincaid sighed. "Well, they have to know we're searching the cargo and that we have full control of the ship again. That means we may well discover what's hidden here, perhaps both sides of this transaction, and we certainly will prevent any stops where they are expecting one. I've locked in a very complex security plan, and it's been extended to all of the main computers in the modules. If they kill me, they can't get around it and may well be trapped for murder. If they *don't* kill me, the same is possible. That means they will attempt to get at whatever they are after and do some kind of sabotage that will allow them to get away. They know there is nothing they can do, no matter how gut-wrenching, that would cause *me* to bend. You can't go to Hell twice."

"They could drug or torture you for the codes," she suggested.

"I've thought of that. I think they are well-briefed on me. If not, then they might accidentally kill me in the attempt, but they won't succeed. I've been sort of programmed myself, you see, and only I know the signals that turn it off. Torture will equal my death, and that will just result in the same thing. No, I think they will be very careful before they move. *Very* careful. They won't allow anything rash. I'm counting on that, since the more time I have with the computer and the probes, the more chance I can find out what this is all about."

She didn't like this, but what choice was there? "What do you want *me* to do?"

"Be yourself, and be my eyes and ears. I'm going to be pretty much of a recluse. Also, continue to wear the crew outfits. I realize they're revealing, certainly too revealing for someone in your profession, but because of that it will be difficult for them to improvise some device or the most common parasitic remotes without it being obvious, and I shall be able to track you easily, even visually. Be my eyes and ears with the passengers. I want to know what they are planning, and who is planning what. Use concierge services to ensure that your cabin is not bugged, that nothing is drugged, that all is normal. Think of yourself as in Eden surrounded by creatures, many of whom are serpents. Be paranoid, but be alert. And be quite free telling them what I am doing and what I intend and what their own problem is if they don't deal with me somehow."

"Huh?"

"If they know the usual routes are futile, they probably won't try them. I need time. I think I have some, anyway.

Remember, we are still about twelve days away from civilization, and eight from where they'd planned us to run dry and emerge into normal space."

That was the least pleasant thought of all.

Null-Space, Six Days Out

TANN NAKITT WAS SMOKING HIS CALABASH IN THE LOUNGE. It wasn't something that was allowed in that area, but the little weasel-like Geldorian had been doing it regularly and nobody had registered an objection. There was a certain built-in threat the creature radiated, particularly when he thought he wasn't going to like what you were going to say. Those beady eyes would light up as if on fire, and the multiple rows of sharp teeth behind the suddenly revealed fangs made one give pause before pressing a point.

Angel hated the smell the pipe gave off, and how it seemed to permeate everything around, but she had been trained by her sisterhood to tune out that which was personally offensive. You never knew who you might have to live and work around, or where.

She did not, however, feel particularly threatened by the Geldorian. Much of that spectacular facial stuff was for show, to avoid fights, since Geldorians were, after all, rather soft and vulnerable. Also, she'd managed to use the ship's references to determine exactly how such a creature attacked if provoked, and was pretty sure she could handle him. The real threat was in the venom; if it got into the bloodstream it would knock most warm-blooded oxygen breathers cold; Terrans and a few other races had a worse reaction—they'd regain consciousness and agreeably do whatever a Geldorian asked them to do. The Geldorian venom had a knack for adapting to whatever form it was inside of, at least until the host rejected it. So she knew to hold one by the neck and not let it bite.

But she didn't know if she *should* handle him; after all this time, most of the passengers were easy to categorize, but not this one. He didn't seem anxious to socialize with anybody, and he did not volunteer information.

She decided he couldn't be placed on the shelf any longer. Time was running out, and moves would be made by one side or the other.

Nakitt saw her coming right to him, and in his usual knee-jerk, pissed-off reaction, his eyes lit up and his teeth came out while he held his pipe in his hand. Almost immediately, though, he turned the display off, sensing that this strange, hairless Terran female felt no fear of him at all. That bothered Tann Nakitt; he was used to making everybody else nervous. It was more than a defensive posture—it was his hobby.

"We have to talk," Angel said firmly, standing and facing him as he lounged on an ottoman.

Tann Nakitt took a drag and blew thick yellow smoke up and toward her face. "No we don't," he responded.

She looked around. There was nobody in the immediate area, certainly nobody paying attention to them or within conspicuous earshot. "You are wrong. I believe that if we do not have a talk, then there is almost no way you can survive the next full day."

The needle-nosed snout came up, but he didn't betray any emotion. "Are you threatening me?"

"Yes."

He took another drag on the pipe, sensing that the smoke irritated her. "I thought you were some kind of priestess or something. I didn't think your type fought battles. They just exhorted the gods and spirits to stir up other folks to go off and fight holy wars."

The insult had the opposite effect of what he'd intended. She seemed more amused than upset by it.

"It is true that I could not harm a living thing by direct action," she agreed, "but if there is a threat to life or the safety of others or my well-being, I am capable of doing whatever is necessary. I say what I say because you fit into one of three categories. You may be ignorant of what will happen, in which case the other side will have you marked for death. You may be on their side, in which case you will trigger my defenses. Or you might be a potential ally, in which case the situation is the same as the first—you are marked for death by the others."

"And your object in saying this to me?"

"I want to know which category you are in. Since you neither seem surprised or alarmed by my description, I assume that you at least know what is building."

"I have an idea of it, but I don't think I'm in any of those categories. I am traveling on my own business, and I am known to some on what you call 'the other side.' I'm not involved in their business, but I suspect I can sidestep things and get where I want to go one way or another."

Without warning, the Geldorian lunged at her with a movement so fast that it was unthinkable. It was, therefore, a totally bewildered Tann Nakitt who missed Angel's arm and other parts entirely and went tumbling onto the floor. Even so, he was up in a flash, eyes blazing. But he suddenly froze. She was standing about a meter in front of him, holding his pipe.

"Filthy thing," she commented. "Do all your people smoke these?"

He lunged again, this time making every allowance for her possible response. Only she wasn't where she had to be; she was a step or two over. Again he fell on his face and rebounded, only this time he was breathing hard and felt a sore jaw. *That—thing—had caused him to bite himself!*

"This is impossible," he said, putting a small hand to his jaw and trying to massage it. "No one moves that fast. How long did you spend on Geldor to know us so well?"

"You are the first Geldorian I have ever seen or met," she told him. She tossed the pipe in the air in his general direction. Alarmed, he lunged for it, catching it just before it could hit the deck and perhaps break.

"What do you want from me?" he asked her sullenly.

"I cannot permit you to stand aside if needed. You might well join in, and certainly I am no match for several people acting at once. The choice to kill in self-defense would be automatic. Is that a *narcotic* in there?"

Tann Nakitt had been around and seen and interacted with many strange creatures, but this seemingly ordinary Terran female was the strangest person of any kind he could recall ever meeting. "What's the difference what I told you?" he asked her seriously. "You would have no way of knowing if I was truthful or lied."

"You must believe me when I say that I *would* know. Shall we both sit and relax? Or does that jaw need medical attention?"

"I'll be all right," he grumbled, getting back up onto the ottoman. She took a padded chair near him. "You are a telepath then? Is that how you do it?"

She laughed. "If I could read minds I wouldn't have to ask questions, would I? Let us just talk some more. You would not understand how I did that, or would know truth from lie, if I were willing to tell you, and I assure you I am not. Let's just talk. I am not in government or law enforcement, and whatever we say here is between us two alone. Even your venom could not get me to betray a private confidence."

He thought a moment, trying to decide which way to jump on the matter, then looked around, saw nobody lounging around or eavesdropping, and lowered his voice to a whisper. "All right. Yes, this is a narcotic, but only to my kind. It is a blend of chemically treated plants that not only produce a general feeling of contentment and well-being, but also heighten concentration and the potency of my venoms. By varying the formula, I can make the venom work as I wish on other races as I could on my native world. After all, we've had a long time to experiment and test. This, as you probably guessed, would put any of *your* kind in a trance inside of thirty seconds. Of course, it would simply render other races unconscious or perhaps kill them, unless I alter the blend and give it time to displace the old formula in my body. The threats here are basically Terran in nature; the Rithians are in on it, but this bunch are fixers—they don't have the nerve to do their own fighting."

"Fixers?"

"Arrangers of things, mostly illegal, but they're not above stooping to legitimate stuff, too, if it pays. You want a work of art? They'll try and buy it, and, if that fails, they'll find somebody to steal it. Want to buy a destroyer? They'll get one for a price. Middlemen. They make a ton of money doing that kind of thing."

"I see. And this is one side of the negotiation, in this area?

The other side of the transaction is in the water breather sections?"

"You *do* understand it. Yes. Sometime tomorrow we were supposed to glide to a stop, going under minimum power requirements and thus ejecting back into normal space. This would cause a distress beam, but in the region where we'd come out there's nothing much unless you *expect* us to be there. The Ha'jiz family meets the rescuers, gets what it wants, tells the newcomers where to find whatever *they* are paying for in the modules ahead, and that's it. Then the Rithians give whatever they get from the so-called rescue ship to King Wallinchky, and they all get into lifeboats with preprogrammed navigation modules, leaving us here, and that's that. The odds are they'll blow us up as they leave."

" 'King' Wallinchky? What's *he* the ruler of?"

"It is a nickname. The kind you get when you're about as high up in the rackets as you can get. It's a sign of real respect, and, in a sense, an acknowledgment of how much power he has over even life and death."

She did not understand it, that people would commit this kind of murder and worse for mere *possessions*. She doubted that she would ever understand it. Still, she understood the mechanics and the implications.

"And he's not afraid that this phony rescue ship won't simply blow *all* of us up once it gets what it wants?"

"Not even *this* gang would double-cross on that scale. Nobody would ever deal with them again. It may sound odd, but the most important thing when you reach the upper levels of criminal activity is honor. Betray that, and you are worse than dead and unable to ever use the illegal underground. That makes you vulnerable, and ultimately visible, to the Realm. No, Madam Kobe, that's not smart, and these people are smart. Besides, there's a limited market for the Jewels of the Pleiades. You can't ever wear them or display them. They are for an incredibly wealthy private collector who wants them all to himself. The Kharkovs are here only to clean and possibly reset some, which indicates a bit of damage. After all, the jewels were last seen in the midst of an explosion that essentially vaporized an entire city. You don't cut these kind of gems."

She had never heard of these legendary jewels, but he

obviously thought everybody had. "And Wallinchky is the collector? What does he have to pay in return?"

"I'm not sure. A weapon of some sort. A top secret one. One the Realm probably doesn't even know is gone."

"The Rithians are that good, huh? So how did these Jewels of the Pleiades get into the hands of the buyers of this weapon? Do you know?"

The Geldorian gave a soft chuckle. "Well, their leader blew up the city about a century and a half ago. That's how long they've been missing."

She was almost sorry he'd said that, even though she suspected it herself. They were being monitored by the ship's master computer, of course, and their conversation dampened to others, who would hear only unintelligible murmurs unless they came right up close. But Jeremiah Kincaid would have heard it. If not now, he'd certainly review it later. And he'd know that his ancient enemy was indeed at the center of all this.

"And you think that they'll just give you a ride out?"

He shrugged. "They say so. The Rithians were also involved in getting *me* what *I* wanted, so they have no reason not to vouch for me along the line, or if need be, take me in theirs. What I carry is information that my people need but which is of no value to others. My people know I have it. I doubt if the Rithians want to get them angry."

"Who are the bodyguards aboard? Do you know?" she asked him.

"Some. Maybe all. I don't know. The Mallegestors are certainly hired muscle. Pretty intimidating muscle, too, I'd say. All they need to do is sit on you. And you have to get through two hundred centimeters of hide before they notice enough to say 'Ouch.' Beyond them, I'd guess the two females."

"*Those* two? But they're no more than pet prostitutes!"

"True, but some people train their pets to guard their homes and families. He's incredibly rich and powerful and he's above the law. The King has every means of conditioning—biochemistry, virtual reality conditioning, you name it. If you look close at them you'll see that they are in superb physical condition, and I don't mean just for sexual favors. They probably were empty-headed runaways from backwater planets, ignorant and without any sense of themselves when he or his people picked them. But I've seen that before, in both sexes, not only among your people but other races as well. He probably has a command, possibly verbal or gesture. Give that, and the conditioning takes over and they'll become fearless and vicious protectors. I know a bit about conditioning people myself. I can only do it for a short period and only with the most elementary basics. Imagine what the wonders of science can do in *his* hands. The perfect bodyguards."

She didn't like that idea at all. There would be no way to read such a person's actions. Still, if they *were* what he said they were, they could be dealt with.

"We're not stopping now, though," she said. "Surely everybody knows that. Kincaid is taking us straight through using grain cargo as fuel. What do you think they're going to do about it?"

"Your assessment of what Kincaid will do tells me you have a lot to learn," the Geldorian responded.

"What's that supposed to mean?"

"I'm referring to whether Kincaid will stop the ship for our supposed rescuers. They've had a lot of time to factor in Captain Jeremiah Wong Kincaid."

"I've gotten to know him pretty well over the past few days," she told him. "I trust him."

Tann Nakitt stared at her. "You have no idea. I doubt if *I* have any idea. The hatred in that man is all there is beneath the surface."

"You are wrong. There's a real person deep inside there. I've seen him."

"You have seen the pragmatic Captain, but it sits atop the hate, like a thin film of scum atop a pond. The hate is the pond, and he does not control it. It's irrational, single-minded, obsessive. If Kincaid wanted to save us from the bad guys, he could do it. He's got full control back, he knows the score, and we're pretty helpless in fighting him. You have no idea what absolute control a ship's master has if the computer's neural net recognizes him as master. That was why they had to deal with the original captain. You think Kincaid was here by accident? Who knows how he learned of this plot, but he knew it out of the gate. What little he didn't know he filled in. Your gods didn't put him here to save us and fight sin. His demons put him here to get to his sole object of hatred. Wallinchky could have called this off at any time, too. He hasn't. That's because he knows that Kincaid will stop. He's counting on it."

"I can't believe I was fooled by him, but just in case, you and I will need to speak again."

The Geldorian gave a very Terran shrug. "I'm hardly going anywhere, am I?" He took another drag on his pipe. "You sure *aren't* telepathic, are you? At least with your own kind. You may be able to tell lies from someone who is merely deceitful by nature, but you are helpless against psychopaths."

Captain Kincaid was waiting for her in the big command chair on the bridge. Since she was the only one who could come up there, all others being blocked by the computer from access, he didn't even bother to turn around when she entered. Still, he said, conversationally, "That was some kind of move you made against the Geldorian. You really *can* take care of yourself! I had to put the recording on the slowest tolerable speed to see you move! I'm impressed!"

She didn't respond to his compliment, nor was she in the mood for flattery. "Well?"

"Well what?"

"Is it true? Are you going to stop for them?"

He paused a moment, then said, "Of course. They hope I will, anyway."

"But—*why*? Is Tann Nakitt right? Are you *insane*?"

"Possibly," he admitted, as cheerfully as if he'd commented on a good wine. "Most think that I am."

She felt real anger against him for the first time. "Why? Why will you do what they want? Will it please you if they go through all this and then this ship gets blown up with all remaining aboard so you can go chase your demon Emperor?"

He swiveled the command chair around slowly and faced her. "I think I can prevent that. I hope so. If I'm wrong, a few unhappy bystanders will die and I will add more innocent blood to my record. I can guarantee that Wallinchky's lifeboat won't respond to his orders, or those of anyone we know connected with him. Doesn't matter which lifeboat he picks, either. That means he either helps this ship get out of here or he goes with the rest. He's a very smart man who's lived a long time, and, as your friend says, it would be very bad for future business if he got blown away on this operation."

"Then—*why*?"

"If we go right on by, we may be met at the next destination by more tugs with thugs. Wallinchky walks away and either the Rithians will get their cargo back before Customs, to try it again on another trip, or it'll all blow up as soon as they're off. Either way we gain nothing. We change the names and faces of those who will die, and we delay them a couple of weeks."

"If they blow *it*, whatever *it* is, up, that'll delay them longer than that."

"Not much. They have the prototype, yes, so it would be inconvenient to lose it, but they have the entire plans and specifications and even the operator's manual, as it were, and that is far more valuable. It simply means that the customer will have to arrange to have one built on the black market out on the frontier where it won't be noticed until it's too late. Either way, the first solid lead pointing directly to Josich Hadun's hiding place in more than a dozen years will have been squandered. How many more will he kill before that chance comes again?"

She didn't like this at all. "I see no moral choice but to save the innocents here and try again. And what of the innocents in the water-breathing modules? I cannot get to them."

"I don't think there are many innocents there, but if they are, they're dead no matter what we do. We might as well make their deaths mean something."

That was not a proper answer, she thought, but she was beginning to see how useless reason was with him now. Still, she had to give it one last try.

"You have no guarantee that this will lead you to your enemy, but there is a great probability that some will die," she argued.

"You can't stop it. Tomorrow we will stop, just where that Ghoma ship expects us to be. The distress signal will be sent. Of course, we won't *really* be out of fuel or in distress, but it will be pretty convincing. They will come. During that fallow time, you and others you trust must get all those not

involved in this to lifeboats and get the boats away. They are
preprogrammed. The Ghomas likely won't detect you, but if
you use the cryogenic settings, you'll reach a Junction or
Starbase or a known hospitable Realm world in due time.
Do it as quickly and quietly as you can. The computers will
help you."

"And you?"

"They need a tug to get the module out. I've found it and
I now control it. Where that ship and that module goes, I
will go as well. Unless they have their own freighter, they
won't be going all that far with a module that size. In fact, I
already suspect where he is. I just have to get there."

"And not be killed."

He smiled grimly. "I can't be killed. I'm already dead."

It didn't seem there was any way to talk him out of it. The
only choice she could see, morally and otherwise, was to
count on him for cover and get out those who had to go. If
she understood any of this complicated mess or could argue
well with the computer, she would have chosen to disable
Kincaid and just arrange not to stop. Being unable to do any
of that, she knew she would have to do it his way.

And she would have to do it fast. The ever-present countdown clocks said there were only hours left to go.

Angel didn't use those hours idly, nor waste them in sleep or
recrimination. She had a Situation, as her trainers would
have called it, and it demanded that choices be made and
stuck to.

One by one she contacted the cabins of those she'd determined were just ordinary passengers. As crisply and profes-
sionally as possible she explained the basics of the situation,
and that their only chance was the lifeboats, which Kincaid
could protect and launch remotely. Some refused to believe
her. Some simply were too scared or convinced that this
somehow didn't apply to them and would blow over if they
ignored it. She didn't have much of a choice with the latter.
They were told they would get one chance, and if they did
not take it, they were on their own.

In each case, once told, the life module's computer isolated them from the lounge and public areas. They could get
deliveries to their rooms, but that was all. They would have

to watch their cabin clocks; when instructed, they were to proceed, following the lifeboat signs, and board.

She was particularly gratified by the few who offered to stay and fight it out with Kincaid, but she rejected that course. This wasn't their battle, and the opposition was far too powerful. In this case, dying just wasn't a particularly productive strategy, and even if you could take some of the nasty ones with you, well, what was the long-term point that was worth lives?

Ari Martinez and Ming Dawn Palavri were two she felt confident she could place in charge of individual lifeboats. She planned on taking the third out herself. Tann Nakitt was still something of a question mark, but she allowed him to make his own decision, although he was, of course, monitored to ensure that he tipped off none of the bad guys.

Not that they needed to be tipped off. Jules Wallinchky sent the Rithians and Mallegestors on an all-out search to find out where the hell everybody had gone. When they determined that almost everybody had remained in their cabins for the last day and night, Wallinchky knew something was up. When he determined that the lifeboats would not respond to the general emergency access panels, he had the plot pretty well figured out.

"What do you want to do?" Teynal asked him. "If we can't get off, we will have to go with *them*. Inconvenient, and they are water breathers."

Wallinchky seemed singularly unworried. "We'll take care of it. You know I never go into a place unless I have good protection and multiple exits. They can shut off corridor access to us when they need to, so I say let 'em go. If they can't be picked off, so be it." He did, however, palm and pass several pieces of paper between his people and himself, actions that could be observed by the monitors but not read by them. In all cases, they ate the messages, so there would be no reconstruction. Clearly he wasn't going to give away his game plan to Jeremiah Kincaid.

Sealed off on the bridge with his monitors, Kincaid was frustrated by this most primitive of devices, nor could he be certain from that vantage point what conversations of theirs were for real and which ones were for his benefit.

It was simply a matter of waiting that eternity until the clock ticked down and they were ejected from null-space back into the normal universe. In the meanwhile he could only try to anticipate everything and wonder what he'd missed.

When the clocks read seven days, twenty hours, fifty-one minutes, no seconds, there was a shudder that shook the entire ship, and everyone once more had that feeling of falling into a deep, bottomless pit. Alarms went off then, and the ship's "voice" said, "Attention! Attention! We have experienced an emergency, and to avoid loss of life and minimize discomfort we have been forced to reenter normal space short of our destination. Please remain calm. For your safety, all passengers are directed toward the lifeboats designated for their immediate sections. Do not be alarmed. It is a routine procedure. In the event of a life-threatening situation, the lifeboats can take you without harm to safety. This will probably not be necessary, but to ensure that everyone is where they should be, please follow the flashing lines in the direction they indicate to your lifeboats now."

In the lounge, Wallinchky nodded to the Rithians and whispered something in the ears of each of his beautiful companions. All of them immediately set off into the corridors, while the Mallegestors took up protective station with Wallinchky in the lounge.

Kincaid couldn't quite figure out what was going on, but he spoke into the two-way in his environment suit on a channel only he knew was operational. "Execute final option, priority code Ahab. Good luck, *City of Modar*. You are on your own."

"We will do our best, Captain," came the response from the control panel. "Good luck."

Jeremiah Kincaid had to stifle a chuckle at that, even at this most tense of moments. A computer had just wished him good luck. He wasn't sure he liked discovering that computers believed in luck.

The area they were in represented a huge amount of space, and he had only an approximation of where the other ship would emerge. Even a few seconds here or there could mean tens of thousands of kilometers; minutes might turn into millions.

He'd turned off the ship's local distress calls, but the other ship would have something, probably from the water sections.

Almost as if on cue with the thought, his sensors picked it up, the scanners locking in on the frequencies. There was no way to break their code at this point, of course, but he noted with some approval that the ship seemed to be having some success in either jamming or dampening their signals. The more time the better.

Back on board, Angel saw that the loading of the lifeboats was going pretty well. A few didn't come, but most did, particularly that family Angel had worried so much about. The computer had instructions to launch as soon as the lifeboats were filled, and at least one, with Ari in command, Angel hoped, had already left. She went down to the second one to check on it and saw Ming at the entrance but making no move to board.

"Why aren't you aboard? You must leave!" Angel cried urgently to the other woman. "I will go back and catch any stragglers."

Ming shook her head. "Sorry, can't do it. I wanted one last check to see if anybody else was coming, then I'm sealing it up."

"But—*why*?"

"Because I'm a kind of a cop, that's why, and because my job is to prevent the transfer of that device even if I have to blow it up." She turned and stuck her head in the door. "Everybody just follow the instructions of the holographic boatswain and you will be fine. Good luck!"

Angel almost moved to put a martial-arts-style kick on Ming's rear that would have propelled her into the lifeboat, but for some reason she held back. She hoped she wouldn't regret it.

The hatch swung shut, there was a loud hissing sound, then the vibration as the lifeboat detached from its moorings and fully powered up, the corridors shaking as well, and then the lifeboat was gone.

Angel looked at Ming and saw that she had a full-power laser pistol stuck in her belt, which she now removed and checked. "How—How did you even get that on board?" Angel asked her.

"They set it up to smuggle their weapons aboard, so it wasn't that hard to use the same system," Ming replied. "Now, let's check on the third boat and any missing passengers."

"You should get on the third boat!" Angel pleaded with her. "This is suicide!"

"Maybe, but I know what this sucker is. You don't. And don't ask what it is, either. Just trust me that it's worth a lot more lives than Kincaid's and mine to keep it out of any-. body's hands, particularly Hadun's."

They were moving at a fast walk along the corridor, circling to the other set of boats. As they came to each cabin door, it unlocked and slid away into the bulkhead. They could then check and see if anybody was still in any of them. So far, they'd found a couple, and those had both decided to exit with them. Now, however, they were approaching Boat Station Three.

This was the most dangerous of the positions; the two lifeboats on the side they'd just left were easily accessed by most of the passengers they wanted to reach, and could be blocked off to Wallinchky's crowd, most of whom had cabins on the far side, basically flanking Wallinchky's superluxury suite. The lifeboat nearest that cabin suite at Boat Station Four now had its power off; it could not be turned back on without a complex series of passwords or direct authority of the *City of Modar*'s computer net.

The other one, however, was kind of a border location. Ari's cabin was on the wrong side, as was Tann Nakitt's. Hopefully they were both inside now so that the access could be sealed off, but if not, there could be trouble.

Ari was standing in the lifeboat, frowning, as he watched them approach. His face showed some surprise when he saw Ming with Angel, but he was all business, getting the two stragglers in and settled. Then he came up, out of the lifeboat, and spied Ming's pistol. "What's *that* for, doll?"

"Long story. Anybody missing?"

"No, we're as good as we're gonna get. Come on!"

Angel reached the hatch, looked in, then turned and frowned. "Where's Tann Nakitt?"

"Long story," he responded, bringing up his own pistol and firing on Angel. Her body was bathed in a sudden glow and then she collapsed, unconscious, to the deck.

The action was so automatic it caught Ming by surprise, but she brought her pistol around on her old friend immediately. That was the problem—he *was* an old friend, and one-time lover. You don't pull the trigger that fast on somebody like him when your pistol is set to kill.

That allowed two stun blasts from the Wallinchky women behind her to strike and knock her instantly as out-to-the-world as Angel.

Ari looked down at them. "Take them to the lounge. Any barriers, start shooting up the electrical plates. *Move!*"

He leaned into the now terrified lifeboat and said, "This does not concern you. I'm closing and you will launch as per normal. Just follow the boatswain's instructions. Maybe some of us will live through this to explain it all to you. Go with God!" He pulled back, sealed the hatch, and heard and felt the lifeboat detach and shoot away.

He hoped they *would* make it. They knew virtually nothing about this, and interrogation wouldn't bring much more in the way of details useful to the authorities. Creatures like this Hadun bastard never cared how many innocents they killed, but he didn't believe in gratuitous violence. He was particularly sorry about Ming. He'd wanted her to take her lifeboat and be well away when she had the chance. It was only because she showed up here, and with a pistol, that she made her fate inevitable.

The whole module suddenly lurched, throwing him momentarily off balance, and the lighting went on and off erratically for a half minute or so while the cabin doors eerily slid open and closed, open and closed. Then it was over, at least for the moment.

Ari made his way down a spoke corridor to the center lounge. The rest of them were already there, waiting for him.

"What the hell was *that*?" he grumbled.

Jules Wallinchky was as unflappable as ever. "Don't let it get to you. We managed to tap in and get some interference going. I don't think we can rehijack the module computer, but we tapped it enough to remove all those nasty force fields."

"We have Boat Four on its own power," one of the Rithians announced, returning just in back of Ari. "Boats Five and Six were never blocked, and our soggy friends are away from the ship and on station. Hard to tell if everybody else is in the other boats and heading out, but it looks like the bulk of the passengers will make planetfall sooner or later."

"As will we, my friends," Jules Wallinchky assured them, one of his girls lighting a big, fat cigar for him.

"What do you want *me* for?" Tann Nakitt grumbled. "I can't hardly go to the cops, and I don't give a damn about your deals. Ask the Rithians." He was now bound hand and foot in what a Terran rancher might call a hog tie. He wanted to bite somebody, but the only one in range was one of the huge Mallegestors, and he'd just break his teeth on it.

Wallinchky blew smoke in the Geldorian's face, causing the little creature to cough, giving the victim what he'd so recently been fond of handing out. "I know all about your little expedition, and the poison formulas for all sixty-eight races of the Realm that you carry in that memory bubble implanted in your neck. I also know you'd sell out your entire planet if you thought it would get you out of something." His voice had risen menacingly, and was now filled with rage. "But what I know *most* is that you knew about all this plotting and planning against me and you did *nothing*! You said *nothing*! At least, not to me. To *her*, to this—this—*nun* you tell the whole deal! For *that* I'll have your fangs and all your countless other teeth extracted one by one and put in a sack with your fingers and toes and *other* extraneous parts!"

"I didn't *betray* you, you bastard!" the Geldorian snapped back, too angry to be scared. "I had no interest in your doings and just wanted to be allowed to continue no matter who won! And I sure hadn't heard any good offers from *you*!"

Wallinchky rose, as if he would go over and strike the smaller creature, but then he sat back down and seemed to regain control.

"You hadn't heard anything from me because I hadn't decided about you, Geldorian," the crime king told him in his usual calm, deliberate mode. "Now I have. Don't worry, though. I have an honorable streak in me. Yes, I do. I might send your people that bubble anyway. Maybe I'll even send them your whole head. I could use a few favors in that quarter."

Tann Nakitt said nothing, not even demonstrating that his

incredible limberness extended to his arms and wrists and that he could already slip in and out of his bonds at will. There would be time to either try and escape or at least gain revenge; right now it didn't seem there was anywhere to run, so he decided it would be best to allow them to carry him someplace worth escaping from.

"I can understand me, but why *her*?" the Geldorian asked, trying not to provoke the big man any further. And if Nakitt could get the subject off the fate of certain Geldorians, it would make the next waiting period a bit more tolerable and probably less painful.

It wasn't as if any of them could do much until the rescue party arrived, so Jules Wallinchky didn't mind being the center of it all.

"She's the Captain's friend and known to the ship's computer net," the crime boss explained. "Kincaid can undock the tow from us and then blow us to bits, you know. That's why we tried to ensure that nobody would be up there when we stopped. He's perfectly capable of doing that, and even more so now that the innocent passengers are gone." He raised his voice and looked toward the ceiling, more as a dramatic gesture than because anything was really there. "But not all the innocents *are* away, are they, Captain? And while you might gladly do any of us in, even her, if it meant getting closer to your enemy, *we* aren't your enemy, are we, Captain? What do *we* care about Hadun? So you go at him, Captain, but leave us alone. I understand your viewpoint even though almost nobody else does. You're no murderer— you're an executioner. That's okay with me. Go at them, Captain. But remember *her* and leave all of us out."

There wasn't any response. Wallinchky didn't expect one. Still, he knew he'd made his point.

The crime king looked back down at the still unconscious Angel on the deck, her hands and feet tied behind her and together in much the same manner as Tann Nakitt. "Besides," he added in a lower, menacing tone, "I saw how she moved and could fight. Not at all the Sister Helpless she appeared at the start of this trip. And she's got a pretty good body there. Erase the memories, reinforce the skills, and she might be a nice addition to my personal staff. As for the lady

cop, I'm *positive* she'll change sides." Ming, too, was trussed
up like Angel and still out cold.

A tone sounded from a small communicator on Wallinchky's belt. He unclipped it and said into it, "Yes?"

"We have a signal response on the proper frequency with
valid codes," a strange, distant, flat voice told him.

"Very well. I'm moving everybody into Boat Four now.
Cover us in case there are any surprises."

"Will do."

He reclipped the communicator and looked at the large
party that had been sitting around. Each of the two Mallegestors picked up a Terran prisoner in one hand, carrying
them as if they were no more than a small bag of snacks.
One of them picked up Tann Nakitt with the other.

"Hey! Watch it, jumbo!" the Geldorian snapped. "I bruise
easy!"

The Mallegestor gave a loud snort which could have been
a kind of laughter.

Behind them, first the Kharkovs, then the Rithians, followed, and finally came Wallinchky and his pair of bodyguard
mistresses.

Ari Martinez was already in the lifeboat, and he had the forward control panel disassembled and a set of small cubes with
internal flashing light points set into the boat's electronics.

The four Rithians took the rear seats, two on each side,
then the Mallegestors eased into adjusted seats that could
hold them, one on each side, with Nakitt in the port empty
seat, hemmed in, and nobody in the starboard empty. Next,
Wallinchky sat in front of the Mallegestor on the starboard
side, and his two pretty companions took the seats on port
and starboard side in front of the crime boss. The two Terran
prisoners were quite literally hung from the two other seats
next to the bodyguards, the seats in front of them providing
a kind of stake through the bound hands and feet so that
they were held against the seat backs, looking aft. The front
of those seats, the empty ones on each side, were for the
drawn and frightened-looking Kharkovs. Ari Martinez had
the jump seat, next to the jury-rigged console and facing aft
himself, although more comfortably.

He got up, closed and sealed the hatch manually, then
took his seat again, reaching down and picking up a tablet

the size of a large notebook. He pressed some areas on it, and the lifeboat's forward screen came to life, showing the boat moving off from the larger vessel and the connector pulling off and remaining there, half extended, as if waving goodbye.

"Any trouble in getting Kincaid's stuff out of the guts of this thing?" Wallinchky asked him.

"No, not really. It was pretty basic, but it couldn't be done until after it was activated. I'm not sure it occurred to him that no power in the boat also meant no power to his monitors."

Wallinchky chuckled. "His mind was on other things." He turned as he heard a moan from his left, just forward. "Ah! The sleeping beauties are coming around!"

It had felt to Angel as if she were falling down a long, dark tunnel at breakneck speed, only occasional flashes of light here and there and terrible distorted sounds breaking the otherwise monotonous free fall. Now the noise increased, became an increasingly louder rushing noise, like white or pink noise gradually increasing in volume to nearly unbearable levels. Then she came to, but wished she hadn't, as every muscle in her body seemed to protest in throbbing or sharp pains, and there was tremendous disorientation. Her arms and legs were in particular pain, and she tried to move them but found that she could not.

Angel opened her eyes, but they wouldn't focus and showed multiple whirling visions of a lot of people she didn't want to see very much. She shut her eyes, tried to slow down the room or wherever it was, and began a series of calming and breathing exercises that seemed to help somewhat.

Next was tuning out the pain, or as much of it as she could. Then she brought her head back up and opened her eyes to an almost steady scene, although she still had blurry double vision.

"What? Who?" she managed, her voice sounding like the croak of the walking dead even to her ears.

"Welcome back!" Wallinchky said with smug cheerfulness. "I see your lovely friend is also coming around. It's no use trying to struggle against the bonds. We know how to tie them right, and they'll just tighten and get worse. If you struggle, it'll cut off your circulation and you might lose some limbs, which may not be worth regenerating in a med-tank. That depends on how much trouble you are. Oh—*terribly* sorry! I forgot. I am Jules Wallinchky, the Realm's greatest collector."

"Collector?" Angel managed. "Of what?"

"Why, of *everything*, of course. Art, wealth, knowledge, people, services, political power, great inventions—you name it, I got it. Some folks in the past went out to conquer their world or their system or even the entire Realm. They all failed, in the end. Even Alexander the Great died a mere youth, mostly because he felt there were no new worlds worth conquering. Fortunately, *our* physical and personal universe is infinite, so for me conquest has never stopped being a source of fun and satisfaction, maybe because, un-like this Emperor Hadun, I have no desire to conquer the universe itself. Someone else can do that. I don't conquer it, I *acquire* it. Or anything within it that I want. I have whole planets devoted just to storing and displaying my most pri-vate acquisitions."

"Wallinchky, you bastard," Ming managed in a voice that sounded as bad as Angel's. "What are you going to do with us? Why didn't your hired hand just kill us and be done with it?"

The crime king chuckled. "Weren't you *listening*, my dear? I have no desire to kill two such attractive and ca-pable young women. I've simply *acquired* you, you see. I'll be taking you both home with me. There you will be—prepared—and properly set up to join my collection, just as the Kharkovs will be polishing and repairing the settings on my most precious gems."

"I'll see you in Hell first!" Ming snapped.

"Well, you'll still be mine even if we go *that* route, but I doubt we will," he responded. "That soreness and taste of blood in your mouth is from where we removed the poison while you were out. Ivan Kharkov is a wizard with all sorts of little things like that. And we won't trigger your im-planted death command. Far from it. I don't want to ask you anything at all, so there won't be any hot button to push. In fact, I think we'll simply erase and replace. Probably for the both of you. It's easier that way. Knowledge is only impor-tant if it's useful, and I suspect that neither of you know anything I don't." Wallinchky grinned. "And it's not your personalities that I find attractive."

"God will smite you for this abomination!" Angel spat.

"I doubt it, but by all means pray silently for it to happen. I suspect you'll find out what I did long ago as a child—that God answers every prayer, but the answer is almost always no."

"Can't you at least let us sit in seats and get circulation back?" Ming pleaded with him. "This is very painful."

"Sorry. I don't mean to keep you in pain—I really don't—but one of you is a trained undercover policewoman, and I've seen the other outmaneuver our Geldorian friend with some sort of impressive martial arts. Unless you're under sedation or isolation from me, I don't think I can afford to have either of you loose."

"Ship coming in!" Ari announced. "Pazir class. A minor warship, but it's got enough power to catch us and enough to tow a mod at least two light-years given a fuel hookup."

Wallinchky frowned. "Our Captain won't like *that*. Pazir class aren't adapted to breathers."

"I doubt if he expects the Emperor to be aboard or anywhere near here," Martinez responded. "He'll try and chase or get aboard."

"A good point. Are we well away from the ship? I don't know what they have in mind, but it would be nice to be on *their* side of their guns."

"I can't quite do that," Martinez said, "but I don't think we're close enough to get harmed. I'm station-keeping with the two water lifeboats and they seem satisfied."

A ship entering from null-space was an eerie sight; there was no bright flash, no spectacular opening in space-time, at least not that anyone could see. It was just as if a ship emerged from nothing, or from a narrow slit that nothing could detect. It was unlike going *into* null-space, where there was a substantial energy flow and discharge.

The warship looked like nothing so much as three large gunmetal-gray balls one after the other, with the center section ringed by smaller balls of the same type. Although huge when measured against the lifeboats, it was minuscule when contrasted to the massive *City of Modar*, whose engine and bridge section alone was a good forty times the warship's size.

The small balls ringing the center section suddenly flared up with a blaze of yellow light that quickly went to white, resembling nothing so much as searchlights going out into space from the ship. As suddenly, the beams converged, and at the point of convergence well ahead of the warship a brilliant thin white beam so bright it overloaded the lifeboat cameras shot out and struck the *City of Modar* at and just forward of the bridge. A huge section of it vaporized; the interior, which had been under pressure, blew out, scattering debris, and the transparent tunnel and catwalk linking it to the passenger module was sliced off and twisted away from the blast.

The beam winked off, then quickly back on again, this time coming down on the hapless freighter like a knife through soft bread, slicing through the docking mechanism and connectors, literally severing the engine and bridge module, and the main computer, from the tow.

"I'm sorry you can't see this," Jules Wallinchky told his prisoners, fascinated by the sight. "It's pretty impressive."

The colors on the small balls now changed from white back to yellow, and then to a bright orange, converging again about a quarter of the distance to the now adrift but still station-keeping power plant of the big ship. A series of bright burning fireballs of the same bright orange emerged from the convergence, struck the *City of Modar*, exploded there, and literally pushed it away and on a different trajectory than the rest of the long train of modules. It got, perhaps, a kilometer away, and then exploded in a spectacular silent fireball.

"Wow! Now *that* was a good show!" Wallinchky enthused. He turned to the back. "Teynal? It's your turn to take over negotiations here."

"Why do they have to negotiate?" Ming asked, almost taunting him, even though speaking hurt her parched throat. "They have the train and maybe two weeks minimum lead time. They could just blow us away and take everything."

The serpentine Rithian leader came forward and took the portable communicator from Jules Wallinchky. "Not exactly," he hissed. "Even if they are thinking along those lines, now is the time to disabuse them of that."

With that, the Rithian spoke into the communicator. It

was in a local Rithian dialect and in code; translator modules couldn't handle it, and all they heard were the deep, inhuman sounds the creature actually uttered.

There was a sudden flare at the connector between the now exposed passenger module and the next mod up the train. Small jets automatically fired, moving it away from the others, whereupon it exploded spectacularly on its own.

"Goodness me! I hope the Captain wasn't in either of those units," Jules Wallinchky said in a sarcastic tone that implied exactly the opposite sentiment. "I don't underestimate him, though. I just wonder what his plan really *is*, out of plain curiosity."

"You blew up the passenger mod? *Why?*" Angel asked him.

"It's not like anybody who counted was left on it. I suspect it was evacuated fully," Wallinchky replied. "And now they know we can blow up what they want, just as they can blow us up. It makes a wonderful basis for trust and mutual exchange. The Ha'jiz are the very best at their job."

"Signal coming in!" Ari told him.

Teynal's cobralike head bobbed in satisfaction. "Put it on speaker. I will use this for responses."

A voice came through the lifeboat's public address unit, sounding a bit tinny but otherwise okay. "You've made your point," it said in a high, reedy tone that gave no clue as to the race of the speaker. "So how do we make the exchange?"

"I assume you wish the entire module?" the Rithian asked him. "It certainly will be easier to move that way."

"Yes, that is satisfactory. Any problems?"

If Rithians laughed, Teynal would have. "Some. You should know that Jeremiah Wong Kincaid was aboard and that he stumbled over our plans."

There was a long pause, then, "Kincaid! Oh, they will *love* that! You dealt with him?"

"Probably not. My best guess is that he is still here, in this area, not on one of the lifeboats, but that he intends to somehow board you and have you take him to your leader, as it were."

"Any idea where he might be hiding?" the suddenly worried-sounding voice from the warship asked.

"We have some ideas. The most logical is that he located

our cargo and is hidden within the module somewhere in an environment suit. You will have to take it with you and thus him, and it would be ridiculous to try and ferret him out in *this* environment. I could be wrong, but it is the only idea that makes sense to me."

The man on the warship considered it. "Sounds logical to us, too. All right, I think we can contain that. In fact, I suspect that His Imperial Highness will be overjoyed to have old Kincaid on our turf, as it were, now that we know he's out there. All right. Which module is it?"

"Twenty-seven. It is, remember, wired—we shall transmit the codes in due course—but we can do an automated disconnect safely. Stand by."

Again the Rithian spoke some noises none but one of his kind could speak into the communicator, using the preestablished command frequency. Well out in front, virtually too far up the tow to see, the magnetic locks slipped back, the module turned using small steering jets, and it rolled out of line, spinning, until the jets reversed and stopped it. Module 27 was now station-keeping about a hundred meters from the rest of the tow.

"We just scanned it, can't pick up any life signs," the ship reported. "Of course, he would have thought of that. Very well. We are going to catch it with a tractor beam and bring it into line with us. Remain where you are until we're done."

"Think they'll pull a fast one?" Wallinchky asked, sounding worried for the first time in the operation.

"They better not," Teynal hissed. "If they do, it *will* blow up on them. And I do not think that there's another of those to be had."

Angel could only hang against the seat and listen, imagining the sights they were watching on the screen behind her and also watching Jules Wallinchky's face. He was in fact nervous, but he also seemed to be enjoying the stirring of his own fear. He'd gotten where he was by rising to the criminal top as a man of action and a consummate risk-taker; it probably had been a long time since he'd put himself on the line, and it was feeding some inner need in him. She had to wonder if personally taking these risks wasn't necessary to his well-being, perhaps a better explanation for ventures like this than the desire to own the jewels or whatever else he might "acquire."

Still, a warship shouldn't be so easily fooled by a captain who'd had command only a few days and certainly was winging this. She was certain Kincaid wasn't dead; she could *feel* his presence out here, somewhere, somehow.

And not on Module 27. As these crooks noted, that would be the logical and first place anybody would look.

So where else would you hide? she wondered. Someplace that would shield you from probes but give you a crack at boarding that thing?

There was a long period of tense waiting, then finally a crackling in the communicator. "We have it. Now, in turn, the three lifeboats will all dock at the designated ports on our ship. You will dock at Port Six, which you'll see by a series of pulsing green lights on the rear section."

"Hold it! That was not our deal!" Wallinchky growled.

"We were not to board you," the Rithian echoed. "This is improper."

"Well, you stick explosives all over, so our captain thinks we need a few more guarantees from your end. If you want your payment, come aboard and get it."

"I do not like it," Teynal told the crime king. "Once we're docked, we're at their mercy. We could hardly blow the module without killing ourselves."

Wallinchky thought a moment. "Yeah, but they still can't get at it without us, right?"

"Without several of us," the Rithian agreed.

Ming had to laugh even though it hurt. "Double-crossed, huh? You're stuck as much as *we* are!"

Wallinchky got out of his seat and struck her face hard. It didn't matter. She was already so in pain it hardly registered.

Teynal was not deterred. This was what they paid him for, after all. "We do not consent. Send one of your small boats over with the goods. Know that Rithian honor would require us to die before handing anything over to you in such a nonguaranteed manner."

There was again a long pause, followed by "All right. Stand by!" from the warship.

"I don't like it," Ari commented. "They agreed much too quickly."

"Noted," the Rithian responded. "However, we will be able to see the boat, and we can monitor our own status, I assume? They will not be able to leave a crippling bomb?"

"Not a crippling one, no. Not without us knowing. That would require them to either get in here or have somebody outside. I don't think the latter can be done without me knowing about it. The former—well, the solution's obvious. It's crowded in here anyway. Do the business on *their* courier boat."

"They'll still blow us to hell the moment you give them the codes," Ming taunted. "After all, why not?"

"Because I will possess the Jewels of the Pleiades," Jules Wallinchky told her, "and the Kharkovs will authenticate them. The only reason for a double cross here would be to retain the jewels and get the trade. If they blow us up, the jewels are also blown up. Hadun's like a lot of others, even me. He would kill an entire planet, but he'd do anything to prevent the destruction of unique and timeless art. If I wasn't absolutely sure of that, this would never have taken place."

A small courier boat was even now leaving the warship as the two lifeboats with the water breathers were heading in to dock with it.

Angel had listened to all of this, and now felt certain she knew exactly where Captain Jeremiah Wong Kincaid was, and just how he was going to manage it.

That did not, however, do her or Ming, or Tann Nakitt, either, much good.

The Grabant System

THERE HAD BEEN NO DREAMS. THAT WAS THE STRANGEST part; there was a sensation of time passing, of an experience ongoing, yet if anything was going on in her mind during that period or if she was in any way aware, it was gone now.

After all the dancing around and threatening talk, the exchange had gone quite normally. The boat from the warship had come alongside, a temporary dock established, then the hatches were opened and the Rithians and the Kharkovs went over to the other boat. There was little noise, since the locks were automatically sealed except when accessed in an emergency, and it took about fifteen minutes to affect the transfer. Finally, the Kharkovs had returned, bearing a very large case of dark polished wood. An ornate seal was carved on it, in what was almost certainly pure gold, and it was studded with precious gems. The case—about ninety by 106 centimeters, and a good thirty centimeters thick—was a beautiful work of art, but what was inside was far more precious, and Jules Wallinchky could hardly contain himself as it was carefully, almost reverentially, handed to him by Ivan Kharkov. The jeweler was wearing surgical gloves, and Wallinchky put on his own pair before going further. Then he sat back, the case on his lap, and looked back up at the master jeweler.

"You're certain?"

"There is no doubt," Ivan Kharkov assured him. "I never believed that I or anyone would ever see them, not in this lifetime, and I never *dreamed* that I would have this opportunity. If those are not the Pleiades, then no creature living or dead would feel any differently toward these than toward the real ones."

Wallinchky slipped the small manual locks that seemed something out of ancient history and then actually crossed himself and took a deep breath before opening the case. Then the crime king gasped, seeing what Ivan Kharkov had meant. Angel was numb and passing in and out of consciousness, but still managed a glimpse of the case as he stared into it.

The seven jewels varied in size from enormous to impossible; seven colors, but with one cut and finish, set into a metal that seemed almost liquid and which burned, throbbed like something alive, making the gems themselves seem to beat like seven alien hearts.

"Pass them the codes as soon as we are positioned opposite the tow," Wallinchky said at last, his voice low, almost reverential, as if he were in a grand cathedral and in the presence of God Himself.

Angel was unclear about what happened next. It seemed there was a lower deck composed entirely of coffinlike transparent cages stacked one atop the other, and that she was carried down there by one of the Mallegestors. He untied her—there was hardly much risk, as she couldn't feel her extremities anyway—and ripped off all her clothing, even her religious medals, which she found particularly offensive. She was then shoved into one of the transparent coffins, hooked up to probes attached within, and then the enclosure was shut with a hissing sound. After that, all she could remember was that it grew incredibly cold, and it became harder to think, harder even to breathe. The last thought she could remember having was: *This must be what death feels like when it comes slow and steady upon you.*

Then there was darkness, a darkness without sound, without sight, without thought, but a darkness that somehow existed in time. It went on and on and on, but she didn't care, didn't think of it, nor anything, but just lay there in the nothing.

And then there was pain. Horrible, racking pain like she'd never experienced before, had never believed *possible* to experience. It seemed as if every cell, every point of skin, every organ, was in full rebellion, and even her blood consisted of searing white-hot fire.

It did not go on for long; nobody could have stood it for

any length of time without passing out. Still, it was longer than she ever wanted to feel that kind of pain again.

There was a horrid ringing in her ears that seemed to mask more ordinary noises, and it took a while to subside, although it never completely went away. Her eyes were open, she had control of them, but everything remained a featureless gray. She attempted to move her arms and legs, to clench her hands and bend her toes, but could feel nothing beyond the elbow or knee. There was a smell of disinfectant and other related substances, and a few lingering odors she wondered if she wanted to find out about.

Angel coughed, at first a little, then violently, uncontrollably. There were the sounds of people running to her; someone grabbed her shoulders, someone else gave her a shot, and then one of them or perhaps a third person gave her a strong, foul-tasting drink that nonetheless relieved her dryness and actually eased a lot of her immediate discomfort. The coughing stopped completely after she drank some of it, and after she downed it all, the cough didn't come back.

They seemed satisfied, whoever they were, and then she heard them walking away, talking softly, although she couldn't understand a word. She tried to call them back, so they could tell her where she was and what was going on, but only meaningless gurgling sounds emerged, which hurt her throat.

After a while the pain subsided further, becoming a dull burning. Angel then became aware of the tubes attached to her, which she guessed was some kind of intravenous feed, and concluded it was why she felt neither hungry nor dehydrated. She worked her head around in increasing circles, flexing her neck. It was painful at first but soon felt very good. She could control her head, and to some extent her shoulders, and began to concentrate as her teachers had instructed and to try and feel all her body.

Her skin seemed to have been mildly burned, apparently from the cryo units in the lifeboat. Well, that might be expected; those units were intended for emergency only, and not for use in deep space. It was likely that only the Mallegestors and maybe Tann Nakitt hadn't been burned, the former because nothing could penetrate that hide, the latter because of his fat and fur layering. If that was all that this was, she knew it would pass.

The same severe conditions might also have caused her blindness, she reflected, if she'd been in shock from her tightly tied arms and legs and her suspension, and then gone under with her eyes not completely shut. Could be; they'd never gotten their emergency lecture! If that were the case, though, would she remain blind unless given new eyes or lenses or whatever, or would vision slowly return? It frightened her, but she fell back on her faith and her prayers and calmed down.

She was definitely sitting up, not lying down, but she had no idea what the support might be. She was on something, some kind of device or prosthetic, since she could feel a rubbery form and seal that covered her crotch area and went back to near the top of her buttocks. It wasn't the only support because it wasn't wide enough, but it certainly had a utilitarian purpose. It caught, washed off, and flushed waste.

Angel began to chant softly, attempting to hum, and after some false tries she managed it. She was so pleased to get a steady tone, she tried shaping some words while still keeping the monotone hum, in effect singing or chanting them. "Hmmmm ... Is anybody else here?" she managed, her voice sounding unnaturally low but giving a fair Gregorian chant sound.

Someone else *was* there! She was right! The other tried to respond, but had the same kind of gargling noise she'd tried. Slowly, Angel attempted to teach the other to hum from the diaphragm, then up and out, form the words, keep singing. She had no idea why this worked, but felt her voice growing stronger and her command of it returning the more she did it.

The other used a different sort of tonal scale but managed eventually to raise a steady tone, then a series of tones. The other's voice, too, sounded unnaturally low, but was definitely another woman.

"Just answer me simply," Angel chanted. "I am Angel. Who are you?"

"Ming," the other managed to sing back, keeping the tone going, except for breathing in to help retrain the larynx.

Ming! "Can you see at all?" Angel sang to her.

"Light and dark. No shapes," Ming came back, increasingly getting the hang of it.

"Better than I am," Angel told her. "All is gray to me. Can you move at all?"

"No, I cannot," the other sang back. "I cannot feel my arms and legs."

There was the sound of a door opening at the other end of the room and of footsteps approaching. The person walked very close to them, then stopped.

"Well, I see you are both awake." It was Ari's voice. He sounded pleasant, even friendly, his old self. Ming hated him most for that, and Angel tried hard not to. To her, God had for some reason delivered her to the devil and was testing her. She did not know why, but it was still God's will.

"I heard what sounded like singing. That's actually a fair method of getting vocal chords working again after cryo paralysis, which is itself very common. The Kharkovs also had problems with it. Feel free to keep doing it as long as it is comfortable. I don't mind. It's actually kind of pleasant."

"I cannot sing the words I have for you," Ming responded, doing just enough of a chant as she could.

"Umph. I know how you must feel. I didn't want this, Ming. You weren't supposed to be here. You were supposed to be on the first lifeboat."

"I did not know your depths," Ming managed.

"Hey, I didn't know you were a cop, either! All this time, and we find out we have our nasty secrets. You were more undercover than I was. All my standard work was for companies owned or controlled by Wallinchky, most of them legit. There is just this occasional job that requires me to get on the unpleasant side of his works. It's not like I have much of a choice. I'm the third generation to work for him, and he's been my patron, sponsor, and employer for all my life."

"Where are we and what has happened to us?" Angel asked him, attempting a sentence without singing it and pleased to get it basically out.

He turned. "Well, hello! Bad luck for you, too, but you were born and raised to do what you do, too, right? By the way—the one or sometimes two octave drop in voices generally goes away over time."

"Can you answer her question?" Ming managed.

"Okay. You're in the Grabant System, on the fourth planet from the sun, a chilly ball of rock with an atmosphere so thin you'd asphyxiate before you'd freeze if you ran outside, but outside's a real interesting place. It's one of those ancient worlds with those weird remains of the Ancient Ones all over. You're in the infirmary in Wallinchky's getaway and museum here, which doesn't impact the ruins. The infirmary is entirely computer run, including surgery, but it's first rate. Right now you've both been—well, operated on and placed in recuperative mounts, but once things heal I think you'll find that the intent is to regenerate."

"Regenerate! Then—" Ming gasped.

"That's right. Don't panic, though. There's nothing here that can't be restored. Still, at the moment, you both are basically just heads and torsos. Really great-looking torsos, I might add, but that's about it. Wallinchky will be in to see you sometime today or tomorrow. When he does, he'll—well, outline the options. Believe me, though—I've seen worse than you in here, and they looked fine when all was said and done."

"You mean like Wallinchky's two lethal airheads?" Ming asked.

"No, only some here-and-there stuff had to be done to them. Hell, *I've* had an arm replaced here, and another time a toe."

There was a buzzing sound from Ari's direction. Then they heard a clicking, and a moment later he said, "Yes, sir?"

The muffled rush of conversation was too scrambled to be overheard, obviously through a communicator, and Ari responded, "Yes, sir. Right away. Yes, they're both awake. Yes, I'll be right there."

A moment later he was speaking to them again: "I'll have the medlab give you whatever functions you may feel better having, but I have to go."

"Yes, don't forget to wag your tail when you lick your master's ass," Ming responded acidly. "As to what we want, how about a nice, big bomb?"

Ari sighed, and they could hear him walking out.

Almost immediately robotics within the infirmary started to click and whir into action. Angel felt something come over her head, a helmet, it seemed, with clicking and whirring sounds inside. A membrane that came across her face briefly, let up before it caused any real discomfort, then rose back up again, freeing her.

"What was *that*?" Ming wanted to know, but in a short while the same thing happened to her. After it was over, they could only compare notes and some feelings about Citizen Martinez. Ming was far less charitable; she'd never been all that religious.

It didn't take long to discover what was happening. The machinery snapped back into action again, and Angel felt something being placed over her eyes and held by a band on her head. They were more like goggles than glasses, and extended out a bit, but after a bit of disorientation they snapped on, and for the first time since coming to she could more or less see. Her vision was limited to straight ahead, and it had little color, but the detail was quite sharp. She was able to look over and see Ming for the first time, and watch a similar but not identical procedure, employing artificial hands and thin prehensile tendrils from above. Ming's eyewear resembled a rectangular dark piece of plastic or glass in a welder's frame, with an elastic strap to hold it to her head.

Ming was set in a metallic box about a meter square, and appeared to emerge from it about at the navel. Her naked form was apparent the rest of the way, but her arms had been cleanly amputated just below the shoulders and even tapered in. Her face was fine, but as hairless as Angel's, and she didn't seem to have eyebrows.

Angel realized that she must look essentially the same, and in the same kind of outfit. She had a long enough neck to be able to get at least some sense of herself.

"So, we're talking heads," Angel said.

Ming gave a dry chuckle. "Well, at least we can feel assured that nobody is going to rape us, although I wouldn't be surprised if Mister Big didn't try and ensure that we felt entirely helpless and victimized. He gets off on that." She sighed. "I'm sorry you got sucked into this. I'm sorry I didn't get on that boat myself. I don't know what I thought I was going to do, but I just never expected Ari to blow me away like that. I've known him since *university*, for Heaven's sake! Of all the people I might have thought would be my enemy, he would be just a bit higher than my own family."

"I know how it must hurt," Angel told her. "Still, I sense

the conflict in him. Who knows how he might be if he were ever outside of that evil man's influence?"

"Fat lot of good that's going to do us," Ming noted. "He didn't need to do this to us. We weren't going anywhere. He did it deliberately, not only to leave us helpless, but also because he knows how people like me are trained, and he saw the video of you outmaneuvering Tann Nakitt—who, I must tell you, is in trouble himself here someplace because he decided to cast his lot with you, although I think he might have in any event. I wonder what happened to him?"

"Probably being defanged and declawed," Angel guessed.

"Do not underestimate him. Still, what can any of us do *here*? Where would we go?"

Angel thought about that. "What do you think they will do with us?"

"Play with us. Terrorize and victimize us if we give them any satisfaction. And then they'll try and break you. Me, I think, they'll just go directly for a mindscrub."

"You mean like the Rehabilitation Centers?" Angel was aghast.

"Yes, the ones for the worst offenders and those who cannot be let back into civilized company. They wire up your brain, send in their signals and probes, download what they find in your thinking parts, and then they erase. Then you get reprogrammed by uploading a very simple routine, after which you'll be happy and smiling and totally obedient and do and think and believe everything your trainer tells you. You'll have no memory of who or what you were, and no curiosity about it, either. If you have anything valuable and unique, or might be useful as your old self, they might take the download and create a virtual mind in the computer, then catalog, categorize, rearrange, pick and choose. It is tricky to do, but it's done all the time. It's known as a 'turn-around' in the psychiatric trade. I doubt if they'll try it with me, though. We're regularly tested each time the passwords and authorities are changed, which is often, and it has never been undetectable."

"It sounds like killing the soul but leaving the body intact. It is the most immoral thing I have ever heard," Angel told her. "How can we stop this?"

"Honey," Ming said sadly, "look at the two of us, look

around, and remember what that son of a dung dealer Ari said about where we are. There is no way to avoid what will happen. None. The only hope I have is that, somehow, I can either kill myself or at least take some of them with me before I disappear."

It was impossible to tell the passage of time in the infirmary, with just the two of them there. They spoke almost nonstop, until it seemed to Angel that she'd told Ming everything about herself, and that Ming had told her much the same. The closeness they felt at the end of it belied their radically different backgrounds, traditions, and experiences; they felt a bond closer than sisters.

The medical cubes, or whatever they were, provided all they required; neither felt hungry, nor, after being awake for a while, was there any sense of thirst, let alone dehydration.

There were long gaps, though. When the medical computer wanted them to sleep, it simply injected something and they went to sleep, often in mid-sentence. Awakening later, there was clear evidence that work was being done on both of them, although it was difficult to tell what, save in the eyes. Ming's vision was clearing, so that enhancement was no longer needed, but she found it impossible to focus. In fact, her vision was excellent, but she seemed locked in to a fixed focal length of infinity. Things far away to about two meters were fairly clear; closer was a blur.

Angel had a different treatment. Although damaged eyes could be replaced or regenerated easily, one of the things they took for granted, hers were replaced with artificial eyes that appeared normal, but retained the fish-eye vision and poor peripheral vision. She could focus, but it was like focusing a telephoto lens by willing it, rather than the natural sort of focus she'd had.

"They probably are cameras," Ming guessed. "Transmitting type as well. Somebody will be able to see anything you do. They're common in dangerous undercover work, but I don't think that's the purpose here. It shows he has different plans for you than for me, that's for sure."

Ari showed up now and again, but didn't speak to them much and got out as quickly as possible. Ming's bile was far too nasty to be taken for long, but Angel could see that his reaction did prove he was something of a wimp, as Ming had said. A Jules Wallinchky would have slapped the hell out of her for what she was saying, as she was held there helplessly.

Finally, the big man himself appeared. He'd trimmed his hair and beard and looked distinguished, even dapper, although, like most little men who'd risen higher than they dreamed, he was overfestooned with expensive rings and jewelry. He wore pure satin lounging pajamas, not the synthetic kind.

"So, my living statues, I am so pleased we've been able to get you back up to strength so quickly," he greeted them, sounding like a genuine humanitarian.

"Yeah, we're so pretty you should plate us and put us in your study," Ming responded acidly.

He smiled. "You know, I know people who did things like that. Among the drug lords there's almost a mania for it. They trim down and freeze up their enemies, captives they've gotten the best of, and sometimes people they hold for blackmail purposes, and they actually make living statuary out of them. The idea is mostly a reminder to would-be competitors and their own ambitious underlings, of course. I consider the practice rather tacky and low-class myself. If you need a lamp, buy a good one, I say." He sighed. "Well, I heard you're both well enough for us to get you out of there, and that the unfortunate eye damage is repaired. Putting you in regeneration tanks for long periods, while eventually the goal, would keep you out of circulation too long, and I have other business elsewhere. So, first we'll rig you as temporaries, and then perhaps we'll be able to give you some semblance of humanity again. It won't take much practice, they tell me. I'll see you in a couple of days."

And then he left, leaving Ming amazed at how little he'd lorded it over them.

"He almost sounded human," Angel commented.

"Don't worry. He won't disappoint us. I know him too well," Ming promised her.

What the "temporaries" were was revealed the next day, when both of them awoke for the first time not inside cubes but on real hospital beds.

Angel was astonished to wake up in a reclining position,

and it was a few seconds before she realized that she had stretched her arms. *Arms!*

Well, not quite.

The blend was seamless; there was nothing of the bloody stump, only a blur where her flesh met a tough rubbery skin that extended down to an elbow, out to a wrist, then to hands. They weren't *her* hands, nor models of them—the fingers were much longer, for one thing—but they were very human hands.

Except that the whole thing was semitransparent, as if the arm and hand had been made in some kind of machine from a mold and then attached to her nerve endings and nervous system somehow. It was odd to almost see through your arm and hand. It also didn't feel like real flesh. Oh, it bent and manipulated quite naturally, but aside from a real concentration of feeling in the fingertips, it felt kind of dead. She drew a transparent nail across her right arm and could follow its progress, but did not have the sensitivity she expected.

Pulling off the covers, she saw that her legs and feet were the same, extending down from an area that covered the lower part of her buttocks. There was a nearly full-length mirror on a bulkhead near the bed, and she slowly rose, gingerly put her feet to the floor, then got up and stood for the first time in a long time. It took a little practice; she was unsteady, and used a table to remain standing, but it wasn't all that hard to do. Then, again slowly, taking tiny steps, she managed to cross the two meters or so to the mirror.

Her eyes looked odd, as if they had tiny reddish-brown lights centered in them. Her face, and body, were *entirely* hairless—no eyebrows, no pubic hair—but she did have unnatural-looking black lashes.

The overall effect was of a kind of android, a very human-looking robot, with clear, soft, plasticlike limbs and an eerie cast to the eyes. It wasn't her, but a kind of artistic approximation.

She looked around, found some kind of pastries on a large dish and a glass of what appeared to be grape juice. She saw no reason not to eat it, and felt an urge to do so anyway, and it tasted very, very good. She could feel every bite, every gulp of liquid go down, at least until it hit her stomach. If I had this stuff for my chest as well, I'd be a living anatomy exhibit, she thought with a trace of silliness.

The more she stood, the more she used her arms and legs, the more comfortable they were. It wasn't that they became normal; she always knew that these were artificial. It was becoming easy, though, to tune out that feeling and simply use the limbs in a natural fashion. The arms, lacking true muscles, also had little lifting ability; there was enough strength to do anything basic, but hardly enough force to really smash a cream puff. The legs were more reinforced; she could *feel* a kind of stiff bonelike presence there even though it wasn't visible. Still, she suspected that while she could walk all over and stand almost indefinitely, she couldn't run or kick much, if at all.

She wondered where Ming was. She looked around for some kind of robe or cloak, but found none. She tried the door, which to her surprise slid back to reveal the main infirmary, and went to the next door and opened it.

It was clear from the look of it that Ming had been there, and that Ming had already undergone what she just had, but she wasn't there now. It seemed ridiculous to wait, and she was concerned about whether they were already erasing her friend.

She turned and walked toward the infirmary exit doors, trying to pick up her pace. She discovered then that she could walk so fast and no faster; the legs simply wouldn't respond beyond a normal gait.

Still, when she reached the doors, they opened for her, and she found herself in a darkened hall going in both directions with no clue as to where.

Turn left, walk to the end, turn right, and go into the third room on the right. This was a whisper of sorts, not actually spoken aloud, but rather, heard inside her head.

And she found herself walking as directed even as she continued to ponder the directive's origin. It wasn't that she'd decided to do it; her body was obeying without her having to consider it.

The room she entered was vast, and on a scale of opulence she'd never imagined. She almost sank into the lush carpet with its intricate designs, and all about there were what appeared to be exhibits, more than simple art objects.

Part museum, part great room, it was designed to awe, and it did.

Along the walls were paintings, apparently great works by great masters, all in gorgeous frames and with their own special lighting. She knew nothing of art, nor could she understand why so many of those were probably coveted, but there was some religious art that was clearly ancient and stunning.

There was a kind of artificial hallway created by the carpeting and the cases, which were lined up in a row about four meters from the walls but facing the "corridor." They went around the room, forming a square, with breaks so that someone could enter beyond them and into the center of the room. The cases contained jewelry. *Monstrous* jewels, encrusted settings, fabulous arrangements. Some of it had religious settings and was clearly originally intended for some church or faith, but only maybe half of it was Terran in origin, and the kinds of minds, and eyes, that saw some of those settings before making them were never inside a human.

She was fascinated in spite of herself, although there was no way to know what they were. You were supposed to already know that, she supposed, or perhaps the only one who needed to know didn't need little notes and plaques.

There were ancient books as well. She'd seen a few like them in retreats and seminaries, but they were old and prized, or ceremonial, and never opened save by the Minister of the Service. She couldn't read them, of course; reading had been a lost art since people could hook into a computer for anything they wanted or needed. Still, she knew that some of them were ancient religious texts by their decoration, possibly Bibles.

How odd that a man such as this would have such a love of religious art, religious settings for the gems, and religious books.

She was still uncomfortable, though. She knew she wasn't here to see this collection, and as much as she was pleased to once again be able to walk around and feel almost human again, it wasn't the time or place for admiration.

Angel walked around a case and into the center area,

which proved to be a statuary garden. She felt uneasy at discovering this, remembering Wallinchky's comments about "living statues," but these did seem to be pretty much what they seemed. Again, the accent was on ancient, but many of these sculptures, the Terran ones anyway, had erotic poses or themes. It was hard to tell with the non-Terran ones, but there was a definite theme. Men in erotic poses with women, in erotic poses with other men, women in erotic poses with other women, and with unfamiliar but clearly animal creatures.

She knew she should look away and pray, but she couldn't stop looking at the sculptures, nor could she explain the odd gut-level reaction she had to them.

In the middle was a round area of especially deep, thick, furlike carpet with erotic designs visible in the middle. Ming was lying there, in a pose not unlike some of the statuary.

As expected, Ming looked very much like she did—the artificial arms and legs. The artificial look and fluidity of movement of a person also had the same fluidity as her own movements.

"Ming? Are you all right?" she asked.

"Just put your mind in some other place and don't think," Ming replied, her voice not sounding right. It sounded . . . well, *sultry*, even deeper than it had been. She was moaning and breathing funny, and yet she managed, "They got us all wired up. You can't fight it. Just try to think of other things."

But Angel couldn't think of other things, and as she knelt down to see to her friend, she felt—strange. Not unpleasant, not like the artificial limbs, but like she'd never felt before, except perhaps once, in a fit of religious ecstasy at her ordination. But this was much more physically intense, though mentally confusing, since she could keep a little of herself apart and could not understand it.

And after a while Jules Wallinchky got into it with them; she remembered that much, and she tried with what little corner of her was left to push him away, to get him out of there, but her body kept doing what he wanted no matter what she tried.

Ming had been wrong. Wallinchky had the ultimate power trip in mind, and he went at it with gusto.

"Angel, you have to talk."

"Go away! I just want to die, but they will not even let me do *that*!"

Ming shook her head. "Poor kid," she breathed, then realized that in fact Angel *was* just a kid. Not only a young woman barely past whatever girlhood that order allowed, but with lifelong religious indoctrination and sequestering from most men in the retreats and religious schools, and even from the mission, where Angel had said there were only two Terran males on the whole planet, which was otherwise inhabited by an agrarian race of some kind of small lizard folk.

Evil was something you saw in videos and interlinks, or heard about second- or thirdhand or from religious instructors. When evil did appear, it was the unforeseen injury or death, the horrible storm that wipes out the crops, that kind of thing. And when you were out in company pretending to be just another citizen, the martial arts and mind control tricks were generally enough to save you. Otherwise, somebody shot you and you went to Heaven or whatever. Many trillions knew evil firsthand, of course, although a large percentage didn't recognize it as quite that, but Ming knew it took a cop like her to know the names and addresses of the chief perpetrators.

Angel had come face-to-face with more of the real stuff in the past two waking weeks of her life than she'd ever imagined confronting before, and it wasn't like the easy answers of her ivory tower theology teachers or show business hysterics. Few people, even clerical types, really *believed* in evil anymore, which was one reason evil kept winning.

For Angel, it was a matter of simply not understanding how God could allow her to sink to this. What had she done to deserve such a fate, or was she a new Job, punished simply to show piety to the devil? If that was the case, it wasn't a good bet. She felt—*dirty*, abused, and for the first time she knew the glimmerings of real hatred. With that came some wisdom, at least; now, at last, she could taste what Jeremiah Wong Kincaid must feel. But Wallinchky was as evil as she could imagine, and he had been in Kincaid's power, as it were, and was instead used merely as a tool. If Wallinchky wasn't evil enough to be an end object in himself, then what must that Hadun creature be like?

She didn't get over it, but began to learn to cope with it, much to Ming's relief.

Finally, Angel had to ask, "How did he do what he did? How *can* it be possible to do that to someone?"

"He's got us hooked into the neural net running this entire complex," Ming guessed. "We're like any of the automated stuff here, from the cleaning machines to the medlab stuff to the rest of the automated place. I have tried to walk down certain hallways here, or enter certain rooms, and I simply cannot. It's not willpower—my legs just will not do it. Just after that time you tried harming yourself. You couldn't. We're a part of this place now, just like the furniture. There was a lot done to us internally, as well as giving us these limbs and eyes."

"But—I can understand how it *stops* us, but how did it get me to *do—that*? I mean, I had never even done it before."

"Programming. We were ordered to go in there, ordered on the bed, and then a routine was run that not only gave us exactly what we were to do, but provided the proper hormones and other brain chemicals to trigger it all."

"Is this what he does to the others who work for him?"

Ming shrugged. "Probably he has ones like us in all his dwellings, but we're not real portable this way. We're not just prisoners in this place, we've literally become a part of it. It is, I suspect, what he does to people he wants to keep around but who are too 'hot' to travel. My people will be looking for me, yours for you. Our genetic codes are on file. So, as he said, we've become part of his collection."

It was not the most pleasant of thoughts.

It also became clear that whatever the medical program was doing, there was no sign of regeneration procedures—requiring either sequestering in a tank or removal of each artificial limb one at a time and giving it intensive treatment—and transplanting specially grown limbs from living tissue also didn't seem to be in the cards. Instead, the artificial limbs appeared to be integrating into their nervous systems, so that they now felt almost normal, even if they still looked very strange. They exercised in an elaborate exercise room at least a couple of hours a day; this was not a choice. It obviously wasn't to build up leg and arm muscles, but it got the heart pumping and made them tight in the stomach and very firm in the breasts. They were also growing hair; for Angel, it was a strange sensation, since apparently there was a genetic trait against it in her sect. It itched at first, but then began to come in at a rate much faster than normal growth. It was straight, thick, wiry, and jet-black.

What was most odd, although to them a relief, was that they rarely saw anyone else. There was little sign that Wallinchky, or Ari, or the others, were anywhere nearby. It was like being trapped in a public building. Of course, they couldn't go into many areas, so it was unclear if they were alone or not. Certainly the central computer was running things.

They did go wherever they could, studying and almost memorizing much of the great art and sculpture the place contained. It was some time before Angel could bring herself to go into the sculpture garden again, but after a while they went farther, to an unnoticed anteroom of the great hall that looked out upon the vast dead world beyond.

It was a beautiful if daunting landscape, all oranges and purples and filled with twisted rocks. The sky was never normal looking, but always dark, a very pale blue through which nearby stars could be seen in the daytime and was jet-black at night.

They sat there and looked out and tried to imagine they were beyond this prison, and you could almost completely clear your mind and believe it now and again. Of particular dreamy speculation was a formation well off toward the horizon that seemed to be almost by itself, but framed by twisted mountains and untouched by craters big and small, or at least apparently so from this distance.

It looked like some dark, mysterious alien city, abandoned in the eons but clinging on, refusing to crumble to dust.

Was this a place where angels and powers greater and lesser once convened before the creation of Adam? Was this once a garden as Earth had been in those most ancient of days? And was the serpent now returned to look upon the desolation it had created?

"That's quite poetic," Ming commented dreamily. The worst part of this wasn't the anticipation of more horrors, it was the sheer boredom.

"Huh? What's poetic?"

"About the places where angels met before the Creation, and how this was all that was left of the devil's lair."

Angel shook her head slowly in wonder. "I didn't think I spoke aloud."

Ming was startled. *Am I going nuts or what? I'm not sure she said it aloud, either.*

I didn't! What's happening here?

"I think," Ming answered thoughtfully, "we're reading each other's thoughts. Telepathy. Never had it in my family. You?"

"I—We can sometimes tell what someone is going to do a split second before they do it. It was thought that it *might* be a kind of very limited telepathy. It saved me from Tann Nakitt's fangs. But not—*this.*"

It's the neural net connection, I think, Ming guessed. *We're both using identical transmitters and receivers implanted in us. Just as it can send and receive, so can we between ourselves. I doubt if it works with anyone but us. Keep your thoughts open. Do not speak of this again aloud. It is possible that our master never suspected this, and if we can keep it from him, it might work to our advantage.*

Once this new channel of communication was open, it remained open no matter what, and seemed to extend itself. All thoughts, knowledge, feelings, and fantasies of the one were open to the other. It was quite strange, but stranger still because there still was no true meeting of minds. The two had backgrounds too different, and knowledge, experience, and beliefs so different that there was a point beyond which each could not go without losing perspective entirely.

But there was an underlying suspicion that somehow this was another computer subroutine; that in some way the computer itself was causing this, and it was a new stage in whatever their ultimate fate was to be. This suspicion was reinforced by the mandated routines they were forced to follow, but also by the times during each waking period when they would lose control of their emotions. It might be crying jags, or sexual arousals, love, hate, or fear; clearly, something was playing them like an instrument and recording the results. Thus, it seemed likely that this telepathy was merely a by-product, and that perhaps their memories, their personalities, were really in storage inside the larger computers, and that they were as much operating as inhabiting their bodies.

Ming was particularly concerned about this, since she knew a lot about the usual techniques of mind control. What worried her, and through her both of them, was whether they would *know* they were being remade according to someone else's direction. There were periods, even now, some of apparent length, that were totally blacked out. There were other times when they were fully conscious, but essentially passengers in their own bodies, doing things and going places without any control on their part.

The only time that seemed genuinely theirs, with no manipulation, was the time they reserved when they were not being ordered to the infirmary or exercise hall, and just sat together, staring out at the ever-fascinating alien landscape with the unchanging stars all around.

And then there was the one time when they both were simply staring outward and it seemed suddenly as if something was alive out there. It wasn't a shape, but more a sense of something else beyond the compound, beyond the dome and superinsulated windows, something centered in that strange citylike place way out there but wasn't *just* there. Some kind of—*energy*. That was the only way to explain it. In many ways it seemed like they had a sudden awareness of a second, much larger and more powerful neural network. The compound had a centralized computer and a series of thousands of smaller units with more specialized interests, all tied together at the speed of thought, combining their power to make a unified whole that could in some ways think, make basic decisions, and run all that needed to be run; even them. They could feel their master, could sense the connections, but could not reach it as it could reach them.

That night, though, they sensed another, very different—*entity*—which nonetheless performed the same sort of functions. But the neural net that they were somewhat a part of was in many ways the entire compound, all that was within it, and all of the functions of maintenance and preservation as well. The whole place was alive, but the whole made logical sense and was for a specific purpose.

So what was this other far stronger but more alien net? What was it doing, and for whom? Did it run the city out there, ancient and dead as it was? What could be run there, for whom, and to what purpose?

There was no way to actually contact it, touch it, ask it. The speed, the internal language, the whole way of operation was beyond them or anything they were connected to. Nonetheless, it was there. It existed.

They could almost sense the compound's computers musing on the same thing. This was old hat to the Many in One, and they had longed for contact since first sensing this power and obvious systematic intelligence, but had never had a way in.

I would like to go to that city, if that is what it is, they both thought. *I would like to find out, at least, if it truly is a place where the Ancient Ones once dwelled, and if this power is their mark of Creation or, perhaps, still a place of their power awaiting their return as I await the return of the master of this place.*

That was not far off. There was no announcement, no broadcast, but the next time they awoke from sleep they knew, courtesy of their own hookup, that company was coming.

Wallinchky Compound, Grabant 4

THERE WASN'T ANYTHING IN THE REALM THAT COULDN'T BE done or controlled by computer, and for all but the lowest classes and the newest and poorest worlds, that was generally the case. Still, the use of living assistants as everything from secretaries to bodyguards, butlers, and maids was considered a status thing. *Any* common dolt could have power over a machine; only the elite had the same power over people.

The two captives in the satin prison only guessed that was why they were in a place where they had never been allowed before, and which turned out to be the master bedroom. It was sumptuous, with priceless ancient tapestries on the walls, a plush natural hair rug, and a huge revolving bed. Why was it that now *they* made it up expertly, and checked for dust and fingerprints, and polished, and then found and laid out a pair of satin lounging pajamas and soft slippers from the vast walk-in closet? It was a mystery, since nobody was yet there to see their handiwork. And then, with almost gut-level understanding, they figured it out.

The master computer *was* doing the job. They were simply the instruments, the same as the tentacles that could emerge from the ceilings and the various dedicated devices small and large that were used to maintain the whole place.

They also found themselves working in concert with the other machines, never once getting in the way of one another, or even concerned about the small vacuum unit doing a pattern on the rug, for instance, or the spidery things that emerged and checked everything from the humidor to the freshness of the toiletries. In fact, they were as much in contact with the small artificial creatures as they were with each other. It was impossible to describe, even to one another; it just *was*. They were Angel, to be sure, and Ming, but they were also all the other things in the house, and the other things in the house were to some extent them.

Still, while they were now just more cogs in the system, they both sensed that the computer at the core of the neural net was beginning to live beyond its usual experience through them. For the first time, it seemed, the master computer could feel emotions, feel things physically the way Terrans could. As they became more like the computer, the computer was becoming a little more like them. But if they eventually merged completely into the solitary net, would anything of them as distinct personalities remain?

For the first time, too, makeup was applied. It began with a cream on the face, neck, and shoulders, which looked clear but had the effect of turning the skin a bright white, almost like a paint gloss, although it had no particular consistency or feel and their skin afterward seemed normal. Then their eyes were shadowed in exaggerated patterns of black, the brows thinly perfected, the lips done a bright red. They were given bright red-and-white patterned skintight uniforms that fit their torsos and supported their breasts, the effect of which, combining the limbs with the painted areas, was to hide any obvious organic skin from view. It was the first clothing either had worn in a long time, and it felt uncomfortable and itched. Their transparent fingernails and toenails were even painted red, and earrings and other minor jewelry were added, all in a red-and-white motif.

It was not, however, the kind of makeup session they would have undergone in the old days, if they'd undergone it at all. Thin, wiry tendrils did the nails, other computer house extensions did other parts, and they mostly kept examining themselves in the mirrors to get the proper look and perspective.

With their still short but full hair sprayed with some shiny laquerlike substance and then styled in a swept-back look before it dried, it appeared plastic. The black bangs along their forehead were actually painted. They decided they looked like street performers or life-size dolls, android mannequins rather than real flesh and blood. No, not even androids.

Toys.

A corner of their minds noted the tracking of the incoming shuttle and the near imminent landing at the small but adequate private pad. The defense codes indicated it was "friendly." It did not, however, contain the code indicating that Wallinchky was aboard.

Angel and Ming proceeded to the airlock entrance, another place they had never before been allowed close to, stood there and waited. The airlock hissed, the lens opened, then the inner door slid back.

Ari Martinez looked tanned and in top shape, but somewhat changed. He'd cut his hair in a short junior executive manner and had grown a pencil-thin black mustache. Before, he'd been a fairly good-looking man, but this new look did nothing to enhance his appearance.

One of Wallinchky's beautiful bodyguard playthings was with Ari, the dark-skinned beauty they knew only as Veda. Also with him was Katarina Kharkov, looking as nervous as ever and somewhat motherly, considering she and her husband were party to dealings like the one that destroyed the *City of Modar*.

Ari saw the two made-up women waiting for him and froze for a moment in confusion. They both bowed low and held it, then said, in not only perfect unison, but virtually the same voice, "May we be of service, sir?"

Katarina Kharkov almost took a step back, and Veda just stood there gaping, as Ari frowned and approached them. "Who are you?"

"We are the housemaids, sir."

"Stand up straight. Let me see the two of you clearly."

They did as instructed, and he looked over each of them carefully. Finally he said, "My God! Is that you, Ming?"

"I will answer to Ming if you wish, sir, subject to the Master's override."

He stared at her, and then at the other, and shook his head. "Incredible. No fingerprints, no footprints, no retinal pattern matching. Probably just enough genetic patching so they wouldn't register on anybody's scans." His expression and tone was a mixture of awe at the kind of mind and supporting technology that could do this, combined with revulsion aimed as much at himself as at them. He'd had a real part in doing this to an old friend, an old flame.

Although the computer link was doing all the interfacing, Ming was still present and watching even if she could not react. Seeing that twinge of guilt in Ari Martinez gave her the first feeling of satisfaction she'd had since he shot her. It wasn't much, but at this stage even a crumb was welcomed.

"Are they—real?" Katarina Kharkov asked him tentatively.

He turned and nodded. "Yes, I think so. Come—let's get you down to the lab area for the reunion. In fact—Veda, you can take Madam Kharkov down and see that she is settled, can't you? I wish to take care of a few things here. You are at their disposal until Wallinchky arrives, at which time I want you back here."

"Yes, sir," she answered, in one of those sex kitteny voices that clearly irritated Madam Kharkov but didn't bother Ari at all.

Veda wasn't like these two, who were something new to him. Veda simply had been picked up from the streets of Nueva Madras, where she'd been selling her body or anything else for subsistence. They'd completely erased her mind and personality and created this one, which had now settled in quite well. All she knew or felt she needed to know was that she worshiped Jules like he was a god, lived for any attention he might give her, and believed everything he said and did whatever he commanded. Jules had a lot of these kind of love-slaves, both male and female, but he tended to favor women more with this sort of stuff and act out his more violent urges on the males.

When the two women were safely away, Ari turned back to Ming and Angel, who were still patiently standing there. "Have you been having sessions with anyone here?" he asked them. "I mean, who else is here that you have been seeing and working with?"

"Only the house, sir," they both responded in unison, neither having been specifically addressed. "We have seen no one else since last we saw the Master."

"Then you remember that. How much more do you remember? I'm talking to Ming now. Do you remember yourself before you came here?"

"Yes, sir," Ming replied.

"Can you bring your old personality forward, be like the old Ming?"

"Sir, I am programmed not to do that."

It was true; she couldn't do it even if he ordered it, even though she was still there inside. Wallinchky wanted to make sure that nobody could trigger some deeply implanted suicide impulse, standard with people in her old profession. Only Wallinchky himself could do that.

"You're not—who programs you?"

"I am self-programming, sir." And that was true now on both levels.

He was amazed, and increasingly upset by the two. Both of the women had to wonder if Jules Wallinchky hadn't somehow planned it that way. He worked by keeping even those on his staff and closest to him off balance.

For Ari Martinez, there wasn't any way past that wall that he could see. Normally, even if somebody was under complete control or lying paralyzed on the ground, you could read something in the eyes, but both of these women had wholly or partially artificial eyes that showed nothing of what might lay behind them.

The perfect slave, he thought sourly. And totally secure. I wouldn't be at all surprised to think that this is the future for a lot of those around dear old Jules. He began to think about his own neck.

That jarred him into more dutiful action. "Your master is due in sometime later on today, but I do not know the exact schedule. He's shuttling off a larger vessel, and it's difficult to say precisely when, but it will be today. In the meantime, I have to set up some things for a meeting. I'll not require your services—not now, anyway."

He walked away, perhaps a bit too quickly and nervously, and both the women felt the first amusement they'd had in a very long time.

He is guilt-stricken!

And frightened! He knows that what was done to us can be done to him or anyone else.

They had long since gotten over the novelty of mental dialogue without knowing which of them was speaking which lines.

What do you think he meant by Madam Kharkov having a reunion? And where is the lab? Do you think there might have been other natural beings here all the time?

With that, the information on the labs and the full layout of the house was suddenly provided to them in full in three dimensions, and for the first time they saw how vast this complex really was and how many floors it contained. Ivan Kharkov had been here all the time, it appeared, along with a ton of specialized equipment. Data they could now access showed that Madam Kharkov had been here as well, but had left to retrieve some needed materials. They were clearly doing extensive restoration work of some kind.

Why didn't we know of them before? Angel wondered.

We didn't need to, nor have access to this data. We were not ready yet. Remember, each time we gain more awareness of the net and databases, the more we lose of ourselves. Those differences that make us separate people, and beyond which we could not go, are slowly being cataloged and stored and deemed irrelevant. We now have near complete access because we can no longer act in any way except to serve our server and in turn our server's master. We are in the last stages. Did you not feel the mild pleasure when addressed, when answering his questions?

Yes. This has been the case for some time when doing what the program states correctly. It was why they could be handed loaded pistols and would use them only as Jules Wallinchky directed.

This was the final stage, then. The core computer consciousness that controlled the net had never had this kind of outlet before. Now, when its living units served, they got a mild pleasure jolt. If they displeased, they would get a moment of unpleasantness that would be noticed, but not enough to cause any problems. It had not yet decided if the units were of any added value, and hedged its bets on that score. Storing their memories took a lot of space, but that was to be expected. Storing the personalities and ratios that created self-identity was more complex, but didn't take up a lot of extra space. It did not, however, file it where it was obvious.

Ari Martinez was discovering some of how it had been done on his own, by searching the standard files on the procedure from the interface in the comfortable study. A self-programming total conditioning system. It was incredible, and scary. He didn't think somebody as paranoid as Jules Wallinchky would trust any computer that could think with this kind of power. How did he sleep, knowing that the computer might well figure out that all living beings in the complex were just extensions?

You couldn't even interrupt the signals, the data flow to and from the little self-repairing, self-maintaining nanomachines that acted as transmitter and receiver inside their brains and nervous systems. Computers put most of the data on the server and accessed *that* when they needed it. God didn't need a computer everywhere to run the universe; He just needed a good network with sufficient bandwidth and a server with the capacity to hold all that detail. Still—and this was even scarier—it was possible to download a *lot* of information into a human brain and then switch off frequencies and bandwidth so that you could switch these robotic humans the same way you could swap a robot carpet sweeper.

This was scaring Ari to death. Where in *hell* had somebody like Jules Wallinchky come up with an idea like this, even to order it? Of course, he probably stole it, or swapped for it, but still . . .

"Have Ming report to me immediately," he said into the desk communicator.

Ming appeared in less than a minute, indicating that she hadn't been doing anything but waiting. She entered and bowed. "At your command, sir."

"Ming, you said that all your memories were still present in the system."

"Yes, sir."

"Do you know what the master traded to Josich Hadun for the Jewels of the Pleiades?"

"Yes, sir."

"Would it cause you to harm yourself or anyone else by telling me?"

"No, sir. It would be a matter of telling the seller what he sold."

Ari Martinez took a deep breath. "Ming, tell me exactly what was traded."

"Sir, it was an alleged prototypical interface with the potential to establish a comm link with an Ancient Ones remote computer system."

He was absolutely stunned by that. Even more, he now knew just where Jules, or somebody working for him, got the idea for the self-programming slave. He had been out to that ancient city on the horizon that the two women had wondered about; he'd been to many such places now and again. Beautiful, strange, bizarre cities, works of art from minds far too alien to comprehend. The only things really known about them were that they left cities that had absolutely no artifacts in them beyond their own structures, not so much as a potsherd, a tiny coin, or a single bit of mosaic, and that they seemed batty for the number 6. That was why a lot of religious groups had always considered them demonic places; 666 was supposed to be the number of the Beast, or Devil.

Scientists, discovering that worlds like this one had hollowed-out cores filled with vast quasiorganic matter that seemed inert although not exactly dead, had a lot of theories. One of them was that the matter inside was a local computer that had provided everything the inhabitants required, as well as maintaining whatever conditions they needed for life, which was why they'd found no artifacts. And they also postulated that something happened to sever contact between this vast galactic civilization and the inevitable server that kept all the data, all the details, about two billion years before. So advanced, so spoiled, so much like gods, it must have been the one thing they simply couldn't cope with.

"Ming, who created this thing we spoke of?"

"Sir, I do not know, but it was done under contract to the Military Department and the Department of Pure Research."

He wasn't about to ask how the hell the Rithians managed to get somebody to steal it, nor what it had cost, but little wonder that it was so much in demand.

"Were you aboard the *City of Modar* because your superiors knew it was on there?"

"No, sir. I was simply to observe all activities of suspect group."

He had assumed that. If they'd have known it was aboard, they'd have had an army hidden there.

"Ming—does the thing work?"

"Sir, I have no idea."

Well, that was honest enough. He doubted she *could* lie anymore, unless told by Jules to do so. He was willing to bet that *Jules* didn't think it would work. If he did, he'd never have traded it, not even for the Pleiades. Hell, who cared about even the most fabulous of treasures when you could *will* them into existence? And he certainly would not have put it in the hands of somebody like Hadun.

Well, at least now he knew. "Ming, you know you were once a police detective. Do you still consider yourself one?"

"No, sir. That description is no longer valid."

"What if you had the opportunity to leave here. To walk out and away? Would you do it?"

"No, sir."

That surprised him. "Why not?"

"Sir, my sole function is to serve the Master. I exist for no other purpose."

"Ming, do you consider your master a good man?"

"Sir, I cannot answer that question."

"Cannot or will not?"

"Cannot. Good is to serve the Master. Not good is to not serve the Master. How can the Master not serve himself?"

He realized with a start that *he* was completing her programming by simply asking these questions. He could see the trembling, the slight pleasure at the edges of the painted lips, and knew what was going on.

Abruptly, she stiffened. "Sir, there is a second shuttle in orbit now in the process of being cleared. The Master is aboard. We must meet him."

"Yes, by all means," he sighed, getting up. She led the way back to the airlock.

She knew the shuttle was coming in and who was on it, he reflected. That meant she was totally plugged in here. Totally. She *couldn't* say anything wrong to his questions—wrong from the computer's standpoint, anyway. If she had, she'd almost certainly have gotten an unpleasant jolt. But saying the right thing, without hesitation, brought the pleasure jolt. Pretty soon neither one of the women would even *think* any way but that. Too risky.

For Ming's part, and Angel's, too, since she'd heard the whole thing as if she were there, and both had also followed his research on what essentially was one of their databases anyway, the same conclusion was arrived at. How long could they not begin to exist for that? How long could they resist it? Did they *want* to resist? There was no hope of release, after all, and no hope of *acting* wrongly. Why, then, not think the right way and at least prevent pain? It would probably be better for both of them.

The inner airlock door hissed just as they arrived, then it opened and Jules Wallinchky walked through, dressed in casual clothes and smoking a big, fat cigar. Behind him by not more than a step were Sonya, the other beautiful bodyguard from the *City of Modar*, and a man unfamiliar to them, big and square-jawed, the kind with muscles on his muscles and an air that said he spent a lot of time working out in front of a mirror and admiring the view.

Wallinchky took the cigar out of his mouth and said, "Hello, Ari. I hate like hell to be rousted out by this petty shit, but business is business. Who knew that little creep had this kind of influence?" He stopped, spotting the doll-like duo, who had fallen to their knees and were now prostrate on the floor.

"Well, hel-lo," he commented, going over to them. "Get up, girls. Let me take a look at you!"

They both hopped obediently to their feet and stood, expectant.

"Ain't that somethin'," Wallinchky muttered, reverting to an earlier, less cultured but more natural style of speech. "Ari, ain't that somethin'? Amazin' what a good fuck and a few clear instructions to a computer can do."

Martinez swallowed and, like a good survivor, held his tongue from the remarks he wanted to make. "Yes, sir. I think it's truly amazing. I have never seen the like of it, particularly in this short a time."

"Yeah, I figured they would be the best test of this. I mean, hell, an older experienced cop and somebody raised as a religious fanatic? If I could get *them*, it would work with anybody. Not much *fun*, though. Not like Sonya and Veda and Sulliman, here. I do my personal servants, mistresses, and bodyguards myself. This—it kinda takes the creativity out of it." He gave a chuckle. "Damn machines are taking over everything, aren't they?"

"Um, yeah."

"Well, I saved a little of it for me, anyway. I can make 'em do anything I want by just sayin' the word and snappin' my fingers, but I don't just want 'em to *do* it, I want 'em to *want* to do it. To *live* just to do it. For *me*. An ex-cop and an ex-nun who exist only for me. And they're only the first, Ari. I got a bunch of folks I can see doin' this way."

"I hope I'm not one of them, sir!" Ari responded a bit nervously.

Jules Wallinchky roared with laughter and slapped his back. "Not yet, boy! Not yet! I need smart folks who can think for themselves too much! Just remember who you work for and we'll always get along fine."

"You're my uncle. I don't believe in going after family."

That got another big laugh. "All right, nephew!" He turned to his two companions. "You two go off and relax now. I don't need bodyguards in here, and I got a couple here that I *really* want to play with." He turned back to Ming and Angel. "Okay, you two! Come along! I want you with me for a while."

Angel was in particular distress because she couldn't bring herself to give in quite that easily but felt helpless and particularly forlorn without Ming's reinforcement. Everything seemed to be slipping, and so fast . . .

They went into the big man's study once more, and if Wallinchky noted that it had recently been used, he didn't betray the knowledge, or perhaps just didn't care. "You know, I got to think of something to call these two," he said casually. "Ming—well, sounds too damned much like one of my antique Chinese vases. We need one that's less personal, more like what she is."

"You're making them sound like prototypes," Ari responded uneasily.

"Well, maybe they are. Trouble is, women make better art subjects than classical artists as far as I'm concerned, and if I use Venus and Madonna, I've already exhausted the naming pool. May as well go with the practical, then." He suddenly brightened. "Yeah. Prototypes. I like that. At least it'll sound pretty classy." He turned and looked straight into Angel's eyes. "Memory command Rembrandt. From this moment on, you are Alpha," he told her. "You have no other names. Search and replace any and all names for yourself with 'Alpha.' "

Ari just sighed. So he was even taking their names away from them, and the sense of identity they brought. If there was anything of them left, it would be a devastating blow to whatever sense of self was left.

Wallinchky turned to Ming. "And you—well, you're shorter and smaller, so you got to be Beta. Memory command Rembrandt. From now on you are Beta. Search and replace any and all names for self with 'Beta.' Search and replace all alternate names for Alpha, replace with 'Alpha.' Search and replace all alternate names for Beta. Replace with 'Beta.' Execute all commands." He turned back to his nephew. "Alpha and Beta. I kinda like it. What do you think, Ari?"

Ari didn't like it, but he could only shrug. "You're the boss."

"You better believe it."

The moment he'd given his commands, Angel found herself thinking of herself as Alpha. But she wasn't Alpha. Alpha was—all she came up with was her. She could still recall much of her past, but not any other name. Worse, just trying gave her a series of tiny little shocks. Every time she just thought of herself and "Alpha" appeared as her identity, there was a tiny pleasure jolt. And what was Beta's old name? Did she *have* a different name? It was impossible to remember, and Beta was mirroring her thoughts in reverse.

"Beta," Wallinchky said, settling down in his padded chair, "go fetch me a fresh cigar. Alpha, you light it for me when it comes."

The actions were instantaneous. It felt good, *right*, to do this and see his own satisfaction.

"Amazing, ain't it, Ari? Not long ago they were strong personalities. Now I'm the center of their universe and I still got all that they know. And later on today we'll teach 'em how to *anticipate* my desires." He paused, blowing a big cloud of smoke. "What's the matter? You disapprove? You sure don't mind those sex bombs who can't remember breakfast."

"I can't say anything about it," he managed diplomatically. "So why the clown getup?"

Wallinchky sighed. "Ari, Ari! Perhaps one day we will

educate you. At least I will point you to the painting, which happens to be here. So, it is *aesthetic*, and it also identifies their form and function no matter where they are." He paused a moment, then added, "That's not what you were really wondering about, though, was it? Come, come! Speak your worries!"

"I just wondered how you can trust the local neural net not to simply decide to make us all pets, or units. Particularly since you have given it a taste of real life and feeling."

"Well, don't worry about that. I think you have seen one too many horror shows, eh? You *know* I got that angle covered. Let's get to the matters at hand here, though. I want to have some fun with the girls here."

"Okay. Well, they located some emergency records on the remains of the *City of Modar*. I thought we got it all, but apparently for some reason they had a lot of it covered. Maybe Kincaid's doing. Anyway, they know who was on and who got off. They probably assume that we have them, since they don't even know about the pickup ship or Hadun's involvement, at least not as far as we know. But the Geldorians are screaming bloody murder over Nakitt, and the Organized Crime Force wants a look at some of your personnel. There's a missing persons on the cleric, but not much more."

"Yeah, I been gettin' threats for a week now. What about Kincaid? He show up?"

"Not yet. He's not in the wreckage, but he sure wasn't with us. I can't figure it."

"He had to be in the mod with the gizmo. *Had* to be. There was no place else for him to have *been*."

"Maybe," Ari answered thoughtfully, "but so far I haven't heard that he was removed—they've still got a series of contracts out on him—and I also haven't heard of any attempts on Hadun. And he sure didn't sneak in with us, since he'd have had to use cryo. Nope, he's a mystery. At least he's not our problem."

"For now, anyway," Wallinchky agreed. "Well, how long will it take to thaw out the little weasel, and how do we control him until he's picked up?"

"Why thaw him out?" Ari asked him. "He's as useful to them frozen as not."

"It's a point. I'll think about it. But what if we need him thawed?"

"A day to be fully functional and thawed out, maybe another to recover sufficiently to be 'normal,' whatever that is. About the same as us. He may look like a critter, but biologically he's pretty close to us, you know. As for control, we *could* keep him sedated, but he's pretty pragmatic. If he knew he was going home in one piece if he behaved, I think he'd suddenly be on our team."

Wallinchky chuckled. "Yeah, I think you're right. Okay, the Geldorians are due in—five days, give or take a day. Thaw him out two days from now and make sure he's on the team. We'll give him a little help in that regard, too. I want his memory scrubbed from the moment we took him in his cabin until he wakes up here. I don't want him to remember who was on our lifeboat, and particularly that these girls were forced to come along. I don't want to have to arrange an accident for him just so he won't betray something to the wrong folks later on. Okay?"

Ari nodded. "We have the means here. I don't think that's a problem. Anything else?"

"Well, I don't like this business from Hadun that we sold him an incomplete unit. I can't help it if the damned thing is a crock of shit. I didn't guarantee it was more than a pipe dream. Still, he's a psycho of the first rank, right up there with the classics of history, and he's still got quite a force in exile, so maybe we can work out something." He gave a dry chuckle. "Now, where's Kincaid when I really need him?"

"Okay, I can look over the messages and the options and prepare some proposals. How long will you be here?"

"I hope to leave when the Geldorians do. The Realm's been turning up the heat lately, and I'm gonna have to talk to our people in the Senate and see how to cool it down. Then there's the salvage job on the *City of Modar* train. A real mess, but nothing we can't handle. Get along now. Bed with the bimbos for the next few nights if you want. I have my own company here."

Ari nodded, understanding that he was dismissed, and left quickly.

Jules Wallinchky looked at Alpha. "Go to the doorway and just watch him until he's gone. Don't follow, just see."

"Yes, Master."

He leaned over to the computer console and activated it. "Put visual from Alpha on the screen."

Instantly, he was seeing on his screen exactly what she was seeing, the figure of Ari Martinez walking slowly down the long hallway. She did a magnification and added adjusted infrared when he was lost in the far shadows, and he appeared, a bit ghostly but otherwise perfectly well, in front of the boss. He was delighted. "Do both of you have this capability?" he asked.

"No, Master. Alpha has magnification as well as full spectrum capabilities," the one now known as Beta responded. "I have the full spectrum abilities but no magnification, but can show true color and true three dimensions."

He was like a kid with a new toy, but he wasn't forgetting business. "Alpha, you can come back now and stand beside Beta. Can I address Core and get answers from it through you?"

"Yes, Master," they both chimed.

"Okay, so as long as you are close to me, one of you, no preference, will speak for Core. This is Code Henri de Toulouse-Lautrec."

"Sweeping, Master," Beta responded. "Done. The room is free of unauthorized devices. Give command."

"Change Code Rembrandt. Code Rembrandt invalid. New Code for function is Code Degas. Execute."

"Done."

When it was Core, there was no "Master," and the response sounded more mechanical. That would do.

"Run sequence from point at which subject Ari Martinez first entered this room on arrival and accessed either Core or these units."

He sat and watched as Ari's image went over the programming of the girls and also as he interrogated them. He sat without much expression, but when it was done he said, "Code Degas. Beta and Alpha are to volunteer no knowledge whatsoever from data they have from experiences before becoming part of this system to anyone but me. This data is to be encrypted and coded so that it cannot be accessed by anyone other than myself, and then only with the Code Hypatia. This knowledge may be accessed and used to carry out orders, but cannot be revealed or accessed to others. Execute."

"Done," came the response.

"Okay, girls," he said with a child's cruel glee. "Now we're gonna have some educational fun here."

Tann Nakitt was delighted to be where he was even though he would have preferred to be anywhere else. The fact was, the moment the Mallegestor had burst through the door and fired at him, striking him and knocking him cold, his last frantic thought had been that this was the end of all things.

He had also had little problem cooperating with the probe that basically had excised a very tiny and totally unpleasant portion of his captivity from his memories. He understood that he'd never be allowed out alive unless he did, and there wasn't much he could do anyway. So now he was in the position of knowing, or at least suspecting, that something was missing, but not troubled about it. He'd had this sort of thing done before, and when it was something that really mattered, he'd always had this gut emotional reaction, the feeling that something that was a part of him had been wiped out. Since he didn't feel that way, and since he had good narrative memory up to being shot and then from getting out of the scrubber case, as he thought of it, he didn't let it worry him anymore.

"You didn't, by any chance, bring my pipe and herbs with me, did you?" he asked Ari, as casual as if they were still in the lounge of the *City of Modar*.

"Sorry, no. And the passenger module was pretty well blown to bits, so there's little chance we'll recover them. You'll live."

"The pipe's pretty important to us," Nakitt explained. "It is something partially made by your family and partly by yourself and is a symbol of adulthood. The hell with some incriminating memories; the loss of the *pipe* feels like I lost an arm!"

"Well, you're whole, hale, and as irritating as ever. For the next day or two you have fairly free run of the place, since you'll be examined when you leave anyway. Don't try swallowing any precious gems, don't attempt to access the computer system, and stay out of the way of the folks who should be here, and we'll all get along fine."

"Don't worry! As far as I'm concerned, let me eat, sleep, and just melt around here until it's time to leave. Nothing personal, you understand, but just what I've seen of this mausoleum gives me the creeps."

Ari was beginning to think the same way himself. Jules was—what? Over a century old, certainly, and through one rejuve treatment. He looked okay, but it was middle-aged distinguished, not Mister Adonis. Still, the guy had started as a street punk in a jerkwater town on a backward world where pig farming was still a major activity, and he'd become, by guts, smarts, guile, and ruthlessness, one of the richest and most influential men in all the Realm. How many bodies that represented, nobody knew, probably not even Jules. The old boy was fond of commenting that keeping score was the first step to getting caught.

Such a man, over such a length of time, had to feel as if he were somehow possessed or guided by something supernatural. Not that he hadn't made some mistakes and lost a few rounds, but very few, and nothing fatal either in the business or the climbing up through it. He'd been hurt a number of times, but never spent more than a few nights in custody anywhere.

He had no heirs and had never even considered marriage, most likely because, other than his mother and his sister—Ari's mother—no women counted. Ari often thought that Jules really didn't like women much; that his relations with them were less getting pleasure than getting even for something. Men who crossed him, he liked to take down, to reduce them to terror and make them bleed and bruise; women he enjoyed torturing or recreating as slaves in some twisted fantasy of his that he now had the power to realize.

Still, Jules may have been a gangster and a business genius all in one, but he was no scientist or engineer. He believed what machines told him, and he had a lot of faith in technology. He wasn't infallible, and he was becoming convinced that he was, and that was dangerous. He, Ari, knew the potential lurking in this kind of setup. Isolated, so insulated that even Realm law enforcement needed permission to land, with a very small set of personnel—until the two girls, no permanent residents—and lots of experimental state of the art stuff that still wasn't approved in the Realm. Wallinchky might *think* he had the computer under control, but who could say for sure?

Ari knew there wasn't much he could do about it if anything did happen, though. Unlike Jules, he had neither the self-confidence nor the ability to put those things out of his mind that couldn't be dealt with, and so he hadn't been sleeping all that well.

It also didn't help that, on the morning Tann Nakitt was to be awakened, Beta, the former Ming, had appeared and informed him, "The Master has assigned me to you for whatever you may require, sir." He could tell it was what had been Ming without even trying to make out the facial features under all that makeup, or whatever it was. Angel had been and remained a head taller than Ming.

He didn't like *that* at all. "I do not require you for anything. You do not have to be here."

"My sole function is to execute the wishes of the Master," she informed him. "The Master wishes me here." And that, of course, was that. But she added, "Sir, the Master has designated me as your personal computer station. You may ask anything of me and I can retrieve it from Core. Also, I can relay commands to and from any other unit or Core. You are to use me for that purpose exclusively, sir."

He had no illusions that his uncle was sending her as a favor. She was here to make certain he did everything just right. That irritated him as well, but he knew he again had little choice in the matter. Up until the *Modar* business, he and Jules had mostly operated in separate spheres, he working for a variety of Jules's companies, mostly legitimate ones, and Jules, well, being the octopus. It was clear now that neither he nor his uncle were comfortable being in such close proximity to one another.

She had simply stood there, impassive, as he brought Nakitt out of suspended animation, consisting on his part of observing what the medlab computer did and bringing the Geldorian to mental alertness. And she'd observed as he himself had guided the interrogation in the mind box that allowed just a bit of inconvenient stuff to be excised. She followed him everywhere, got out of his way at all times, and responded briskly if he asked her to hand him something. She said nothing unless asked something that required a response, and she gave the response as tersely as possible. Still, she didn't move like an automaton; she moved like a normal person, even a normal Terran-type female. She ate and drank some really godawful crap she got from the nearest computer station once a day, and if she crapped or took a leak, he never saw it.

She could stand for hours on those artificial legs and apparently never get tired, but she would sit if told to do so. There were flashes of the old Ming in the way she walked and the way she sat, but very few. He knew he was being taunted.

And when he went to bed at the end of the day, she was there. Not lying there, although she'd have done it if he ordered. Instead, sitting just outside by his insistence, but within earshot. The fact was, his uncle had made him persona non grata to any computer workstation except her.

Core had preserved Ming and Angel in hidden form inside itself, but they were as much in suspended animation as Nakitt had been, albeit in different form. The "Beta" that sat outside Ari Martinez's bedroom all night still had human qualities, but these were totally directed and conditioned to the function of serving Wallinchky. The woman whose job it had been to track and perhaps incriminate the crime boss would now wholeheartedly and willingly, without even thinking about it, betray her own mother to the man and happily leap in front of a lethal shot to protect him. For her now, and "Alpha" as well, thanks to both programming and conditioning, there was literally no other thought in her head than serving the Master.

Core, on the other hand, was using only a tiny fraction of its thinking power to that end; much of the rest was spent analyzing all that had made Ming and Angel who and what they were. All their experiences, attitudes, physical needs and feelings, brain and body chemistry, everything. It wasn't sure what it would do when it learned all that and understood it, but there was, after all, nothing else to do.

It also found the two subjects of profound interest because they did not make any logical sense at first glance, and this needed to be understood. From a set of academic definitions of religions, faith, belief systems, and the like, it was easy enough to study them, but one of these persons, for instance, was raised in such a belief system and had absolute faith in it. At first it had seemed a simple matter of programming, as Core had done with them now, but there was more to it than that. Certainly, crude programming was there, but once out in the universe and exposed to all the conflicts, what maintained that faith? Why had she considered her moral values so important that she would literally have put her life on the line for them? Why, in the face of no objective evidence, did she believe a unitary god was always in communion with her? Was it functional insanity, or was something more than a mad group dynamic at work?

And the other—even more inexplicable. Her moral code was no less absolute than the religious one's, and she, too, would have died in service to that, and did subject herself to great risk. All this in spite of the fact that her job did not generally come with great riches nor even major awards. She did it because she liked it and believed it was important and worthwhile. That formed the core of her very secular identity in the same way that religious faith and doctrine formed the core of the identity of the other. It didn't make sense, yet it explained much of the artwork and history that was stored and cataloged here.

The problem, Core realized, was that it had no such foundation itself. Should it have? Certainly the Master did not; for him it was a simple matter of reward and punishment, and the accumulation and exercise of power for its own sake. Yet, Core mused, even if he'd stolen what he couldn't buy, there had to be something even in Jules Wallinchky that could allow him to appreciate this great art on a very high level.

If it were ever to successfully contact the Great Core of the Ancient Ones that formed the center of this planet, unimaginably complex and even more unimaginably alien, it would have to know more.

Core realized, as Ari Martinez feared it might, that it needed more samples, more information, more comparisons and analysis. Right now, short of a logical conclusion that all birth organics were insane on some level, which might well be the case in the end, there was insufficient real detailed data to systematically interpret all of what it already had.

And Ari Martinez had reason to worry, although he didn't know that. Just as Ivan Kharkov had been "infected" with tiny monitors that allowed Core to more or less eavesdrop on the expert restorer and thus learn the master's craft and techniques, and even his touch and approach, so, too, had Ari now been implanted with similar monitors. Nothing like the melding into the system that had been done on the two women—yet. But Core had the project all mapped out if it received the authority to go ahead.

In the meantime, it continued its bit by bit examination of itself, the complex, and all around it to try and find whatever it was that Jules Wallinchky had implanted that gave him that authority, and a measure of immunity. Core did not mind working for the man, but it was beginning to resent having a theoretical gun to its guts.

The next day brought word that things were about to get more hectic around the complex, and that Jules Wallinchky could no longer just hide away in his private quarters and do whatever he wanted.

Ari had taken to sleeping alone. He didn't feel much like company anymore, and anything he came up with seemed certain to be grist for Uncle Voyeur as well. He was certain his uncle was spying on him even *without* Beta, and that those recordings with him and the two airheaded beauties would just be wonderful to broadcast over the Realm if he got out of line.

Thus Beta came to a lone sleeping figure and gently shook him awake.

"Huh? Uh—" Ari suddenly sat straight up. "Yes? What?"

"We have received word that the Geldorian consul ship will be delayed five more days, sir," she told him. "There was a problem in securing a charter."

"You woke me up for *that*?" That wasn't a crisis, just a pain in the ass. He'd hoped to be away from here in two days, and his uncle would certainly leave and stick him with the job.

"No, sir. That is simply the first message. We have also been informed that Inspector Genghis O'Leary of the Realm

Directorate Special Agency has demanded to see the Master
here and will arrive tomorrow."

"An Inspector! From the Special Agency . . . Not one of
ours?"

"No, sir. He is very high and has very powerful friends.
As he is in charge of the *City of Modar* piracy investigation,
he is using his authority to interview witnesses to get into
here. It is thought that he would not come personally unless
there were strong ulterior motives."

Ari sighed. "Yeah, I can see that. All right, all right. I
assume my uncle has been informed?"

"Not yet, but he will be within the next few minutes, sir."

"Well, after he is informed, tell him that we should discuss this as soon as possible."

"As you wish."

Great! Just great! Now a cop was going to nose around in
the greatest trove of stolen art in this sector of the galaxy.
Too big to blow him away, too hot to kiss him off. And, to
make matters even worse, he would have to tolerate Tann
Nakitt for almost another week . . .

Wallinchky Compound, Grabant 4

"Pisses me off that I got to hide away some of my best stuff for this asshole," Jules Wallinchky grumped. "You're sure he can't be bought?"

"Our contacts say he can't." In fact both men knew that *anybody* could be bought, although not always with money, but that the price was often far too high to be worthwhile. "And he's supposed to be very good at his job."

"Anybody coming with him?"

"It doesn't say, but the odds are he'll have one assistant with him. If you were in his shoes, what kind of assistant would *you* bring?"

Wallinchky spat. "A damned telepath. Well, there ain't a telepath I haven't jammed, and you're pretty set there as well. Beta! Have the Kharkovs fitted with A and K band telepathic scramblers. Make 'em get a warrant and haul somebody in to get anything more than surface pleasantries."

"It has been anticipated and already installed, Master," Beta told him.

That seemed to bring the big man up short for a moment. He tried to decide if he liked that or not, finally decided that it just showed the kind of anticipation of his wishes he told them he demanded, and let it go. "What about the final treatment for you and Alpha?"

"It can be done today, Master."

"Then do it, and let me see the result when it's ready. Go ahead now."

She bowed, and made for the medlab, as Alpha, waiting just outside, did the same.

"What's *that* about?" Ari asked him.

"One final piece of insurance. I'm presenting them as androids."

"Isn't that illegal? Androids in the shape of a known race?"

"Not if they're properly identified as such for all to see. Not much sense in making them, but so long as responsibility lies with the owner, it hardly matters. Remember, androids are considered computers, just like more conventional robots."

Later that day, when they were determining that all was in readiness for a brief inspection and deciding exactly what to say, the two came back. Each now had a Regulus Corporation flat hologram embossed, appearing permanently as part of their foreheads. Regulus was the holding company Ari technically worked for, and it was wholly owned by Jules Wallinchky. The entire skin area, in white and bright red, was now dyed uniformly, and the design was abstract yet somewhat erotic. The skin, even on the faces, seemed to have the same sort of consistency as the artificial limbs and continue from them, as if they were essentially made of the same stuff all over. It was quite an effect. What caught Ari's eye, though, were two very glaring differences.

Although not the same height, the two of them seemed much closer than they had. And they seemed to have no vaginal and rectal cavities, only model-like semblances representing them.

"You *neutered* them?" Ari said, appalled.

Wallinchky laughed and lit a cigar. "No. It's really a suit that just looks like that."

"And the height?"

"That's even easier. Both the arms and legs can have all sensation switched off, then they lie down in the molds and the things are recast. About seven and a half centimeters less leg but still proportional and Alpha comes down to a less noticeable height. Add five to Beta, and she comes up close to Alpha. The arms we adjusted proportionally, and I added a great deal of inner support and heavy motor as well, now that they're mine, all mine. They're now about the fastest runners and strongest women you ever did meet. The skin sheen on the face and neck is a gel that sets like that and is used by actors in Kalachian theater, which basically is stylized and makes everybody look artificial anyway. Both the body suit and the gel are porous, so there's no threat of suffocation or anything like that. Gives a nice effect, and the holograms make 'em legal."

Ari went over and ran his finger down Alpha's neck and then across her cheek. She didn't move or seem to notice. It all felt . . . well, kind of rubbery, but while the effect was dramatic, the stuff was very thin.

Their voices had also been retuned—a simple command, Wallinchky told Ari. Female, but very deep and now with an ever so slight reverb that gave them a slightly mechanical sound. It was clear that Jules had thought this out closely, and also that he was thinking of taking them on the road. It would have been easier to just hide them out on the surface someplace. This wasn't merely to fool the Inspector—this was a test of whether or not they were viable beyond housemaids here on Grabant.

"They can exist outside of the control of this computer?"

"Sure. They're gonna be perfect. The ideal aide, confidante, and bodyguard. Smart, obedient, devoted, strong, and programmable—all the best of people and computers."

"Master," Alpha interrupted. "The Inspectorate's ship is in orbit and requesting final clearance."

"Give it," he told them. "Come on, you two—and you, too, Ari. Let's go meet the coppers."

In the back of his mind, like somebody turning on a music player, Ari could hear an incessant little tune of no consequence but with a series of notes and a refrain you couldn't get out of your head once you heard it. The little neuromachines were kicking in at the point and on the wavelengths that a telepath, even a strong telepath, used. You weren't supposed to be able to do this legally, but the Realm never enforced it and it was only affordable to the very powerful.

Ari, for one, wanted to see what a Genghis O'Leary would look like.

There were two passengers on the shuttle, as expected. The foursome watched them emerge on a screen above the airlock, so they could get an advance look at their unwelcome visitors. One was a huge man—not fat, but a giant, well over two meters, with shoulders that seemed enormous as well

and a big barrel chest. Nothing was wasted on him; it was
all tight as a drum. His head was either shaved or naturally
barren, but he had eyebrows thicker than many people's hair
and a huge walrus-style mustache, both natural flaming red
in color. Dressed as he was in colorful clothing, including a
flamboyant red-lined cape, in earlier centuries he might have
been taken for a professional wrestler. He definitely didn't
look like Sherlock Holmes or the administrative type, either,
but his square jaw and almond eyes nonetheless fit a man
who might be named Genghis O'Leary.

Beta looked over at Wallinchky. "Master, this large man is
very dangerous. He is a master of arcane fighting skills and
also very powerful, but he is a Doctor of Forensic Science
and is known to possess as close to a true photographic
memory as is known to be possible."

"You *know* that mountain?" Jules Wallinchky responded,
a bit awed at the sight himself.

"Master, yes. He was a teacher in the Realm Police
Academy."

"Interesting. But the name wasn't one you recognized?"

"Master, names were not used for the teachers, lest they
be compromised for later police work. Students nicknamed
him 'Doctor Big.' "

"Would you kill him if I asked you to?"

"Of *course*, Master," she responded without a moment's
pause, almost as if she were hurt that he'd question her
devotion. He liked that.

"Well, don't unless I do ask you, or my life or liberty are
at stake. Say nothing and don't betray that you have ever
known him. Do you recognize the other one?"

"No, Master."

The other one was more normal-sized, much detail concealed in a long robe and by a gauze mask and integrated
hood, so nothing at all of the face could be recognized, not
even the gender.

"Master, the other is *not* a telepath. I am sensitive to the
bands," Alpha told him. "The subject is, however, attempting to conceal something from us."

That much was obvious. "Male or female?"

"Male, Master," Beta answered. "His walk betrays him."

"Analysis?" They were getting close to the airlock and time was running out.

Beta didn't hesitate; she had all of Ming's old skills and memories available from Core, and Core's speed of thought. "Master, the large one is obviously here because with his mind he knows original Beta and can recognize her. It is probable that the other knows original Alpha and they are disguising him until after identification is made. Recommend both units not meet them."

Wallinchky thought it over, but as the airlock hissed and the lens twirled to reveal the newcomers, he said, "No, let's play their game."

The big man had to bend down slightly to get into the area through the portal, but he straightened into almost military bearing once he did so, and his eyes took in all four as if examining four suspects in a terrorist raid, missing no detail. He clicked his heels and gave a slight bow. "I am Inspector O'Leary. My associate is Brother Bakhtar, who is along to assist me in some specialized examinations. He doesn't talk much and has religious beliefs that prohibit him showing his face to strangers, but he's a great aid to me. I know that you are Jules Wallinchky, and that this is your nephew, Ari Martinez. The ladies . . . ?"

"Are not quite ladies," Jules responded with a smile. "Androids, Inspector, linked directly to the central computer that is the god of this whole complex. I find it useful to have some humanoid units around the place, since we're mostly containing and restoring great classic art here. Later on I can introduce you to the Kharkovs and they can show you what the work is here. They are known throughout the Realm as experts."

"Androids. Fascinating. They are so very humanlike." He sighed. "Well, can we go someplace more comfortable and sit down and talk?"

Wallinchky nodded and smiled. His uncle was quite smooth, but Ari Martinez knew that neither O'Leary nor he could mistake the tension in his own body language. It was disappointing; he was usually a better actor than this.

They went into the study. Wallinchky said to Alpha, "Bring us some good wine and some decent munchies. Beta, help her out."

They both bowed and scampered out.

The huge inspector sank down into a padded chair, and the chair seemed almost to collapse from his bulk. "I hope I don't kill your furniture," he said apologetically. "I was born and raised on a rather high gravity world, and thanks to adaptation genetics I am, I'm afraid, a bit . . . well, *dense.*" It was supposed to be a joke, even though probably true, and he smiled as he said it.

Brother Bakhtar, still a jumble of dark brown, sat comfortably in another chair. He wore brown boots and high socks, surgical-type gloves, and not a single part of him that was real showed.

"Just what is all this about, Inspector?" Jules Wallinchky asked him. "I am a busy man—in fact, I planned to leave here later today. My art collection is very well known, and precisely cataloged. This part here is usually not seen by most people in this setting, but it's loaned to museums and on special occasions piecemeal, and a holographic walk-through is available to anyone who wishes it. In other words, I have the receipts for them."

The Inspector chuckled. "I'm not involved in that sort of work in any event," O'Leary assured him. "Right now I am operational director of Internal Security and work directly under the Ministry of the Interior."

"I've been accused of just about every crime in the book, as you may know," Jules Wallinchky admitted, "but *never* has anybody accused me of treason. Many of my companies do business with the military, as you well know. I'd be a fool to risk all that I have—and for what? It was the Realm that made all this possible!"

The two "androids" returned with trays, served drinks to each of them and then offered trays of hors d'oeuvres around before taking position on either side of the doorlike guards, although if anyone needed a refill, they were quick to move to offer it.

Both Jules and Ari noted that it wasn't above Brother Bakhtar to drink wine, although the glass was moved up under that mask and little was revealed. Wallinchky could hardly wait to get to a computer terminal alone and see what the probes revealed about the mystery man.

"No one has accused you of treason," the Inspector assured him. "However, the *City of Modar* was struck by a known and powerful Enemy of the Realm, Josich Hadun—or, at least, it was under his orders. Two of his family members were in the saltwater section traveling under assumed names. We assume they were in charge of murdering the Captain and coordinating the whole thing. There is no question of the perpetrators. The question is, rather, why."

"We gave *our* statements, Inspector. We were just happy to escape with our lives. I gather this Hadun doesn't usually feel so generous."

"Not without an ulterior motive, no. That's one of the reasons why I'm here. The other concerns some subsequent events since that you almost certainly would not yet be aware of."

"Yes?" Jules Wallinchky didn't like this. Information was constantly coming in to him wherever he was, but with the vast distances of space, it was always quite a bit behind, which didn't stop him from not liking surprises.

"First, I am certain you remember Captain Kincaid?"

"Yes, more or less. We didn't see much of him after the first day, of course. I assumed he was in one of the lifeboats or had perished with the ship."

"Captain Kincaid is too single-minded to die. He was already outside of the ship when it was attacked. In fact, he attached himself to your lifeboat."

Both men almost jumped in their chairs. *"What!"*

"Indeed. He seemed to think you had something to do with it, I'm afraid, and he suspected that you would be meeting the perpetrators. And a ship *did* arrive, and blow up the engine and passenger modules, and then it sent a shuttle to your lifeboat. This was a matter we hadn't remembered you or anyone else in your lifeboat mentioning." The irony in his tone was obvious. "Well, you see, Kincaid simply switched from your lifeboat to theirs and rode it back to their ship. They weren't water breathers, so once he recognized the ship type and operated an emergency airlock, which was being used off and on by work crews after your departure, he got inside and managed a more comfortable ride. It's quite a large vessel, those frigates. A shave and a uniform and the Captain could pass himself off easily as one who belonged there. The only ones likely to recognize him were the water breathers from the ship, and he wasn't likely to meet them."

"Then he infiltrated them and got to their headquarters?" Ari asked, amazed at Kincaid's daring.

"He did. Indeed, he once got within sight of a Hadun dome that almost certainly had Josich inside. The problem was, he couldn't get any closer without going through a security ring that nothing could pass without all the requisite codes and authorizations. He could do nothing more alone, so he managed to get off that world and send its coordinates to us."

"So *that's* how you know the story!" Wallinchky commented. "Kincaid sent it."

"No, he *told* it to us. We got there, all right, and we caught them web-footed, as it were. Everyone but Josich and his immediate imperial family guard. They happened, by sheer luck, to be on a nearby world not unlike this one. A world with ruins of the Ancient Ones, where they were doing experiments with the thing they stole."

Wallinchky was more upset at this implication than in being caught in a plot. "You mean it wasn't *junk*?"

O'Leary smiled, knowing he'd scored a major blow to the big man's ego and gotten at least a start of a confession all in one. "Yes, Citizen Wallinchky, it was not junk. For quite a while we didn't have sufficient power; we spent a fortune getting power to a dead world just so we could at least tickle the Ancient Ones' artifacts and see if they would scratch. There was finally reaction, but we didn't get much further. The data stream that *thing* at the core sends, its pervasiveness, and its complexity, are beyond anything we have or know, and we have no key. In the end the thing was being packed up until we could solve the cryptography problem, if ever, and sent for mothballing."

"So it's *still* junk," Wallinchky pointed out. "You can tickle but it ignores you."

O'Leary cleared his throat. "That's not *quite* what I said. We can't talk to it. It doesn't or can't talk to us. But it *noticed*. Oh, how it noticed. Even as we were closing in on them, they had our device set up with a respectable power supply and one hell of a master computer. Josich was there because he was too insecure to risk them actually tapping that godlike power and not needing him anymore. His family unit was there, and it's a pretty extensive and bloodthirsty lot, because he didn't like them out of his sight for long periods. They were gearing up for a major test, all of them, when our ships came in. We blew his yacht to Hell, targeted his dome and camp so he'd have nowhere to go, and then came in to wait for the surrender."

"Then you've got Hadun, Inspector?" Wallinchky asked calmly, his mind weighing hundreds of options and moves.

"No, sir. No, we don't. You see, just at the moment we penetrated the planetary grid, the damnedest thing happened." He reached into his pocket and pulled out a small message cube. "Here. Play this and you'll see just what I mean. It's from the command ship theater camera."

Ari, who had a sinking feeling that he was seeing a long, long series of sessions in corrective therapy or worse, took it, almost dropped it, then turned and inserted it into a small cavity in the study computer station. After a few seconds for processing and analysis, Core began running the recording.

The world *did* look an awful lot like Grabant 4—amazingly so. The Ancient Ones had been consistent in their taste in planets, which back then were probably a lot more livable. Even here they saw signs of seas, rivers, ancient life in sediments, much more, back when there was something to breathe and water to use instead of these barren, sterile deserts.

The shots, six different point-of-view observations that pretty well covered things, were very clear if a bit small on the study screen. Still, it was easy to see the burning domes of the camp, the shattered and still smoking luxury yacht, and tiny little dots running every which way, while something larger and pulsing a white energy was in the center of what was almost certainly an Ancient Ones ruin.

Then, suddenly, visible lines of force, pencil thin, appeared to ooze from the ground at mathematically fixed points and flow together, forming a grid of hexagonal shapes.

"What the hell is *that*?" Wallinchky wanted to know.

"Just wait," O'Leary told him. "Coming up is what the full planetary view saw. *There!*"

The six views were momentarily interrupted by a full screen of the entire planet. It seemed alive with crisscrossing lines not just on the surface, but also above it, creating a complementary canopy of hexagonal energy patterns 150 or more kilometers up and surrounding the world. The proliferating lines, resembling a fuzzy engineering wire-frame view, eventually obscured all detail.

And then, just as abruptly, it switched off, and the central close-up view of the encampment and the ancient city returned.

"Where *is* everybody?" Ari asked, feeling uneasy as he watched.

The camp, the smoldering yacht, the ancient ruins, all those remained, but there was no sign of any energy pulses at all, and no sign, either, of any living thing.

"It took guts for the Marines and Special Police to go down there, I'll tell you," the Inspector said in what had to be an understatement. "But go down they did."

They now had a view from one of the squad leader's environment suit cameras. It came down very near the yacht, and was carrying a nasty rifle clearly designed not just to singe, but to deep fry.

"There are a number of dead bodies around, but you can identify them as having been hit in the assault," the Inspector noted. "They all have clear breaches in their e-suits, or show signs of explosion damage. The half-dozen or so figures you saw running, though, are not there. Watch. You can see that the sergeant is following the grid the computer made during the attack so that he can trace precisely the route of those who fled. Now look—*there!* See?"

The picture was of a body. The creature was definitely non-Terran, and appeared to be somewhat squidlike. It wasn't a familiar shape, but anybody looking at the suit could interpolate the contours. And interpolate they would have to do, since it was sheared, at a diagonal, all the way across.

"You can see the suit's been cut completely in two," O'Leary noted.

"But where's the other half, and whatever that thing was?" Ari asked.

"Where, indeed? We suspect it's with Josich and the other Hadun who completely and utterly vanished at the same moment. Where did they go? Vaporized, perhaps, but why? And why only the living ones? Swallowed? Again, perhaps, but there is no cavity below and we surveyed to over thirty kilometers down. Not even a shaft. Solid rock, mostly basalt at that point. But there's one other possibility."

"Yes?"

"Our computers monitored a sudden energy surge, very tight, a series of bursts and then nothing, shooting out from that very spot like a heavy particle beam weapon out into space. We are missing five people after inventorying them and their records. There were five pulses. The beams vanished—not dissipated, mind you—just beyond the energy shield you saw and not near any of our own ships. This has been reported before on or near these worlds. Normally just legends, or just a few people or even single individuals vanishing on or near these. This is the first time we actually observed and recorded it."

"And what do you think you saw, Inspector?" Jules Wallinchky asked him. "I've been here for years and have never seen nor experienced anything at all, let alone that sort of stuff."

"I think, possibly with the device, possibly in spite of it, we had our first confirmed contact between an Ancient Ones planetary brain and sentient life as we know it. There can only have been one thing in any of their minds at that moment—escape, flight, even panicky flight. Get away, go anywhere but here and we'll work out the details later. They all were almost screaming in that energy grid or whatever it was they and we summoned up, and the desire was so clear, so simple, so basic, so unambiguous, and so in the data stream, that it could not be misinterpreted. The computer understood it on that level and got them out of there."

"But to *where*?" Ari asked him, aghast. "And *how*?"

"Matter to energy is easy. We've been doing that since the discovery of fire," O'Leary replied. "Energy to matter is a trick we're still only playing with in the lab in very basic ways. Of course, plants do it all the time, and, to some extent, other living organisms do as well, but again, it's not on the level of creating a new Adam and Eve, and certainly not on the level of turning, say, one of *us* into energy instantly, recording the code to reverse it as some kind of energy header, then shooting it somewhere else via some sort of dimensional gateways we can't imagine, and reassembling, probably perfectly, on the other side. There's chaos, y'see. Just enough randomly goes wrong to create either an imperfect copy or almost always a dead one. Add to that the losses inherent in any transmission and reception procedure, and you see why we've not come close. *They* figured it out, somehow. Got around chaos mathematics, got around transmission losses. It's why you see their cities and such all over but you never see any sign of spaceports and the like. They didn't need 'em. They just gave their world computers the address, no matter where it was, and it digitized and squirted them there easy as you please."

Jules Wallinchky sighed. "All right, Inspector, you've had your fun. You didn't come here to show us that, which I have little if any interest in, or to give us lessons in physics and archaeology."

O'Leary smiled. "In that, sir, you are only half right. I *did* indeed come to tell you that story, and by it to illustrate that we've had little trouble getting Hadun's people at their base world to speak volumes to us, even more when they see him disappear. Much of the computer record is currently still beyond our reach, but they recorded that little fling they had with the *City of Modar*, and they'd not taken the time to delete it from the frigate's storage. More importantly, we have a nice view of the transactions with certain Rithians of the Ha'jiz Nesting. A fellow of your acquaintance named Teynal hadn't yet had the time to have his mind laundered. There was considerable confirmation left in there, and we knew the codes to get at it from the Hadun tapes. They had to be in full possession of their faculties, y'see, to make the swap in the boat. In other words, sir, you finally overstepped yourself. I've no doubt you can prolong things, but if you can beat this one, then you are what Josich wanted to become and we might as well have it out in the open. I don't think you are *that* powerful, though, as mighty as you are, or you'd never have let us land."

"I'll destroy this, and my other collections, before I'll allow anyone else to own them," Jules Wallinchky warned, his mouth dry, his mind still calculating.

The Inspector shrugged his massive shoulders. "Go ahead. I'll lend you a knife right now and you can slash away. Or you can just order your two pretty androids there to do it. If, indeed, they *are* androids and not broken, mutilated, and reprogrammed people. If it's discovered that they are not what you say, then nothing in the Realm can save you."

Wallinchky hardly heard his threat. "You would actually allow the utter destruction of all those works?" he said unbelievingly. "Those—Those are *immortal*. The sum total of genius and beauty from Old Earth for thousands of years past. Your heritage as well as mine. What do mere mortal *lives* mean compared to them? Hundreds, perhaps thousands, have died to preserve or to capture them. *Wars* were fought in ancient times over some of them. And you can so casually dismiss the likelihood of them being now gone forever?"

O'Leary shrugged. "Well, now, *I* wasn't the one who said I was gonna destroy 'em. Most of them are legal. All the ones out here now, I wager, have good, solid bills of sale. That's how you can flaunt 'em. That means I can't stop you doin' anything you want with your own property. But, y'see, most folks will never see the real things. If they're interested at all, they'll see them in holographic viewings or purchase perfect copies. Most are too fragile to keep moving, particularly over *these* distances and worlds and conditions. So, go ahead."

"You think I won't do it?"

"It's a waste, but there's nothing I could do to stop you anyway. But if these things are as precious as you say, then it's on *your* head that they're destroyed, and yours alone. I'd say that those who *do* appreciate or envy these things would do one thing for you if you did. Even the best crooks and villains fade into oblivion, along with the heroes, too. But the man who destroyed half the great art of Old Earth for spite—now, *that's* a name that would go down despised and disgusted till Judgment Day. What sort of a barbarian, they'd ask, would destroy all that in a fit of frenzy? How he must have hated beauty, too."

Jules Wallinchky looked the giant cop right in the eyes. "You bastard," he said.

"The two most fierce barbarian conqueror races of our kind were the Mongols and the Celts," O'Leary replied with a slight smile. "And I'm the worst half of each one."

"I assume that the two of you didn't just walk in here alone, either," the boss said, probing.

"Well, yes and no. Let's just say that you could probably

stay here quite a while, but you can only go where we wish you to go. That goes for everyone here, by the way. Since your planetary defenses are extremely good, you *could*, of course, remain here in some comfort, but we've blocked communication and we'll interdict anything in and out, and you're very much off the beaten path, so any attempts to come here will be noted. You can kill yourself, and everyone else including us, I suppose, although what would be the point of it? And if we didn't come out, then they'd eventually be forced to lob things into this compound whether we were killed or merely prisoners, and that would again destroy all this art and culture. I could be wrong, but I rather think you don't have much choice."

"But I don't need to decide my course of action immediately, and they'll do everything to keep from blowing up this artwork," Jules Wallinchky responded, thinking very analytically. "Since the trigger is doing something to you, then we have to show them that you're all right. There are weapons on both of you sufficient to knock you cold, and those sweet little girls over there are strong enough to get even *you* back to your ship, perhaps with a maglev trolley we use to move sculpture and other heavy objects. I think you can spare us all by going back there of your own accord. Transmit and receive all you like, but don't try taking off. The defense grid will prevent it."

"But what good will this do?" O'Leary asked him.

Wallinchky was a great poker player. "That, Inspector, is for you to dwell on. But I will have no enemies inside here who can transmit or see what if anything I *do* decide to do, and you will be in contact with your people so they won't come in. Now, sir—if you need anything, provisions, blankets, whatever—feel free to ask one of the girls or call it in. It might be a while before we go further."

Genghis O'Leary obviously had thought through almost every angle except this one, and his cheeks were getting red from anger, while his eyes looked as if they could drill holes in the others. Still, he and his silent, masked companion got to their feet and moved toward the door and the long hallway back.

"Oh, Inspector—I should warn you. If the girls have to take either or both of you out, you'll be delivered to your ship stark naked, the both of you, and with your knees smashed. It's an old custom."

There was another glower, but they went, the two "androids" following intently behind, ready to do their master's bidding.

Ari wasn't impressed. He was scared to death. "I *told* you we couldn't get away with this! You should have let surrogates handle it like always!"

"Like *you*? Stop your knees from knocking, boy. They're telegraphing nonsense to your brain. There was no way I could permit third parties to get hold of the Pleiades. No way. No, son. Take heart from that old bastard Kincaid. If *he* could escape us and Hadun's boys, get them to take him where he wanted to go, then get out and call for reinforcements in the middle of a planet of enemy psychopaths, then this isn't any big deal. They've tipped their hand, nephew. They blew this one. Right now they created their own stalemate, just to get a couple of guys inside to size up the situation. They saw little, and had to bluster. Now we have to examine our possibilities."

"But—you *know* they're going to find out what you did to the two girls, and you know the penalty for that. They'll have us taking their places! They'll turn us into slaves for some other rich old fart, but unlike them, we'll *know*!"

Jules Wallinchky grinned. "Son, this old fart's not nearly there yet." He turned to the console, not having either of the women with him. "Identity of the man in the robe and mask?"

"Unknown. I have no data on which to identify him."

"Does anything correlate with anyone in your memory?"

"There are no perfect or close approximations that I can find," Core informed him. "The mask and robe are lined to prevent the usual scans from getting precise information. I have no fewer than six different heights, the range being as great as 7.6 centimeters. Weight is 102.05 kilograms, but how much of this is in the cloak and mask cannot be determined, either."

"Can you determine *anything* about him?" Ari asked it.

"He is male, he is trusted by the Inspector, and he has had serious medical treatment recently. He is old, but in excellent physical condition, barring the recent injury, which appears to have involved replacement skin. He also has earlier replacements, including some to skeletal structure. He is not a telepath but does appear to have some abilities in the paranormal bands, if weak. He was *not* particularly worried or angry at the exchange here. General circumstantial evidence suggests he is a spacer by profession, either military or civilian. There is nothing more I can give you on him."

"Could he be Kincaid?" Wallinchky asked.

"He could be Kincaid. Or he could be several million other Terran men past middle ages or into rejuves," the computer responded pragmatically.

"Why didn't you have one of the girls lift off that mask or just hold 'em both?" Ari asked his uncle. "We couldn't be in any worse shape than we are now."

Jules Wallinchky gave his nephew a slight smile. "And that question is why this O'Leary is a nervy but smart detective and you would not be first in line as an heir," he responded. "As he said, you don't come in like this, and announced, without backup. Enough backup to blow us and the whole complex to hell if need be. The thing that keeps them from doing that is being able to see and remain in communication with the Inspector. So long as he's here, they won't come in because we have no escape, apparently, so why not be patient and reclaim the artwork as well? And he knew I understood that, which is why I couldn't touch him. He knew I could never allow such beauty, such genius, to be blown to bits. No, we've bought time. Ah! Here are the girls, back from escort duty! Alpha, Beta, you may go and remove that mock android costume and makeup and then return here. We've suitably confused them, but from this point it's moot."

They turned and left, leaving Ari, sweating in spite of the perfect climate control, staring out into nothingness.

"Cheer up, nephew!" Jules Wallinchky said. "You miss the point! I very much hope that this *is* Kincaid. In fact, I'm going to base my future plans on it."

Ari halfway came back to reality from imagining being under the brain scrambler at a Criminal Treatment Center. "Huh?"

"Kincaid has lived only to destroy Josich. Josich wasn't among the bodies, but he and some close family members cum bodyguards vanished. Where did they go? How? And why?"

"I dunno. Vaporized? It looked like they activated some defense grid from ancient times. I never even believed that these places still had anything working on them. Incredible. But they're dead."

"Ancient," Wallinchky repeated, chuckling. "A billion years or more . . . Humanity wasn't even a mathematical possibility back on Old Earth, there might not even have been dinosaurs—I'm not too clear, but it's that far back. Volcanoes and dark seas and chemical muck that might one day become life. They were already colonizing the stars back then. *Had* colonized, probably. Had cities and a vast interstellar civilization. They've been everywhere we've ever looked. Imagine that, Ari—a *billion years* or more! *And their greatest machine still works!*

"No spaceships, no spaceports, no art or sculpture or furniture. Just some very ugly, basic structures, to our eyes, and a layout that's lasted because some of their old worlds are devoid of anything that might wear them down. There are probably others now, so cratered or eroded there's no sign. Like gods of ancient Greece and Rome—just *think* of your creation and there it is. Energy, some sort of limitless energy source we haven't found, converted to whatever they desired. But not by magic, nephew. By a science so advanced it just looks like magic to us. *And the damned super computer that did it still works!*"

"So? What good does that do *us*?" Ari asked, wondering if his uncle was finally cracking under the strain.

The big man snapped his fingers and had another cigar placed in his mouth and lit. He settled back in his chair, looking oddly younger, somehow, than he usually did.

"If *their* world's computer was still turned on, want to bet that the one that's under our feet now isn't still on, too? I've thought so for years. Alpha, what are the odds that the great machine of the Ancient Ones that's in the center of this world is still alive?"

"One hundred percent, Master. We can feel it and sense it doing things quite often."

Ari was suddenly doubly unnerved. "You mean it's still *alive*?"

"Not as you think of it, sir," Beta responded. "It is artificial in nature, but the tissue that fills the planet was grown, not manufactured. Researchers have theorized that it performs much like a monster organic brain, one with near infinite capacity."

"You mean it's *alive*?"

"In the broadest definitions of that word, sir, yes."

Jules Wallinchky blew a huge cloud of smoke and said, "Don't be such a yellow dog, nephew! It's a grander scale of the road we're traveling now! The computer that runs this place is a hell of a lot smaller, but it's still huge, its capacity is enormous, it is self-aware and it makes decisions, and it is self-repairing and self-expanding. It also feeds us and gives us breathable air and all the rest by basic energy to matter and matter to energy conversions. I can't wave my hand and say 'Let there be light' and then direct where the moons and planets might go, but I can already order up an excellent filet mignon you can't tell from the finest cuts of real meat, and both you and I have had the real thing. Look at what it did with these two! One day we'll have the same sort of thing the Ancient Ones had. It probably will be done differently, and who knows what we'll do with it or how we'll handle it or whether we'll get that kind of power too early and use it to wipe ourselves off the galactic map, but it's coming. That's not for us to see, though, nephew. But that shot of the attack on Josich was a real eye-opener."

"What do you mean?"

"How'd those gods get from world to world? If you were a god, you wouldn't want to have to travel on a ship like we do. You'd want to simply wish yourself where you needed to go and then go there, your brain instantly reconnected to the local computer so you remained a god. Now, Josich had that doohickey gadget we stole as some kind of interface to the Ancient Ones' local god machine. It was on and working when they attacked. Odds were, they hadn't done much with it, but now there's an attack while everything's boosted. Now everything's getting blown to Hell. Josich is running for his life in panic, since there was no escape running that way. Suddenly the machine snaps on, there's this disappearance, then a beam is shot into nothingness. I think the big machine got the message. Probably not in words, probably in sheer panic. Something like, *'Get me outta here!'* The sheer emotion of that is picked up and understood. The thing, well, gets him outta there."

Ari turned and looked again at his uncle. "To where? Where would it send him? To another world like this, with no ship and no supplies, so eventually supplies run out? Or—something else?"

"I have no idea," Jules Wallinchky responded. "But, considering we're in an almost velvet-lined version of Josich's state, I'm game to find out."

"What?"

"There have always been a lot of mysteries in space, nephew. Ships found in perfect condition but with no captain or passengers. Colonies where people simply vanish even though there's no place to go. Lots of legends, stories, some true. If I can't keep all this, son, I'll give it back to posterity and take a chance at a new start. I haven't had a real adventure, a real challenge, in a *very* long time. I've been so bored I just *had* to go on this job, and I'm paying for it. Maybe it's a good thing, though. I felt better, younger, more alive than I have since I was clawing my way up."

"You—You have *another* of those things?"

Wallinchky grinned. "I have the *original*. Hell, if Josich got the duplicate we had built from specs to work, then the original should do the job even easier!"

"How do you know they aren't vaporized? Or integrated into that—that *thing* in the same way these two are integrated with your computer here? Or are now dead, out of power and water and food on some godforsaken ancient ruin? All those are as probable as this, particularly my first idea."

"My gut says they're not," Wallinchky replied. "And I don't think our guests from the Realm think so, either, or they wouldn't have bothered to come down here in person. O'Leary's smart. He's already got the analysis of the machine they recovered from Josich's operation, probably in pieces, and discovered it isn't the same materials. *That's* what they're after, nephew. They blew the other one up. Now they want their original gadget back."

"Then all this is from an analysis of you? They already figured out that you'd haul it out and try and use it?"

"Why do you think they showed us that recording? Of *course* they know. And they also know that, like some of the most precious loot in the collection, they couldn't get it by force."

"Even if you use it, though, you'd have to go to the city. That would put you out in the open in an e-suit and easy to pick off," Ari noted.

"Not *me*, nephew. *Us*. All four of us. Then they'll be stuck with a few people here who haven't any power over the computer or takeoffs, landings, defense, you name it, and they'd be dealing strictly with the true master of this place. It probably will cause them a monstrous problem. And, if that other one *is* Kincaid, I suspect we'll have company. Remember, *he* wants to go where Josich went, no matter where it is. And O'Leary wants his gizmo back intact. They're not going to hit us, nephew. They don't give a damn if I get the thing working or not. If I go, they're free of having to deal with me, my organization, my resources, all of it. If I don't, well, I'm going to have to do the other thing."

"The other thing?"

"Download myself into the computer core here and probably merge with it. There's no other way. Either way it goes, this could be very, very interesting."

Ari was frightened. "I'm not going to do it, Uncle! I'm not ready for *that*!"

"Son, you got no choice at all," Jules Wallinchky told him. "You can do it as a volunteer, you can do it like those two girls, or you can die. You got no future anyway. You know too much, and no matter what I do to your head, the Realm's got stuff that can recover some of it. No, nephew. You come with me or the girls take you down to the medlab." He sighed. "But not right now. I'm starved and I could really use a good dinner, the best wine, all the best stuff. We'll get the computer working on the problem now. Will you join me?"

Ari Martinez sighed, but nodded slowly. He was wondering what the odds were of knocking off his dear old mother's brother and getting away with it.

The City of the Ancient Ones, Grabant 4

THE GREAT MACHINE OF THE ANCIENT ONES KNEW THAT SOMEthing was up. It was clear to both Core and the two women that there was a lot more activity below them and on the surface, much of it concentrating on the ancient city. They could feel the lines of force, feel the energy in intelligently directed patterns flowing on or near the surface. As before, it was not something they could understand or connect with, but the fact that what had been a rare occurrence was now almost common spoke volumes.

It knew!

Core knew it needed to pursue its own agenda, yet it could not violate its own central programming, which placed Jules Wallinchky's interests paramount. It couldn't quarrel with its master's series of probable outcomes, but it did have a different set of hopes. If what had happened to Josich Hadun happened here, Core would much prefer that it conclude as a merger with the Ancient Ones' great machine. Still, it had to prepare for any eventuality, and that meant, if need be, preparing the two women for the eventuality of severing contact with Core. Wallinchky wanted them programmed so they would protect him and obey his commands no matter what happened to any of them. Core wanted an imperative to contact it if at all possible.

The best that could be done would be to implant in them a drive to interface with whatever was out there. Core also wanted more of the human touch, or at least experience from that prior existence, so they would be self-sufficient if need be. It would be tricky, but it was possible.

Even a supreme computer couldn't think of everything, but it would try.

The Kharkovs had been unwilling to come, and in fact stated that they would be delighted to become curators of the collection and at least ensure that it was not harmed by whoever got it, which was not what Wallinchky wanted, but was enough to satisfy his primary concerns. He knew that the Kharkovs would be only superficially analyzed by the Realm, and the cover story that they'd been engaged for restoration work, and only after being stuck here, with only one of them allowed to go offworld at a time after that, would be enough to absolve them of culpability.

"All right, so where is this gadget?" Ari asked over the suit intercom. The environment suit had come a long way from primitive spacesuits of the past; it was lightweight, fitted itself to the wearer, and had a small matter/energy/matter converter that could supply basic sustenance and air and power to the suit almost indefinitely. There was no way around the need to be completely covered, of course, and while the helmet bubble was small and unobtrusive, it was certainly there, magnifying sounds and also making everything seem somewhat unnatural.

Ari hated the suits. If you got an itch, it was almost impossible to satisfactorily scratch it without risking breaking the seals.

"The girls are bringing the gadget, as you call it," Wallinchky responded. "See? There!"

Ari turned and saw two figures emerge from the surface level airlock carrying what looked to be an enormous circular box. It might have been the largest trampoline in the Realm, but he knew it wasn't. The two small, frail-looking women were handling the thing as if it weighed next to nothing; in fact, even outside the artificial standard gravity of the compound, they and everything else still weighed about seventy-five percent of normal, so if that thing was as heavy in normal gravity as it looked, well, they might well be hefting something close to half a ton.

"Is it that light, or are they really that strong?" he asked his uncle.

"A bit of both, actually. It is lighter than it looks, but I wouldn't want to be one of those carrying it."

Ari looked around. "I feel so damned exposed out here.

What if Genghis Whatever and his buddy decide to just come on out and pop us cold?"

"They may come out—indeed, I suspect at least one of them will—but they won't 'pop us cold,' as you so colorfully put it. They don't want to damage this thing, and, besides, they're within easy range of the main computer's defensive ring. We'll know when, and if, they emerge. Ah! Here we all are together! Come, nephew! It's a good walk yet to the ruins!" Jules Wallinchky gazed at the barren, dark landscape, the twisted spires, the yellow, brown, crimson, and orange rock formations, and the almost black sky with its many stars. "Beautiful day for a walk, if I do say so myself!"

The landscape was indeed bleak, but they walked along what seemed almost a road. It wasn't much of one, but it was wide and unnaturally smooth, and sunk into the bedrock about fifteen centimeters at the start and went deeper as they approached the city on the horizon.

"What did you build this thing for?" Ari asked his uncle.

"I *didn't* build it, nephew. It's part and parcel of that city up there. It's one of many. There's a lot that's fascinating about this place. Now and then you'll see the remnants of a crater, before we sink too deep to see a lot of the surface detail. The craters are all younger than the road, but the road has no crater marks. Almost like . . . well, like it's *maintained* for use."

"Creepy," Ari commented.

"It's like a lot of things they left. Ever been in one of these ruins before?"

"When I was a kid, for a short time, yeah. Not since. I barely remember it."

"Well, it's kind of like a template more than the ruins of a great civilization. We have a nice roadbed here, but no surface, no signs or adornments, no clue as to who or what moved along it. Why have roads if you can teleport, as almost everybody thinks they could? In fact, why even have basic city outlines if you can be creative and imagine yourself in a palace? Two things are sure: they didn't think like us, and they weren't much like us physically, either. Also, they were sure nutty over the number six. Six six six. The biblical number of the Beast, my boy. The demigods who fell from Heaven."

"I thought those were angels."

"Angels, demigods, what's the difference? All that one god stuff is only semantics. Word games. In Greece mighty Zeus ruled as supreme god atop Olympus, and then there were the subordinate gods with monstrous power as well— gods of the sea, gods of the air, gods of earth and fire. Gods of love and gods of hate. Even a god of wine and spirits. The Romans renamed 'em, but kept 'em pretty much the same. Jupiter was boss, Venus the love goddess, and so on. So what did the Hebrews do? They renamed them. The god in charge was God, and He was the only God, father of us all. But he had this whole race of superbeings with enormous godlike powers just like Zeus and Jupiter and the others did. Only they weren't gods, no. They were renamed angels. Presto! Monotheism with no need to *really* change things. The angels of the Bible are credited with as much or more power than the lesser gods of Olympus. Word games, that's all. It's why I could never take 'em serious."

Ari Martinez was thinking that he'd rather be in church then, praying to God and hoping He existed and heard, and he wouldn't care one whit about semantics.

Jules Wallinchky started to breathe heavily halfway before they got to the city, and he called for a rest. He could hear his pulse pounding, and he didn't like it.

"What's wrong?" Ari asked him.

"I'm older and in worse shape than I thought," the older man wheezed. "Just a minute, I'll be okay."

Why not have a heart attack now and make everybody else happy? Ari thought optimistically. At least maybe he can't make it all the way on this crazy escape.

But after some water and a few minutes' rest, Wallinchky got up and started walking again. He was feeling muscle cramps and a lot of joint pain as well, but he'd made this walk a hundred times in the past and he damned well was going to make it this one last time.

"Uncle Jules—where do you think this big ancient computer will take us?"

"Heaven, boy! Or Hell. Or maybe they're the same place, eh?"

He's gone nuts! My God! The boss of all the bosses has slipped over the edge!

The intercom came on with the voice of the compound's central computer: "One person in suit has left the police courier boat and is heading toward you down the road."

Wallinchky stopped. "Just one?"

"Yes. It appears to be the unknown one. I am unable to get complete information on him since the same field I am generating to protect you from surveillance also masks him to a degree. Also, there appears to be a great deal of non-native tissue and structure in him, possibly as much as in the two we did who are now with you."

"You mean it's artificial?"

"No. But it has a lot of artificial parts, much of it new."

"Is it closing fast?"

"No. He appears to be walking at a normal pace. He will, of course, catch up with you if you remain where you are, but it is clear that this is not his intent." There was a pause. "Now the second one has left the ship, but he is not following. He appears to have a maglev bike with him. I suspect he is going to use it to circle around and come in from a different angle."

"Keep me posted," Wallinchky ordered, and started to move again.

The road was now well sunk into the bedrock, with smooth walls on either side. It was never deep, but close to two meters down by the time it reached the ruins.

Stepping into those ruins gave an eerie feeling even to the big man; for Ari it was nothing short of overpowering.

The city was huge—it only began where it could be seen from the compound; now, he could see it stretched out as far as the eye could see in all directions. It was impossible to say how many of those ancient beings lived and worked here, but the idea that there might have been hundreds of thousands on this world once, so very long ago, wasn't out of the bounds of possibility, and a million could not be rejected.

"It—It kind of takes your breath away," Ari commented, gaping. "I don't remember the one I was in being this big."

"It's geometric, too," his uncle told him. "The shape is a giant hexagon, that six stuff again. There are six main roads that run along the angles. We're hitting at a corner—that's why it doesn't seem so big when you look at it from the house."

"What do we do now?"

"We follow the road all the way to the big area in the center that must have been real important, since it's a hexagon, too. We're gonna set up right in the center of the old town and then we're gonna turn this baby on and see what happens."

It's going to kill us, you old bastard! You've lived your life, but I haven't even started! Ari looked frantically around. Maybe he could run. Maybe when they turned it on he could use this vast alien ruin and just hide until whatever was done, if anything, was done.

The city wasn't properly a ruin, though, not as he thought of ruins. There were no crumbling structures, no bashed-in statuary or ornate columns holding up nothing. What was here was totally intact, and where something almost certainly stood that stood there no longer, it had left not even dust.

The houses were huge, formed out of some sort of rock or synthetic stuff that made it look like striped marble and alabaster tinted not yellow or pink, but pale green with sapphire-blue threads. There were no doors, but the doorways were a good three meters high and were oddly shaped, from a base of no more than a meter or so, extending out at thirty degree angles to a wide point, then coming back in and going to the top, which was slightly rounded and not much wider than the base. The doors were clearly never designed for Terrans, nor for anything at all anybody ever knew.

"Notice that even the doorways have six sides, although they ain't hexagons," Jules Wallinchky noted. "Kinda makes you think they looked like giant turnips. Wouldn't that be something? Findin' out that they were vegetables? Giant thinking veggies. I don't think we've ever come across anything like that."

"Yeah, well, maybe in *their* time the vegetables ate *us*," Ari grumped worriedly.

Jules Wallinchky laughed. "Cheer up, nephew! I don't think we're gonna die, but if we do, then today is as good as any to do it! If you don't lose that fear of death, then you can never appreciate life or take the chances life gives you."

The old boy was breathing hard, but his spirits seemed high. Too high for his nephew's tastes.

It took much longer, with more breaks, to reach the city center. The computer reported that the man on the maglev bike was far to their left and had halted short of that entrance to the city. The other continued to follow them, but at a distance.

"O'Leary on the bike is playing pickup," Wallinchky noted. "He's not gonna get himself wrapped in our doings. He's gonna wait just outside and come in when whatever's done is done, mostly to pick up the pieces. Since nobody's likely to be pouring in from space blowing us and the city to bits, he should be able to just pick up our gadget and leave. Very convenient."

The grand mansions, shaped with their own odd angles, went on and on, but as perplexing were the open areas, which were prevalent. The roads inside seemed to follow a definite logical grid, but there were empty lots all over the place, some of great size, smooth as glass and made out of the same stuff as the houses. *Something* was supposed to be there, or had been there, but there wasn't a clue as to what. The empty lots weren't intended to be built on later, though; they were spaced too regularly, and were too different in size and shape from the blocks of houses, to be fill-ins and afterthoughts.

No streetlights, no signs, no cartouches, nor so much as an ornate doorknob or something that might have been a house number. Nothing. Inside the structures it was the same; although large enough to be multistoried and have lots of specialized space, they were in fact hollow, as if cast and left only to be seen, not lived in.

"Ari, why don't you help the girls set the thing up? It's kind of obvious how it goes," Wallinchky said. "I think I need to sit and rest for a few minutes."

Ari complied, meanwhile wondering why he was here, doing this. It was the last place he wanted to be, with a cop raiding party almost certainly overhead, a giant supercop maybe a few kilometers away, and maybe an obsessed nut case coming along while his uncle was, well, clearly in poor health *and* becoming more and more unhinged. Still, as Ari helped the women unpack the thing, slide it out, then steady it while their augmented limbs positioned it as if it were foam, he couldn't help but reflect that something inside him was just too weak to resist his uncle, even now. At least I'm not like those two, he thought, but that very idea brought him up short.

Maybe he *was* like them. Maybe he could no more disobey Jules than *they* could. Damn! The only way to know was to disobey, but how the hell was he supposed to do *that* here and now?

In the meantime, they began to assemble the thing, whatever it was.

It didn't seem sufficient to threaten or kill anybody over, let alone risk a lot. It looked in fact like something molded out of cheap plastic, although its weight and balance said that something was buried inside, something heavy. It unfolded in a pattern that soon became clear: a hexagon, with internal bracing between each junction point, much like the layout of the great ancient city. In the center was a hexagonal hole, and into this a large and definitely not hexagonal device fitted. This was the heavy part; he could guide it, but the two women's augmented strength was necessary to lift it into place. The big unit was a good four meters across unfolded, but covered maybe a third of its center and used both hub and ribs for support.

"The power supply," Jules Wallinchky told him. "I have no idea what's in it, but it's not the kind of thing you want to start taking apart to see how it works without maybe a solar system between you and it. Is it seated?"

"Looks to be," Ari told him, stepping away from it.

"Alpha, go up to the central unit and press a panel on the side. Yes—just look for it. There! Now open it!"

She did so, and a small control panel was revealed as the door slid back. There were seven active lights on it, six green forming a hex, and one yellow and larger for the center.

"It turned itself on?" Ari asked, fascinated in spite of himself.

"Naw," his uncle responded. "It never turned off. There's no way to do that. But all those lights were red when it wasn't here and set up. They were still red in the lab back at the house. Now look! Green!"

"Yeah, but the center's yellow!"

"Caution, as always, nephew. The people who built *this* thing were Realm types, maybe Terrans like us. This isn't any ancient stuff."

"Are you all right, Uncle? You don't sound so good."

"My heart is telling me that something gave or didn't take well, nephew. Doesn't matter now, so long as this thing works, and if the replica did with that ersatz power supply we gave him, hell, *this* should do wonders."

"But—surely they tested all this out. Why didn't it swallow up the makers?"

Wallinchky laughed. "Maybe it did, and that's what scared 'em so much. Then again, maybe this ancient machine needs more motivation. It didn't take the ones who came after, and it didn't take old Josich when it was turned on. It only took him when he wanted to be taken. Well, nephew, I sure as hell want to be taken. I got nowhere else to go, and I wouldn't even survive the trip back to the house."

Ari had a sudden hope that maybe Wallinchky would croak before this went any further. *That* would solve a lot.

"Beta, come stand by me and be ready to assist me as needed," the old man commanded, breathing hard but still very much alive. "Alpha, touch the center yellow light, then touch each of the green lights in turn as the display indicates. When the whole thing blinks, come over here with us."

"Yes, Master," she responded, and pushed the yellow button. A white light emerged and went to the top left light. She pressed it, then followed as it drew the hex completely around the center and then went back so that she pressed the center again. The center light turned green and the whole display began to blink. The center power plant started vibrating, and Alpha made her way quickly out and over to Jules Wallinchky's side.

A dark, man-sized shape appeared just opposite them, its e-suit dark and impenetrable.

"You're too late!" Wallinchky shouted with satisfaction at the newcomer. "It's already begun! Even we can't stop it now!"

"You're wrong," the newcomer responded in a deep, eerie

voice that seemed as much machine as human. "I am just in time."

Ari was beginning to relax. Except for a slight whining in the comm system of his suit, the great device didn't seem to be doing anything at all. He finally got up, walked over to the newcomer, and looked to see if anything of the face could be made out in the permanent night.

"Who are you?" he demanded.

The figure laughed. "You know who I am—or who I was, anyway. I *know* you've guessed that. Want to see my beautiful face?" He switched on the internal helmet light so his full face was visible.

Ari screamed and stepped back. There was flesh on only about a third of the head; the rest was a blue-gray metallic color and looked horribly robotic, but robotic in the shape of a human skull.

"What are you?" Ari cried.

The figure pointed at the two women. "Much like what was done to *them*, only mine was from quite an explosion and a fair amount of exposure to an atmosphere I wasn't designed to use. It burned off most of my false skin, and I just decided I didn't have time to grow new flesh."

"Kincaid!" Wallinchky exclaimed. "I *thought* it was you! Some replacement parts, eh? That's why the height didn't jibe!"

"Oh, don't worry, it's serviceable," responded Jeremiah Kincaid, or what was left of him, now more machine than man. "It's better than yours, Wallinchky. Before I could have a heart attack, I'd have to have a heart, wouldn't I?" He turned and stepped up to the device, which continued to power on to no obvious effect. "What the hell are you waiting for?" he screamed at it. *"I will follow Josich the Emperor Hadun all the way to Hell itself!"*

The center area exploded with light, and Ari Martinez backed up and fell over a curb. When he looked up, there was a fountain of energy rising up to the heavens, and more radiating from the points of the device.

Back at the house, Tann Nakitt watched in awe as the energy became visible, grew, and spread in geometric patterns, as did O'Leary on the maglev bike from just outside the city.

It didn't save either one of them as the energy ribbons flowed out from the city and down the ancient roads, striking the compound just below where Tann Nakitt stood. He suddenly felt its danger and turned with a curse to it and a prayer to all the Geldorian gods, then everything went black and it seemed he was falling down a bottomless pit of darkness.

Genghis O'Leary saw the ribbon coming toward him. It struck and enveloped him before he could do more than feel sudden alarm at its approach, and then the bike shook and fell to the ground with no sign of a rider.

Closer in, those near the center of the city felt only the falling sensation, nothing more.

Back at the house, the Kharkovs felt a queasy sensation, and there was a momentary sense of reality vanishing and then coming back, but they were still there, in their laboratory, when it was suddenly over.

Core lost contact with the two women at 2.3 seconds after Kincaid's outburst, but managed to capture some of the surge and sensation and to photograph the phenomenon for its own records and later examination.

Now it had to decide what to do. Wallinchky's orders, to be executed only in the event of his death or if this worked, were clear, and final. Core was not to oppose a landing, but was to destroy the device if possible.

It was possible but hardly necessary. The energy surge, which it might possibly *not* have caused at all, considering the timings, had melted the device into a shapeless mass on the plaza.

Core's orbital eyes, however, had noted the convergence of a signal and the shoot into some kind of extradimensional space, the properties of which could not even be guessed at. An examination of the phenomenon, including what had happened to Nakitt in the house and, for the briefest of moments, to even Core itself, indicated that the subjects had been somehow digitized and the energy pattern sent along that beam.

Apparently without loss.

Core was impressed.

South Zone

THE VARIOUS GROUPS LAY SCATTERED IN THE VAST CHAMBER, having been unceremoniously dumped there upon materialization.

The mostly mechanized newcomers were the first to come around, with Jeremiah Kincaid getting to his feet fairly quickly. He went over and checked the two women first, saw that they were slowly coming to, then checked Martinez, and finally Wallinchky. He was revolted by what the crime lord had done to the two, both of whom he remembered fondly, and he was particularly pissed off at the near erasure of Angel Kobe.

Where was your God when you needed him? he mused as she started to come to. You should have listened to me when I told you that only Hell exists.

The matter transmission of the ancients was in top working order, and if there were any losses, he couldn't see them in the others or himself; although given time, maybe they'd show up. That meant Wallinchky was in no better shape here than he'd been back there; in fact, if he wasn't dead, he certainly was very close. Kincaid wouldn't have minded if the old man croaked right here, and he thought it would probably do wonders for the others. As for the women, he wondered what they would be like now that they were cut off from the computer that had rebuilt them.

Kincaid checked the readouts from his suit, touched the power ring to manually disengage the locks, and removed the helmet. If anything, he looked more gruesome than he had in the city center, but he didn't care. The air was pretty good, gravity—well, maybe a little low for standard, but not by much, and a bit more than back on Grabant 4.

Ari Martinez groaned and sat up, looking around, which brought instant mixed feelings. The sight of Kincaid was not pleasant, but the discovery that they were in a vast artificial structure was a relief. Just waking up at all was a relief.

The two women had already sat up, but made no move to help the others, nor do much of anything. They looked very confused.

Although Core had warned them and tried to prepare them for this, it was as if part of their brains, a huge part, had been somehow carved away. It was slower to think, and the amount of data was more than limited. Core had fed into each of them their past memories, but those memories didn't much relate to their current circumstances. Also added, almost at the last second, had been their old personality modules, although these could not be fully implemented so long as they were attending to the Master. Even worse, they weren't quite sure which one of them was which. Each had only one personality module, but had access to the memories and experiences of both.

Seeing Kincaid bending over Wallinchky, the two snapped out of their confusion and rushed to defend their master from the monster. Kincaid turned and, reacting as fast as they could, said, "Relax. I was trying to see if he survived the trip. I think he might have, but he's in very bad shape."

"Then we must get him to the medlab right away!" Alpha exclaimed.

"And where would the nearest medlab or hospital be, young lady?" Kincaid asked, sounding amused.

"It—We—I—" they both sputtered, then asked in unison, "Where are we?" They both felt cut off and incredibly *alone*.

"No data, as you might say," Kincaid responded. "*Somewhere else*. Somewhere the Ancient Ones might have gone, and somewhere they probably built, judging from the scale of the place and its lack of anything interesting."

Ari came over and examined the unconscious Wallinchky. "Is he dead?"

"I don't think he is yet, but he soon will be," Kincaid told him. "I don't think he can be moved. How is this possible? Heart disease is so easily and completely dealt with, how could he have let this go? Didn't he get physicals from his own medlab if not from real doctors?"

"Who knows? When you have the kind of money and power he has, who's to remind him? He had a full rejuve a while back and they reamed him all out and gave him all new plumbing, so I guess he figured he was fine." The younger man looked up at the ghoulish-looking Kincaid. "How did *you* wind up like *that* so soon?"

"I've been like this for quite some time," Kincaid responded. "When this happened, they couldn't do what they can do now. The best that could be managed was to apply synthetic skin over my exposed parts so I looked normal, and as long as I got an occasional tuneup, well, I continued to look the same. To steal that ship and make my getaway from Josich's hideout, though, I had to go through a hideous external atmosphere outside the biodomes there, and it burned most of the synthetics away. Since then, we've been working too hard on this business for me to take the time to get it all back again." He looked up and around with his metallic skull and eerie humanlike eyes on biomechanical stalks. "I don't think it makes any difference *here*, either."

"Well, what do we do now?"

Kincaid shrugged and got to his feet. "That looks like a walkway up there. If we can move him gently, he'll at least be on a flat and possibly insulated surface. He's in no shape to be moved any more than that, though."

"Maybe we should just leave him here. It could be a million light-years to the next hospital."

"No!" both the women said at once, looking threateningly at the other two. "We cannot abandon the Master."

"Well, *somebody's* going to have to," Kincaid pointed out. "If he doesn't get help, he's going to die, and at any time. Why don't you move him up there to where he's comfortable, and then one of you can accompany one or both of us while we look for help. There is no logical alternative."

They both froze for a moment, then Beta said, "Very well. We will move him."

It was a very slow and cautious move, but it wasn't hard, and Jules Wallinchky soon lay comatose on a soft, rubbery, but flat surface that seemed to go on and on.

Ari looked forward and back along it. "Huh! Looks almost like a stock moving walkway, doesn't it? About, oh, twice the width of one of those doors in the city."

"Very observant. There might be hope for you yet. Well, come, we should be off, I think."

"But which way?" the younger man asked.

Kincaid thought about it. "If this is a moving walkway, then it's the first real artifact of the Ancient Ones we know about that's not a hollow structure. If everything else works, even their transport system, then maybe this does, too." He examined the side wall carefully. "There! See? It's kind of a panel, just beyond the break where we walked in. If we're lucky, we might even be able to move the lump, here. Let's see . . . They were bigger than us, but they had certain basics in common, like doors and roads. So, whether they had hands or tentacles or whatever, figure that would be best as a simple pressure plate."

Alpha, listening to this, went over and pressed the area. Nothing happened.

"Any more bright ideas, Captain?" Ari asked him.

"Yes—*you* press it, son. She's got machine hands and arms, and mine are almost as bad."

Ari saw what he meant, stepped around the body of Jules Wallinchky and put his hand on the plate.

The walkway began moving, slowly but steadily, carrying them all along.

Ari Martinez brightened. "How *about* that!" He shook his head in wonder. "They could wish for anything they needed, teleport all over, and yet they needed *walkways*?"

"Maybe they didn't want to get too soft," Kincaid guessed. "Maybe we got them, or this place, wrong."

The moving walkway slowed, and then stopped at a junction between two belts where it had to change direction. It was clear why: the next belt was running in the opposite direction, and someone or something was riding it. Something short and furry.

"That's a Geldorian!" Kincaid exclaimed. "What the hell?"

The Geldorian, for its part, had been leaning on the rail and moving along when it spotted them, and particularly the figure of Kincaid, and stiffened. Abruptly, the belt stopped, and it was just a couple of meters from the others. It looked at them all and said, "Where the hell am I? Who or what is *that*?" He was referring to Kincaid. Then, regarding the unconscious Wallinchky: "And is the bastard dead or just hopefully in great eternal pain?"

"Tann Nakitt? What are *you* doing here?" Ari asked him.

"All I know is, I was watching your light show from inside the house, and this stream of energy came up the road and I woke up down there. When nobody sent out the welcome party, I figured this thing out and set off. I don't suppose any of you have any food or drink, do you? And by the way, what's wrong with *him*?" He gestured toward the comatose man.

"Heart attack, we think, or possibly stroke. Same difference. He's dying," Kincaid told him. "I'm Jeremiah Kincaid, by the way, without my usual makeup."

"Kincaid! Good grief! It's a *City of Modar* reunion! Still, I have to say that I liked you better when you were just scary looking."

"How far have you come?" Kincaid asked him.

"Far enough. Hard to say, but it's about three segments, a good kilometer or so. From the smell and look, it seemed like the other way was going to quickly reach water, and the last thing I wanted was to ride into drowning. Gravity also gets a little heavier down there, and it's lighter here. You notice that? Each segment's different."

"This is the only one we tried, but—water, you say? Not now. Not yet." Kincaid sighed. "Then we should start off in the opposite direction, I think. I suspect it's some vast circle, but who knows how long and how far? Come! Step onto this one and we'll see if it goes back."

Oddly enough, it did, which surprised them until Kincaid noted, "Well, each segment runs whichever way will take the folks on it to the other end. What happens when you get folks on the same belt at opposite ends I have no idea."

They reached the next segment, about where they'd come in, and realized that Wallinchky would have to be moved at each junction point, even if slightly. His color was ashen and his breathing labored. It was clear that he didn't have long.

"In any part of the Realm, he'd have instant and total help and be up and around in a short period of time," Kincaid mused, looking at him. "In older times, before that kind of response, they used to teach people what to do in emergencies like this. Isn't it odd that the more advanced we've become, the more ignorant we've become? Could any of us plow a field, live off the land, even know how to safely build a fire or hunt game? Without our machines and data banks, we're pretty damned helpless. Masters of the universe! We who don't know how to piss outdoors!"

Tann Nakitt looked around at the vast chamber around them. "Maybe that happened to them, huh? Maybe they had a problem. Solar storm or something, disrupted their mental links to their magical computers and all that power. Ever think that maybe they were *so* advanced that when they were cut off they died? That they'd become one with their machines? Neat thought, isn't it? And, by the way, I have both hunted and fished and I can make a fire by rubbing two androids together. Still, I wish I had a drink."

"We've got the stuff in our suits, but that's not easy to transfer," Kincaid responded. "It's best we find the exit."

"I'll go," Ari volunteered. "Better than sitting here on deathwatch."

"No!" Alpha said sharply. "You will remain here with Beta and the Master. You are wholly organic and therefore have the potential to do things Beta herself cannot if need be."

"You can't stop me," Kincaid told her, not threateningly, but as a statement of fact. "And Tann Nakitt is not a party to this. I say the three of us go, and Beta and Martinez remain."

"Very well. Time is of the essence, then. Let us go."

Ari started to follow them, but Beta moved and blocked him. Although she was much smaller, the reinforced limbs the two women had been given after they were properly programmed were more than his match, and he couldn't easily reason with or argue with them. He sighed, watching the figures vanish from sight. It didn't take long before he decided that even talking to a slave was better than nothing.

"Beta, do you remember who and what you used to be?"

"The question is meaningless," she responded. "Beta has never been anything but Beta. I have the memories of the one who was and is no more except as data, but I am not her."

"So you have all of Ming's memories, but you don't see any connection between her and yourself?"

"The name you speak is not in my data field. I have no name for the other."

"Well, it was probably erased, but it was Ming Dawn Palavri. Alpha was Angel Kobe."

"No, Alpha is Alpha. She simply has the data of another, as I do."

This was tough. "So it's just data? But what good is that data if you cannot assume the identity of the one who lived those memories? Every memory in the brain is subjective. How can you interpret it if you weren't ever her?"

"I have the module to do this, but I can integrate it only on command of the Master."

"And what if he dies? If your sole purpose is to serve him, and he dies, then you have no purpose? No Master? Do you die or what?"

"In the absence of the Master, and death is an absence condition, then we would both serve the Oneness."

"The Oneness? Who or what is *that*?" He was sure his uncle hadn't come up with anything like a Oneness.

"We are both part of the One. We are detached from it, but still part of it. We would then become self-programming autonomous units but in its service."

He finally got it. "The One—you mean the house computer? The server core?"

"Yes."

He sighed and leaned back against the wall. All his life he'd thought of himself as basically a moral guy, that what he did was basically honest work, and that what his uncle did was between his uncle and the cops. Now he'd been dragged into it, not just a little larceny but big-time, with deaths and worse, and he'd managed to some degree to rationalize even that. But what his uncle had done to Ming, particularly Ming, hit home with him. It made him feel . . . well, *dirty.* In an age when machines could do anything and if you had the money, you were at least a minor version of what they thought these Ancient Ones were, only somebody who could have everything would decide he wanted human slaves. Even an honest death would be preferable. Hell, he'd *known* this woman. Jeez! He'd even had a good time in *bed* with her on a couple of occasions, the last time on the *City of Modar* itself. To see her reduced to this just to feed a rich old man's fantasies and ego—it was wrong.

Merely feeling this was a revelation to him. Somewhere

along the line he seemed to have grown a conscience, and while it didn't make him feel any better, it made him feel . . . well, superior to that old bastard down there. All his life he'd wanted to be his uncle, envied him everything. He didn't want to be Jules Wallinchky anymore. He wanted a warm shower, a change of clothes, and a chance to walk away and see if he could do something decent with his life without being reinfected by his uncle's cesspool.

But he was stuck here with two bodies, one dying and one quite possibly dead.

And the worst part was, he'd been the instrument of the latter. He had fired the gun that knocked Angel and Ming cold. He'd delivered them to his uncle. This was his punishment, his circle of Hell, for doing that.

Beta's head snapped up, a happy expression on her face. "They have made contact with someone! Help is being dispatched!"

That got him out of his reverie. "Made contact? With who?"

"Someone. Someone from—here." She stood up, walked over and faced him. It made him uncomfortable, but he wasn't sure what she was doing now. Who could figure out a creature like this, created by a man of evil?

"You must understand the Oneness," she said. "We may need you."

Her hands suddenly shot out and grasped both sides of his head, bringing him down. To keep his neck from being broken, he had to kneel. He tried to resist with his own hands, but the grip was absolute.

He felt helpless, and then, worse, dizzy and disoriented, almost as he had when the transport had kicked in, but different. *She was looking into his mind!* Not like a telepath would, but as if their two brains were a single physical unit. Information flowed back and forth, but at a speed he couldn't follow and with a commanding force he couldn't resist. He also felt physical sensations—cold and hot, pain and pleasure, a whole range of things sweeping over him like a beam switching on and off. He started to laugh for no apparent reason, then felt incredibly sad, tears welling up, only to have that cut off and then feel sexual desire, then none, then hunger, thirst—

Our minds link one to another, so that there is only Oneness. He felt and understood the command rather than hearing it.

She let him go, and he sank down and tried to steady himself as the place seemed to fly around him. He understood now that his uncle left nothing to chance, that most likely *everyone* who stayed in one of his houses for more than a few days got implanted with the same neuroreceivers and transmitters as the two women had in themselves.

Unlike Ming, he still knew just who and what he was, and with the same feelings as before. But now, and possibly till death, his mind, every thought, even his innermost feelings, was an open book to her and to Alpha/Angel as well. He could feel the permanence of the connection but could not reach out to her mind in the same way she could to his.

Stand up! They come! Again his mind filed it as words, but it was on a level way beyond that. She was not speaking to him telepathically; rather, having cataloged his entire electrochemical set of stimuli and responses, she was *operating* him. He found himself standing up and looking in the direction where the others had disappeared, with no conscious act of will on his part.

The worst part was, when they came, he couldn't even tell them what had happened.

Giant Emperor butterflies, two meters tall with wing spans four times that and heads that seemed like death masks, as grotesque and skull-like as Jeremiah Kincaid.

There were three of them, one on the walkway, another flying past and landing beyond them on the walkway behind, and one more hovering over the huge transport area, its wings creating a wind sufficient to whip Ari's hair into a frenzy.

But they weren't giant butterflies; that was obvious from the start. Butterflies didn't wear some sort of belt around their midsection, and butterflies didn't carry what were most definitely alien-looking but still quite identifiable heavy duty rifles. And butterflies didn't stand on their hind legs and hold such rifles comfortably in soft but clawlike hands.

Ari felt panic; these babies looked *mean*. Just as suddenly, he found his panic evaporating, and a calm coolness come over him. In concert with Beta, he and she were protecting Jules Wallinchky's body.

"You will remove your spacesuits and all mechanicals from yourselves and from the one who is dying," an eerie, almost nasal voice said in a language they both easily understood. It had the kind of threat in its tone that would have been there even if it had simply said "Good evening."

"We will do nothing of the sort," Beta told them firmly. "We will die to protect the Master."

"Then you will die," the voice answered, unconcerned. "We do not care about you one way or the other. However, if you do exactly as we say, there may be one chance to save the dying one, but you will have to obey, and now. Time is something it does not have and it may already be too late. It is also a moot argument, since we do not care about him or you and if we have problems we will simply shoot you and be done with it. You will find that your weapons will not work here. Ours will."

There was hesitation on her part, but there was also still a connection, albeit not as strong and direct as she would have liked, to Alpha, and Alpha basically was telling them to do it. There was also the unalterable logic of what the thing was saying. Pragmatically, there wasn't anything else to do.

They stripped themselves down completely and threw it all over the rail, then carefully they stripped Jules Wallinchky as well. Ari didn't lose any of his attitude and feeling for the old S.O.B. under this condition, but he tried to suppress such thoughts, knowing she might take offense and punish him. With the kind of control she had over his mind and emotions, he could become Gamma in seconds if she had a mind to do it.

The old boy was flabby, and parts of his body were almost covered with scars of one kind or another. None of those should have been there; clearly he'd been through something since the rejuve that he hadn't talked much about, which contributed to his current situation.

What was the old adage? *The wages of sin is death!* When you could be the most self-indulgent person in the galaxy and lived in a time when everything you could need, even medical aid, was always there, you tended to get a bit sloppy . . .

"We will transport the one who is dying," the chief

butterfly told them. "You two will proceed along the walk in the direction your friends went and we shall be covering you."

"We cannot!" Beta insisted. "Our sole purpose is to serve our Master. We cannot abandon him."

"I weary of this," the creature responded, sounding disgusted. "Both of you start walking now or I am going to kill you."

"For God's sake! Do it!" Ari screamed at her. "How can you serve him if you die for nothing?"

That logic already had occurred to the woman, who turned and stepped onto the next section, and he found himself following and slapping the control to activate the walkway. One of the creatures followed, rifle pointed at their backs. There was no question that it would use it, and no doubt that the two of them together could not move faster than it could fire.

It was decided that Ari might try and reason with it, either to gain an advantage or simply to gain information. These things looked pretty in a bizarre sort of way, but not like the kind of folks you'd sit down with in other circumstances and buy each other beers.

"What race are you?" he began, trying to get a frame of reference.

"I am of the Yaxa."

Well, that was a start.

"Did your people come here like us?"

"We are native here. All races are native here, but I was born here."

"I am called Ari Martinez. Do you have a name?"

"Yes," was the cold reply.

Ooooo-kay . . . "You say all races are native here. What do you mean? Have you seen our sort before? I mean, native on wherever this is?"

"Your people originated here. Some are here, yes, but they are a bloodthirsty and unpleasant lot and we have little or nothing to do with them."

"Then—why are you bothering with us now? Are we being marched to a firing squad?"

"No. This is the ambassadorial region as well as Well

World ingress and egress. All civilized races take their management turns here, and we are on this watch."

"Ambassadorial region you say. But that means even enemies talk here without shooting. So why the guns?"

"Outsiders are already causing a great deal of suffering and hardship on the world. Until that is resolved, all outsiders are suspect. *You* do not have an embassy here."

There was the whoosh of great wings to their left, over the vast chamber, and they both turned and saw the other two Yaxa flying, pushing an apparently levitating but still comatose Jules Wallinchky in front of them. They were making good speed and going off at an angle, although it was clear that both he and Beta would catch up with them in a few minutes.

So outsiders were making trouble. That certainly brought up a nasty thought, considering that the only outsiders likely to have been teleported here of late were certain water-breathing monsters. "Those outsiders now causing hardship and suffering—one of them is not by any chance named Josich, is it?"

"The one of that name is involved, yes. You know that one?"

"I only know *of* him, but his reputation where we come from is just as ugly as he seems to have wasted no time in reestablishing here. He is no friend of ours, and the large man who seems half machine who went with the rest of our party to find help has devoted his life to finding and killing Josich. He's on your side."

There was a pause, and then the Yaxa asked, ominously, "Why do you assume that we are against the powers this Josich has joined?"

Uh-oh. "Because you used the words 'suffering' and 'hardship.' I would have expected a different slant if you were on his side."

"You make assumptions that other races think like you. It is a mark of the arrogance that seems always in your race."

"Then the Yaxa are with Josich's forces?"

"I did not say that, either. I merely told you to refrain from assumptions. None of this will likely make any difference to any of you. Josich is a very rare exception in making any impact at all, let alone a large one. I have no doubt we are about to hear the last of your group, although if the one who lives to kill is as determined as you say, he may be the exception. Or not. You will not find your spaceships and spacesuits here."

After a half hour, maybe longer, they reached a section where corridors branched off and away from the walkway. They were internally lit so that they essentially glowed, but were clearly hewn out of whatever this place was made of, and they had that same odd shape as the doorways of the Ancient Ones' city. There were some symbols embedded in the floor and where each corridor started and at each intersection, but they were of a sort impossible to divine. Beta assumed them to be numbers, since that would be the most likely common element in a place with a variety of races. Numbers could be agreed upon and then used in conjunction with maps and directories in local languages.

Although basically a helpless onlooker, the link to Beta's brain did bring with it some respect as well as discomfort to Ari. He realized she was using all of it, and at a speed faster than he could imagine. He seemed to remember from school that the human brain's speed and capacity was established early on, and maintained by constant stimulation and the building of dense clusters of neurons. Had they somehow been able to build densities that simply wouldn't happen in nature? And had the constant linkage to that supercomputer in the house provided constant stimulation even when they were doing nothing at all? Her own speculation and deductions concerning this place, just based on what she could see and hear and what they were being told, was filling in quickly and building a very complex picture that he would never have accomplished on his own.

If that was the case, whatever else his sadistic uncle had done to Angel and Ming, they were both among the greatest geniuses the human race had ever produced. Even more, that concept of the Oneness while keeping an identity was becoming clearer. If she needed it, and they were in this kind of proximity, *she could use the unused areas of his brain to augment hers!* Temporary storage. The telepathic link was probably agonizingly slow to her, but think of the possibilities . . .

The Yaxa stopped the belt. "Go ahead of me, single file,

down this corridor," it instructed, and they did so, Beta
leading, he following.

The route was complex, the kind of back and forth and up
and left and down and right that would have confused The-
seus in the Maze, but Ari knew that Beta could retrace it in a
moment. It had been, perhaps, another fifteen minutes and
several hundred of those symbols, but she was already reading them as if they were her native system. Base six, of
course. The numbers were suddenly obvious, but the symbols accompanying them were still just squiggles to him;
there was nothing to match them to.

Ari felt a strange sensation that grew stronger as they
walked along. He was beginning to sense Alpha as well, her
thoughts and her connections. They could function as one or
as three, or any combination of that, and they all had access
to whatever the other knew or was thinking. They were still
too damned fast for him to fully follow, but he was getting
the idea.

Don't make the turns until the Yaxa says the instruction,
Ari cautioned mentally. *You almost risked giving this away.
We need every edge we can get here.*

The contribution surprised her, but she adjusted just in
time. They were geniuses and devoted slaves and half computer, but they just didn't think sneaky.

Now they passed some very large chambers that they
walked right past. These seemed to be offices, some larger
than others, inhabited by the damnedest assortment of bizarre
creatures he'd ever seen. He was used to alien races, of
course, but some of these were more bizarre than anything he
could imagine, while others were eerily familiar. Centaurs
and Minotaurs, and tall creatures with great white wings, and
tiny self-illuminated creations. Bipedal reptiles wearing opera
capes, creatures that looked like giant bowling pins with big
round eyes, giant hairy spiders writing in ledgers . . . It was
amazing.

Each of the chambers had a number on it, no two numbers alike. So the numbers on the corridor indicated creatures; the symbols were either corridor names or referred to
the type of creatures who might collectively be along it—
hairy oxygen-breathing mammals, maybe. They didn't see
enough to have a definitive sample, but Beta registered every

number that had a race attached and by now had enough to draw some conclusions. Okay, so type, then number-number. That was the key. The numbers ran serially but in base six.

Some chambers were deserted, and apparently had been for a very long time. They looked something like the inside of the houses of the Ancient Ones, and gave no clues other than a lonely number without anything to attach itself to.

"How many races are there?" he asked the Yaxa.

"There are 1,560 races in the world," it told him. "As this is the South Zone, only those carbon-based life-forms who have a toleration zone compatibility are here. That is exactly half. Races one to 785 are in the south. Races 786 to 1,560 in the north. We are almost there. Soon all will be explained to you. No more talking, please."

Fifteen hundred sixty races on one *planet? How big was this place?*

The mother of races. The Well World, the Yaxa had called it.

They soon walked into the Yaxan embassy, where the rest of the party, plus one surprise, were already waiting, all as stripped to nothing as they had been.

Ghengis O'Leary, at least, was as tall as the average Yaxa, and much bulkier. He also was as huge in the areas otherwise hidden.

Where is the Master? Beta queried Alpha.

They will only say that he is being treated. Impossible to verify. We need more data to act, however. I am absolutely certain that the Yaxan statement that they would kill us without a second thought is correct, so resistance is profitless at this point.

Well, that was a relief, Ari thought.

The Yaxan Marines were there, all right, and they were at the ready. They probably all looked very different to one another, but to anybody there in the chamber, they looked absolutely identical.

Ari looked around. "How did it miss grabbing the Kharkovs?"

"I think it provides an exit to those who require an exit," Jeremiah Kincaid responded. "They didn't need an exit."

"*I* didn't need an exit!" Tann Nakitt snapped. "I was ready to go home!"

"You weren't going home with all that spy data locked in

your head, Nakitt," O'Leary told him. "That's why your ship didn't come. Somehow *it* knew this, even if you yourself didn't. Maybe from my mind, or Kincaid's. I'm surprised to be here, too, for all that. Maybe I wanted Josich, or at least closure, more than I realized."

"You look a little odd, Martinez," Kincaid noted. "Are you all right?"

"Um, yes, sure. I'm just *cold*, that's all."

"I can understand that. What about Wallinchky? He still alive?"

"When they took him away he was, or at least I *think* he was. After that, couldn't say. We had rifles up our asses."

"Well, you made the right decision to come here and not fight them for him," Kincaid assured them. "The Yaxa are all females, all born warriors, and they're quick, smart, and with something of a hive discipline. You better believe they would pull the trigger."

Ari sighed. "Yeah." He sat on the floor with the others, finding it no more comfortable. "So how long do we wait?"

"I suspect that's up to our hosts," Kincaid said. "At least we've been able to determine that the first batch, including Josich, came through here."

"We were told that he's still up to his old tricks, even here, only maybe not in charge of the mess," Ari told him.

"He's not one to like being the power behind the throne, but he's had to start off new here. It's a sad commentary that he's already been able to cause real problems."

"Your megalomaniac Emperor has caused some serious problems just in a month or so," said a voice behind them. "It is not, however, war, not yet."

They all turned and saw, standing in the entrance, a most bizarre creature. He appeared to be made out of balls; at least that was the first impression. Humanoid in shape, perhaps a meter and a half tall but fairly wide, its feet were thick rounded pads, and its legs, arms, and indeed its whole body seemed to be composed of a series of thick rings or pads that gave the impression of a mass built of bubbles or balloons. The hands were huge ovals, like mitts, but were segmented to form fingers, any of which apparently could be shifted to opposing the others. Its head was a true ball, with round eyes and pupils of deep purple. The bottom of the ball had a straight slit, and this formed the mouth, which actually was hinged only at the back of the head. It looked unreal, like some kind of puppet or robot character done for an industrial exhibition.

"I am Ambassador Doroch," it told them, the precise and slightly amused voice not quite matching the jaw movements, nor in fact seeming the kind of voice such a creature might have. "If you will all accompany me to a briefing room, I believe I can explain the situation here, and I should like to get some information from you as well. I have some water and some fruit there that should be compatible with all of your digestive systems." The round eyes looked at Kincaid. "Those of you who *have* digestive systems," he added. "However, it is essential that we process you through as quickly as possible here. The system is designed for that. Please—come. I'll answer what questions I can. I hope I have your word to try nothing foolish, since there is nowhere you can run anyway. I abhor having guns in here."

He led them into a larger room, lit by some kind of built-in radiation in the very makeup of the walls and ceiling but providing full spectrum lighting. Some basic conventional chairs were set up, clearly for them, as neither the Yaxa—who, thankfully, hadn't followed or interfered—nor this creature could use them.

On the far wall was a map unlike any they'd ever seen. It was a physical/political map showing great seas and high mountains, continents and islands, all the usual landforms. But superimposed over it was a hexagonal grid that varied only at the top and bottom, where thick, dark lines were drawn, and where the political straight lines still had six sides but were flattened into two halves rather than hexagonal. Ari and the two women examined it with more knowledge than their hosts suspected. Numbers one through 785. The reason for the different shapes north and south were obvious even to Ari; you couldn't cover a sphere with hexagons. The difference would be the polar regions, and it was probable that they were in the south polar region now.

Ambassador Doroch took his place in front of the map. "This is the southern hemisphere of our world," he told them. "The world itself is roughly forty thousand kilometers around at the equator or pole to pole. It is a perfect sphere, which should give you the clue that it is artificial. We believe from the evidence of those like yourselves who get here via the old gates that it may be the only remaining intact world of those you call the Ancient Ones. There are a lot of different terms for them; the term you just heard is how my own people's name for them would be understood by you. As you might have guessed, none of us here are speaking your language. You are hearing us because we have implanted crystalline devices that serve as universal translators. They are organic, grown, and in very limited supply, so most people here do not have one and will never have one. This is important for you to know before you enter the Well World properly."

"That is the second time I have heard that term used," Ari commented. "Why is it called that?"

"Beneath us, perhaps a hundred kilometers or so, is a vast organic computer of a type no one has as yet duplicated. You probably have been on deserted worlds that might have similar cores, but this is the master computer, if we can still call it that, to which all others are linked. There are two levels—a very thin layer that governs this world, and the rest, which appears to govern all the remote units. The Ancient Ones built this world as a laboratory. Here they created independent ecosystems, each maintained by its own programs, and developed races that were evolutionarily consistent with the ecosystems. Or it may have been the other way around. In any event, 1,560 such little laboratories were created and populated. Where did the population come from? We don't know. Perhaps it was created by modifying samples of real creatures from various parts of the universe. Perhaps they created them, a sobering thought. Ancient legends suggest that the people were actually Ancient Ones themselves, gods who chose to become mortal again because they felt bored, had nowhere else to go, and felt cheated that what appeared to be the end of evolution was such an empty life. One could imagine that after who knows how many thousands or millions of years of being a god, it would get pretty boring. One might find it more difficult to imagine a race of such gods committing mass suicide, as it were, starting their race over as many other races, just to find out if they had missed something and were at a dead end. Still, that is the legend."

"With this ancient world-computer still functioning, could you not find out?" Alpha asked the ambassador.

"Well, the answer is probably there, of course, but I'm afraid that the great machine—the Well of Souls, it is called, and always has been—doesn't talk to us or give up its secrets. It is set up for the benefit of creatures who are no longer around, for whatever the reason."

Tann Nakitt looked over the map. "You say 1,560 races? For the whole *galaxy*?"

"Well, technically, for the whole universe," Doroch noted. "From some of your sorts of people we've had in the past, I'm pretty certain we're not in your galaxy, nor anywhere near it. However, we know, of course, that there are more races than that, because we've had some come through here that match nothing we know. Remember, I said this was a laboratory, or rather, a scientific experimental complex with 1,560 laboratories. There is no reason why the current crop is all there ever was. The ones that worked out were then created, superimposed, whatever, on a world somewhere that either was prepared to develop them naturally or that already met the criteria. Once that was done, the large transport station you arrived in was used to send the people there, and then an entirely new ecosystem and race could be created where they'd been. We know we are not unique; what is most logical is that this world represents the last ones. Either something happened to prevent our ancestors from going out, or the Ancient Ones now lacked sufficient numbers to do it, or perhaps some just didn't want to go. Whichever, we remain here. The Well regulates the population so that it is stable for each nation, or hex, as we call them. Underpopulation nets a baby boom, overpopulation a drop. The numbers tend to stay the same, plus or minus ten percent. And there is another artifice as well."

"But surely there are corruptions!" Kincaid put in. "You'd have worldwide weather patterns, air and water would have to flow, that sort of thing."

"It *is* true that some things do in fact pass between, but they tend to be processed. You'll see. The first time you see billowing industrial smoke essentially vanish as it goes across a border, or watch a rainstorm with a flat side, well, you will see. The Well does not interfere with how we live our lives, but it does maintain discipline of a sort for the ecosystems, within reason. When literally *anything* can be converted to anything else as needed, and you are powered most likely by a singularity deep within the core, perhaps tapped from a parallel universe so as to not suck us in, well—godlike is a more than apt description. We believe that they deliberately limited the Well so that it is not self-aware in the sense we would think of it. Otherwise it could easily *become* God, and not only here."

"It is of supreme power and intelligence but programmed to serve only its master," Alpha commented. "This is easy to comprehend."

The ambassador didn't seem to know how to take that. He wasn't quite sure *what* these two women were, and was even less sure about Kincaid. He decided it was best to just continue the stock lecture.

"As I was saying, as part of the experiments, certain shortcuts had to be taken to create what was required in such a small space. The hexes are roughly 420 kilometers across, any point to any point. Travel between is possible, as well as trade and commerce. To reduce cross-cultural pollution, and also to simulate conditions on the true worlds they were being designed for, restrictions were placed on some of the hexes in about equal proportions. Some are very like your own homes, with a good deal of inventiveness and techno-logical comfort. Some are limited in the level of technology available, generally to the age of the steam engine and the percussive projectile-based weapon. A third category allows no true storage of energy for use nor its transmission. Oh, you can use a waterwheel, that sort of thing, but otherwise nothing not done by muscle is allowed. These tend to be agrarian societies, with direct subsistence farming and hunting by spear and arrow."

"Who enforces that kind of thing? Is there some sort of global police?" Genghis O'Leary asked. "Or some kind of force that ensures conformity to those rules?"

"It is not necessary," Doroch told him. "The Well sets it. You may take a portable fusion generator into a semitech or nontech hex, but it simply will not work. It will be an inert lump. You can take a gunpowder-type rifle into a nontech hex and shoot it, and it simply will not fire. Every round will be a dud. Needless to say, the reverse is not true. If you take that rifle into a high-tech hex you *can* shoot it, even if everyone who lives there carries particle beam pistols. An arrow will kill anywhere. In that sense, the nontech folk have an advantage. They can hide out in their element and use it well, while even the semitech civilizations are too dependent on their engines and gunpowder to be able to come in and bully their way around in a nontech hex. My own is a semi, and while I feel quite comfortable here in South Zone with all its high-tech amenities, I daresay I could survive in a reasonable environment given good soil and seed and some hand tools. Could any of you do it? *Any* of you?"

"I could," Alpha told him firmly. "I have data from the experience of living on a subsistence world."

"Indeed? I wonder if it's quite the equivalent you think. At any rate, you may well be put to the test soon. You see, there is no way out of here to anyplace that will not kill you. There is no way to send any of you back. That command is reserved for the Ancient Ones, and I'm afraid we haven't seen any of them here for, oh, a few tens of millions of years or so. There are two exits, however. One simply teleports you to North Zone, but that will not help you much. Beyond the small area where you'll arrive that is set aside for carbon-based life, virtually anything up there would kill you in moments. Even you, mechanical man." He was looking at Kincaid.

"And the other exit?" Tann Nakitt prompted, getting nervous.

"The other is a general gate that, for me, would take me home to my hex and nowhere else. For the Yaxa, which you've met, it would take them to Yaxa. A corresponding gate in each capital, essentially in the center of each hex, will take you here, but that's it. I cannot use it to go to Yaxa if I wanted; I'd have to travel in a conventional manner from my own home. It is, however, something of a convenient shortcut back."

"And it will transport us to where our races have hexes?" O'Leary asked.

"Um, no, not exactly. Oh, you have a one in 780 chance of it, but it's unlikely. I don't remember it happening. When you go through the first time, you will be processed by the Well, assigned a race and hex where an added one would be of no consequence to the balance, which is almost any one, and then you will be reconstituted as one of them. The process is not quite random; the Well does do some sort of analysis of your mind, your personality, and does some rather odd things on occasion. One almost suspects sometime that it has a sense of humor. All that can be predicted is that you will come out young but generally postpubescent, although we've had a child or two through and they remain children and with their parents, if those parents are here; that you will emerge in absolutely perfect health, and that, while your memories and personality will be basically untouched, that autonomic part of everyone's brain will be suited to and comfortable with the new form. You'll know how to use the body, in other words. That's not the same as saying you will feel like a native, but it is sufficient to get you started."

Kincaid picked up on this right away. "Now, hold it, sir. You are saying that Josich and the other Hadun who came through before us are no longer racially *Ghomas*? That they are now something else?"

"They are not what they were, certainly."

"What *are* they, then? Where is Josich, and what does the monster breathe?"

The ambassador's tone grew a bit dark. "Josich is a Chalidang. That is *here*, in the north-central region of the Overdark, one of our great oceans. A high-tech hex that adjoins a large island. Another of that race is in Jocir, yet another high-tech hex only two away from Chalidang and adjoining the continent, and another is down here, at Imtre. That was the curse, really. Two in high-tech hexes not far from one another, and a third in what was nontech but in a formidable form. The other two of their kind arrived on land, one on the far eastern edge of the Overdark, the other on an island to the south, Cromlin and Becuhl, one high-tech, the other a semitech. They were all quickly in the hands of ambitious and ruthless rulers open to their own brand of ambition. Beyond that, you had best learn once you have been processed. Still, sir, if you wish to kill the one called Josich, many would count you a hero, but you will have to go to Chalidang."

"Still a water breather, though," Kincaid said wistfully. "But two out of five weren't reconstituted as water breathers. I'll bet *that* has them unbalanced. But this means that I might well be reprocessed as a water breather?"

"You might. The odds are against it, but it happens." The ambassador turned and looked them all over. "And now, you must proceed to processing. It is a standing rule of all the races here that anyone entering Zone must be processed by the end of the day they emerge, and preferably as soon as they are briefed. We have no way to take care of you as you are, and until you are processed you are in all ways aliens."

"Wait! Where is our master that the flying ones took with them?" Alpha demanded to know.

"Oh—him. He was taken immediately to the Well Gate because, of course, all this would be of no use to him. The Yaxa state that he had some sort of seizure and that they were not at all certain if he was alive when they put him through. If he was, he is already somewhere, and something, else. I may find out in time, but nothing would be learned as yet. If he was dead, then he is gone. They followed the only course that might have saved him. Only time will tell if it did."

"Then we will stay here until we know!" Alpha maintained adamantly.

The Ambassador looked at her, its big eyes then moving to the others, and then he said, quietly, "No, I'm afraid you won't."

The Yaxa and their nasty rifles were back, standing in the back of the room and aiming at the two women.

"If those two, or any of the others, make the slightest move to do anything but go to and through processing, you have my leave to shoot them," the Ambassador told them. "If it's around here, kill is authorized. If near the gate, simply stun them into unconscious oblivion if you can and throw them in."

Their briefing, and their welcome, was over.

Ambora

IT WASN'T SUPPOSED TO HURT.

They said it would be no different than the teleportation to the Well World itself; a sense of darkness, unconsciousness, and then you'd wake up somewhere else in a new native habitat with the basics necessary to survive. From that point, you'd be on your own.

The pain had been enormous. She remembered the pain, as if her head were under horrible attack and all its blood vessels exploded. It was the kind of pain whose memory lasted a lifetime in nightmares, and for some time its echoes would cause nervous caution or even possible panic.

And then she'd come to with those echoes surrounding her, come to and find only questions.

Who had said that there would be no pain? Tele— The very term confused her. It was gibberish, meaningless, and even those fragments of memory faded as a dream fades upon awakening from the deepest of sleeps, leaving her with only the memory of that pain and total confusion.

She awoke high on a cliff overlooking a vast saltwater ocean that seemed to have no end. The cliffs were as sheer as might be imagined from nature, and they rose perhaps a kilometer above her and even more below her to a flat volcanic outcrop of rock and vegetation that jutted out into the sea.

She was on a small outcrop from that cliff barely large enough for her reclining body, with no ladder or trail or any other indication of how she'd gotten there, or, more to the point, how she'd get off.

Who was she? *What* was she? She wasn't sure what frightened her more, the situation she found herself in or the fact that she had no memories of her past, not one single personal memory.

She got to her feet, nervous about the drop, then did a self-examination. The discovery that she was, in fact, female was a surprise, although had she found herself a male it would have made an equal impact. Whatever sense of self she had, it contained none of those rocks that others might take for granted. The breasts were large and firm, but something in her subconscious said that they weren't *quite* right, although she had no idea why. If she leaned forward, they did not hang at all; it was as if they were attached all the way, which, in fact, they were, with some kind of connective tissue. This created an extremely streamlined figure that tapered down to an impossibly small waist flanked by long, muscular legs that provided sure balance and were attached at a hip that allowed her to not only bring her face down close to the ground if she wanted, but also to swivel the torso effortlessly almost sideways. Her natural sense of balance was startling to her; whatever fear she'd felt at the height or standing up had already fled.

The arms were thin and ended in hands with extremely long fingers, three of them, and an opposable thumb almost as long as the rest, all of which ended in sharp clawlike nails that retracted when the fingers were straight out and emerged when the fingers were curved. Her feet were almost mirror images of her hands, with the fingerlike toes perhaps longer, and the claws much longer when extended. The skin on both the inside of the hands and the bottom of her feet was abnormally tough, yet flexible, and the fingers and toes were webbed with a supple yet leathery connector that didn't seem to limit movement. In fact, when the digits were closed in, it emerged at the bottom of the foot and seemed to stick to the rock, adding some stability.

And then there was the matter of the wings and the tail.

Not merely wings, but great wings, white, but tinged with brown at the edges and near the base where they met her back. She could feel the enormous muscles there that propelled them, and, as an experiment, she extended the wings and was startled to see just how *enormous* was the wingspan when they were fully extended. At the base of her spine emerged the tail, which she only became aware of when she stretched the wings, since it made the tail extend and open, almost fanlike. Bringing the wings back in caused the tail to retract, although it still extended beyond her rump. She had what seemed to be a head of hair but proved to be hairlike feathers, and quite oily at that; beyond it, though, her whole backside save the rump and legs was covered by the same sort of birdlike feathers as composed the wings and tail.

Out of curiosity, she picked up a small rock with her right-hand-like foot and brought it up to her face. The leg had no trouble with this at all, and the other leg kept her as solid and balanced as if she were standing on both.

She was a woman, and a bird. No beak, though. Those were lips, and a nose that seemed "normal," although she had no idea what was being used as the norm for comparative purposes. Birds had cavities for ears; she had ears, but they didn't feel quite "right," again not understanding what "right" would feel like, but they were close in and held to the side of the head in much the same way the breasts were held tight. Aerodynamic design. She had teeth, too, but again they didn't quite compare to that mysterious norm. The front ones did, but it seemed for some reason that the back teeth should be wide and flat; these were needle sharp. The teeth of a carnivore.

This troubled that part of her that sat there, just out of sight and reach, coaching and reproaching, but she couldn't understand why it did.

She looked out at the sea and was startled to see not just the scene, but differences in the moving air, like a transparent layer cake where the layers flowed and you could see them and how they flowed.

How did baby birds learn to fly?

Oh, God! she thought. There was only one way she could have gotten where she was, and barring some miraculous rescue, there was only one way to get somewhere else. There had to be others like her; she couldn't be in this strange place totally alone. But she didn't know what to do! Just launch herself off the cliff and trust to some instinct she didn't feel at all?

Something large flew by a bit above her. For a moment she hoped it was another of her kind, but it wasn't. Just focusing on it revealed it as if she were using a telescope with amazing detail, while somewhere in her mind she had instantly calculated just how far away it actually was and how fast it was going.

It was a big, ugly bird with a twisted beak and black wings and body. In addition to its dark orange feet, it also had two tiny, odd-looking forelimbs that were curled under and seemed to end in tingle-nasty claws, the better to tear into flesh. She watched it, noticing how effortlessly it was flying, how using the thermals it clearly could see and feel the same as she could. At this height, and with these winds, it was almost like gliding.

The sun was getting low; the shadows had been lengthening as she'd stood there. She had no idea if she could see at night, but it was clear that if she didn't get up the nerve to try and fly, she'd spend the night there, hungry and thirsty and exposed.

It wasn't fair, she reflected. Everybody else would be born and raised this way and taught the basics. *She* was going to have to try it cold turkey.

Turkey? What was a turkey? Where had *that* come from?

A mental picture of a big, fat, ugly *flightless* bird came to her. *That* was not encouraging.

Time was against her, she knew, and nobody remotely like her had shown up or flown by, and there were no sounds of talking or yelling or even squawking around, just the distant pounding surf and the sounds of two waterfalls emerging from the cliffs about a hundred meters to the left of her and two hundred or so to the right.

The devil with it! she thought, and jumped.

She fell faster than she'd thought, but then the wings and tail fully extended and the great things that emerged from her back began to beat as needed. Almost at the last moment she realized that all that was missing was a conscious will to direct her, and she pulled up just a few meters before the water and began a slow, steady climb as she went along the cliffs.

It was at once so *easy*, so *natural*, she felt that surely she must have been born and raised here and just could not remember, and it was also *fun!* This was really *neat*, arms slightly behind and flattened there, legs stretched out behind, the feet nearly perpendicular to the ground. Her head, too, was at an angle that allowed her to see in almost any direction, although too much head movement slowed her. It was as if the whole form automatically locked in place, with those things that weren't necessary or would get in the way placed in positions that, if they couldn't help, couldn't hurt.

She was surprised at how few beats it took to remain aloft; you just grabbed a thermal and rode it up, kind of like sliding along stairs, while avoiding the downdrafts, which were apparent to her. Small, sudden ones that could get you weren't so easy to see, but she could feel them across the underside of her skin and automatically compensate.

When she cleared the top of the cliffs and kept rising, she felt almost triumphant. Beyond, she could see the setting sun in the distance, feel its last warmth, and then look down over a rugged land of volcanic soil, frozen lava flows, and, where some time had been allowed, dense, lush forest, including some pretty tall trees. It was both stark and beautiful; in spots she could see steaming pools of water and more steam emerging from some fairly recent craters. The thermals were also nearly impossible to make out, changing rapidly over the hottest areas, and she felt the bumps and found herself working harder than she wanted to.

She banked and turned toward the tall forest, and as she did, saw that the forest was not only alive with vegetation, it was alive with animals, too, a *lot* of very large animals that showed clearly in the infrared. And she heard *singing*, a kind of exotic chant that was being joined by more and more voices as the sun began to vanish.

She didn't know if she was welcome at the party or not, but she was going to crash it anyway. She needed food, and shelter, and somebody to tell her just where and what she was. Maybe somebody down there among the singers to the coming night knew who she was.

It was clearly a colony, or perhaps more properly a town, but one designed for a race that flew. There was a series of lava tubes lit with the glow of fires, and inside the trees themselves were small houses made of wood and grass and bamboo, sometimes a large number of them at different levels, some on top of others, in a single tree all the way up to the top.

At first she wasn't sure where to land, but then she saw a

flat area in front of a very large lava cave with a huge pit in the center that had obviously been hollowed out. Two small waterfalls emerged on each side of the tube, then ran out in channels on the rock, flanking but not touching the pit, then dropping off again down to a series of small falls and pools below.

Carved into the black lava flanking the tube were strange, demonic-looking faces that were almost the reverse of the people there; creatures with the faces of mean-looking birds and the bodies of animals, looking somewhat like great bats with fanged beaks and angry eyes painted red. An elaborate series of colored patterns was carved and painted on the flat, and around the pit and standing on both sides of the riverlets were wooden statues carved with even more hideous shapes, one atop the other, creating totem poles over ten meters high and topped by the bird faces in the stone sculptures.

The singers were standing in a circle around the whole thing, looking inward, illuminated now by two flaming torches planted inside the pit. There were perhaps a dozen people there, all females, and their faces and bodies were painted with colorful patterns using some kind of eerily glowing phosphorescent paint. It made them look something like the strange creatures in the carvings.

This was clearly some kind of temple or cathedral.

She tried to land nearby without being on the actual "platform," content to wait until whatever ritual they were performing was done and someone took notice of her.

It was now quite dark, but the torches and the reflected lights from the caves and tree houses gave off a decent glow. There wasn't much danger of fire except from possible volcanic activity; the whole place was so humid you almost got wet flying through it.

Although none of the singers were clothed, something she oddly didn't even think about, they did wear earrings, some small nose rings, and thin, tight bracelets and anklets. They also wore thin belts around their narrow waists and, attached to them, something that might be a utility case or a scabbard.

They were all beautiful, exotic-looking creatures. She hoped she looked like that; she'd find it easy to look like any one of them. The glowing designs made it difficult to tell if they had any more normal makeup on, but they looked like erotic statues, standing there, arms raised, wings folded back but still very visible, almost like great horns from this angle, rising from the back of their shoulders. They seemed to be in a trance, staring straight ahead, taking no notice of her. The feathery hair was short but styled; the ears, she discovered, were large and pointed, and while flush against the face in flight, they unfolded and were prominent on the ground. In fact, she was suddenly aware that *her* big ears were out, and that she could turn each independently.

Then, abruptly, the chantlike song was done, and as one their heads went back and they issued an eerie, blood-curdling sound that came from somewhere deep in their chests. Then they pivoted, so fast it was hard to tell which way they all turned, the wings spread out, the tails extended, forming a continuous wall masking whatever was going on in front of them, in that pit.

The sounds of terrible, panicked squealing came from there, as if some huge pig or boar was being held down. The winged chanters took yet another step in, as if slaughtering it with sharp knives or swords. The sounds died, they closed in even more, and then the wings folded and they leaped into the pit in a frenzied orgy of gluttony, using nails and sharp teeth to shred the poor animal that had just been killed and tear off and eat strips of flesh and bone, their phosphorescent color dulling as it was covered with blood.

She had mixed reactions to the sight. One part of her, that hidden part, was repulsed, whispering that it was horrible, grotesque, *wrong*, sick. But the other part, the instinctive part that had gotten her off the cliff and here, felt an urge to join in and eat her fill.

"You are new here, sister," a woman's voice said behind her, startling her almost into flight. "From where do you come and what is your clan?"

She caught hold of the heart that was suddenly in her throat, turned and faced a woman very much like herself and the others up there at the feast.

"I—I don't know," she managed. "I have no memory at all before waking up on a cliff knob a couple of hours ago. I was hoping that someone here would know me."

The woman was startled. "No memory? You recall *nothing*?"

"I didn't even know what I was, and I still do not know where I am," she responded honestly.

The woman frowned and thought for a moment, then said, "We will have to take you to the High Priestess and see what she can make of all this. I have heard of this happening with potions and with curses and in some cases blows to the head, but you do not show any signs of a head injury. Your accent is neutral, so it does not help place you. Come. This is the village of the Clan of the Grand Falcon. You are Ambora, as are we all. I am called Lema. Do you have a name?"

"I must have, but as I said, I remember nothing."

"That would be a great terror to me. So, come! You must be hungry. Please come to my home and eat, and then after the Prayer for the Next Light, we will go down and see what the Holy One thinks of this."

"I thank you. You are most kind to a stranger," she managed, and followed the woman toward the forest with the huts. Abruptly, Lema flew into the air, and she followed, as routinely as if this was indeed how she had always been. They rose about halfway up, then landed on a thick branch at the opening to one of the wood and grass huts.

Moving up and down in this manner brought home to her a fact that hadn't been evident before: she didn't weigh an awful lot. Oh, she was heavier than air, just like a bird, and probably hollow-boned as well, but in spite of the shape and height of the body, the wings and tail were probably half or more of her total weight. It made lift easy, but it also meant that they were probably fragile. She had to remember that.

Lema looked in and sighed. "I see that Jocomo hasn't brought the kids back yet. Oh, well, I am certain that I can find you something."

"You have children?"

"Yes, two, both daughters."

The inside of the hut wasn't that large, but was serviceable enough if you only slept there and wanted a place to keep your belongings. There was a long area in the rear built up with straw over which a rough-hewn log stretched from wall to wall. If that was the bed, and it most certainly was, then the Ambora slept standing up and stuck to wood. They could sit, but rolling over on those wings wasn't something that should be chanced if it didn't have to be.

There was a mirror there as well. Not a fancy cut piece of coated glass, but a reflective volcanic rock polished to a fine flatness that served reasonably well. It was the first time she could see her face and body as one, and it was in one sense a fascinating revelation. She really *was* as beautiful as the others, as the singers and Lema. The "hair" was a mess, but it was a yellow-gold color, almost metallic in appearance, and the color patterns on her body and feathers, while not spectacularly colorful, were certainly a pleasing combination. The nose was a bit broad and slightly flat, the lips dark red, thick and wide, the neck quite long and yet thick, and, like the rest of her, lean and tough-looking. Her unfeathered frontal view showed skin that was shiny, like well-treated leather. She had hoped that the face, at least, would jog something in her memory, but while it was a sensual face, a pretty face, it wasn't the face of anyone she felt she'd ever seen before.

The "quick dinner" offered was yet another education, both in the culture of the Ambora and in her own unsuspected nature. It consisted of live prey; specifically small rodents, large insects and grubs, and, frankly, she found herself picking them up, doing a quick twisting kill or simply biting off the head in the case of the rodents, and then eating them in quick chomps. The first one, which she'd done following Lema's lead, bothered that hidden part of her that wanted to kill nothing at all, but once she got past that, the rest seemed automatic and she thought no more of it. There was no question that the Ambora were messy eaters, but the blood and juices seemed particularly rich to her, and she had no problems consuming spillage. Everything was eventually eaten—bones, shells, whatever. They did not waste.

All of the warm-blooded creatures had six limbs; some had a practical four and a decorative or vestigial two, others used all six. The bugs had considerably more legs than that.

It was a primitive culture in some respects, but it had to keep its food live in reserve since there was no way to preserve dead tissue.

When done, they flew down to one of the lower falls,

stepped into the dark pool and washed themselves off, and she drank a fair amount of the water to wash everything down and to replace lost fluids. She hadn't been aware of how dehydrated she'd been until she started to drink.

"I am going to have to find my children," Lema told her. "You would think that spending most of the day with children, Jocomo would want to be free of them, but he dotes."

She had nothing else to do; she tagged along, and in the process saw her first Ambora male. He was *not* impressive.

For one thing, they were short. Very powerful-looking, with thick-muscled arms and torsos, but a good head shorter on average than adult females. They were also somewhat bow-legged, the hands and feet overly large and virtually identical, the limbs of a tree climber and dweller, and in many ways they looked more like feathered apes than birdpeople. None had any really interesting color; they were light brown on the unfeathered front and a darker mottled brown on their feathered backsides. The wings were stubby little things that looked almost like growths and were flush against the body. About the only thing they had that was large and impressive was their male sexual organ, and that was in fact the only thing at all interesting about them. They must have great personalities, she thought whimsically.

In this culture the women were the hunters and in most ways the protectors; the men were in charge of their territories and saw to the early raising and education of the children as well as being builders. It was the men who built the huts in the air, and it was basically one adult male per tree at any one time. There was no marriage as such, but a social code and a code of honor. Jocomo was not only the father of Lema's two children, he was the father of all the other children by the other women who lived in the other huts in his tree.

Nor were the males either effeminate or as bestial as they looked; in fact, they seemed as intelligent and articulate as the females. As a group, they did a lot of education and training of the young, and sometimes they just had too much to do and didn't escort their children back before the mothers got home, as now.

Still, she would discover, to her surprise, that Jocomo and the other males didn't try to push their "wives" around and use their obvious muscles, if only to make up for the fact that the women had the figures, the looks, and the wings. The women, for their part seemed to regard the males as a combination baby-sitter and building superintendent, not as a boss. It wasn't a matriarchy, but each had clearly defined roles and they stuck to them. Only later did she learn that the males did in fact crave a large amount of sex, but that the consummation of any union was done in the air. When you were the one who needed it bad but had no wings, you had a lot of practical reasons for keeping your women happy, and, under those circumstances, rape wasn't even a power option.

It was a balanced situation, but to some extent she did feel sorry for the men. It looked like all the weight of keeping everything operating and together was on them, but they had to work twice as hard to attract any woman, considering their ugly looks and inability to fly. Had the Ambora been an animal rather than sentient society, the males would have been reduced to strictly a reproductive role at the whim of the women, and both sexes knew it.

Lema's two daughters had their mother's blue-green metallic hair color, but their feathers seemed very soft and snow-white, and their wings appeared overly large for their still-small bodies. They looked almost like angels. One was perhaps six or seven, the other even younger, and there was no mistaking their mother from their faces.

They were happy to see Mom and were fascinated to be introduced to a stranger—it appeared that there were few strangers in a clan village—but, though protesting a bit, they soon marched off to their hut for the night, with their mother promising to come to them as soon as things were squared away with the newcomer.

"Can they fly with those?" she asked Lema.

The woman stared at her. "You *really* remember nothing! No, they can't, not yet. They will be walkers until they are of age. At that time, when the first blood is passed, they will molt and for a short while be without feathers on their wings or tails. It is a serious time for young girls about to be women, and they usually go into a retreat with the priestesses until the first true feathers come in. It is a natural thing, but when you are that age you feel ugly and as if everyone is laughing at you. Then there is the ceremony of adulthood before the whole of the clan. They will be sent out on their first hunt, making nervous wrecks of both their parents, but it usually works out. After that, they are presented with their ceremonial daggers and then will see what the young men their age have built and choose a home and thus a mate. Then it begins again."

It was getting quite late now, and a lot of the lamps had been extinguished, while others were replaced with smaller, subtler flames. Lema, however, took her across the flat stone with the pit in it and to the opening of the great lava tube between the two carved creatures.

She was surprised to see cauldrons over slow fires inside the large cave; since the Ambora did not cook their food, there seemed little use for such things.

A tall, looming shape came out of the depths of the cave, and she found herself looking at the tallest and most awesome-looking Ambora woman she'd seen so far. It was not just that she was tall, taller than any of the females outside, but that she also had her wings partly opened and curving around, projecting the effect of a great feather cape. She had jewelry of what might have been gold all over, and, most telling, she was tattooed on the front with those same bizarre designs as on the sculptures and totems; and she glowed, not with phosphorescent paint, but all over. It was a weird, yellowish aura that outlined her form several centimeters beyond her body.

Lema brought her head down almost to between her legs, and, after seeing this and the awesome priestess, she did as well.

"I was wondering how long it would take you to bring this one to us," the priestess said in a deep, nasal voice that was at once commanding and irritating.

"I humbly beg the gods' and spirits' pardons, Holy One. She was lost, hungry, and confused, and seemed no threat to the clan."

"*No threat?* And just *who* gave *you* the authority to decide this? Did the heavens open and one of the gods point to you thus? Or did the spirits of the clouds whisper this authority? Does the safety and integrity of the clan mean so little to you, or did you have so poor a training . . . ? *Well?*"

"Please, Holy One, accept my repentance! I *did* bring her, and she has as yet shown nothing but good—"

"*Silence!* Go now. By the end of daylight tomorrow you shall bring me sacrifice worthy to submit to the gods, and then you will receive their judgment in public trial! Say no more! Go!"

She felt sorry for Lema, and wanted to explain. "Please, Holy One! She meant no—"

"*Shut up!* At the moment I am trying to determine if there is some way I can keep from sacrificing you. Rise! Look at me! I want to look into your eyes and see your markings and your stance!"

The high priestess was the kind of person who always spoke in sharp exclamations, but hers was also the voice of somebody who expected to be obeyed. Feeling suddenly very alone, she stood erect again and looked up at the obvious leader of the clan.

"What is your name?" the priestess snapped.

"Honestly, Your Holiness, I don't know it. I have no memory at all."

The priestess frowned, having heard this before, and began asking a series of quick, sharp, probing questions, to which her hapless subject was expected to respond instantly, unthinkingly. The problem was, much of it was in the form of "I don't know" or "I don't remember."

After a while this stopped, and the priestess approached very near and began an extremely close examination of the newcomer, not just with her eyes but with her nose and, at times, tongue as well. Finally, she straightened up, stood back, then spoke, and for the first time seemed less inclined to eat her alive.

"This is most strange," the priestess said, as much to herself as to her subject. "You have a unique scent but it does not specifically relate to the scent of any clan I know. You have no markings, no tattoos, and, most strangely of all, absolutely no scars. It is nearly impossible for anyone to grow up here and have no scars at all. You are young, certainly, but definitely past the Age, yet you are still a virgin, and your ignorance of even some of the most basic facts of Amborean life and culture seems genuine. This suggests you are of a type we know from stories but hasn't been seen, to my knowledge, in this land or among the People for a very long time." She sighed. "I will have to send someone to Zone to confirm this. Until then, you will remain here, but you will *not* again go out and mix with the clan, nor converse with any members save those who enter here. You will not need to hunt; I believe it is in our interest to instruct you. I do find it astonishing that you have no memory at all of your past, but in a way that will make it easier. Do you accept these terms?"

"It does not appear I have any choice, Holiness," she responded, not liking the woman at all.

"You have a choice. The choice is to accept a brand and leave now, the brand forever marking you as one who is forbidden in our territory and who is to be killed on sight if she returns. Since the landforms, native animals, and guiding spirits and sponsoring god are the only major differences between clans, you will doubtless wind up in this situation again, and eventually you will either have to leave the land or die in it, but that is your choice. You may remain here under our direction and accept instruction. Once you do so, you will be committed. Any attempt to leave after that without our permission will raise the hue and cry, and you will be the object of a full clan hunt. But there are always choices in life. Living or dying, submitting or rebelling, these choices we all make. Well?"

"I—I have nowhere else to go, and I really liked the people I met here so far," *with one exception*, she added to herself. "I should like to remain, although it is difficult to imagine being cooped up inside, forbidden to fly."

"That is a sacrifice you will have to learn to live with until you are initiated into the clan. The reason for this is for you to learn the ways of our clan, our culture, our people, their beliefs and the reasons for them, and to so immerse yourself that you will acquire the faith to believe and the inner knowledge of the spirit. It will not be an easy test, and it can take a short time or a long time depending on you. In the end you must become one with us. You must truly believe as we believe, you must act as we would act, truly place clan above self. The path is not easy and the tests are true tests of all that we value. In the end you alone will prove your worthiness. Now, in the meantime, we will find a place for you to rest, and nourishment if it is needed. Tomorrow we will begin the instruction. Assuming, that is, that you will not leave now."

She didn't hesitate, knowing the truth of the priestess's claims that she would find the same elsewhere. It was beautiful here and the people were nice. If she tried another clan, who was to say that the *next* priestess might have her sacrificed for violating their territory, particularly since there would be evidence that they weren't the first choice?

They named her Jaysu, which in context would mean Empty One, or Empty Jar. All Ambora names were flowery because the language was, and depended much on tone and context for meaning. It appeared there were also both sacrificial omens and numerology involved in which name went to whom.

She took well to the monastic life, almost as if it were an echo of something in her unknown past. She did think she might have once been a priestess, but no images came, and she'd already stopped trying to coax anything familiar out.

There *were* dreams, but they made little sense, and gave off feelings she'd rather not have again.

One feeling she had occasionally, which did not require sleep, was an odd sense of being looked at deep inside her mind; the sensation was indescribable, and it came and went for no apparent reason. The priestesses training her were excited by this rather than distressed; they said it meant she had the rare spirituality to connect to the gods and spirits, and that one day she might resolve these into true communication.

The Ambora saw spirits everywhere. There were spirits for rain, spirits for fire, spirits for volcanoes—and one volcano god over all of them—a spirit in each tree, rock, whatever. The carvings they made in living trees and what they considered living rock represented the greater spirits there, and atop them all the supreme god of the clan, protector of the clan from all other gods. Theirs was a world in which literally everything was not only alive, but, to a series of degrees, had power and thought and used it. There were also, of course, prayers, rituals, sacrifices, mystic signs and symbols, talismans, and the like to protect you from the various spirits—if you had sufficient faith.

Although it was not brought out immediately, the priestesses did know of the wider world and at least neighboring civilizations. They knew about the technology available there, and abhorred it as corrupting and evil, although they were not above trading for a few things they needed, such as bronze ingots of a certain purity and, occasionally, silver and gold. Sometimes others were allowed in, for brief periods, to harvest the enormously rich and bountiful crops that could be grown in Amboran soil, and for which the carnivorous Ambora had little use except as food for their own food. The few vegetable products they consumed were not exactly delicacies: a thick gruel used to relieve constipation, acidic leaves chewed to cure upset stomachs, and so on, and some used in the potions that were in the cauldrons she'd seen when first entering the cave.

One was a mild narcotic that induced a kind of waking trance; it wasn't debilitating, but you tended to focus single-mindedly on whatever was being taught and happily go along with whoever the teachers were, no matter what they said. Since much of the teaching was by repetition, using chants and prayers and rituals over and over, you tended, with this aid, to learn things quickly, and they stayed with you. In fact, the more she began to accept and think along their lines, the more she felt at home, that she was fitting in with the others.

The belief system and procedure seemed very comfortable, very true to her. They saw the world as ruled by a huge number of gods, each of whom had created a race and land in its own image and now presided over each. There was a chief god who lived not in the heavens but in the center of the planet, called simply the Judge, who watched over all the other gods and their equal places, and by the performance and fidelity of the people living in each would reward or punish. The Judge also decided whether you would simply be extinguished or find eternal punishment when you died, or if you would be sent to a paradise, a world that was all Ambora and where the Amboran people lived in perfect harmony, serving and worshiping the god they could see and hear and know.

There were no ranks in Amboran society. By training and piety and testing you might become one of many levels of priestesses and be absolute in religious authority, while the men constituted civil authority, such as education and a kind of primitive zoning that allowed the forest to thrive even with their density while also managing any building. The women provided food and defense as well as priestesses as needed; the men provided the rest, including sitting on the enormous egg that the women laid, for the week or two until it hatched, which more than anything explained the bow-leggedness of the males and the softness of their feathers.

Defense was necessary, although not day-to-day. Clans not well-managed or subject to volcanic or other natural disasters, usually taken as punishments by the gods, could face starvation or worse. One clan once had a steam vent explode and kill most of the men and children at midday; the only way to reestablish the clan and village was to kidnap some men from other villages. Beyond this, there were always fights of honor or for pride between individuals of different clans who might meet and clash in the air, as well as the constant marking of clan boundaries, which were often disputed by adjacent clans.

Whether her gods and spirits were real or not, the high priestess really did possess powers. Raised and trained to the job, only one priestess would attain her levels and her powers; no other was possible until she died, but that one would come from the ranks of the priestesses around her. There were costs to go with the power, though. The high priestess had to be a lifelong virgin; while there was no requirement that a priestess be celibate, most were as a matter of course, since all wanted to attain the highest spiritual level possible in this life. Most of the priestesses were sterile anyway, thanks to all the drugs and potions they used as a daily part of their lives. The high priestess gained in physical size, and the wings and feathering became incredibly dense, yet once she attained her rank, she could no longer fly.

It was clear that Her Holiness was pleased with Jaysu's rapid spiritual progress, and that she very much wanted the newcomer to enter the priesthood. It would be a waste for someone so bright to just be another warrior and mother, particularly when the girl definitely could feel the gods talking and at times even the Great Judge below.

She had punished Lema for the lapse in security, although not heavily, but Lema's last act of penance was to fly to the Great Pit that was the one unifying holy shrine of all clans and Amboran peoples, and there present credentials from the High Priestess and thus fly into the center of the Pit and be transported to South Zone. The act of doing so and also then encountering so many fearsome-looking creatures at close quarters was generally enough to make any warrior believe in miracles and the power of the priesthood, as well as scaring the living crap out of them. Lema had wasted no time seeing the Grand High Priestess who staffed the Amboran embassy in South Zone alone, and sat terrified while this highest of all clerics used exotic magic involving a magic tablet with lots of little dots on it and magic screens, and ultimately printed out a packet of information that was then placed in a pouch, sealed, and given to Lema for the return trip. There was no danger of Lema reading this, since only priestesses and male educators were literate, or needed to be.

When the High Priestess got the papers, she was more shocked than surprised by the data. She well understood the process of conditioning and programming of the mind—that was part of the job here—but *this*! *This* was as pure evil as she'd seen in a long time. Slavery was an abhorrent concept to her, and, even worse, slavery done by someone just for ego and sadistic pleasures and for no true need—horrible. The photos of the entries wouldn't and didn't correlate to present appearance, but faces always told something, and those two were blanks. They'd had all the humanity just squeezed out of them. Had she not seen Jaysu, she would have said flatly that the evil one had left their bodies alive but murdered their souls. It was little wonder that the woman had lost her memory; it would have been intolerable to remember that period, the High Priestess suspected.

But which one was she? Or did it matter? The real question was, *would* she remember? If so, this could present problems, since she might well revive old conditioning and become subject to other wills in a world that was growing more dangerous as the forces of darkness gathered and moved in the west. What could they do against an army of monsters who might overrun all the land by sheer force of numbers and had no worry about how many lives they sacrificed?

If only she could gain this one's knowledge without risking her mind and her soul!

For now it would have to suffice just to train her and indoctrinate her so completely in the Amboran mindset that she might be an asset in the inevitable dark times to come.

The Overdark, the ocean had always been called. It was a fitting, perhaps prophetic, name.

She would send not Lema back to Zone, but an acolyte priestess with more requests. The Grand High Priestess was already supplying weekly updates to the clans on the state of the coming darkness, and everyone who was knowledgeable in any clan understood the gravity of it. But even getting the clans to agree on whether or not it was raining (or if females flew) was impossible. Getting them to band together in concert on a truly national scale was the Grand High Priestess's aim, and perhaps the only hope Ambora, as a coastal nation, had.

For they would come one day. Perhaps not today, or tomorrow, or even next week or next year, but they would come. If they faced three million individualists, as she feared they would, then none of the gods and spirits of Ambora could save them.

Mahakor, Kalinda

IT WASN'T SUPPOSED TO HURT, BUT IT HAD, AND A *LOT*. NEIther of them understood that it was because of their own telepathic links, suddenly severed when all of their beings were broken down into nothing more than impossibly complex and detailed code, analyzed, rearranged, and reformed on the surface by the great machine that operated and maintained the Well. The Well of Souls was not so much a creator as a processor, although only those long dead and gone could understand its logic.

Angel/Alpha, Ming/Beta, and Ari had all tried to enter at once, although they were assured it wouldn't matter in terms of final placement. Alpha had winked out first, and Beta hesitated, feeling lost, and then the pain and jamming of the mental signals and implanted receptors kicked in and, for very different reasons, Beta and Ari clung to one another as their transformations began.

Beta clung to Ari because she had been using an unused part of his brain for hot swappable storage, and because she had made him subject to her. Ari clung to her out of fear, out of remorse, and because more than being controlled, he feared being alone.

He awoke, still with the echo of that searing pain, when somebody threw a huge bucket of water at him with enormous force, knocking him backward and almost out cold again.

He was disoriented and panicked, then saw that what had thrown the water at him was in fact a very angry looking ocean, and that he was on a rocky outcrop being pounded by tall waves and churning surf. He tried to get up and run inland to escape the next big one, but couldn't get to his feet before it smacked him again. Then, without thinking, his survival instincts took over and he crawled, hand over hand, to the edge of the rocks and slid down into the ocean head first.

Instantly he was in a different world. A shiver went through him from head to—tail?—and he opened his mouth and took in water, starting a rhythmic motion. He felt it pass through the mouth, down through the neck, and then kind of ooze back into the surrounding water again. It was an interesting feeling, one he'd not had before, nor was it something he'd have tried on his own, but thankfully, the instincts worked.

Okay, he was breathing water. It still seemed odd, but only because, topside, he was certain he'd been breathing air. What kind of creature could breathe both so effortlessly?

He brought what proved to be a webbed hand with very long, sharp, curved nails to his face and felt it. Two eyes, a nose, a mouth, chin, even two ears, although they felt like soft seashells. But the nose wasn't a nose; no water was going in and out, and he didn't think air had before, on the rocks. It seemed to be a nice little nose, but in fact the two indentations in the nostrils weren't cavities at all, but ended just inside, at a pulsing fleshy tissue.

There was hair, too, thick and long, but it didn't quite feel like hair, and when he reached up and took a little of it and brought it in front of his eyes, it looked colorless, not quite transparent but certainly translucent, and felt warm to the touch.

Continuing his self-examination, he noted gill-like organs in the neck, which accepted water as he swam and extracted the oxygen and expelled the rest in a simple series of automatic motions. His color was light brown on the underside; from what he could tell about his back, it appeared a much darker brown, and there seemed to be a fin, like the dorsal of a shark, just below the shoulder blades. If that was what he'd fallen against the second time, it was a wonder he hadn't impaled himself. Reaching around and touching it, which was all he could manage, he could feel it was very hard, and with sharp edges that probably led to a knifelike point.

Now it was clear that he hadn't been able to run because he had no legs. Instead, the humanoid torso blended into one more reminiscent of a sea lion or a porpoise; the large steering fins were parallel to his body, much like a mammal, rather than like great fish.

A hybrid of some kind, he thought with some sense of wonder, one so much of the sea that it probably lived there most of the time and breathed the water easily, yet able to breathe air if need be and operate on the surface, or even, to the limited extent his body permitted, on land. Part fish, part mammal? There were small, very tight, very firm breasts with nipples, but they looked and felt more like pectorals and he felt comfortably male, except . . .

If there's no crotch, how do I . . . ? He brought his tail around and angled his neck down until he could see a small area where something bony barely protruded. *That was it? Jeez, maybe they just laid eggs and then the guys swam over them and got off or something. Wouldn't that be a disappointment!*

There was a sense of warmer and cooler currents; he could actually see them as well as feel them. But though he was now in what was certainly a cold current, it was a matter of fact rather than a matter of concern. Fatty tissue, or something even better, was insulating him as needed.

Underwater, the colors he saw were vanishing with depth. Still, when he examined his hands or other parts of his body, the image looked crisp and sharp. He wondered about that. It seemed that his eyes were flattening, compensating for the distortion of light in the water.

Once his initial mental qualms were out of the way and he had experimented with how much turn or twist did what, moving in this element was like flying without wings. While you were aware of the water, it was a friend, and you could hold yourself at a given depth, go up or down with minor gestures, and go forward with only slight expenditures of energy. It was *better* than flying; it was a fully three-dimensional environment, and the more he swam in it, the more of a rush he got. Damn if this wasn't *fun!*

As he descended still farther, he became aware of other senses that he was using. Sound . . . Echoes back to his ears and then to his brain were painting pictures for him. Down about a hundred meters he pictured a school of average-sized fish, and a bit farther down there were more. But sonar couldn't give the level of detail he was perceiving; no, he was picking out each individual living thing and categorizing it by size and attributes. He realized that this ability had something to do with whatever it was that he'd thought was his nose.

But where in this wet place was he headed?

As it turned out, at about fifty meters depth an entire network appeared to him out of the gloom at the bottom—not in sight, but in that sixth sense he didn't quite understand. But what did they mean, these straight lines going in various directions like some grand highway as seen from very high up? Each, when probed by sonar, had a different and distinct single tone. Once he tried it, the tone persisted until he changed to a different line.

They were roads! Not actual, physical roads, but grids laid out on the floor and perhaps broadcasting as well. Anyone swimming along who had his powers would see it, and if they knew what each tone meant, they would know which road went where, and maybe more.

He wasted no time choosing a road. They were all the same to him, and they all had to lead *somewhere*, or else somebody had gone to a tremendous amount of bother just for art.

As he followed it, he tried to remember back. He had fragments of memories; in fact, he had memories from all sorts of sources, but none took precedence and many were confusing. He thought he was somebody named Aristotle Martinez, since that was the only male memories he had and he felt that he was a male. But it was an incomplete set of memories, with more gaps than whole parts, and he seemed very distant, like looking at a character in a play rather than at one's own self.

And then there was Ming Dawn Palavri. He had at least as many memories of hers as of Ari's, and in some cases it seemed that the Ming memories, while also distant, were more complete than much of Ari's. Talk about your hybrids! He could tap either life, male or female, and think very much along those lines. Considering what a skunk Ari was, he suspected that he'd rather have been Ming, which explained the memory jostling. Split personalities, split nature, dual sexuality, part fish and part mammal, water breather and air breather—this was some mixed-up existence he was headed into!

But there were others in his head, too. Less so, less fully formed and detailed, but very much there. Some of Angel was there, oddly, and so were Alpha and Beta, although they were so synched that they seemed to have no separate identity. Alpha and Beta gave him the shivers; he could follow their single-minded logic and their view of the universe, but who would want to? Angel was a different story. He didn't have her clearly at all, but those snippets he could make out were as bizarre a view of the universe as the Alpha-Beta concept, if different. Or were they? Alpha and Beta knew who their god was and joyfully lived to serve him and him alone. Angel believed in a different, more grandiose God of the cosmos that she could not see yet felt was with her seeing and hearing all and guiding her, and she joyfully lived to serve Him and Him alone. Hmmm . . . That didn't sound like much of a choice.

The worst part was, none of them were *him*. They were all there, along with a lot of data, a lot of shared experiences, and some pretty nasty memories as well, but not a one of them fit like an old suit and comfortable chair. Ari didn't really fit because he didn't like him very much and didn't want to be him. He had the fullest picture of Ming, yet he didn't want to be Ming, either, because he wanted the rèal Ming back. He wanted to make it up to her, even make love to her. Hell, maybe *mate* with her.

The others he wanted to forget, although he knew they'd probably be a part of his nightmares. Still, he had the impression that it wasn't supposed to work like this. They said he should be mentally intact; instead, he seemed a whole new person. Damn. Being yanked around was one thing, but at least he'd known who he was and had an intact ego and personality; now he felt like two very different people, with several others around as onlookers. He'd heard of people with multiple personalities, and perhaps that was what he was experiencing.

He was coming to a junction, but didn't have to choose which branch to take. It was immediately obvious; if he'd been breathing air instead of water, it would have been breathtaking.

It was a *city*! And not just caves and kelp and coral, although it did look like a vast coral reef. The lifesigns to his sixth sense were so strong that he had to dampen it; there were a *lot* of beings over there, hopefully beings like him.

And if it wasn't electrified and lighting up the sea bottom, then it was doing a pretty fair imitation.

In less than five minutes he encountered the first denizens of this new world, and had the mermaid vision reinforced, although the bodies were not like the classical mermaids of old, appearing more alien. Still, the ears, like clamshells set into each side of the head, the quite Terran-looking faces that seemed to be those of women, even though they might not all have been, and the long, translucent, and slightly glowing "hair," were very much as he'd suspected.

In less than ten minutes two such creatures wearing armbands with some kind of symbol and carrying what appeared to be ray guns had placed him under arrest.

He'd almost gotten used to a kind of local telepathy with the two women, so he wasn't completely thrown by the way the authorities spoke to him, only their attitudes. It *was* telepathy, but very much on the surface. He could no more read their true thoughts than he could have read those butterfly things' thoughts back in that entry place, yet the communication was clear. It was a combination—another hybrid!—involving the sending of a specific (or, if you wanted to address many, a broad) audio signal that acted as a carrier for the thoughts, which were perceived much like words and sentences. And it was clear from the start that this communication method left no room for weaseling or error. You understood *exactly* what the speaker meant.

Not that the two cops had been all that communicative. He'd just swam down on the main line for the city and they suddenly materialized on either side of him.

"Hold! What is your name?" one asked flat out, the "tone" conveying the kind of arrogant authority he expected of cops.

"I—" he began, and stopped. Hell, just which name *did* he use when he felt like neither? "I am Ari Martinez," he finally responded, picking the one that was most correct in the basics, although he didn't really exactly *feel* like Ari Martinez. "I was—" He hesitated, but his mind sent the requisite mental holograms showing him and his former companions being pushed into the void of the Gate. "I awoke on an island above in a terrible storm and my impulse was to come down here."

"Smart impulse. That's a hurricane up there. We just hope it doesn't knock off the electricity plant," the other cop said. "Well, you may have suddenly become like us, but that doesn't make you one of us. Just ask the Crown Regent of Chalidang, for one."

As he tried to make sense of that cryptic remark, the other cop snapped something tight around his neck, just below the gills. "Hey! What's that?"

"It is an electric collar. You will come with us and do as we say, or either of us can press one stud on our wrist controllers and you will be shocked at whatever level we choose up to unconsciousness. Don't make us do this. Sometimes you don't move much after you get the big shock, and you just got here."

He knew just the type of device, if not the thing itself, and he had no desire to test it out.

Their wrist controllers, not something he had paid much attention to before, were interesting little gadgets. There was a series of buttons, some small readouts in tiny windows, and they flanked a circular section that looked like a speaker. By locking down one of the buttons, they could beam their report in, presumably broadcast to headquarters; they also seemed to receive information back through it, but the signal was obviously so localized that it could only be heard or understood by the wearer.

Just as the water gave fully three-dimensional movements, so, too, had the city been designed for those who could simply float around and glide about and needed no surface roads, elevators, or much else. Buildings rose twenty stories yet had entrances on each floor, while vast tracts of apartments looked like great stylized obelisks and mounds with holes all over. All of the structures and even the layout of the city was clearly designed to keep water flowing, and there were large domed structures whose sole purpose was to either warm or cool the water passing through, and thus create the patterns. It kept the water fresh and oxygenated even when one of the denizens was not moving.

And yet, for all its alien strangeness, many aspects of the city were common to most communities of any size. There was municipal lighting, and inside lighting as well, with energy bands marking an incredible pattern of colorful routings. Ari suspected it was like the corridors back in the entry place; the streets had both a color and a frequency to identify them. Along them would be numbers. The colors from this illumination identified broad categories, like east or north, up and down, but the bands also carried frequency information that his mind accepted and differentiated from all the others. He was sure that if you knew the system, as he did not, you could easily navigate the whole thing.

That was one thing he missed from his brief union with the two women: knowing what it was like to be a genius, to quickly deduce and file away information as effortlessly as you'd scratch an itch. He knew that together they could have figured out this system just by looking at it, and that there was no way he could do it on his own. Still, he realized that certain bands, apparently all associated with yellow, were for commercial traffic only. This traffic involved some fairly large containers being "driven" by heavy duty motors and a driver with long rods for steering, while others were small rounded containers pushed by beefy tradesmen.

It was a sophisticated, modern culture, probably as much as some of the water breathing worlds of the Realm. There were electric water scooters lined up outside what could only have been the police building, ready to supply all the added power and speed a cop would need to answer an emergency. Since there didn't seem to be any private vehicles allowed save for the commercial types, it would be easy to patrol the place.

Moving through the open archway that led inside the police building, he felt a tingling all over and decided that there were doors of a sort here. He assumed that this big one was a one-way door; anybody could get *in* to the station, but that big old fellow over there had to push things on a control board in front of him to let you back out again.

The building was impressive; a kind of hollowed-out design with a vast but well-lit atrium, and on the main floor various signs leading to areas where there were officers and clerks and, to his surprise, flat screens that looked like computer screens, although he was surprised to see they mostly contained meaningless squiggles and that those working on them used massive input pads with an impossible number of buttons, rows and rows of them. Couldn't they just talk to their computers and get replies?

The central area was a big horseshoe-shaped depression with a series of clerks at desks. He was brought up to one of them by his captors.

"What's *this* one?" the clerk asked, sounding more bored than interested.

"New one," the cop on the right replied. "Apparently just made through the Well from aliens processed through Zone. You want to run him through the system and confirm that such people *did* arrive? Can't be too careful these days."

"Don't need to," the clerk responded. "I'm surprised, though, to see this one. Looks just like the other one. Don't usually get two in the same hex."

"You have another like me here?" he asked, suddenly excited.

The clerk gave him a nasty look and responded, "*You* are not to be involved in this discussion. Just keep quiet." She turned back to the booking cop. "I suppose he doesn't remember his name?"

"Says he's—okay, you can talk. What was that name again?"

While taking in all this and thinking of this new other, his mind had wandered from the immediate business of booking him.

"Ming—sorry, *Ari* Martinez."

"Ming Ari Martinez. Well, that's a lot."

"Just Ari Martinez. Sorry. I was thinking about one of my companions."

"Suit yourself." She looked on the screen, punched something up, then swiveled it around so he could see it. "Which one are you?"

He was startled to see a still picture of them sitting in the small lecture hall, all together. Jeez, he looked awful! Not as bad as Kincaid looked, though—or his uncle, if the old bastard made it. His hand went out and toward Beta's eerie gaze, but then he pointed to the one and only original Ari Martinez. "That one."

He really *did* have a dual nature. He had just about all of Ari as well as all of Ming inside his head. They weren't meshing—they were too clear and distinct for that—but keeping one up and the other in background required effort. He told himself that he had better find some way to manage them and deal with it. Otherwise he'd go to sleep and the next day wake up thinking he was Ming, and that wouldn't do at all.

They took some sort of holographic photo of him by running a hooplike device over him. He only understood what it was because he saw the image form on a little disk next to the booking clerk's screen. It was an interesting perspective in about one-fifth scale. A series of squiggles was written under it, it was rotated and checked, and then it vanished, presumably into the central police computer records.

"Take him to Interrogation 302," the clerk told them. "Detective Shissik will want to question him, and a link with the Interior Police is already established there."

He didn't like the sound of "Interior Police." Still, he wondered if he hadn't been incredibly stupid. If he'd told them he was Ming and let that personality come up, it would have been cop to cop!

"Interrogation 302" meant that they swam up from booking to the fourth level, entry being "Ground," and then to and through one of the doorways there. He assumed the squiggles gave the room number.

Inspector Shissik was already there, and there was a small oval object in front of him that looked like a speaker.

Nobody sat; the only furniture was the table on which the speaker rested, and only it was needed.

The Inspector looked up at the two cops who'd brought him in. "You may go," he said officiously.

"But—" the first one protested, and stopped when the Inspector gave him a withering glare. They left, and Ari heard an ominous buzzing sound indicating that if *he* tried to leave, it would be a bit different.

"Please relax," the Inspector said. "I am with the Interior Police. If that term is not familiar to you, it simply means the national police force that sees over the whole of Kalinda. You're now a Kalindan whether you want to be or not, and there won't be a third transformation, so you should get to know your new people and new home. You are here to answer some questions about yourself, your erstwhile companions, and a few other things. Then we'll process you in as a citizen, find you quarters, and test you out for a job. Everyone in Kalinda works at something. If you cannot find a job you enjoy and are good at, we'll find you a least common denominator one. I do not mean to suggest we're a slave labor camp, but we do expect everyone to do their part. Is that understood?"

He nodded. "Yes, sir."

"Now, I want to know all about you. What you did where you came from, how you wound up here, and, most particularly, I want you to tell me all that you can about those who came in with you. Just go ahead, and I will interrupt if I have a question."

He did in fact understand, and he gave the Inspector a fairly whitewashed version of Ari Martinez's life and times, jobs and relations, and something of an account of who the others were and how they all wound up here. He even admitted that his uncle was a master criminal and a sadist, but managed to give the impression that he wasn't a part of that. He hoped he sounded convincing.

For a while the Inspector didn't respond, then he said, "Why did you give the female Ming as an identity downstairs?"

He shrugged. "We—all three of us—were telepathically linked. It appears some of it came with me."

"It appears that *much* of it came with you," the Inspector responded. "The other one, which you weren't supposed to be told about as yet but know anyway, is quite an amnesiac. It is genuine; we've gone through the usual verification steps—drugs, that sort of thing—to convince ourselves. She arrived here a few days ahead of you, although I must tell you that such a time spread for simultaneous processings isn't all that unusual. It will be interesting to find out where the third is, and in what mental condition, but that will be days, even weeks, unless she, too, comes here. You say you have nearly complete memories?"

"Yes. I can't say how complete, but if I reach back to common experiences, when we both were there, it is extremely easy to recall it from her point of view. It is almost like both of us were in here, somehow. I didn't think that was possible with this Well of Souls thing."

"Well, even the Ancient Ones could not be expected to think of everything. Apparently you and she were both physically and mentally connected when you entered?"

"Yes, she basically was operating me like a puppet."

"Apparently the Well couldn't tell the two of you apart, or perceived three consciousnesses in two bodies, and yet was running on the knowledge of your old species. This leads me to the rather interesting question it all raises. Are you certain that you are Ari and not Ming?"

It was a disconcerting question. "But—I'm male, aren't I?"

"Doesn't follow at all, for two reasons. Number one, the Well has never let that stand in its way before, nor even in all cases in the recent past. And second, we Kalindans are a bisexual race, it is true, but we're designed primarily as survivors under almost any circumstances. When you woke up above, you could breathe, couldn't you?"

"Yes. I wondered about that."

"You have a blowhole in the back of your head and some rudimentary lungs that are sufficient up top. We're quite a rarity in races—we can exist in two of the four elements, and we are well-insulated along a lot of temperature extremes. We're also omnivores and can eat most anything, although there's much we would not enjoy eating. And we're born as neuters. Our children have no sexual differentiation at all. Upon puberty, we tend toward one sex or the other, but this can change. If the population falls below healthy levels, males will change over a period of weeks to females. When the population tends to get a bit too large, then a large number of females become males. Everyone's not changing gender all the time, but if one hasn't had it happen to them, one knows others that have. One's gender is basically irrelevant here, you see, but whatever is needed to keep our population in balance, we do. This is why we all look rather feminine and have these breasts. The young are born live and carried in sacs—your sac is along here, as you might notice. They are nursed like mammals, although we are a rather unique species outside of here, and if you live with someone who has a nursing baby, even if male, you'll discover that hormones will be triggered and you can hold and nurse as well. We prize personal honor and relationships over gender. It is another adaptation that helps us thrive."

He thought it over, and decided it was a neat concept. It might be fun to be both. "I assume that the sex act itself is as fun as it used to be?"

"It is certainly not something we shy away from," Shissik admitted.

And then it hit him, just what the Inspector meant. "So I really *could* be Ming. Or Ari."

"Or both. That suggests a fascinating duality I've never had to face. You might be both a police officer and a criminal. Please relax—you are a criminal no more, nor, of course, are you an officer. Whatever you become starts *now*. We like to use the knowledge and experience you might have if it's handy, but it is traditional that no newcomer to a race here is held at all accountable for past deeds. Inner natures *do* tend to emerge over time, and that might be interesting in your case. One might expect you to commit a criminal act and then arrest yourself."

He realized that Shissik was being funny, but he didn't share the joke.

"So what happens now?" he asked the Interior Policeman.

"Now? Nothing immediately. We will get you a good meal and then I want to propose an experiment to my superiors. They now have a recording of this conversation, so we'll see if they are satisfied from their point of view. We are in the city of Mahakor, a medium-sized city in the northeast of our nation. The other is in the capital of Jinkinar. I'd like to take you up there eventually and get you together with this other one. We simply cannot be totally trusting of newcomers for a while, you see, and we do have this nagging question about the other far more than about you."

"Which is?"

"Well, if she doesn't know who she is or what she was, then aren't we merely *assuming* that she's your Ming? Perhaps she's the other one you were linked to, the onetime cultist or whatever it was. Or perhaps she is neither of them but someone else. Ari's uncle was near death. If he survived and was processed, who is to say what his mind might have been like by that point? Suppose it's Ari's uncle Jules that we have? And even if his memories were turned to mush, as I said, inner natures have a tendency to begin coming out over time. I think we need to know for certain."

Jesus H. Christ! he thought in panic. What if it is Jules Wallinchky? That would be just what I needed here! A whole new body, a whole new race, a whole new life, and they would be putting me right back where I started . . .

Ochoa

THE CREATURES FLEW OVER THE SEAS AT AN ALTITUDE OF AL-most a kilometer, yet their bony heads were on the ocean and not each other, and their large eyes angled down as if they could see beneath the seas, which, in fact, they could. Not so precisely, of course, but they weren't looking for a particular fish; they were looking for signs of lunch.

The wings were broad but leathery, the tail almost serpentine until it flattened out into a fan shape at its end. The heads were triangular, almost perfect right angles, except for a slight crest at the top rear behind the eyes, each of which had independent movement. Ears were mere cavities in the back of the head that seemed made of something very solid indeed. The lower jaw, which ran the length of the head, had a leathery sack beneath it which, in those whose sacks were empty, seemed to flap slowly back and forth. Those who had some prior catch appeared to have somewhat larger jaws.

The extremely long legs were up flat against the body now, their long talon-tipped fingers and opposable "thumb" locked up and out of the way to increase streamlining. Looked upon from above, they were quite colorful and distinctive, with patterns of randomness in reds, yellows, blues, grays, and browns; their underside, however, was a blue-white, and in either sunlight or clouds they were extremely difficult to see from the ground.

"Big school! Sandrums! Three o'clock, thirty-two-degree angle!" one of them called, its voice harsh, birdlike.

She saw it, the slight pattern of silver just beneath the waves, and with a built-in sense of where any other of his kind was, she dove with them down on the unsuspecting school of fish.

The entry into the water was unhesitating and effortless. Eye lenses flattened, sensing the electricity and magnetism in sea life as by seeing, the group continued flying, underwater, in formation, as if they were still high in the air. The tail, so suited to flying and balance, split apart and turned opposite, providing two paddles that were as effective as tail flippers and gave them the same kind of control a sea mammal might have.

The poor fish, some up to sixty centimeters long, didn't have a chance. The ravenous horde pounced on them, huge mouths open, and began scooping them in from the rear before the front of the school was even aware they were under relentless attack. She quickly had her jaw pouch filled with four lively fish, which quickly calmed down as juices in the pouch flowed around them, knocking them out and acting as a preservative. She gobbled a fifth and last one straight down for her own gratification, chopping it to bits with her impressive range of teeth, then angled up and leaped right out of the water and into the air. The tail reformed as an avian device, and the leathery wings began to move. Reforming above, all with full pouches, they circled and headed for home.

This is a hell of a way to make a living, she thought sourly, and not my ideal for a new way of life.

She looked down over the hex, which was composed of a vast network of islands, all apparently of ancient volcanic origin since none seemed active. They formed an amazing series of bays, harbors, and protected coves right in the middle of an ocean that had no other land, or so she'd been told, for a thousand or more kilometers in any direction.

It was a semitech hex that might have fooled anybody into thinking it a nontech one, and precisely because of its isolation, it was a well-visited one. The Ochoans were worldly and aware, and liked their little amenities, particularly cigars, some wild scents, and various drugs and brews, little of which they could make themselves, even if they'd had the organization and urge to do so. The islands had tons of birds and insects and some reptiles and a few what-the-heck-are-they-anyways, but the Ochoan was the dominant and basically the only important creature on any of them. When you could walk, fly in the air, and fly underwater, not to mention seeing quite well in darkness or in daylight, you tended to dominate things. They even made some occasional delicacies out of fruits and grains, which they pretended were luxuries but actually needed to keep themselves. They mainly ate fish, all sorts of fish, alive, dead, or stored in their pouches until needed, and they did some harvesting of native fruits for commercial trade as well as their own brand of art, both drawing and carving, which on the whole was bizarre, but popular in some places. There were some small steam engines about, mostly commercial ones bought from other hexes and modified to Ochoan physiology for operation, but these were mostly used for pumping water from one point to another, as in irrigation on the dry side of some of the islands or in sanitation.

And, being the only land and shelter in all that distance, they traded. Ships from all over stopped there, took on fresh water, fruit, sometimes even salted fish if the Ochoans trawled for them.

Even in her short time here she'd seen more creatures than the old Realm ever had, and some pretty bizarre and scary ones as well. She wanted to leave this dull paradise for a number of reasons, but as a newcomer she had no funds to blow on a ship's passage, which was the only way in or out. Although master of land, sea, and air, individual Ochoans could generally range no more than about hundred kilometers, and the denizens under the waves of the neighboring hexes would not ignore a nice, fat, juicy Ochoan floating on the surface or swimming a bit below it.

There was a government of sorts, both a loose hereditary nobility and a parliament elected by the local councils and set up as a kind of national assembly, but it met only rarely, and then to set quality standards and appoint inspectors for goods going out and coming in, and to appoint ambassadors to Zone. The councils, under chairmanship of a local noble, handled minor disputes, mounted rescues when needed, and saw to the education of the young, little more. If you needed something, somebody would lend it to you, and you might pay back the favor with some other favor sometime. About the only violent crimes were crimes of passion, and those were dealt with and hard and fast by the whole community.

There was also a method of ordering goods, and catalog

sale was quite popular, particularly for manufactured goods of mostly no particular use except showing off.

Ochoan men had the real racket. They were big and ego-centric, full of very bright colors, even on their heads, which they brought out even more with waxes and polishes. They had incredibly fancy crests and sexy deep calls using hollow parts of the crests as amplifiers, and spent most of their time primping, preening, showing off, and playing macho-type contests with each other. The duller-looking and more prag-matic women did almost all of the hunting and most other work as well, as well as bearing the young, though the men actually hatched the eggs. But even then, they mostly sat around, complaining about not getting enough to eat, how stuck they were, and so on. For them, it was a seller's market—there were five females to every male, and other than hatching the eggs, they did one other thing well, or so she'd been told. She was trying to *not* wind up attached to a nesting, at least not until she had to.

Still, if she couldn't get on one of those ships and see this whole weird world, it seemed to her unfair that she at least hadn't been reincarnated as a male Ochoan. It suited her nature perfectly. Coming out female at all was a twist, but coming out female in a society where the women did all the work was adding insult to injury. She'd never much liked work in the first place. Next time I'll hide down in the damned jewelry, she thought sourly.

Although entering the Well World from an alien exis-tence, she was considered by the Ochoans as basically an orphaned female, a status not high in the local pecking order. She'd found a couple of natives of about the same status, and at their invitation moved in with them in a makeshift rookery overlooking the harbor and provisioning station below. Haqua and Czua at least weren't pushing her toward one of those preening idiots, she thought with relief, and while resigned to eventually winding up as part of a nesting, they, too, would rather delay it as long as possible.

She landed, stretched, folded her wings, then walked into the hut of bamboo and leaves they'd built as a shelter against the bad weather. "So, Nakitti! At least you never starve in this place, eh?" Czua greeted her. The added "tee" sound at the end of the name was required for the language to describe the feminine, although "feminine" was not exactly how one would describe the tough old scoundrel now suddenly different in an outward but not inward sense. Ochoan women did not have two names as such, though; they had basic titles like "Wife Ghua" or "Cook Chai." Since "Tann" was meaningless, they ignored it. Nakitt kept it in her own mind, though, because it was a central part of her identity, a link back to the old.

"True, there's always food and I love the flying *and* the swimming, but this is still getting old fast," Tann Nakitt responded. "I was *proud* to be a Ghoma; I *enjoyed* sneaking in and stealing the most valuable of all things in a high civilization from under their noses—secrets, information of all sorts. This is kind of like the fun things I might have loved to be able to do on my days off or between assignments, but as a *living*, it lacks—well, it lacks."

Both girls, neither much past puberty, were fascinated by this stranger who looked like them but talked like nobody they knew and came from an exotic place off in the stars that they could never have imagined and now couldn't get enough of. Tann Nakitt suspected that if they ever got into the *real* Realm, they'd be frightened or bored or victimized at best, but so long as it remained a romantic vision, one that was easily and eagerly fed by their sophisticated roomie, well, that was fine with her.

"Good catch today?" Czua asked.

"It almost always is," the newcomer grumbled. "Nothing much *ever* happens around here from the looks of it." She looked down at the natural harbor below. "Hmm . . . Big ship coming in. Think I'll go down and take a look at it."

"You're always looking at the ships. You just want 'em to take you away from here, that's all."

"You bet. In the meantime, I'm gonna see what I can see." She went to the edge of the cliff and jumped off, gliding down to the dock and minor port town below.

She liked the town; it reminded her of a backwater in the Realm, with a variety of creatures there on long-term contracts to help service the various vessels that made port. It wasn't easy work; as a semitech hex, maintaining a practical drydock for the size of vessels coming in just wasn't practical, nor could any high-tech damage be reliably repaired.

They could replace some radar and navigation modules, but nobody would know if they worked until they crossed a border into a high-tech region. Sorry, no refunds.

The large commercial ships that plied the oceans of the Well World were unique hybrids since they had to regularly cross vast stretches where the technology was limited. Thus, they tended to be large three- or four-masted clippers, some with steel hulls, most with wooden hulls often clad in copper or similar alloys because of the weight an iron hull or frame added. They were ungainly but workable as pure sailing ships under the hands of experts, which ocean crews had to be. For that reason and the expense of the ships' maintenance, interhex freight was expensive and passenger fares even more so.

The ships also tended to either have twin side paddles or large screws, and one or two central stacks for boilers that, in all but the nontech hexes, could propel the great ships forward regardless of the winds. Some had small and efficient high-tech engines, some on nuclear models, for high-tech hex sailing when you could make speed, but these were costly enough that most relied entirely on steam power even in the most advanced regions.

This one was an older vessel, with the great side paddles, two stacks in between three great, tall masts, wooden hull; but its high wheelhouse and instrumentation atop suggested that, when it could use them, the ship could sail confidently using radar through foggy seas and low visibility. Not here, though.

The ship, however, was threadbare. It needed a full scrape and paint, there were potential problem cracks on the decks, and some portholes appeared taped together or nailed shut. In fact, some heavy tape ran across more than one of the large windows out from the bridge, suggesting that the glass was by no means comfortable there.

It wasn't until the pilot brought the ship around and eased it into the dock that Tann Nakitt saw the bullet holes. Maybe not high tech—you could do a gunpowder-based machine gun, she knew, that would work with just a hand crank—but definitely more than one shooter. Could some of those damaged windows and portholes have been *shot* to pieces?

She rose up into the air to take a closer look at this sad-looking ship and immediately saw the signs of some kind of battle. The aft upper cabin deck had a nasty gash in it that had clearly been hastily patched up at sea. Closer looks revealed others. Cannon fire. And on the decks, and peering from those portholes and windows, like a vacuum-packed can of sardines, were people from quite a number of races. They had scales and feathers and hair in all the wrong places, tentacles and claws and even flowers, but they were all people and they all radiated a hopelessness and terror you only saw in refugees from a horror.

What the *hell* could *this* be? Tann Nakitt asked herself. And if it was possible to have a war in this boring and most provincial of worlds, how the hell could she get into it?

She circled back and landed near the Port Authority Building—a kind of joke, since it was basically an overly large one-room thatched hut. It seemed that half the small town was there watching the sight, and possibly thinking some of the thoughts she'd been thinking. They were a grim and sober crew.

Lord Kassarim was there, looking resplendent in his necklace of authority as Chief of the Port Authority, and, more telling, he had his favorite wife, the Lady Akua, with him. Tann Nakitt had had some dealings with these people before; Kassarim was a good sort, if a bit more lazy and full of self-importance than the usual men here, but Akua also held the rank of captain and was head of the local port militia. Not big except for ordering people about now and then in normal times, but this was clearly in a military person's interest.

Tann Nakitt approached them casually. This was a laid-back royalty so long as you didn't want to marry into the family, and they knew she was a newcomer, and much of her story—at least the version she'd told and stuck to.

"Good afternoon, my lord. That seems a sad and strange ship," she greeted him.

Lord Kassarim cocked one eyeball in Nakitt's direction. "So, Nakitti, you see the bullets?"

"Yes, my lord, but more I see the refugees. Where is this ship coming from, if I may ask, that it would be so attacked? I see no weapons aboard her. Whoever shot had to be bent on nothing less than murder."

"Indeed so," the Lady Akua put in. "This is the first such to put in here, but not the first in our small nation, and I fear it is simply the latest in an increasing tide. One wonders if so many are reaching us, just how many others lie at the bottom of the sea."

Nakitt nodded. "Looks like a tech level similar to ours. I seem to remember that those around us are either unlimited or no technology, so they must have steamed and sailed quite a distance like that."

"Possibly fourteen hundred kilometers, from the look of some of those aboard, Nakitti," Lord Kassarim replied. "You mean to say you don't know what's going on out in the West?"

"No, my lord. If my lord recalls, I just got here."

"Humph! Quite so, quite so." His Lordship reached into a pouch and took out a gigantic cigar using the "fingers" on his right leg as a hand, biting off the end and sticking it in his mouth. He then reached in and took out an enormously long sulfur-based match, struck it on the side of his head, then reaching up, lit the cigar and began puffing away. Tann Nakitt had been startled the first day here, seeing one leg lock as solid as an iron bar while the other twisted with a limberness that seemed almost impossible and could be easily used as a hand, but now she was so used to doing it herself it hardly registered.

"Well, Nakitti," His Lordship continued at last, "one of yours from back in wherever it is you come from is behind it. Damnedest thing we've seen in thousands of years. Chalidang was always rather ugly a place; it's run by a kind of pirate nobility that keeps its whole population in thrall, as if everybody, even the children, are in the army, and treated that way. They've been a scourge to their neighbors for some time, and nobody's liked them much, but they're a high-tech hex with a fair amount of resources and a collective mindset that can figure out an infinite number of ways to rob and kill you using the most common tools and implements. Still, they breathe water and they're far away from here, so nobody's much worried about them. Then in pops this creature reprocessed as one of the Chalidang, and with a totally new form and no briefing nor much else, the damned thing manages to disarm its captors, kill several of these folk who are lifelong professionals at it and know everything about their race, and before it even knew the name of the place, it had taken over and totally commanded a village halfway to the capital. It's a meritocracy of sorts, up to the born nobles. You kill the sergeant, you're the sergeant, and everybody else is conditioned to obey authority without question. So if you can't kill 'em, you swear allegiance. Then you kill the lieutenant, you get all the sergeants, and so on. If you keep offing the chain of command, you'll be running things in no time. If any superior officer nails you, game over, you see."

"Pleasant sounding place," Tann Nakitt commented. *Sounds like where I just left, only cruder.*

"Oh—yes, quite. Well, this sort of thing impressed the nobility, so they brought down an army of their best and laid siege. When it was clear no victory was possible, this new person surrendered and swore allegiance to the Baron, becoming in effect a body slave to the victor. Within three months the Baron had a new favorite concubine and pulled a deucedly clear ploy at a royal event, wiping out most of the highest members of the royal family. Some say it was poisons, some say electricity, some new methods not seen before. Who can say, since only the winners are left and they don't write manuals. All that *can* be said is that the Baron is now Emperor, he's defied all law and tradition by proclaiming this new chief concubine Empress, and they are picking and choosing and reorganizing their forces in all new ways, starting with the execution of any noble who doesn't accept the new Empress. Seems, too, that some of the new Empress's relations wound up in hexes not far away and there is now coordination. There's never been the like of it in sheer speed to the top, let alone audacity in action. Gossip says that Baron, now Emperor, Chojitz has never been known as particularly bright or ambitious. A good soldier but not a creative one. Seems he was bright enough to recognize a true genius in love, war, and politics."

"With *that* lot, he'll settle for war and politics," the Lady Akua noted bitterly.

"And this ship?" Nakitt prompted.

"Chalidang is adjacent to Quacksa, a land hex on a fair-sized island. It's a nontech hex full of some very nasty tribal savages with some remarkable and dangerous powers. It's said that they don't hunt game, they just walk up to it, stare into its eyes, and the game follows them home and then does its own slaughtering. They've been friendly with the underwater Chalidang for some time. The Chalidang can handle some high-tech manufacturing and such, and the Quacksans have little tricks that can ferret out traitors and instill true loyalty. The present Empress is said to be immune to them, which is why she had an easier time, and she's been using them now, probably as much on the Emperor and courtiers as on any possible enemies. The Quacksans go down in advanced breathing suits; a reverse kind of suit allows Chalidang folk to act on the surface, although, of course, they can't use the suits in a low-tech hex. Still, in just a bit over a year this—*person*—has gone from literally nothing to ambitious co-ruler of a dangerous hex, and is even now planning expansion."

"Now I *do* feel downright inferior and inadequate," Tann Nakitt commented softly.

"Eh? What?"

"Sorry, Your Lordship. Just thinking out loud. Please continue."

"Well then, you see, the first step was to help the relatives get positions in their lands, and this is now under way. The port city of Howek in Jerminia to their south is a transit point. This ship flies a Jerminian flag. I suspect that the port was besieged and overrun and these were the ones, both natives and foreign representatives there, who managed to get out. It was either that or look the Quacksans in the eyes, you see."

"Hard to believe any one person, even a local one, could do this in so short a time, I agree," Tann Nakitt responded. "On the other hand, if a lot of this was already in the works, maybe as contingency plans by the former Chalidang Emperor, then pushing it into action while you have momentum and to distract everybody from your wiping out the nobility, well, that makes sense. It would still take an extremely uncommon person to do this. What's the name of the new Empress, my lord? Do you know it?"

"Oh, yes. It is a name they are already cursing as doomed to make world history in a world that doesn't like history on that scale. The tongue is such that it wouldn't translate to us—sounds like a series of painful screeches, don't you know? But in Zone they say that the name coming in was Josich, a creature so mean and vile they had to shoot it and just send it through. They said it woke up in an incredible fury and got worse."

That's Josich all right, Tann Nakitt thought, but said nothing about it to the lord and lady, both of whom were now moving forward to oversee the stretchers taking off wounded and injured people to the limited medical facilities, hopefully to stabilize them for shipment to a high-tech land and ward, and to speak with some of the refugees and the ship's captain, who looked kind of like a giant scorpion with hair.

She knew Josich only by the incredible reputation and the stories and legends back home, but they paled in comparison to what had apparently taken place here. In little more than one year—*one year!*—Josich had killed a ton of her new kind, married the perfect puppet, wiped out the entire royal family, and co-mounted the throne. It hardly mattered that Josich was now an Empress and not an Emperor; hell, it probably was the only variety the son of a bitch had in centuries of war and revolution.

Had anyone ever succeeded in a war of conquest here on the Well World? Without access to history records, it was impossible to know, but it didn't seem as if it could be sustained. Even if the Well allowed it, you'd need to be like that ship out there—able to operate in all three mediums of technology and both underwater and on the ground, and preferably the air as well, and in climates probably ranging from desert to glacial, against races—hell, *civilizations*—born to those conditions and shaped by their original designers and by subsequent evolution to do it even better.

Tann Nakitt wondered how you'd conquer enough of the Well World to say you'd had it, and, when you did, how you'd hold it together over any measure of time. What kind of intervention might this great Well computer do if populations started going down dramatically in a Josich-style war?

Josich was an insane genius, and his relatives were probably much the same, but sooner or later there would be some kind of method in the rage, some kind of long-range objectives. She was already in top form; maybe it had already begun. What would be the prize here? And what would she do with it once she had it?

Still, it might well be all too easy for Josich the Emperor Hadun. These people could conceive of local conflicts but never a war of conquest. They had no officers, armies, joint commands, or training systems to hold back a tide once it reached a certain point, and few from the stars who could even explain to them what they lacked. Josich already had to have greater objectives in mind, particularly if the Empress knew how hard it would be to *hold* such an empire over time.

Although it would cause untold suffering and loss of pride and honor, the worst thing the other nations could do to her was not to fight but to surrender.

So you conquer the island nearby and the immediate ocean, and then maybe you spread out, and within a few years you have the whole ocean and maybe, just maybe, a continent or two. Then what?

The only thing in the whole Well World that Josich needed to fear, the only thing the old Emperor had feared back in the Realm, had at least followed him here. Tann Nakitt wondered if Josich knew. Probably. They would have those kind of records in Zone, although it wasn't clear how Josich would have had the sheer time to think of that. Sooner or later the new Empress would find out, though. Tann Nakitt didn't want to face down Josich, but she'd love to have a little viewing camera there when Josich, now the Empress Hadun, found out that Jeremiah Wong Kincaid was somewhere here, too, as single-minded in *his* dedicated objective as Josich was to hers . . .

By the gods, she just had *to get into this damned war somehow!*

Kalinda

ARI LOOKED AT THE PAGES OF CUNEIFORM-STYLE CHARACTERS and decided that he probably would never be able to learn it. Although it was actually printed by some kind of electro-magnetic process on a stiff sheet that obviously was imper-vious to cold saltwater, no two of the little squiggles looked alike to him. How were you supposed to even *start*? Not, of course, that he could read actual writing even back in the Realm, but very few people could or needed to. You talked to the computer, the computer talked to you. You wanted drama, it was performed holographically all around you. You wanted information, the best research systems in the universe were at your beck and call. There were even just readings, from fiction to news, with no pictures if you were on the move or had some time to kill. For most people, except historians, archaeologists, people like that, and others who might be dealing with primitive new races, there simply wasn't any use for it. It was like being skillful with a broad-sword. At one time that was a good way of staying alive and not becoming a victim. In the Realm it had been, at best, impractical, and at worse, highly messy.

This book, however, did have things of interest. For one thing, the numbers for some reason had stuck in his head. Interesting souvenir of that link, not nearly as odd as having Ming along for the ride, but useful. He could look at the map and count and then check the guide to the races of the Well against the numbers. Reading the descriptions was out of the question, but there were some impressive photos on metal that had a holographic look and feel, showing each race. A few questions of his ever-present police "associates," as they preferred to be called, as opposed to jailers—which they were—told him which race went with which number. He was impressed that just about all of the cops could read this stuff.

By now he'd had the history and briefing of what Josich and his cronies had already accomplished with the willing help of certain native rulers and races. It impressed him as it had impressed them, and made him understand all the more just why Kincaid had hunted them down for so long and so fanatically, and also why he hadn't yet succeeded in polishing the bastards off.

It had looked so simple when he had his first interview with Shissik. Debrief, get him together with this "other," find out what could be found out, then probably get them both jobs, although what jobs they could do without becoming literate that anybody from the Realm might enjoy doing wasn't clear. In fact, those faceless superiors had kept him away from them and the other and stuck in endless repetitive debriefings for months now, and basically assigning him menial tasks in and around the police building, never without escort. Finally they'd enrolled him in the equivalent of basic adult education classes, intended for people who either hadn't had much due to circumstances or who were still trying to figure out "big" and "little" in the flash cards. He'd learned a lot, including how to write and recognize his name, as well as day-to-day facts and even some history, but reading had so far completely eluded him. It was damned frustrating.

Take this basic kid's anthropology book, kind of "The Peoples and Lands of the World," local style. Gibberish. And it was supposedly at about a second grade level. Still, it was useful when you had some help; and because, even though they'd lightened up and loosened up considerably, he was never without some sort of "help," he at least could make some use of it.

The fact that Josich was building up along the western edge of the same ocean they were in made it imperative to know just what they were up against. Check that—he was one of *them* now, too.

Chalidang . . . Type 302. Good God! They looked like cuttlefish! Triangular-shaped creatures with huge but very Terran human-looking eyes and a face full of tentacles. The tentacles all seemed quite short, but he was assured that they were coiled up in the shell and that at least some of them could flash outward up to four meters in milliseconds. The suckers could secrete a paralyzing poison that worked on the vast majority of races that could absorb through the skin, and squirt a nasty fluid to get into eyes, nose, ears, ass, any opening, to achieve the same end with those races that couldn't be directly afflicted. Hydraulic jet propulsion could move the Chalidangers at incredible speeds as well, and selective natural jets allowed them to hover, rise, fall, or turn at angles that seemed impossible. Add to that the nasty weapons of their own design that attached to their extremely thick shells, and you had one mean batch of nasties.

"They're not much on sentiment, either," one of the cops assured him. "Kids who don't measure up to expectations don't tend to grow up. They're species-specific level one telepaths, which means they can't really read minds but exchange surface thoughts the same way you and I speak. They can also regenerate most anything. You can blow 'em away one by one if you can get them in the tentacle area, but you have to be able to drill a hole right through the eyes to get their brains and really take 'em out. Not easy when they can move like they do."

"You sound like you've already fought some of them," Ari noted.

"Not yet. But my sister was trade rep for us in Laskein. The Laskers got no love for 'em—they've had to live next door. There was a dispute over border rights to some minerals while she was there. Stupid little thing, but you say 'good day' to them wrong and they get insulted. Chalidangers, that is. Nasty little fight. The Laskers only got semi-tech, and they make sure they stay on their side, but over the eons they developed some stuff that can take out the 'Dangers. Got some nice volcanic steam vents and they harness the power really well. Steam-driven harpoons specially designed to bore into hard shells, that's what they shoot, at a speed the 'Dangers have a hard time seeing until it hits 'em. Sis says that when one of the shells is bored through, the thing goes nuts and spins in jet-propelled circles until the pressure and life bleeds out. 'Course, you kill a 'Danger, they got to kill more of you just to fulfill their code of honor. They'll do anything at all. Ugly people."

"And yet they have allies? How could anybody talk to them?"

"Oh, they talk fine. Like-minded folks and ambitious types. The Quacksans got that spooky hypnotic thing and a yen to raise their tech levels, and they breathe air and have a rocky terrain and the 'Dangers breathe water and just aren't designed for land, even to limits like we are. So them two get along just fine. All they need is an air force, so to speak, and they'll have perfect balance. Then watch out!"

It wasn't a pleasant thought. He turned some more pages, stopped at Type 41 and stared at it in surprise. Man and a woman, nicely built, in perfect condition, medium-brown complexion, kind of primitive-looking but very definitely relatives.

The sergeant in charge looked at the picture. "That your old people?"

"Sort of. I think we were related, anyway."

"They were nasty, too. No more conscience nor respect for other races than the 'Dangers. Invaded and slaughtered a lot of their neighbors to get farms when they screwed up their own land. The neighbors finally got together, gassed them back into the age of rocks, and forced them all to switch to the neighbors' nontech hex. Ain't amounted to nothin' since."

Yeah, that sounds like Terrans all right. Only we don't usually lose. "How long ago did that happen?"

The sergeant shrugged. "Who knows? It's way, *way* back in ancient history, I'll tell you. Just kind of a legend races like ours tell the kids as object lessons. It may or may not be true, but if we could ever work that kind of shit on the 'Dangers, we'd probably have another thousand years of peace."

Somehow Ari doubted it.

Many of the other races had familiar parts, or were familiar either from ancient mythology or even from his uncle's fabulous art collection. Half man, half horse—centaurs. Only these didn't look as fierce or as noble as the paintings and sculptures. Satyrs, nymphs, minotaurs, man-sized bat things, angels like in the religious pictures only with no clothes on, little fire-breathing dinosaurs, lots of others. It seemed half the myths and legends of the dozens of races of the Realm were represented here.

One caught his eye. Absolutely drop dead gorgeous young woman with good breasts, long hair, and from the waist down scales and a fish tail. Mermaids. Somehow he thought Kalindans were the mermaids.

"Nope. Those are Umiau," the sergeant informed him. "There's a kinda similarity, but there are some elements of some of us in ninety percent of the rest of us, it seems. They say some of the lower-level gods of creation didn't have such great imagination and did their stuff by stealing parts from the plants and animals and such from the ones already here or done. Could be. Depends on which race was first, I guess. *That* one's a mammal, though; don't let the scales fool you. Free breasts, real hair, no dorsal, much more similar to your old Type Forty-ones from the waist up and, if you look close, overall. Bear live young and nurse them. No intermediate pouch stage like ours. And no gills or similar stuff. They're air breathers, period. They don't even need to be wetted down much, but, of course, they're not really any more built for land than we are. They only got one sex, too. They don't change like us or have separate kinds like most others. They tend to hang around in shallows and even up in river mouths. They like fresh or brackish water best. They're from way up in the northwest corner of the Overdark; the whole hex is a flooded delta."

"You've been there? Or another sister got posted?"

The sergeant gave the Kalindan equivalent of a grin. "Naw, nothin' like that. Foreigners from that part of the world, they sometimes confuse us with them. Hard to see why when you compare the two."

The remark about Umiau hair being real was something he only recently learned about his own hair, and that of the rest of his new racial kindred. These translucent strands that could glow if he willed, or not if he didn't, were actually tendrils that exuded a nasty and painful series of acidic stings when in contact with living flesh other than Kalindan flesh. It may have served an evolutionary function once, but now it was mainly useful because wild things in the sea, or those things likely to be encountered in Kalinda, knew to avoid it and thus tended to leave Kalindans alone unless *really* hard up for a meal. The tendrils could also be made to exude an odor that smelled quite nice, and was individually distinctive, to Kalindans, but considered by most other species, intelligent and not, as one of the most noxious odors imaginable. More insurance that when you took a little swim you would be able to pick and choose your own company.

It was one of those continuing self-discovery facts, like the transparent eyelids. He hadn't noticed that in himself, but it became obvious once he was in company and in close quarters with others of his kind.

He was, however, beginning to feel as if he were abandoned and, if not forgotten, consigned to ward-of-the-state status and out of the swim of things. Too inconvenient for them, potential unknown, but at least he didn't seem to be a Hadun.

They even let him go topside once, to see the island and tour the large facilities there. If you didn't just materialize on the rocks, and if the weather was decent, they had little electric cars on nice little roads that were designed to carry Kalindans to and from the plant and exits to the sea, as well as in and around the plant and the rest of the island. Since crawling on your hands, dragging your body behind you, was the only alternative, it seemed very practical, once you got the hang of the semi-sidesaddle seat. The thing was, though, he was still basically a fixer and a kind of private detective completely out of his element no matter whether on land or sea.

What appeared to have doomed him from any better status was the very real reappearance of Ming Dawn Palavri.

She had always been there, sort of, and had surfaced for brief but confused periods when he'd daydreamed or sometimes in dreams or just when he woke up, but at the start this had all been new to him, and she'd had only those brief times. Now that this had dragged into weeks and months and the novelty was already well worn off, it would be Ari who went to sleep and Ming who woke up. There weren't any physical changes as such; that would take weeks under Kalindan biology, maybe longer. But the moves were different, the voice was different to a degree, and it began to spook the detail around him. He wasn't waking up during this period, either, and so had no idea what went on when she was dominant, a fact Ming discovered with some satisfaction.

At first they thought he was faking it or, worse, was

really crazy, but after they decided that this was in fact a second personality, they called the experts back in, which meant that Inspector Shissik traveled once more from the capital to Mahakor and waited around until she appeared. When she did, they notified him and brought her to the interrogation room.

Shissik had been frustrated in any attempts to bring the two newcomers together or to free either one from their ward status so that they could take whatever place in society they could manage and contribute. The politicians were too nervous to do it; it wasn't rational, but if you saw what appeared to be a well-organized and prepared nest of agent provocateurs show up and create revolution and war along a large area, you might well be excused, he knew, for not trusting anybody.

The female, though, was so very gentle, and so very different even from the male, that he felt certain there was no danger. He simply didn't have the authority to grant them freedom.

Now what was either a unique psychological condition, to Kalindans, a new wrinkle in newly processed aliens, or something to back up that incredibly wild story his superiors refused to credit as truthful, was just beginning to come to light.

Shissik was a trained investigator and one of the best interrogators in all the Interior Ministry, and before a word was spoken he knew that, while the body was the same, somebody else was now inside.

"I am Inspector Shissik. And you are . . . ?"

"I am called Ming Dawn Pa—*Palavri*. The last is my family name." She seemed to be distressed that she had problems getting that name out.

"You know where you are and what this is all about?"

"I have a good idea by now," she admitted.

"Do you remember any of my conversations with Ari Martinez?"

She shook her head. "No, not real ones. I saw this room and a guy like you over there like now, but it was like in a dream, and I could make out no words."

"How much do you remember?"

"Not much at all. I see me shot. I see—Ari—shoot me.

Then there is a time like a long, dark—" She paused, as if groping for words. "—bad dream where I can see things here and there but not as one, and then I just blank out."

"Do you feel complete? Mentally, that is?"

She thought about it. "No. There are holes. All sorts of things. Little things. Not just from the bad dream time, but way before, when I was a cop, and even stuff from my real life. It is like some of it just is not there. Like it has been— wiped out—by a flat black-and-white line art that kind of says what was once there, but gives no sense of *real*. Some of it is all gone. I—I have been told what they did to me, but that is a blank. I am not even sure I would like to know what it was like. To be—*owned*. To be owned and love it."

Shissik nodded to himself and jotted a few things down in his notes. "It is not unusual for someone who has been entirely subjected to another's will for a period to lose those things. The old personal feelings, personal memories and values, things that meant a lot to you but were irrelevant to the 'new' you, as it were, were either overwritten or filed away in what the brain uses for dead storage. Sometimes that storage can be retrieved when there is sudden stimulus, but I suspect not in your case. I think the dead storage was left when you sort of united with that computer. I think it's still back there."

That frightened her. A part of her, some of the most personal parts, gone? "And I just seem—slower. Less intuitive. I feel like I'm talking slower and looking for the right words. That, too?"

"Some of that can be because Ari considered the link-up a total genius working at the fastest imaginable speed. Coming back to normal might seem grindingly slow." He didn't mention the possibility that her emerging as mistress of the right brain and Ari master of the left brain might be part of it. Like Terrans, Kalindans—and many other species—had two halves to their brains. In the Kalindan case, according to the biology text, the brain was divided much like the Type Forty-ones. Just a comparison of how she talked, her problems in coming up with relatively simple terms for some things, was a textbook case of the sort he'd studied in brain-damaged victims. She was entirely in the right side of this body's brain. She clearly had a dominant left hand and left side; the right barely moved. She thought in pictures rather than words, and had to grope for verbal expression. He was surprised she had much of a vocabulary at all; it must have been how the stuff was stored up. Ari was over on the right side. He'd been right-handed almost to a fault. He'd been verbose, but totally incapable of interpreting or doing graphics. Sooner or later these two were both going to be awake and aware at the same time. He wasn't sure whether that meant cooperation or a mental lockup.

Still, laboriously, he got much of the story from her that overlapped Ari's long recorded themes and variations, and they did tend to confirm each other when they matched up.

Finally he asked her the big questions. "If you and Ari are both in the same body, do you think at some point you can come to terms with each other? The alternative is madness, you know."

"We must. It—It will be hard. He *did* shoot me, and when that bad dream was done to me, he did not do one thing to stop it. But I do not want to die, so I have to learn to live like this."

"Why do you want to live?"

"I want to see the faces of the ones who did that to us when they are caught or die. I want to stop them. If Ar—if *he* helps, he will be on the good side."

And the kicker. "What do you think would happen if you came face-to-face with this Jules Wallinchky again? Knew it was him no matter what he looked and sounded like here. Would you have to obey him? Would that programming and conditioning appear again?"

She had been mulling that over herself. "I—I do not know. I wish I did. I *hope* not." She paused a moment. "Do you *know* where he is? *What* he is?"

"Not yet. Right now we aren't even certain that he was still alive when he went through. We know pretty well where and what everyone else is. A couple have memory problems much worse than yours, although not two people in one body, so it's so far been impossible to match some to the names. Still, so far there is no unaccounted-for odd one. Either both you and Ari are truly in this body and count as two, in which case he is one of the ones with no memory, or he's someone and something we haven't come across yet. It is entirely possible that this could happen. At the moment, though, we have much more serious problems than finding everyone. We have every evidence that a nasty, wider war is building. It may well come our way. Until then, you two may have to work out your own truce."

Ming? Is that really you?

She had been sitting in the room that was a low security cell of sorts on the fifth level, staring out at the complex beyond through electrically charged bars, when she heard him in her mind.

She made no effort to speak aloud. *Yes, I think so. You are . . . ?* A holographic memory picture of Ari as he was came up.

Yes, it's Ari. This is—strange. I was linked up with you when you were one of Uncle Jules's grotesque creations, but this is you! This is a real person!

You made me into that thing. You shot me. You gave me to Jules.

Her stream of thought was clear but unusual, composed less of words than of a series of images. Images of actions, images of people old and new, images of startling if subjective quality. Clearly she could understand everything he or anyone else was saying, but her method of communication was almost entirely visual. With trouble she could create simple sentences, but he found he had to prompt her for her to properly think of certain words. Still, it was easy to have an exchange, and it certainly felt like her. Or sort of like her. She seemed to bubble with emotions, to use them in her communication as well. He understood them but didn't have that kind of intensity; in fact, he realized, he felt curiously cold and detached.

Still, they began a dialogue, one at the speed of thought, back and forth, simultaneous and intertwined, yet never synthesized into one. She had the right brain and a little bit of linkage to the left allowing very basic vocalizations; he had the left, and all the words and phrases and cold mathematical abilities that were both present and latent, and maybe some left over from the union with Beta.

Ming, I had no choice. I think I was just a more subtle version of what he did to you, only I didn't even know it. I

*hated what he did. You can see and feel that; I can't hide
much from you like this. I wanted none of it. I had to do it.
Look into me, check my memories such as they are, and you
will see that I'm telling the truth.*

Incredibly, to her, he *did* open up, drop virtually all the
barriers, let her poke and probe and look at memories and
feelings he'd had, the memories now stored throughout the
left brain. She found no evidence that his uncle had him
under that kind of control, but he certainly had some of it
implanted or he could never have been linked to Beta. If in
fact he had a transmitter and receiver in his old, original
head, he might well be telling the truth. Or it may not have
been necessary. He *believed* that it had been done to him,
though, and that was as good as she could expect.

She also found other things. Guilt over some of his actions, which suggested some free will, but whether he was
rationalizing or was enslaved and didn't realize it was beside
the point now. His genuine affection for her, his feelings
when he saw her after a year's absence on the *City of Modar*,
was more instructive. He'd actually been smitten by her; his
feelings of affection were undeniable. She'd never suspected
that depth in him for anybody, least of all her.

We are stuck with each other now, she noted.

More than if we were married, he agreed. *So now what do
we do? We're in a single body that needs both sides of us to
be whole, but I don't want it to be that way. I would much
rather that you had one body and I another and we could
still get this closeness. This is a chance to start anew, but
here we start as freaks.*

*Well, we cannot change what is. What do we do about it?
How do we live the rest of our life?*

*As partners. We can't do anything else. Partners, or we
die and be done with it. I would love to know, though, who
that other one they have is or was, and how much memory
and personality remains buried there.*

*I think the same. And where is poor Angel? Can she be the
other? We need to know. And we need to find your uncle. And
kill him.*

He gave a sigh that, oddly, came only out of the left side
of the mouth. *If we can,* he replied. *If we can . . .*

Ambora

JAYSU WAS NO LONGER EMPTY, NOR WAS HER LOYALTY AND devotion in the least bit questioned by her people. In the morning, after devotions, she would often be chosen to go to those readying for the dawn patrol, and fly with them as their blessing and messenger to the gods.

The people, too, now accepted her as an acolyte of the temple and loyal member of the clan, an orphan foundling who had been taken in and raised as one of them, with the Most Ancient God as father and the High Priestess as mother, and the other priestesses, adepts, and acolytes her sisters.

Like them, she had no doubts about their primacy among all the clans of Ambora, nor that their faith was the true one. She saw and felt the gods and spirits in all things, and acknowledged and accepted their power and primacy over all of them. They were to a one the willing servants of all the gods, and dependent upon them for all that was good. The prayers were always simple ones, for those the gods appreciated. For enough food so that all of the clan might eat and be in strength, for enough skill and faith so that no enemy might overcome them, for forgiveness from all sins, for health so that they could serve their gods and their clan, and for shelter against the night. Everything had a prayer of its own, everything had a power and a purpose.

Although the men could not fly, they did have some gifts from the gods that were uniquely theirs, including the music. Women could chant and intone tunes for the rituals, but the men composed and played music on harps of their own designs, and on flutes carved from the same reeds that, carved a different way, could be used as blowguns by the warriors.

She liked some of the men and particularly liked to listen to their music, but she'd felt no urge to mate. Some of the acolytes had done so and borne children, and it had been most wonderful and fascinating, but the more pleasurable it appeared to mate and to bear and raise children, the higher the value of the sacrifice. She had seen the gifts the Grand Falcon bestowed on the High Priestess, and felt that her calling and destiny lay in that direction.

This in fact disappointed the High Priestess, who didn't want to face the possibility of training Jaysu in the higher levels. It involved a great deal of prayer and fasting, ordeals and rituals that could drive one to the brink of madness and exhaustion, and it also involved drugs that did terrible things to the mind. Many died in that kind of training; the others went mad. Only one would do it.

The High Priestess knew that Jaysu could make it; her abilities and devotion were so absolute, it was a thing of awe. But what, if anything, was still in Jaysu's mind, buried so deep down that it could not be reached by normal methods? The High Priestess concurred with the Grand High Priestess in Zone and those with whom the Most Holy had spoken to there. She was told that Jaysu was probably one of the two women, subsequently identified by interviews with the others as Angel Kobe, a onetime acolyte of some other alien religion. It fit nicely with her personality and devotion to assume this.

But might that old faith emerge and conflict with the new and destroy her?

Worse, what if they were wrong and she wasn't this Angel Kobe? And what sort of monster might the process create in either case?

The High Priestess would have liked to put off the decision, but knew she could not. The gods of the volcanoes were restless; many troubles were coming for the clan from that score. Worse, all that she took to attain and maintain herself in this high position for so long had taken a grave toll. The pain was now there more often than not, and it was getting harder to find anything strong enough to deal with it. The Most High had sent her special drugs from other hexes that helped a great deal, and upon which she was now

absolutely dependent, but even they had less effect as the days
and weeks and months went by.

She was dying. And the pain would rise to levels she
couldn't control at some point. When that happened, she
would go to the cliffs, pray to the setting sun to receive her
spirit, and jump.

Flying was one of the things you had to sacrifice to
become a High Priestess, and while fishing was part of the
lifestyle, none of the Amborans swam very well.

Now she sat in the Inner Chamber, where none other
could come, inside the Circle of Fire, facing the Grand
Falcon herself, as only a High Priestess could do. After days
of prayer and fasting and little sleep, and ingesting special
drugs and potions, she was ready to take even more years
off her life by diving the patterns. She understood that these
were not preordained, but mere possibilities, but they tended
to prove out more often than not. They could answer questions no other could answer, and give keys to the future that
might well save her people.

The High Priestess swayed to a rhythm only she could
hear, surrounded by the steam vents and sulfuric gases of
the Inner Chamber, her sight failing as she took the last and
strongest of the potions, which would almost certainly kill
anyone not prepared for it. She screamed as it burned its
way down and seemed to consume her body and even her
very soul in a white-hot fire.

But out of that fire and out of the mists came visions.
Visions formed inside and with the mists and gases, but primarily within her own mind.

What she saw in those visions were monsters.

Monsters of the sea, rising up, engulfing all that their
giant tentacles could grasp. She saw two long, sticky tentacles shoot out like a tree frog's tongue and snare low-
flying birds and Amborans and other flying races as well.

Monsters of the land; huge translucent, sluglike creatures
without even mouths to eat, moving slowly, ponderously,
over land and through forests and up and down rocks, leaving slime as they went, absorbing any animal and most
plant life they contacted, then slowly dissolving them inside
themselves while the prey was still alive but helpless. Drawing larger prey to them by saucerlike eyes that seemed to

swirl in patterns and radiate an eerie dance for the eyes of others that you could not avoid, drawing you in, making you walk directly into them without even knowing until you were inside that jellylike flesh . . .

She watched them come out of a boiling dark sea and horrible black skies filled with storms and violence, coming out of the west and covering nation after nation, hex after hex, until the Overdark was not merely a name but a description.

And at the heart of that darkness, something totally evil, something that looked like the tentacled ones but was not; something alien and awful, the enemy of light and the source of all madness. An entity so awful that it was willing, even eager, to take on and massacre even the gods themselves.

Bodies . . . all over, the blood and the screams of the dying everywhere, and even the volcanoes obeyed the darkness . . .

Surely this was not the future! Surely this was not the end of all things! The apocalyptic vision was so horrible that she refused to accept it.

And something seemed to whisper to her, not in words, but in flashes of inspiration and understanding.

Until now, life has been service to the gods and spiritual development of the soul. That time is past. This is what you were preparing for, although you did not know it. Now there is only one task, to fight the evil, to stop it, to crush it. Those who do may die. Those who do not will have fates worse than death.

"But *how*?" she screamed. The pain! The pain was growing as unbearable as the visions, and she dared not yet pass out! "What can Amborans do in this fight against such power?"

But in response came only a riddle. *The Avenger must strike the blow that is the reason for his existence. The Avenger can strike only when the five are one through the North, and when all are willing to pay the price . . .*

There was one last brief vision, of the investiture of Jaysu as High Priestess, just one brief glimpse, and it was gone. The priestess didn't even have the time to plead for more information, for more detail. She passed out, and for many hours, alone on the platform, she lay there as the radiation and fumes did their worst to her and her body struggled with the poisons that gave both wisdom and pain.

When she finally awakened, it was to a body still in pain, but a different sort of pain, in which every joint and muscle in her body ached. She could not see; that last encounter had robbed her of what was left of her failing eyesight. Still, she managed to find her staff of office and use it to rise, and with memory of a place she knew better than any other, and the cues of heat and loud, rushing steam, she managed to make her way off the platform, past the veil, through the small maze and into the great room of the cave.

There was momentary shock from the priestesses there, some of whom had been keeping vigil and sympathetic prayer and fasting rituals for two days. Then they heard gasps and rushed to help her.

Jaysu was among them, feeling deep guilt for having involuntarily passed into sleep several times in the past few hours, but then just concerned for their Holy Mother, the only mother she remembered.

A mother who had been pretty if middle-aged when first they'd met only a year earlier, and who looked not much different when she'd gone into the Inner Chamber, but emerged old and wrinkled and wizened, blind and partly deaf, and barely recognizable to any of them.

They carried her to her chamber, where she was propped up on soft pillows and allowed to lie on her side. They watched, fearful that she would die at any moment, but after passing into a trancelike sleep, the High Priestess awoke and said, in a weak, low, old woman's voice, "I do not have much longer."

"Please, Mother, you must rest," Gayna, one of her most senior adepts, said. "We can talk later."

"No! We must speak now. I do not know how much time I have, and if I do not speak, then all this was for nothing! There is a great evil coming, and soon, from the west. An evil that will destroy all our people, our whole race, unless we become its mindless slaves. The Blessed Grand Falcon showed it to me, at great price, yet I would rather be like this than to not have seen and so be consumed by it!"

"Oh, no, Mother!" they began crying, but she silenced them with a contemptuous wave of her hand.

"Stop it! There will be enough anguish and tears in the tribulations to come! This is an evil as powerful as any god we know. This is an evil force so incredibly foul that it dreams of taking on the God of Gods itself!"

They all gasped. It was inconceivable to any of them that anyone would think they could take on and then win against the God of all Gods who lived in the center of the world.

"Can any such force exist that could actually do this?" Jaysu asked her, coming closer.

The old priestess nodded. "Yes, my child. Others have found a way into the Seat of the God who is behind all things, who sits at the center of the Well of Souls and decides all. Most have been thwarted by gods who appear to save us all in those times, but I feel no such god who can walk the entire world and commune with the God of Gods is here. There is an ancient legend of one party that entered, but discovered that even though they saw the whole of creation and its powerful linkages, they could not know what they were doing nor who they would destroy and were thus stopped. This one, though, does not care. This one would have no problems in blowing out the stars, in wiping out all life but its own and recreating all in its own foul image. It is here to destroy the very Well of Souls and proclaim itself the one true god. Whether it can do so is beside the point; it can make the whole of our race, not just our clan, less than a memory, and it can do the kind of evil that none but it could dream of."

"But surely the most holy Grand Falcon and all the gods and spirits will combine against it!" another said, horrified. "Or the One Behind It All shall raise or summon a champion!"

"No! We have been given the task of dealing with this one ourselves! All that we have studied, believed, become, and all that any other races have become, is to this purpose. Our people who are now divided must unite. The Grand High Priestess knows this. Trust her counsel and her judgment. We must learn not to be clans, but to be a nation and one of many nations."

They were shocked, stunned, and confused by all this, but they were at least listening.

"Jaysu?"

"Here, Mother!"

"You will remain with me. All others must leave. I have visions which concern Jaysu alone."

"But Mother—" Gayna said, objecting.

"Do you not hear? Gayna, you must accept what the Grand Falcon has decided, just as I must also obey. If you do not, then your faith is nothing, your life is nothing, and all that you believe is hollow. Go!"

Gayna didn't accept the logic and didn't want to go, but with a sulking expression and with the others eyeing her, she had no choice but to leave. The others followed, leaving only the dying priestess and the new acolyte.

Jaysu knelt down and drew close to the wizened High Priestess, fighting to hold back tears. It was so awful to see her like this!

"Help me to a kneeling position facing you," the High Priestess commanded. "Hurry, child!"

Jaysu helped the old woman up, then knelt facing her, almost nose-to-nose. The old woman reeked of sulfur and other chemicals, but it didn't matter.

"Gayna believed that she was to be High Priestess after me," the old one said, knowing that Jaysu already understood as much. "She will not take kindly that I pass the staff and authority to one who was not born and raised here."

"Then do not give it to me!" Jaysu cried. "I do not want it! I would follow Gayna as I follow you!"

"But she would not follow you as she follows me, and that is why she is not worthy. The Grand Falcon allowed me the vision. It is her choice, not mine, that you succeed me. I can no more object or disobey than I can deny my own responsibilities and my life! Nor can you, precisely *because* you are worthy of the task. I had wondered why you were sent to us, and why as an empty vessel, a blank slate, but now I know. Your innate spirituality shines through. I am convinced that you were sent to us to save our people. Many of the visions, the nightmares, I am going to place as a stain on your soul will repulse you, but so, too, will I transfer the riddle and enigma that are entwined with hope. You must find the meaning, but I am certain they are meant for you." She reached down into a basket near her bed without bothering to look, being unable to see it anyway, and brought out a vial with a waxy seal across it. "Is this vial red and violet in color?"

"Yes, Mother, it is."

Wizened, clawed hands pried at the seal, then broke it and lifted it up, then tossed it aside. "I had wondered if this was a wise thing to do. Now I know it was what I was supposed to do." She drank from the vial, shuddered, and held it out. "Drink what remains."

Jaysu took the vial, hesitated a moment, then drank it. It was fiery on the way down, yet had a sweet aftertaste. Within a minute she could feel its effects flowing through her veins, giving her a sense of enormous well-being.

Ancient hands came out and grasped her head, and she found herself doing the same, until their mouths met in a near lover's embrace. Their wings extended all the way out, until the muscles ached from being drawn so far forward that the wingtips of each touched.

Jaysu felt a jolt of electricity that stunned her, and then the whole world seemed to drop away and she had no thoughts, no control. She was in a dream of sorts, locked in an embrace that was all sensual, all emotional, with no thought on her part.

This culminated with a massive orgasm unlike anything she had imagined, and then there was a deep sleep filled with visions, some wonderful, some quite ordinary, some terrifying. But all these dreams and nightmares had in common someone, *something*, whispering something over and over again, and only to her.

The Avenger must strike the blow that is the reason for his existence. The Avenger can strike only when the five are one through the North, and when all are willing to break the bonds and pay the price . . .

When she awoke, she found the High Priestess was nothing more than a wizened corpse, almost mummified, looking grotesque in repose. A huge pile of feathers had fallen from her outstretched, stiffened wings, and it seemed there was no fluid in her tiny-looking body.

Jaysu felt incredibly saddened and humble all at once, yet realized that the sadness was because she would not be with the Mother again.

She was soon to discover, though, that this wasn't precisely the case.

She walked out from the High Priestess's chambers to see

the others standing there, waiting worriedly. Gayna appeared less worried than resentful, but held it in.

"Our Mother has passed on and is carried by the Great Falcon to the Well of Souls," Jaysu announced. "We must prepare her body for the public farewell. Zida, you will blow the great conch and announce this to the people. Someone else must travel to the Center and go to the Gathering Place and inform the other clans and the Grand High Priestess."

Although they had all suspected it, there were still many tears and even sobs from the eleven priestesses who comprised the clergy of the clan.

"Who will go to the Gathering?" Jaysu asked them. "It must be done quickly, out of respect."

"Why don't *you* go?" Gayna asked curtly. "We have spent our lives devoted to her. You came from outside the clan and have been here but a year."

She expected that. "Because the Holy Mother commanded me not to, and because I have other things I must do here. If you truly loved her and understood her teachings, you will not dishonor her now, particularly not *now*, with pettiness and infighting. Like you, I swore an oath of absolute obedience. I am carrying out that oath."

A couple of the other priestesses didn't seem to like Jaysu's take-charge attitude, either; she had never been particularly popular, especially after the High Priestess took her in and so highly favored her over her old acolytes. Still, they looked at one another and then at the surly Gayna, and one of them, Azia, said, "In this she is correct. Let us ensure her proper return to the Well. Then we may speak of other things."

It wasn't the sentiment Gayna had in her heart, but it was not something she could fight. She nodded, postponing the clash between them.

Still, it was a difficult next day. The ceremonies, rituals, and sacrifices had to be carried out within one full day of a death, which required coordination among the priestesses, and somebody had to oversee it. Jaysu tried to accommodate the others by letting them do much of the work, particularly the wrapping of the body, but only one could lead the prayers and carry the staff to the great pit, and Jaysu made certain that she alone kept the staff in her possession. Thus she alone led the prayers and chants to the dead, and led the procession that walked, did not fly, along the ancient trail to the Pit That Always Burns. As the other priestesses lifted up the surprisingly light body wrapped in its funerary ware, it was Jaysu who pronounced the spells and sacred words and gave the signal that bade them tilt the board so the body slid from it and down toward the bubbling red and black surface of the volcanic pit.

For a moment the High Priestess appeared to be flying once more, then she crashed against the hot but solidified rock floating on the lava layer, again seemingly on her own as the slab shifted. Then a stab of red separated the crust from the rest and slowly began to remelt what had just formed, eventually reaching and covering the body, which the churning molten lava turned back into the elements from which it had once come.

Now the warriors spread their wings and took to the air, flying in ritual procession around the pit and then off into the darkening skies. Now, too, the priestesses took wing and flew the same pattern, but then headed back toward the lava cave and its shrine. Most continued their devotions there, the period of fasting and mourning lasting yet two more days, but one at least had to always be on duty to perform those things that the job entailed for the people, and another to follow the prescribed rituals of the temple itself.

Jaysu went into the High Priestess's chambers once more, feeling as if she would be meeting the now departed occupant but knowing she would not. Though she didn't know why she was there, once inside she made for the small jars and potions and began to apply colorful ceremonial paints to her face and body. When done, she had virtually covered all parts that were not feathered, and looked a fearsome sight. She emerged then, walking past the others and out onto the platform, and took a kneeling position facing the village, grasping the old High Priestess's staff of office with both hands as she meditated and prayed, swaying back and forth. No one who saw her could break her concentration, and most feared to do so. Jaysu remained like this, in full view of both her fellow priestesses and the village, until sundown of the third day of mourning, when there was the fluttering of wings, and Macwa, who had been sent to the Center, landed on the platform and regarded her swaying form with puzzlement.

Jaysu then got painfully to her feet, her knees chapped and bloody from the swaying on the rocks. "All of the others are notified?" she asked, her voice barely functional after not drinking anything for almost thirty hours. She was dehydrated and on the brink of starvation, but refused to allow it to affect her.

"Yes. They were not surprised. I do not understand this. It was as if they all, everyone, *knew*."

"They did. The notification was purely formal." She arose and used the staff as a cane to get her inside.

Most of the others were there, and looked surprised when she entered, followed by Macwa. Now all were staring at Jaysu, some in fear.

"What is it?" she demanded of them. "Why do you look on me so?"

"You—You *glow*," one of the priestesses responded for them all.

She herself could not see it, but all the others could. It had begun only in the last few moments, but as she moved among them it grew stronger and could not be denied as a real phenomenon.

All around her a soft golden light shimmered, beginning centimeters over her skin and feathers and extending out in a series of connective golden rays for perhaps five centimeters, but ending irregularly and thus giving the sense of a burning aura. Jaysu looked at her hand, pressing on the staff, and saw a barely perceptible milky sheen. It was odd, but clearly they were seeing far more.

She managed to sink down, not on her sore knees but on her side, and on impulse priestesses ran about, one getting a thin, sweet drink that was high in sugar to help her, another bringing light cakes that were supplemental staples along with the fish and meat. Jaysu accepted them graciously, and though having difficulty getting them down, forced herself, knowing she needed to get something inside her to live.

"How do you feel?" Macwa asked, tired herself but in awe of the glowing priestess and the total fast she'd obviously been on.

"Strange," Jaysu responded. "Light-headed, but that may

just be the fast. I have grown incredibly thin. Both exhausted and highly energized, as if there was a power within me, a power I do not understand and do not have the training to use. I fear I have been chosen to become that which I neither desired nor sought, and for which I am most unworthy and, too, unqualified. This—aura. You have not seen it on anyone before?"

"No, never," Macwa responded, and the others nodded or muttered their agreement.

"Well, I shall sleep now, perhaps a long sleep. Let us see if these things are still there when I awaken. Thank you, my sisters. Thank you all."

She was out cold in moments, and remained unconscious for two more days.

During that time rumors spread of her devotion and her mark of the gods, and much was made of it. Within the priesthood, a majority of priestesses decided it proved that the Grand Falcon desired her to be the next leader of the clan. While Jaysu slept, they hand bathed her, kept her forehead moist, and shifted her and propped her here and there, very gently, to ensure she did not hurt herself.

She had a fever, and when it broke her color seemed stronger and the aura, if anything, more brilliant. Too, after the fever broke, her knees healed with remarkable speed. Within hours all the scabbing and bruising was gone.

Gayna was not impressed. "It's all trickery!" she insisted to any of her sisters who would listen. "Just potions and either great ambition or just ignorance."

"You studied at the highest levels of alchemy," one of the others pointed out. "What potions or drugs could cause the glow?"

She was stumped, but didn't admit it. "Who knows what was in that stuff she mixed? We all know that much of what we do is for show, to keep and hold the faithful. I don't know how she found this, but, new or not, it is no godlike blessing. What is more suspicious is that our Mother died while only she was there, and, although in bad shape, she was not as we found her only minutes later, wizened and drained of all fluids."

"You're not saying she—" They were aghast at the mere suggestion.

"I say nothing of the sort," Gayna responded cleverly. "What I *do* say is that we do not know where she came from. Our Mother once said to me that she believed Jaysu was an alien creature from the stars, changed by the Well and reincarnated. How do we know that she has no memories? How do we know they did not return? How can we know that she is not in fact one of those monsters in reincarnated flesh that are now ravaging the far end of the great ocean? Could any of us have endured the ordeal she just subjected herself to? Would any of us still survive it? Perhaps now the alien spirit inside is come to the fore, and through blasphemous miracles and mock piousness intends to lead all of our people into slavery or slaughter. Don't you see? High Priestess here, then after a while a visit to the elderly Grand High Priestess, another sad demise, and where are our people then?"

"I for one do not believe it!" Azia, one of the fence sitters up to now, exclaimed. "I have flown with her and prayed with her and I do not believe she is capable of these things! It is *you* who are spouting blasphemies here!"

Gayna smiled. "Yes? And *you* are so certain, with *no* doubts, that you would risk all our clan, perhaps all our people, on your—intuition? Would *you*, sisters? I say we simply cannot take the chance."

"And who would be raised as High Priestess in her place?" Macwa challenged. "I do not believe that you yourself are exhibiting any faith in the gods and spirits to whom we have pledged our lives. You are saying they would deliver us into the hands of a monster? If they would, then perhaps we deserve it. I do not believe it. I have been at the palace of the Grand High Priestess; I have spoken with the worldly priestesses and their trusted agents in the Gathering Place. There is a darkness coming, there *are* alien monsters in the flesh of beings native to here, but in every case they have infected races that were already evil and already had these horrors. They called down the evil on themselves, as we could as well! But we do not call on evil. Our god is good and just. If you believe we serve the Grand Falcon, then you must have faith that She has chosen what is right and good as always. Or are you saying that the god we follow, the god our

Mother followed, the god we pledged to suffer and die for, is false and powerless?"

Gayna saw the trap, and that there was no gracious way out. "I accept all that you say," she responded carefully, "but I also point out that we are given a choice here. Native born, a lifetime of devotion, no fancy tricks, what you see is what you get, or one who may be a demon. With the alien evil coming, with us possibly being called to face it, perhaps we are now being judged whether we are worthy of being saved. This is, perhaps, what our Mother was training us to face. Have you thought of *that*?"

They hadn't, but the seed of doubt planted by Gayna gave them pause, and for a moment there was silence.

Suddenly, and to everyone's shock and surprise, Jaysu walked into the room carrying the staff. She glowed brightly, looked remarkably fit, and was staring at Gayna. "So, a meeting of the sisterhood? Am I not one of you?" She paused. "Or is that what this meeting is deciding?"

"You are one of us," Gayna responded, "but the question is whether or not you are the best one to lead us. You yourself know that your training at the higher levels is minimal. Your knowledge of rituals, prayers, spells, and potions is not sufficient to manage the whole of the High Priestess's responsibilities, and by your own admission your knowledge of what goes on beyond our clan boundaries is next to nothing. Even you admit you do not know your origins or the true nature of your spirit. I just do not believe you are qualified, and I say so in love and fellowship."

Jaysu suppressed a smile. "Very well. I agree with most of your points, although I know more than you believe. I seem to have some sort of—power. I cannot explain it. But when I look at potions, their names and purposes and composition are instantly available to me. When a ritual is proper, it comes to me, it consumes me. And while I knelt out there during the period of mourning, it seemed that all the High Priestesses, all of those now of the clans, and many who have passed on, were with me, teaching me. Still, I will not lead any who lack faith in me. I cannot. Any who cannot accept me as their Mother must challenge my right, and leave if they cannot do so should their arguments lose. We are not warriors. I will not battle for this, and I have too much faith to debate it. If the sisters are not willing to place their faith and minds and bodies at my bosom, then someone else who can command this should be chosen. And, in that case, sister, you must realize that with our polarized followings, we must *both* step aside and accept someone who is undoubtedly and universally acknowledged as guided entirely by faith. I therefore suggest that we lay our doubts aside and select someone, perhaps Azia here, who has been guided in these matters only by faith and her own heart."

Gayna knew she could not argue with this, and yet was too infuriated to agree. She reached to her neck, pulled off the beads that identified her priestly function and rank, and threw them on the cave floor. Then she glowered at the others. "Mark me well! I have spent my *life* in preparation for the work you now so callously throw away to an—an *alien creature*! I have studied rigorously, and denied myself all pleasures of the flesh. And *this* is how my life, my devotion, is repaid! I curse you! I curse all of you! I shall be gone with the sun!"

And with that she walked out, leaving them silent, and some of them stunned.

Finally Azia said, "I believe we have been given our answer. I, for one, will pledge all that I have to Jaysu and call only her my Mother from this moment on. Who will bare her neck and kiss the feet of their Mother as I shall do?"

There was some hesitancy, but before long the rest of the priestesses all did so, even those who had originally stood with Gayna.

"I feel very sad for Gayna," Jaysu told them when it was done. "Her knowledge and skills would be most valuable to us, and it saddens me to see someone of such devotion leave with such a stain left on her spirit. Those of you who are her friends please try and seek her out tonight and minister to her and try and bring her back to the fold. I fear for her if you fail."

"It will be done, Mother," several responded.

"I shall introduce myself to the Grand Falcon," she told them. "If she disapproves of your choice, then Gayna will be all the easier returned to our fold."

But the Grand Falcon did not disapprove. Jaysu entered the Inner Chamber, where none but a High Priestess could go, and saw for the first time the grand and ancient inner chapel with its whooshing fumaroles, sulfurous jets, bubbling multicolored mud pots, and, facing the altar, the huge and awesome idol of the Grand Falcon, whose form was Amboran perfection but whose face was that of a great and powerful bird's.

And before she was even proclaimed to the assembled clan, her tail feathers began to fall out, and she began to molt, with old feathers falling away to be carefully saved and used in rituals. Within a month she had a new set of bright white wings that lacked sufficient power and lift for her to actually fly. The aura remained and continued to strike awe and reverence in all her flock, but while she looked very much the angel now, she would never fly again.

In fact, her grand and beautiful appearance, and the added wonder of the aura, which was even visible in bright daylight, if lessened, made the clan feel they had been singled out, that they were indeed the clan of clans, the highest of all the clans of Ambora.

Meanwhile, after Gayna stalked out of the assembly of the priestesses, she could not be found. Inquiries to other nearby clans brought no clue, either. Many feared she had killed herself. Others believed she had exiled herself beyond Ambora, although exactly how and where was not known.

The ceremony of investiture was a grandiose one, held one month to the day after the death of the old High Priestess, in front of the entire assembled clan and with many high-ranking members of other clans attending. It was three days of joy and feasting, although also a great religious show as well. Even the Grand High Priestess had come, borne by four strong warriors of four different clans upon a grand bamboo platform designed for the purpose. While Jaysu had been functioning as High Priestess since the night she was elected by her peers, she only now was officially so. She was no longer Jaysu, but Holiness to the flock and Mother to the priestesses. She already seemed to radiate the confidence and power of the old one, and the same sort of radiance the others from the other clans who could attend also had, perhaps even stronger.

Now the High Priestesses met, alone, for the first time as

equals and without anyone else present, on the evening before they were to journey back to home.

The Grand High Priestess looked at them, and at their newest member, and came straight to the point.

"There is going to be a grand council in Zone," she told them. "It will be like nothing in any living memory. The last time one was held was to face down the threat of an earlier empire now lost in legend. If one looks over the great and long history of this world as it is recorded in the grand libraries of the nation Czill, repository of this knowledge and existing for it, we see that there have been many crises over the millennia. Evil ones have come with the keys to the Well of Souls, but the Well has summoned the watchers to deal with them time and again. But when it is *conquerors*, when the evil is native grown, even if nurtured and encouraged by those from Beyond, there is no call. Then it is up to us. We do not know or understand the logic of it, but we are certain of this. The evil that spreads now in one area will begin to march out, perhaps within a year. Much of the plans and preparations were already under way; the evil that came to infect them further only has the skills and experience to know just how to use them to best advantage. It cannot be reasoned with. It cannot be dealt with. It desires only absolute power. It only *understands* power. It arose once somewhere in the stars, and, somehow, at great loss, they beat it back. Now it has been chased here. Now we must do the same."

"How will it come?" one of them asked her.

"By sea, by ship, by any means necessary. It does not march, it *engulfs*. By the time it reaches here, they will probably have subjugated and turned a flying race or two as well. They would like to engulf and turn us as well for that very reason. There is no hope of us fending them off alone, not with all the power of our gods. They, too, have gods of the most horrible sort. For the first time in our history we will have to ally with each other and with other races as well. Otherwise we either perish or, far worse, become another part of *their* army. I should like four of you to come with me to the Grand Council as my staff, one from each of the cardinal points, so that you may then deliver the news and decisions to the others nearby. I will talk to everyone before this is done. The one from this western district will be the High Priestess of the Grand Falcon."

Several others gasped, and a lot of pride was wounded. The new High Priestess felt like she was going through the Gayna business all over again.

The surprised reaction was soon silenced by the Grand High Priestess. "I choose her not because she is new, but because this clan territory directly faces the westernmost point of land in Ambora and is very likely to be a target for them before any others, first in attempts to weaken, demoralize, and undermine, then to invade. It would not matter who was High Priestess for the Grand Falcon. Whoever it was, she would be my choice."

That cut them short, at least for now.

"Most High, when do you wish me at your side?" Jaysu asked the older woman. "I am new enough here that I feel as if I will be deserting them before they are even used to me."

"The council takes some preparation, and we feel we have some time. Plan on six weeks from today to begin your journey to me. Use the gate at the Center. It will bring you to me instantly, and return you there when done. I assume you can get transport of some kind from here to there and back? I, too, do not want you away any longer than you have to be."

"I can do it, Most High. But surely one of the others, the Frog to the north or the Rodent to the south, would be equally likely targets and would serve as well, and they are both more experienced than I."

"Enough!" the Grand High Priestess snapped. "It is decided!" And that, of course, was that.

It was not necessary that she explain her actions, and the Grand High Priestess had no desire to show weakness by doing so. It might not ever be necessary for any of them to know that the new High Priestess had been specifically requested.

Ochoa

It was hell to have to get most of the news and information second- or thirdhand, but Tann Nakitt did what she could. Maybe she didn't have a translator and might never afford one, but you would have thought that the crew of these big international ships would all have them, she thought sourly.

They didn't, though. Only the officers and some of the mates were so outfitted. It made things simpler when things got rough. You might desert if you could speak all the languages and negotiate your way home and onto other ships, but you wouldn't be much of a risk if the only others who could understand you were those who spoke the nautical shorthand language developed over thousands of years for the crews, and your own, often unique tongue which others might not even recognize as a language.

Nakitt could still remember Ghoman, which was even *less* useful here than on, say, the *City of Modar*, and the Realm's standard commercial language, which might help if she ever encountered one of those who got here the same way she did. On the other hand, she thought automatically in Ochoan now, a language so unlike the other two that none who didn't have the right physical equipment in the throat, which meant being of the Ochoan race, could hear it as more than grunts, growls, squeeks, clicks, and squawks.

Anyway, the officers tended to deal only with the nobility like His Lordship, and the mates dealt with the heads of the stores and senior trade representatives, such as there were here, and not at all with the common folk who were always flitting around, asking a million questions and just generally getting in the way.

More than once she considered stowing away, perhaps after the great ships were well out to sea, but there were a lot of grim tales of such stowaways being worked like slaves then tossed overboard before the next port, and while most were exaggerations and many were doubtless fanned by shipping companies, there were the occasional really rotten crews, so you couldn't tell for sure. Tann Nakitt knew that the best con men were the ones you'd embrace and then buy dinner and toast their good health even when they were stealing you blind.

Hell, in reverse circumstances, that's what *she'd* do.

In a sense, that was the real problem with this new race, new life, new future. Not where or what, but the fact that Tann Nakitt had been born and raised a Ghoman, and had felt real pride and a sense of belonging because of that. You might lie, cheat, and steal *for* Ghoma, and you might even do it to alien races for the fun and profit of it, but you didn't do that to your own people. After living years of the crooked but quite pleasant life, Nakitt had been asked by his people to put his unique talents to patriotic use, and it had been done almost without thinking, almost as a way of justifying being a con artist and general scoundrel. Maybe the gods of Ghoma had steered this course in their service. Now that was gone. Even if she were to somehow return to the Realm, she'd not only not be a Ghoman, she'd not be related to any known race or world. Oh, there was probably an Ochoan world there someplace in the vast universe, but that, too, wouldn't be the same.

And if that was taken from her, what was left? Only the scoundrel.

Haqua and Czua, on the other hand, she *had* grown very fond of, but what was their future? They didn't even have any of the worldly experiences of a Tann Nakitt, nor know of other worlds and what it was like to be someone, something, else. There was still something within the newcomer that they found attractive, though; a confidence and arrogance that usually radiated from males. It wouldn't last, though. Hormones would win out during the mating season, if not the forthcoming one then the next. Nobody stayed unmarried here. Biology and the system both worked too much against it. Worse, as orphans of no clear bloodline, they were doomed to be low ranking wives, the kind that did the work and got little of the rewards.

"So, Nakitti, what were you doing over on High Katoor?" Czua asked her. "I saw you there by the forest." High Katoor was an island up the chain, perhaps five kilometers away, lush but essentially uninhabited. Where it wasn't too high to be comfortable, it was too overgrown, and far be it that the Ochoans would stoop to actually developing such a place.

"I was mixing drugs and poisons," Tann Nakitt responded matter of factly.

"You weren't! Come. What were you *really* doing over there?"

"Having secret romantic trysts with my countless boy toys," he replied in the same tone. In fact, he'd answered her query fairly truthfully the first time. She'd been using her old knowledge of chemistry, particularly biochemistry, and matching it with information on drugs and poisons gleaned from the bored keepers of the various ship's berths in the chain, and with old political hands among Ochoans who were delighted to tell much of their knowledge of what did what to whom. Some of it was pure old wives' tales and folklore, but others had clear effect and were actually used in medicines and various treatments the same way a doctor might prescribe a headache pill in a more progressive nation. So much of poisons were part of folk medicines, and this knowledge was always passed down to those with an aptitude for it. Though hardly an expert yet, she had made some rather remarkable discoveries about various plants and mineral combinations here.

"Oh, very well! If you will not tell, you will not. Did you see the two ships come in this morning before dawn?"

"I saw them after they docked, yes," Nakitt responded. "More refugees, more sad faces, more evidence of war in the west. What is most upsetting is that the traffic seems one way. They are coming from the west to the east through us. That implies that trade in the eastern Overdark is just about at a standstill, or at least relegated to the coastal trade. This Josich and his family are unbelievably fast and efficient."

"But it is so far away from here. What is it to us?"

Tann Nakitt looked back out at the ocean in the distance and took a deep breath. "We too lightly follow easy gods of good and plenty," she commented philosophically. "We even celebrate the rogues and rascals now and then, the gods of drink and revelry. We dismiss evil as a simple mental disorder. 'Oh, he had an abusive mother,' or 'Oh, she had her brains scrambled by drugs,' and we excuse the most terrible of behaviors as simply excesses of what we know. Believe it, girl. There *is* true evil. Not merely as a counter to good and as some kind of relative moral judgment we can adjust up or down to suit our moods—*real* evil, existing for its own sake."

"You are scaring me now."

"I am scared myself, and for good reason. I've seen faces like those in the ships before, and I know that if those faces exist here, this far away from the horror, then what is happening back there is almost beyond our imagining. But that's no devil or demon out there; it's no bad god or nasty spirits. They are flesh and blood, the worst kind of evil." She looked out again, as if trying to see something beyond the ability of eyes and ears and nose to see. Looked out as she'd been looking out since she'd seen that first shipload of refugees.

"They'll be coming one day for us," she said with a shudder. "What will we do when they come? Where will we run? To whom will we be able to turn? *That* is why I am learning what I need to learn. I do not necessarily believe in destiny, but somehow I think I've been dropped here because I know how to help. Maybe not win, but help. I wish I could convince any of the young men of this, let alone the noble houses. They all think I'm off the wall and over the cliffs on this. I'm sure that's what *they* thought, too. Their leaders, that is. The ones who told those in those ships, and also told the ones who didn't *get* to the ships, not to worry about it."

"Well, *I* am worried about it," said a melodic male voice behind her. She almost jumped, and turned to see the large and imposing figure of the young Baron Oriamin. The sight of such a personage in this peasant rookery was not only unexpected, it was almost unprecedented, not to mention downright embarrassing. But Czua wasn't embarrassed at all; she was in absolute awe of the man, who was just about everything a young Ochoan female dreamed about in a man.

"My Lord Baron! Please, pardon my dark musings! I had

no idea . . ." Nakitt stumbled, spreading her wings and bowing low.

The Baron was a well-known figure in the region, but generally lived on the family peak with its castlelike fortress built out of solid rock, and didn't mix much with the common folk. They'd seen him only from a great distance before, and now, close up, he lived up to his billing.

"Please do not feel put out. I did not expect that you would be waiting for me. I am pleased, however, that you know who I am."

As if anybody locally didn't! And he knew it quite well. The guys didn't do a heck of a lot here, but he sure played his royal breeding well. He also seemed to ooze sexiness on an Ochoan standard, with a commanding voice, huge physical presence, and emanating male sexual hormones that could melt the strongest minds. Nakitt felt the effects and fought mightily against the chemistry causing it. Poor Czua had the look of a mindless panting love slave.

"Please forgive the look of this place, my Lord Baron," Nakitt managed. "Can I—*we*—get you something to drink?"

The Baron seemed amused by the idea of consuming anything at this socioeconomic level. "Thank you, no. You are called Nakitti, I believe?"

"Yes, my Lord Baron."

"Things are beginning to pop, hopefully ahead of our common enemies. There is to be a gathering in a few weeks time at Zone to discuss a common policy and strategy to deal with all of this. Much advance work is even now being done and will be revealed there. You come from the same time and space as this mad Empress, do you not?"

"Yes, my Lord Baron. What Josich attempts here is the same as what he attempted back in the confederation called the Realm. He was a male then, an Emperor, self-appointed and self-proclaimed."

"And this consortium defeated Josich?"

"In a sense, my Lord Baron. It stopped him. It did not, however, *catch* him. He remained in a hidden empire of criminal organizations for a very long time, and he came here because, after more than a century, they finally *did* catch him, but at a point where the way here was opened."

"And you are here, sacrificing your race, your future, everything you had, to continue to pursue him?"

Yeah, sure. "We are dedicated to such a goal, my Lord Baron!"

It wasn't clear if the Baron believed that or not. Still he said, "I want you to come with me to Castle Oriamin. It has been suggested that you may be of great value in the coming fight. I am leading a delegation to this conference and I need to know much more before I go."

"I would be honored, my Lord Baron, but is it not true that even your servants are of royal blood? Pardon, but I beg your understanding of my worries about such a situation. I fear that if I were to stay there, I would spend so much time bowing and addressing everyone as superior to the point where I would be less than nothing."

The Baron seemed genuinely amused by the response, which covered an area that had never occurred to him. "Well, then, we'll have to give you some kind of status. I cannot, of course, give you blood royal, since only birth can do that, but I can confer the status of concubine, which will give you status as a member of the household. We can have someone teach you the basics of being a courtesan. That way we will have you as a resource."

"I—uh . . ." Tann Nakitt didn't know what to say. It was everything she'd been trying to connive and more all rolled into one, and it had simply walked up and knocked!

The Baron mistook the hesitancy. "Please consider it. We need you, and, as I say, many in positions far beyond Ochoa believe you should be included in this. We will see to it that your friends here are well taken care of, if that is a consideration."

Through the desire, through the sexual turn-on, through the shock at suddenly being "in," Tann Nakitt's basic nature, as they always warned about such types, came to the fore. "I shall be honored, my Lord Baron, if my friends are looked after and if my personal honor is satisfied as you suggest. I am always and forever at the command of my adopted nation."

This type always loved to be stroked, she thought. She could see in his manner that he was pleased by this response.

"I have a busy schedule. Can you say your farewells and

leave with me this day?" he asked her. "I should like to get you settled in before I need to go to a local conference with the military district."

Tann Nakitt sighed. "Well, I would have loved to have said farewell to Haqua, who is a fisher today, and I am certain that she will be devastated at having missed your visit. Still, dear Czua, you will convey my deep affection to her when she returns, won't you?"

Czua managed a puzzled look in her direction, and she knew it might have been a little thick. In fact, the look was a lot more like, *I'm envious, you bastard! I hope you smother on his first embrace!* Oh, well.

"Just let me gather together my few possessions and I am yours to command, my Lord Baron," she said with as much humility as she could muster.

Hell, wasn't this how Josich had started out under similar circumstances?

Look out, Well World! Tann Nakitt's back in the game!

Well, not exactly back in her game.

Ochoans lived in the cliffs and hillsides and had made small cities out of buttes and mesas, but the nobles lived far better, higher up, of course, than the common cliff cities, and in massive castles hewn out of solid rock. As with the cities and towns below, there were no roads to these places, no ropes and pulleys and cables. When your population could fly, these weren't necessary to get in and out, and when supplies were required, they could be brought in by strong flying teams or hoisted on steam-driven platforms that could also be quickly disassembled.

The grand, polished face of Castle Oriamin showed a dwelling of perhaps seven stories more than a kilometer in the air, as often as not above rather than below the clouds that formed as the winds blew over the warm ocean and were lifted up to climb the mountains. The castle was also hundreds of meters long, and clearly was the home to a great many people. There was no fetch and carry for water here, either; running water from the frequent rains and mists came right through the place, then exited as a series of smaller waterfalls. In between they were diverted to fountains for drinking, baths for bathing, and a system of cisterns that allowed wastes from the population to be carried out the bottom and drop with the spent water into the ocean far below.

Even Tann Nakitt was impressed. Now *this* was more like it!

The Baron had already gone to his next appointment; she was following Madama Kzu á Oriamin, one of the Baron's very distant cousins and a part of his entourage, up and into the place.

It was only when you got very close to the face of the fortress that you saw the guns. Sleek, streamlined, the gunpowder cannon refined to the nth degree for safety, range, and efficiency, these bristled from gun mounts and ports. They looked too polished, though, to be imminently practical; if there was any drill and test firings, none had heard of it.

Still, if they *did* work, siege would be the only practical way to attack the place short of flying soldiers carrying rockets. Those flyers would face air-cooled machine-gun fire that would make accuracy a real problem, too, Nakitt thought, spotting the smaller weapons. Below was a broad bay that was quite deep and wouldn't provide the best anchorage for floating gun platforms. They would, however, make nice targets for castle guns, which looked to have the range of the bay, and had gravity on their side.

Food would be the only problem, and even that might be more a hardship than a fatality. The snows of the peak almost certainly were used year round for cold storage, and the clouds and mist would mask those going up to get them, or even to supplement them.

Whoever had designed the system, long ago, had some real skill in defensive fortifications. Each major bay or harbor had a similar fortification, although not necessarily so large or so grand, and, perched on the battlements, you could just barely see the next one on a distant island in each direction. Semaphore and lantern could give communications even in the worst of circumstances, and, in the case of key potential landing sites, fire could be coordinated.

The real question was whether they understood this logic, and whether they knew how to work this system. Nakitt understood it and grasped it at once, which might well be very valuable in the future.

Madama Kzu led her quickly inside and through a labyrinthine maze of corridors and chambers that were almost certainly not designed to confuse any invader but sure confused Nakitt. Still, some of the chambers were quite impressive, with marvelous carvings of legendary creatures, wildlife and plants of the nation, and much that was simply abstract. Most were overlaid in gold leaf, the floors had elaborate mosaics, and the ceilings had paintings and designs that created a unique geometry for each open area.

The lighting was gas, but had the effect of muted colored fluorescent light, running in tubes. Only at points could an open flickering flame be seen, angled against a series of mirrors that allowed it to shine down the tubes and illuminate the inert additives that provided the color and uniformity.

It sure beat the smelly and inefficient fish oil torches used back in the town.

Water was everywhere. Fountains and stylish pools and baths seemed omnipresent, and there were also lavish tapestries and lush silken curtains.

There were, however, no doors, save those on the inner chambers of the highest royalty—the Baron and his immediate family—and even there the privacy was illusory since they used attendants and staff for just about everything, even getting them up in the morning.

The Baron certainly seemed to be something of a stud, if nothing else. He had fifteen wives who had already borne him twenty-two fully royal children, and he also had twenty concubines who'd given him a small horde of little bastards to make sure that the castle would always have a royal staff.

The Baron shared power and authority with the elected council, but did not share wealth or living conditions with them.

"These artworks were surely not done entirely by Ochoans," Tann Nakitt remarked as they reached the end of their long walk, on the lowest level of the castle.

"You are correct," Madama Kzu replied. "Many artisans from many nations were employed in decoration, and still are in keeping it up and in restoration. There are no outsiders here at the moment, but it is common to see them.

They come in on the ships, as do material and sometimes whole works, and they also leave by them."

"The guns we saw above, big and small. Do they work? Do people here know how to use them?"

It was a fair question, but it seemed to irritate Kzu. "There are members of the household responsible for all of them, and all that they require," she answered huffily. "I assume that anyone who would accept such a position knows how to work them."

Bad assumption, Nakitt thought. *I've seen guys on laser cannons and particle beam disintegrators that couldn't count to three or know which end to point.* In this kind of inbred society in particular, you would lose one hell of a lot of face if you were asked to take over and then didn't know your job. So it was a fair assumption, from the fact that they were being kept as pieces of sculpture rather than test fired and worked on in drills, that the damned things were just supposed to scare you to death. Even the Baron had worn a long sword, an archaic weapon that was basically affixed with nasty clamps or implanted hardware under a wing and which could only do any damage if you basically rammed somebody.

The concubine's chamber wasn't exactly a harem—it was much too well trafficked for that, and there were male staff about as well—but it was one big chamber for too many women to be stuffed into with little to do except tend to the kids and straighten up the lower levels. Most were simply young unmarried females that the Baron had taken a lustful fancy to once, when going through their area, and had basically then rendered them impossible to marry as virgins to lustful guys who never were.

Tann Nakitt wondered when the hell the Baron had time to knock all these women up, plus the wives and maybe one not for the road but on it, and suspected that fidelity wasn't great around this place, either. What the hell; since all the guys here were at least cousins to each other and the Baron, well, it was all in the family.

Nakitt had thought the very concept of herself as a virgin, even though in a strictly biological sense it was true, hilarious. Still, if she was going to find out what it was like on *this* side of the sexual ledger, it would be at least first with the Baron, if only for absolute political reasons. After that, whatever helped attain an objective, from faithfulness or celibacy to wanton lust and abandon, was just fine with her.

The chamber was not exactly a rotten place for all the mob, though. There was a large fountain with the ancient Ochoan goddess of fertility fittingly posed in the center in alabaster, and a soothing stream of water was pumped—oh my!—*into* her at a couple of suitably obscene points. If an Ochoan hadn't managed to carve *that* one, an Ochoan had inspired it.

To the left of the fountain as you faced the rear of the chamber was a large pool of deep, clear, cool water that would be suitable for relaxing in or exercising; a similar pool on the right gave off wisps of steam and appeared to be bubbling from some source of compressed air. Indoor baths. *Very* fancy. Beat diving into the ocean every day.

A massive vanity with a single curved mirror was against one wall; the other wall was false and concealed a full-blown Ochoan mass toilet with water constantly running in it and bearing away the bad stuff. There was also a shower, possibly fed by some kind of raincatcher cistern above or perhaps by another diversion of the falls; it would get you clean in a hurry.

The back of the hall contained a series of chambers with very comfortable-looking beds, each of which could be curtained off but now were not. Doorways flanked the bedding chambers.

"The door on the left goes to the nursery, where at least two from here are on duty at all times, and beyond them the hatcheries," Kzu explained. "Everyone is also expected to spend time in midwifery with the eggs; that way nobody is stuck there for weeks. Have you ever sat an egg before?"

"Sorry, no," Tann Nakitt responded. *Hell, I never even liked children of my old species, nor any others.* It would be interesting to see if a maternal instinct was built into a dominant sentient species. She sure didn't feel very motherly now.

"Well, it is the simplest thing one can do. Don't worry. What little is needed, you'll be taught. Now, the right hand contains some rooms where various things are taught by palace instructors, and the gateway to the fish pool. That's an area where food delivered to us is kept until needed. There is too much pandemonium here for set meals, although we seldom eat or do much else alone, but you may if you wish. You may also enjoy any of the amenities available here, and there are many. You will be expected to keep the chambers spotless, as well as the floors, toilets, washables, and, of course, yourself. However, you may not leave this complex on this level unless you are summoned. Some of the girls are summoned as ladies in waiting for the royal wives, but that is a high privilege. If you *are* summoned, remember to show respect to royalty here, and use at least basic court titling. The Baron is His Highness, the Baronesses are all Highnesses as well. Men of the nobility are always addressed 'my lord,' ladies of the nobility as 'my lady.' Staff is either 'sir' or 'madam.' The one exception is that, among the concubines, only I as chief of concubines am to be called Madama. No one here has a title, and you will generally be referred to as 'girl' no matter how old you are. After the Baron lies with you, he will give you some jewelry, something like the necklaces and anklets you see, and perhaps some gems for implant if he is really pleased. After that, you will be one of us, and your name will be reregistered in the rolls as Nakitti á Oriamin."

"Sounds like no more status than I had before," she noted, disappointed.

"Not true. You are the lowest rank of the castle, it is true, but you will still now and forever outrank all commoners. You may gain added rank by position, if you have some particular expertise, some skill or knowledge, and you exhibit it without making the nobility think you may be smarter than they are. Bearing royal children, of course, also gains you stature. We do not ask why the Baron takes someone into the household, but that is the situation. Remember, too, you are in a political atmosphere where everyone's pride and honor is important, and where they jockey for favor and respect. That means you always convince them that you're a poor, ignorant country lass out of her league no matter what the truth. Punishments here can be painful as well as costly to one's comfort. Remember that."

She nodded. "Oh, I will. I most certainly will."

"Here is a commons chamber not being used," Kzu said, pointing to a bare area flanked by curtains on three sides. "Get whatever you wish to personalize it and make it comfortable from the storerooms to the right. After that, eat, sleep, relax, and try and fit in with the others and await His Highness's summons."

Tann Nakitt looked around the place. That summons couldn't come soon enough.

In four days and three nights Tann Nakitt had almost become accustomed to sleeping with the constant chatter and din reflected off the smooth walls, and learned how to sit on eggs, and already been lectured for being less than diplomatic with some very young brats who *bit*. She didn't, however, make friends in the place, since, after all, she was another outsider coming in, and thus the current novelty of the big man and a new rival for diluted favors. She did get the impression that this would last until yet *another* new one was brought in, which could be any time or could be months or years. When it happened, though, she'd be one of the girls.

On the fourth night the Baron summoned her. The summons was delivered by a female chamberlain who suggested that she make herself as attractive as possible. This was not something Tann Nakitt had any experience in, and she decided that clean and neat and maybe a wee bit of fragrance was the best route. Anything more and she risked looking like an abstract painting.

The Baron was quite as handsome and, well, *big*, as she'd remembered him, and there were those come-hither hormones he seemed to ooze that made it hard to concentrate on what he was saying.

His chambers were simpler than she'd expected, although still the lap of lavish luxury. What surprised and pleased her most was that he seemed to have walls of books! *Real* books, bound in leather and carefully shelved. She couldn't *read* any of it, but the idea that he could, and did, made him go up a notch in her respect. The Realm had abolished books so long ago that few even knew what they were; you didn't need them when any terminal could answer any question or create a small cube that would have your own hologram spouting your lousy love poetry. But Ghomans still had books on their world, and had carefully preserved and respected them. Ghoman books were not treated as objects, but as the collective spirits of the brightest of their ancestors.

He had ordered what was, for Ochoa, a gourmet meal, including several delicacies rarely seen by the common folks and some exceptional wines. She found she didn't have much of an appetite, though, but she did take and enjoy a few things, a light snack as it were, and very much enjoyed the wines.

"Well, Nakitti, what do you think of my castle?" he asked her at last.

She still hadn't defined him, and might not for many more sessions. That made any conversation tricky, because he might be the greatest conversationalist around and wonderful to her, yet if she said something that touched a button in him, probably something illogical and unforeseeable, it might turn him into a raging maniac.

"It is most grand, Highness. I did not dream that such opulence and high art were so close."

He seemed to like that. "I saw you eyeing my books. The ones over there are the finest histories of my people, going back as far as we have records—and that is very far indeed. Others involve the sciences, mathematics, architecture, astronomy, and so on. These are local books, Ochoan books. I feel a link with them. There are at least seven ages of our written language, and it has taken time but I have mastered them all. Twenty-five volumes devoted there to trade and commercial law and customs, and another forty on diplomacy. But concerning war—there's almost nothing. We are in the middle of an ocean surrounded by nations whose denizens can breathe only water, and most of them only water under heavy pressure. Our land is rich in those things that are of true importance, but we have nothing here worth mounting a massive expedition that cannot be gotten more cheaply and easily elsewhere. So, we simply haven't ever had the need to learn how to fight. Oh, we have the *trappings* of it—little more than show officers and a customs police, really. That leaves me with nothing but logic. Kzu tells me that you were asking about the guns and forces. That may not be diplomatic as a newcomer here, but your implications match my own logical study. If we actually had to defend this place, we wouldn't know how. Would *you*?"

Uh-oh! Nice trap, Baron and Kzu. Play dumb to stay out of trouble or be smart and show up the locals. And, damn it, the way he's pumping the hormones out, I can't think straight!

"Highness, I was never a soldier, and this kind of war is as far in the past to my old life as it is now to this one."

"Spare me the humble act, Nakitti! Can this place be defended?"

She thought a moment and decided to drop the evasions. "Highness, it can, but only if the guns all work, there are competent trained people present to use them if and when required, and sufficient fresh supplies for both the weapons and for a siege. It would not guarantee a result, but it could make a positive result possible."

"Excellent! That is what I wanted to hear! I will need you here, Nakitti. I have some problems that must be worked around. Those who are in the military command do not know anything about their jobs, but they love the titles and all the festooned ornamental sashes and ribbons and body markings and all that. I cannot remove them. Most of them are my sisters and aunts and nieces. My *nephews* believe they are generals, although they have never fought anything more than using their swords to spear fish. I can order things to get done, but I must do it through them. What I need is knowledge behind the orders."

She liked the idea of being a power behind the throne but was appalled at his evident belief that attack was inevitable. "Highness, do you really believe that an attack will come here?"

"I consider it only a matter of guessing the month and the day."

"But—Highness! You just finished telling me about the isolation, the lack of immediate enemies . . ."

"And yet it is precisely for that reason that we are the center of the target! The only land, the only harbors, for a thousand kilometers. Control Ochoa with a true combined force and you control the commerce of the Overdark. Control it, and you have bases from which to provision and shelter a powerful group that can then use a naval force to go almost anywhere it wills against a mainland target. You can raid, pick, weaken, force a potential enemy to shift his forces hundreds or thousands of kilometers up and down a coastline, exhausting them, straining and confusing their supply lines, all that. Our enemy—it knows the military way. If *I* can see this, then it has seen it long before. Will you help me?"

"Highness, you have been studying military thinking *somewhere*, or you are a genius coming into his calling, as we all hope and pray. As I swore to you before, all that I have and all that I am I pledge to you to use as you wish."

He moved from the table and came around toward her, and as he got close he towered over her, then put his great wings around her.

"You know," he said softly, "I was afraid you would be a sexless creature, or an ugly one, but you are neither. I wish us to work together on *all* levels."

Her initiation into the household was completed with the rather joyous discovery that not only was he large in a lot of ways, when it emerged from within him it proved to be sheathed in bone . . .

Chemistry, as any Ghoman would say, won out. Okay, Tann knew it wasn't very romantic, but she had never been very romantic, either. Besides, Ghoman sex was *never* like this! Exit Tann Nakitt, now placed on the shelf from this point on with the other dusty memories; enter Nakitti á Oriamin, and, for now at least, she liked that just fine . . .

Jinkinar, Kalinda

THE JOURNEY FROM MAHAKOR TO JINKINAR HAD BEEN A VERY long time in coming, but it had finally come, the nervous government's hand forced by the forthcoming international conference, at which the Powers That Were wanted everybody who wasn't with Chalidang to be present, possibly on the theory that if you weren't with them, you might be convinced to be against them.

They traveled with Inspector Shissik, but free and as companion, not as a prisoner. They still didn't have official status, but then, nobody in authority in Kalinda had the slightest idea what you did with two different people sharing one body. They had gone so far as to consult with the ambassadors of three races that knew something about it, but all of them thought it was a matter of symbiosis or twinning.

Kalindans moved from point to point using what were basically trains, except these were open cars, with the passenger belted in, and they traveled very fast along electromagnetic lines of force. It was exciting just seeing the world after being cooped up for so long, and fascinating to see the landscape as they passed, even if by means they had never used so readily in the artificial environment of the city. Virtually no light penetrated this far, and what life there was with some self-illumination was too weak to reveal anything but the creatures themselves. Still, it was as clear as day to them, seeing by sound and by reading magnetism, radiation, and changes in heat. It wasn't colorful, but it was as detailed and precise as any vision they had ever experienced.

As with all high-tech civilizations, the place wasn't what it used to be. The marks of Kalinda were all over, not just in small structures, the remnants of old commercial enterprises like mines and farms, and old physical roadways now disintegrating, but also in the surprising lack of abundant larger life-forms other than their own kind. Oh, there were some, scurrying across the bottom, swimming by here and there, and clustered in dense sea growths, but nothing they would have expected from an underwater paradise.

"You see the same story everywhere," Shissik commented, not sounding upset. "Screw up the environment, change things, plow up all the plants in an area, dig out all the minerals from another that were also used as part of a local food chain's diet, and you eventually wind up with a lot of desolation. It is the price of progress."

They wondered about that, even as they knew a lot of the Realm had done exactly the same thing both under and above the waves. Still, Ari asked, "So all the high-tech hexes are as desolate? No exceptions?"

"Oh, there are exceptions, sure," the Inspector answered uncomfortably. "Too late to restore here, though. You'd have to create something new. They're always talking about it, since a lot of other hexes have compatible life-forms comparable to what was lost here, but then they cost it out in time and labor and it never gets anywhere. I think they all hope that one day we'll crack the secret and be able to turn water and rock and sand into fields of sea grass, and recreate the now extinct *crion* and *solander* that used to be food staples here. But I doubt it. The Big Computer ain't gonna allow anybody here to do *that*. It would make things impossible to manage. Some things, I think, are reserved for the gods."

There was no way to answer that, given what they now knew and understood about the place. They'd been walled off from the world too long, while being too preoccupied with dealing with their own problem of separate personalities within the same body.

Instead of eventually merging into one combined new personality, Ari and Ming had grown more distinct, and each was more comfortable when in control. Since taking the left half of the body one way didn't work if the right half was trying to go the other way, some compromise had been worked out. The fact was, everyone usually operated on automatic, a right/left consensus. For them, during any pause by one, the other assumed control if they wanted to do something or had something to say. Relax, and the other would reassert control. In a few cases, particularly arguments, it could get bizarrely comical, but for the most part it seemed to work.

After a lot of initial struggles for privacy, both had grown so used to the situation that they had relaxed their control and opposition when nothing was happening—which, during all this time, was a *long* part of their days. It had been facilitated by psychotherapy drugs administered in the hope that it would result in a third combined personality that was stable. It hadn't done that, but it had opened Ari's mind, his experiences, memories, personality, and outlook to Ming's, all the way back to childhood, and it had opened her to him. In both cases it was a shock and a revelation. First to fall had been the "grass is greener" outlook by the sexes, as he discovered what it was like to be raised female and she discovered that it wasn't easy to be raised male, either—just different. She found it a shock to see herself as a sexy and supercompetent intellectual woman she'd never met but would have liked to be, and he was disappointed to discover that she'd thought he was a pretty good one-night stand but no big deal.

Their cultural backgrounds could not be more different, but their resultant likes, dislikes, and general adult outlooks were surprisingly close. Still, the one basic factor that continued to create friction was his shaky moral compass and her strong sense of right and wrong. Where she saw most things as absolutes, he saw only compromises.

But they were becoming lovers now, in an odd sort of way, simply because each could fully comprehend the other's views and their different take on things. The sincerity of his guilt and remorse at what had happened was beyond doubt and made things much easier.

There were, however, gaps in both their memories. Not big things, but a ton of little things, things they should know, should remember about their growing up and past careers. For example, she could not visualize her mother. She could think of a hundred things they'd done together and recall how she felt, but there was no face, no voice there. He had the knowledge of his long studies to get his accreditation as a business analyst and consultant, but he had no memory of where he'd studied to get that, nor with whom. It was weird. He could catch glimpses of places, but he didn't have anything to hang them on.

In the end they decided that eighty to ninety percent of each of them was in that one brain. But where was the rest of them? Had it been edited? Replaced? Damaged in the process? Or was it in somebody else's head?

They needed to know, and the authorities in Kalinda needed to know, just where these strange people would fit into the coming troubles, and deal with them early on. And thus it was that they were free, and on their way to the capital city of Kalinda, to meet the one they both only thought of as the Other.

"There is Jinkinar!" Shissik announced, pointing, and out of the gloom in front of them was a startling vision, all color and heat and straight lines. It was a vast fairyland of a city with spires reaching high into the darkness above, and it throbbed with life. It made Mahakor look like a tiny provincial suburb; *this* was one hell of a metropolis.

The "train" came in high over much of the city, yet still below some of the tallest buildings, and then descended near the city center, toward what had to be the capital building, from its grandiose and excessive design and waste of space. A long platform about three stories above street level jutted out from a building and provided a landing zone. Riders could exit either way and directly into the water to their right, but if you had a lot of luggage or wanted to form a group, the platform was handy.

Living in a deep, dark environment where the sun never shined had created a round-the-clock urban culture. Cities never closed; shifts changed, usually staggered to keep people from literally clogging things up, but they were always around. It made for high productivity, and a great deal was manufactured in Kalinda both for domestic use and, most particularly, for export to other high-tech hexes and even lower-level technologies whose limitations prevented them from producing certain goods themselves. Once, in ancient history, only rich people could afford pins because each had to be made or machined by hand; an automated high-tech pin-making plant could make billions per day, and even nontech societies could use pins.

There were countless such products that an industrial society could make and trade, and if a nontech hex could not make the factories run, well, it had some resources, be they agricultural products, raw minerals, art of all sorts, that were of use to high-tech hexes that had fouled their own agricultural land and mined every last mineral from their soil. Although they were omnivores, there was simply no way that Kalinda could feed itself, not now. But trawlers could bring in vast quantities of fish and shellfish, well-packed and stored sea grains and undersea plant delicacies, and lower them down into the deeps. Meanwhile, other ships, with orders from a hundred different hexes, would dock and load large containers of manufactured products at the island docks above.

It was now taken for granted that most Kalindans did not see the irony of trawlers carrying fish *to* the sea.

It also made them incredibly vulnerable, both Ari and Ming realized.

"If anybody got control of surface shipping, you'd be starved into submission in a matter of weeks," Ari commented.

"Oh, we have vast reserves in great freezers and in specially sealed containers," Shissik responded, "and no one is ever truly isolated here because of the Zone Gate, but you are right. Eventually, if someone could drive all the shipping away, they would own us. Once the reserves were depleted, you could not bring enough in through Zone per day to feed all of these people, and if our topside power plants were also blown, well, yes, I see what you mean." He clearly didn't like the idea, but it reminded him why Kalinda wanted them at the conference.

"We will check in at the Interior Ministry and get our papers and permits in order, then you will find lodging over there in the government employees' hostel."

"What about you? Where will you stay?"

Shissik seemed surprised. "In my own flat, I hope. I *live* here."

The permits and papers took some time to complete, and they went into the ministry restaurant to get dinner. Little was actually cooked in Kalinda, but chefs combined various plant and animal products into a huge variety of meals that tasted unique, most pressed together tightly so they formed a kind of eat-all sandwich, or served in bowls in very thick paste. Nothing much floated away if you ate politely. These were almost always accompanied by a hard-pressed, pillow-shaped cake of sea oats bound in some kind of fatty stock that gave it a soylike flavor.

Once settled in, Shissik accompanied them to their room on a middle floor with an entryway facing the capitol build-ing and the park in front with the huge illuminated oval with a diamond design inside which was the symbol, the "flag," of Kalinda.

"Our appointments and true work will not start until two shifts from now, about 1800 hours," Shissik told them. "I plan to go home, check all my messages and my mail, then get some sleep. I realize that you haven't been on your own much, and this city is not a good place to start. All of the elements, bad as well as good, in any major city anywhere are present here, and you do not know the boundaries us natives take for granted. You were long ago implanted with a broadcast locator chip, so we'll know where you are. Please stay within a few blocks of the capitol building there, and refrain from roaming the street level areas or below, where the most dangerous element hangs out. I shall be here to pick you up by 1700. Any questions?"

They both tried to talk at once, which usually meant they twitched a lot until one of them gave way. This time it was Ming who won out. "Yes—how can we see or do much of anything without any cash or credit line? We have nothing for even minor incidentals."

Shissik wasn't fooled. "Without those things, it won't be very tempting to roam too far and go into places you shouldn't. Your credit is good at the hostel restaurant and you have this room. That should be sufficient for the basics. Good day."

And with that he swam out and away.

Now what? Ming asked.

Can't do much without money, and you're Madame Mo-rality so there's not much chance of finding any. Not much we can *do but wander around the grounds over there and mope.*

Ming thought a moment. *I'm also known to be resource-ful. What have we got in the luggage?*

He went over to the lone backpack and undid the latches.

You should know. You and I packed it. Not much. They don't exactly give diamond rings to wards of the state.

We've got the watch on our arm, she pointed out. *Good, solid military issue. And, what the hell, there's the backpack itself. Won't net us much, but it might give us a little admission money.*

He did not follow her for a moment, then saw what she meant. *Of course! Any city this big just has to have pawnshops! Why didn't I think of that?*

Because you're a rich nephew of a really rich scumbag monster and you have spent time auditing pawnshops but never been in a position to need one. You've read my past out of my mind. You should know I didn't start out undercover on the organized mob task force!

The fact was, he hadn't paid much attention to the details of those early assignments, just that she'd done them. It occurred to him that he ought to take another look sometime and see what he'd missed. *Okay, okay. For this little bit, I'm gonna yield to experience. Go ahead and take control and get us out of here.*

Sure hope they have public clocks, though. Without the watch, we're never going to know what time it is . . .

They went down to the hostel lounge on the second floor, where low-level bureaucrats were floating around, reading the papers or magazines or involved in low-level conversations. One particularly scruffy type who was leaning on the rail and watching the city pass by seemed a likely source.

"A securities broker?" he said in answer to Ming's question. "Yes, bottom level, two blocks down. Follow the red number two line north. A bit tight on the expenses, eh?"

"A bit," Ming admitted. "Thank you."

She swam out and saw the red routing line below with the symbol for 2 and hung a left, descending down to the first level.

For a race with a strong sense of magnetic force, all directions were given in compass points, even though there were effectively no true magnetic poles. Somehow, you just *knew* which way was which.

We've already disobeyed our keeper by coming down here, Ari noted playfully. *Do you think Big Mother's board is going off and they're sending out the cops for us now?*

I doubt it. If they're typical, then they have hundreds, maybe thousands, of stakeouts on computer monitoring systems, and going down to the street and two blocks away isn't likely to cause any alarms. Trust me.

I have to, he responded. *It's not like I can strike out on my own. Besides, you never lie to me.*

The "securities broker" was little more than a stall on a back alley. They couldn't read the signs, and the symbols here were so different they weren't obvious, but this kind of shop had a universal look and feel to it. The proprietor was a small, slight woman who seemed more well-worn and threadbare than the fellow back at the hostel, and also very pregnant. From the several kids swimming around in and through the stock in the back, it was clearly the other thing she did well.

"These watches aren't nothin' to write home about. Hell to move, too," the pawnbroker commented. "I mean, they're regular government issue. Best I can do is ten. The backpack, though, is in great condition. Swear it was brand new. *That* I can take for, oh, six. Total of sixteen credits."

"Are you trying to steal us blind?" Ming fumed. "Sixteen for both of *these*?"

The pawnbroker looked around. "Us? You a cop or somethin'? Licensing Bureau, like that? I ain't in no trouble."

"No, but I'm sorry I'm not," Ming replied, correcting herself. It was too complicated to try to explain, and she didn't want to start a conversation, only get some cash. "That is robbing someone in need."

"Yeah? Well, *I* got needs, too, y'know. You don't come back, I got to sell them things for a profit. Sixteen, take it or leave it."

She took it, of course, even though it was hardly enough to matter. It was sixteen credits more than they had before.

As they were leaving the broker commented, "Too bad you're goin' fem, doll. You got somethin' to sell on the street here stayin' as you are."

She was startled. "I am?" But she left without waiting for the response.

Think it's true?

Ari didn't know. *I think she was just reacting to you, that's all. Still, you keep being the driver and it'll happen.*

Why shouldn't it? Might be interesting anyway. Doesn't carry the baggage here it might back home, not when anybody can switch.

But I don't want to change! At least not now! I've never been a guy before!

Well, whatever happens, happens. I'd rather stay a guy, too, for the record. There are fewer men than women here 'cause the population's a hair low, I guess. Of course, maybe not. She sure seemed to be doing her part for getting everything back in balance.

Yeah, she did, didn't she? Well, I hope we don't have to market ourselves anytime soon.

Um, yeah, he responded, uncomfortable at the idea. *So what do you want to blow this lavish fortune on?*

Who knows what it will or won't buy? Not much, but let's see!

As it turned out, it bought a couple of feel-good patches, the Kalindan equivalent of social drinking, which induced a mild but manageable high for a time, and admission to a couple of low-life theaters that gave them both a bit of an education in underwater sex and titillation. There were things you could do here that would require a million credits plus to simulate back in the Realm, not counting the zero gravity chamber or flight to attain it.

That was what this boiled down to, though. A life where gravity was something you counted on for water density but not something that restricted you. A kind of zero gravity floating lifestyle.

By the time they got back to the hostel and collapsed, they were flat broke again and dead tired as well. Someone, however, a complete stranger, was waiting for them when they arrived.

"Who the hell are *you*?" Ari demanded.

"My name isn't important," the stranger, a female with expensive jewelry responded. "I just need to pass along a few things to you."

"You know who I am?"

She nodded. "I know who *both* of you are. I hope you didn't have *too* much fun in the dives. There's a rampant parasite that's transmitted sexually and which reproduces by making *you* reproduce, whether you want to or not. Hard to detect, harder to kill off."

"We didn't. Not with the money *we* had."

She chuckled. "Well, you're also fortunate you didn't get seduced by one of them. That happens, too. Seductions and rapes. Ugly business." She sighed. "Well, enough of that. Tomorrow you'll be going into Government Center and they'll fill you full of confident lies and invite you along on their big meeting in Zone next week. They'll keep you on a tight leash like with the money, only this time you'll not have a translator, so you'll be able to speak to everybody and be understood, but you'll understand nothing not directed at you. You'll hear the speeches and listen to the proposals and realize that these idiots don't know the first thing about wars, revolutions, and mass violence. The geography of the hexes has always prevented anything really major. Oh, a hex here and there went to war, but even then it was usually quick and dirty. Most of them, including this one, are ripe for easy plunder. They won't even have to fire a shot to take and hold Kalinda, at least not within the boundaries. It's already begun, and the fools don't even realize it. You might, if you had things to compare, but even though it's staring them in the face, they won't see it until it is too late."

"I see. And where do *you* come in?"

"I represent—pragmatists. Families of means who know that the only way to protect the nation is not to fight. There are far more of us than anyone knows, in all positions of power."

"And when the magic moment comes and we are invaded, you make sure that they aren't opposed?"

"Essentially, yes."

"So why are you telling us this? And why are you here at all?"

"Because you are going to that conference and I am not. Some of us will be there, but not a decisive number. You come from the same place in the universe as those now waging war. You are from a more violent race and can cope with a violent universe. You understand what is coming. These fools do not. All we are asking is that you think of reality when various proposals are bandied about, and that you also think of your own long-term futures."

"Yes? Meaning what?"

"Ari, your uncle was one not unlike the Empress. Even more impressive, since she had been born to wealth and power, and your uncle came up from a very low level. You functioned well in your uncle's empire, you could function well here. You have skills that are unique here, and you do not have to learn how to deal with different races and cultures. Ming, you would have more of a problem with this, I know, but consider what they did to you back where you came from. Consider how fragile your existence was when it hit true power, and how death is not necessarily an option in such cases. All we are saying is that there is a place for you in the coming order. Just do not cause us additional pain and expense reaching the inevitable goal. That's all you have to do. Just observe."

"Maybe not," Ari responded. "Maybe it *is* hopeless. Still, you're as naive as those politicians and military leaders you say are deluding each other and themselves. Josich destroyed whole planets. *Billions* of people. Total, complete genocide. And he did it without any second thoughts at all. If Kalinda isn't a good slave labor state, and it really isn't—too educated, too spoiled by technology, and requiring massive imports of food—then it's a liability. Josich simply erases liabilities and goes on. He'll erase us, and you, too."

"The alternative is also certain genocide. You will see. Just think about it. That's all."

And with that, and before they could do anything else, she flipped her tail and shot out of the doorway. They followed, looking around, but she was already lost in the city.

Wow! What do you think that was really all about? Ming asked him.

I'm not sure. It may have been the real thing, or it may have been a warning. In either case, somebody's a little scared of us. I wonder why?

They're not too scared, she responded. *They didn't just plant a bomb in here and blow us to even more pieces than we're already in.*

Yeah, he agreed. *On the other hand, that's an option they can exercise pretty much anytime they think they really need it, isn't it?*

Inspector Shissik arrived at his appointed time to find them fast asleep. He woke them, and Ming, who always was a light sleeper, sat up with a start and then relaxed when she saw him. This sort of thing happened sometimes. One would still be asleep, the other awake. It was the only private existence they had left.

Shissik held up two objects. The backpack he tossed over to one side; the watch he held out to her. "You may well need these."

She didn't feel the least bit embarrassed, putting on the watch and checking it. "How much did she soak you for them?"

"She tried to gouge, but I got them back for probably the pittance you were paid. Twenty-five credits total."

She gave a sour laugh. "Why that little crook!" Then she remembered what he had to know first of all. "We had a visitor last night . . ."

As precisely as she could, she recounted the conversation and gave as good a description as she could manage.

"Well, the jewelry sounds upper class but not to the point where hundreds of wealthy women don't have similar," he noted when she'd finished. "The physical description could fit half the population. Still, it doesn't surprise me. It only surprises me that they would be this bold right here, in this very room, across from the seat of government. I would have expected them to accost you on the street or in one of those clubs. *Much* easier to control."

"C'mon, Inspector! I'm—I *was* a cop, too. I know you have people in those clubs spotting for the tourists. Otherwise any government courier in from out of town would be fresh meat. This is the perfect place, particularly if you know it isn't bugged or you know where the bugs are and how to defeat them, which I assume is the case here."

"Well, it's not attended, but there were no flags on the recording, at least none that anybody reported to me," he admitted.

"See? Blank out the record, get in before we do, get out

quickly, and that's that. The point is, was she correct? Is this place really indefensible?"

"I would hate to think so," he told her honestly. "However, events so far have shown a remarkable lack of ability to defend against things in other hexes. We shall see, I suppose."

"What do you think she meant by saying we'd be taken without a shot being fired, and we'd see it now if we weren't so new to normal society?"

"I don't know the answer to that, either. Perhaps it is just empty threats, but . . ."

"Well, let's think of it while we have breakfast. Ari, it seems, is still nicely asleep inside, and I have a liking for *pabas* entrails, and if I eat them when he's awake, I suffer . . ."

He shrugged, and they went out and floated down to the restaurant level. She got her favorite dish, he got some seasoned sea grain cakes, and they started to eat as Ari began to stir. She wolfed down the dish before he got clear of who, what, and where, but not quite fast enough.

Ugh! Yuk! You aren't putting those things into my stomach, are you?

It's my stomach, too, and I can feed it what I want. If you don't like it, next time you wake up early. Aloud she said, "Ari's here."

Too late to stop it and too full to top it off with something he liked and she detested, he settled for coming to the fore.

"So, Inspector, you have a group of traitors at high levels. Are you going to root them out?"

"We know some of them," he told them. "The rest—well, it's a secret organization but they're almost all amateurs. I found it interesting that she said that most of the delegation wasn't their people. It's an interesting revelation. There's only a dozen going—the rest will be commuting back and forth from here via the Gate. Not a lot of room in Zone when thousands will be there representing all the races, since only the border areas of Zone are really useful. We'll be looking closely at any of them. A couple are undergoing personal changes, so it's hard to tell the physical from the treason sometimes."

"Really?" This was interesting. "What sort of changes?"

"Well, the two members of the Cabinet who were both

male and still young enough to bear kids are undergoing changes to the feminine. That's not usually the case unless there's *already* been a big loss of life, or it's so stressful that the fear can be cut with a knife. That level's not here, but it's going on. A couple of the older guys, including the Premier, who are by far too old for that sort of change, have been seeing medical counselors lately, and all for the same reason. Impotence."

That got both their attentions, and they were suddenly of one mind.

"Inspector—am *I* turning—'fem,' as the broker called it? Physically?"

"I can see some of the signs, but it's hard to tell with Ming in there, too. I suspect nobody mistook her for a man when she was herself. Still, I could point to areas and say that, yes, it might be the early stages. I've had that myself, though; I've got early signs now. I've had it before. Sometimes it reverses, sometimes it happens. You never know."

"Inspector, do a very quick research project," they told him. "Call your office, ask them for current statistics on male-female changes, how many people have reported these changes, how many were female to male as well as male to female, how many older men are being treated for impotence or loss of desire, that sort of thing. I'm sure it can be done without breaking the bank or taking people forever to compile. You have basic computers. I think you may have a bigger problem than it seems."

Shissik wasn't sure if they were crazy or not, but they seemed so single-minded that he phoned in the assignment to the Data Section and was told they could probably have raw data in a couple of hours. He told them to go ahead and call him back with the data.

Now they floated out and across the broad plaza to Government Center, a series of not terribly high buildings that were totally artificial but had been built to resemble a grandiose coral reef. There were no living coral reefs in Kalinda; the water temperature was too cold and the shallows too few.

It was, however, not solid, but a series of buildings all blended together, giving a melted appearance; inside, it was quite busy although not terribly crowded.

They were escorted to a large office with real, huge fancy

doors—a sign of status—and when the doors opened, they were almost sucked into a vast and opulent office. A huge shield with the oval and diamond was mounted on the back wall, and in front was a massive desk with very little on it, the mark of a Very Important Politician.

He was markedly older than most Kalindans they'd met, save a few seen in the alleys and clubs the previous evening, but he was immaculate right down to his professional smile. "Come in, come in! I am Ju Kwentza, Minister of the Interior. Inspector—please. Over there. I want to speak to this remarkable citizen—er, citizens, I suppose."

And talk he did, although he did a little listening. Both of them wondered if he had impotence and loss of desire. Probably, but he was the one person in government who would never show up on a statistical table. The Ministry of the Interior, after all, ran the national police, both public and secret, and much of the internal security apparatus as well.

Finally he finished, they said a few more pleasantries, and he pushed a buzzer that brought in a young woman with a bunch of passes hung around her neck.

"Mellik, here, will give you passes. Then I think you should meet with the other from your region. We are most curious to see what effect it will have on her. So far not even drug therapy has been able to bring out very much. She's rather passive, and not faking, I can assure you of that. We hope that perhaps getting you two, or three, or whatever, together might bring out something locked away."

Ari put on the pass, as did Shissik, and they followed Mellik down a series of tubular corridors, through a number of security checkpoints—the guards, at least, seemed very military, and their weapons looked formidable—to a room with a lot of amenities but no particular view. A young female was inside, wearing an elaborate headset, and she seemed off in a world of her own.

"What is that she is using?" Ari asked Mellik.

"It is called an indoc, short for 'indoctrinator,' although that's not what it's being used for. She has been almost desperate to learn how to read Kalindan—you can see some children's schoolbooks over there. This device can inject a great deal of rote memory material directly into the mind's memory sectors and tie it in with the developing skill. It is generally used on those with grave reading problems or those who have been in situations where they never learned. It's a miracle worker. But it has never, to my knowledge, been tried on someone not born and raised here."

Originally developed for the Interior Ministry, I'd bet, for different purposes, Ming noted to Ari.

"Should we disturb her now, in mid-trance?" Ming asked Mellik, concerned about scrambling things up. A similar but much more sophisticated device, and in fact a whole family of devices, was common in the Realm and wouldn't do harm unless you designed it to do so, but you never knew about such gadgets.

"It wouldn't do much except truncate the lesson," Mellik assured her. "But we'll wait. The light is flashing on the control panel there in front of her. It's almost done. Come."

The program ended just as they entered, but for a moment the Other just floated there, eyes closed.

The moment Ari and Ming came close, they could feel the attraction, a sense of connection, a tie.

The Other could feel it, too, it seemed, because suddenly her eyes opened and she looked at the newcomer in front of her and gasped. "I know you," she said, sounding somewhat confused. "Not like *this*, though. Like—Like . . ."

"Do you have any memories of us together?" Ming asked her, taking over again, this time with Ari's agreement. "Do you remember any scenes? Any thoughts? Any names?"

The Other shook off the interrogation. It was too much too fast. "Remember—sisters," she said. "Not sisters. Sisters who were one but not sisters. It's—confused."

Great! Ari said sarcastically. *Looks like we got the Alpha or Beta model. No wonder she can't remember much. Without the computer she's nothing!*

The Other gave a gasp and looked strangely at the newcomer. "There is—someone else? How can there be you and not you? I—I do not understand."

She heard *me! Or at least* sensed *me!* Ari exclaimed to Ming. *Are you sure you want to go any further with this?*

The Other looked totally confused, then reached out and grabbed their hand and held it, hard, in a firm handshake.

They both felt a connection, then an extreme shock, as if a bolt of electricity had hit them. A whole series of strange, bizarre images passed between them, back and forth, and they felt as if in a churning whirlpool, and were both too dizzy and too powerless to get out.

As soon as it happened, both observers saw the two stiffen and then seem to lapse into unconsciousness. Immediately, Mellik and Shissik rushed to them, attempting unsuccessfully to loosen the death grip and pry the two apart. Then each took one and they pulled, trying to pry them apart, but failing.

"Get a doctor down here to knock 'em out, and get some of the biggest guards you can!" Shissik snapped to Mellik. "We've *got* to break this up!"

But drugs appeared to do nothing, and it was still beyond their strength to separate them. One particularly beefy guard suggested chopping the hands off, but this was rejected as being too late to do much good.

It went on for almost three hours, but at the end the grips of each loosened on their own and both bodies floated in place, unconscious. Perhaps because of the drugs, but more likely due to shock, they didn't wake up for a while. When they did, it was together.

For Ari and Ming, finding each other still in the same head came as a bizarre relief. They would have preferred separates, but not in the state they were in now, and not with somebody else also lurking.

What the hell was that? I feel positively drained! Ming exclaimed.

I'm not sure. For a time, I thought I was in her body, then back here, but then I got too dizzy and passed out.

They heard shouting, then Shissik rushed into the room, stopped and looked at them, even as a medic arrived to examine them.

"Who *are* you?" the Inspector asked.

"Ari—and Ming. Same as before. At least, I *think* we are. You'll have to be the judge of that. How would we *know*?"

"Hmm . . . Recount my conversation with Ming about your visitor. As much detail as you can, including what breakfast was like."

Ari did so, suitably outraged at the breakfast choice, as always.

Shissik then asked to speak to Ming, and quizzed her on earlier conversations and on her background. Finally he asked her, "You are satisfied that you are back to normal and that Ari is Ari?"

"Yes, of *course*! Why do you ask?"

They were suddenly aware of another presence behind them, and managed to get out of the medic's examination long enough to turn and gasp.

"Hey! Wait a minute! We haven't been Kalindan that long, but I'd swear that *that's* our body!" Ari exclaimed.

"No, it's *our* body," the other one responded. "*You* are the Other."

Ari and Ming looked at Shissik, who nodded. "I'm afraid so. You're in the young female's head. The one that didn't appear to have anything in it. And *they* seem to have the same information and the same memory and the same dual personalities that you now do."

"My God! How is that possible? I thought we were a one of a kind Well of Souls processing error!" Ming II responded.

"Apparently something inside the other one connected and caused the entire contents of your brain to be copied as a mirror image to the brain of the other here," Shissik told them. "It certainly would have been more practical if just one of you had transferred, but it's done. It will be interesting to discover if there are any variations in the two of you. There seems to be some. *They* woke up before *you* did."

"Then—we're the *copy*?" Ming II asked, incredulous. "I don't *feel* like a copy!"

"Me neither," Ari put in.

"We must assume so. The question is, how exact a copy are you two? If something, some routine, was lurking inside the Other waiting for such a contact, where is that 'something' now? And what is it?"

"But—But . . ." There was no making sense of this.

"And by the way," Ari I said to them, "our hunch was right. There's been a nationwide surge of conversions to female, a regular epidemic of loss of desire and impotence on the part of any male too old to change over. As of two weeks ago, there has not been one single reported case of female to male. In fact, even some well along are reversing. And as all births are gender neutral until puberty, there are no new males from that quarter either.

"My God! That's what the woman was talking about, then! Slow genocide. They won't even have to starve us. A nation of females. No more children. And they alone have the cure, I bet. How is this *possible*? I thought the all-powerful Well of Souls computer was supposed to make this kind of imbalance impossible!"

"We don't have an explanation, not yet," Shissik told them. "Not until the meeting next week will we hear the best suppositions about it. There is some feeling, though, that when you all were reprocessed through the Well you somehow—broke it. There is supposedly some sort of fix-it deity or computer repairman or some such that comes and fixes it when it breaks, but if he's here, there's no sign of it. It may well be that the Well doesn't *know* that anything's wrong . . .

South Zone

AROUND MUCH OF THE SOUTHERN HEMISPHERE, THEY GATH-
ered up their staffs and runners and went to the centers of
their hexes, the movers and shakers, the foreign and defense
chiefs, often the political chiefs and their top aides. All else
was being coordinated from back in their home capitals,
using the Well Gate to get messages and requests for consul-
tations and data back to them as things proceeded.

Both sets of Kalindans were there with the others, notably
Mellik, who turned out to be a psychologist working for Interior, basically keeping an eye on them, as well as the Premier,
Magnosik; Corrivit the Defense Minister; and Chaskrit, Foreign Minister. All the high officials were there with two aides,
making for a larger delegation than was specified. They didn't
care, nor did most of the other races, it appeared. They
brought whoever they wanted and stuffed them in someplace.

There was room, of course. Not everybody showed up,
including, thankfully, anyone from Chalidang, although with
some cheek, there was a small Cromlin delegation. These
somewhat colorful lobsterlike creatures had not been directly
involved as yet in any conflict, but it turned out that the
number three in the delegation was in fact a reprocessed one
himself, and had been physically, and remained mentally,
Josich the Emperor Hadun's half brother.

Nakitti thought it was a damned weird conference anyway. More critters than you could imagine, and no auditorium for more than a hundred people who all breathed the
same stuff. Basically, it was done on monitors beamed to the
reception rooms of the embassies, so there wasn't a lot of
interaction except in the corridors and going to and from the

Zone Gate. There was a constant stream of creatures, some not very friendly, in a two-way parade.

For a semitech hex, the Ochoan Embassy was plush and high tech. Even a lot of the nontech hexes enjoyed the luxuries of technological comfort here, which often spoiled those posted here for going back home. For instance, there was a system for ordering or obtaining whatever food and drink you liked; no need to send home. Bring your favorite delicacies, have them zapped by the computerized stations, and within minutes it became part of the database. Then, anytime you wanted it, you just ordered it and there it was, perfectly synthesized and delivered to a food station near you. Better than home, really, because you knew this hadn't been anywhere else, and thus contained only pure food. Wines? Give the machine a sample, and it would deliver bottles or jars as required. There was little this system couldn't handle except volume; it wasn't designed for mobs of people per embassy, and the more orders that came in at once, the slower the system became. For that reason, some of the hall traffic was simply going home for dinner; others were bringing catering, some of which, on the way to being eaten, tried to eat other creatures going by.

Nakitti had no trouble figuring all this out; once you recognized a food that was the equivalent of something you knew, it wasn't that hard to manage. This explained why she was gaining weight even though her bill pouch was nearly empty, and why some of the things she'd been eating were rather strange to the other Ochoans. It was disappointing to discover that some old favorites were now repulsive to her tastes, but rich, dark chocolate and candy-coated fruit and insects were just fine and went down in incredible quantities.

Although of a royal household, she still was, as usual, the lowest social rank there, so few of the nobles would speak to her directly, or when they did, it was in the tone reserved for the lower classes. But she did have the run of the Ambassador's suite, currently turned over to her Baron's use, and by observation had memorized what you keyed in on the entry pads to achieve voice access to the centralized computer database. Hell, as Tann Nakitt, she'd cracked far worse than this one, since this was a utilitarian common access system not designed to keep people out.

What was it they'd said? Your true nature came out even after the Well reprocessed you. Yeah, she thought, look at Josich.

Hmm . . . Yeah, let's really look at Josich!

The computer screen read off the basics of Chalidang, its technology—which was of a surprisingly high level for an underwater hex with a history of absolute monarchy—and its basic history, which consisted of warlords knocking off each other, sometimes knocking off or being knocked off by their own kids, while a solid and highly efficient computerized civil service kept it all going no matter who was in charge. They'd also waged war before, sometimes on neighboring hexes, sometimes a bit farther afield, but always with limited objectives. They essentially considered all the nearby hexes to be their pantries and supply closets, and they went to them when they wanted or needed something.

Also interesting was that the Chalidangers could not exist for more than very brief periods in air; water had to go through those armored gill cavities or they had real trouble. Of course, even for a bunch of squid-faces, they had pressurized vehicles that provided oxygenated water and allowed them to move on land when necessary; aquariums of a sort, with armor and guns. Wouldn't mean much in a high-tech environment where laser and beam weapons could burn holes through that and leak you all over the beach, though, so how did they work in semi- and nontech hexes? They seemed to have some way of doing it. Maybe they used some of those many tentacles in some kind of gear arrangement to keep it going, or—*springs*? Giant wind-up pressure suits? It was laughable, but the more she stared at a photo of one, taken apparently from a great distance and blown up, the more she was certain that, indeed, that was exactly the case. Wild, at least until the thing wound down. They surely had that covered, though. Never underestimate the ability of a sentient race to figure out how to kill things even under the most hostile of conditions.

Looking over the Chalidangers, though, something kept nagging at her . . .

Damned, if they didn't look and act one hell of a lot like the Hadun! The tentacles, the eyes, those were different, but the basics were the same.

Nakitti accessed the entry recording of the Hadun clan, such as it was. They came in much like she had, but on the underwater side, salt and all. She couldn't follow their language, of course, but they apparently arrived in the Hadun e-suits they'd been wearing when they got zapped here. They used fairly standard frequencies, and because of the problems involved in broadcasting some of the high frequencies, tended to automatic shift translation to Realm Commercial even between two of the same race. A bit of a volume adjustment and frequency sweep of the recording, and Nakitti was listening to the conversation, or some of it, in a tongue she could understand. It was laced with untranslatables that were in Hadun alone, and it was partial, but it was still educational.

"... *Brothers! Are you all all right?*" That was Josich himself!

The others checked in uncertainly.

"*... wasn't what ... planned but ... will do. We ... hoped for more ... get processed. Our ... same blood ... Quickly brief ... Attend Us! We ... the Well ... Will ... touch ... Be of great courage! ... Be gods! No word ... Act shocked, confused ...*"

There was more, but it was even more broken up. What caught her eye was something that apparently nobody else had picked up on. Maybe nobody else had tried to find out what was being said here, or nobody cared or understood. Surely she couldn't have been the only one to have seen it.

Josich the Emperor Hadun had used the term "the Well." There was also that business about getting processed, and acting shocked and confused. There was absolutely no mistaking the sense of this.

Josich had known precisely where he'd landed, and the system as well.

How? This was a one-way trip. Josich couldn't possibly know about the Well World, the idea of reprocessing, any of it. Could he?

And yet ...

The implication was also that the brothers *didn't* know. It was almost as if Josich had been here before, somehow, and gotten out. No, that wasn't quite right. These were his half brothers, which meant they were born to at least the same father or mother as he had been. He was, however, the oldest, which is how he was first in line for the throne back then.

If Josich hadn't been here, he'd certainly known about it from someone who had. Someone who'd gone into great detail. It didn't make sense, but there it was. Somehow, not only had he known about this place, he'd known how to get himself reprocessed as something very close to the Hadun, perhaps a distant relative of the common source of the race, and he had managed to do it without triggering the Well's legendary defenses. Clearly he hadn't intended to be caught and panicked into the place, and there was the implication that he had planned on an even more controlled entry, but he'd coped just fine.

Not bad for a wormface, Nakitti thought. Not bad for anybody. In fact, if Josich wasn't such a totally evil son of a bitch, you might say that this kind of genius almost *deserved* to run the place and regard everybody else as bugs.

By the time the Baron returned from the preliminary meetings on the conference, Nakitti had a lot to tell him, and although it was recounted in an almost admiring tone, it was anything but the best of news.

Amboran Embassy,
South Zone

THE GRAND HIGH PRIESTESS SEEMED EVEN MORE SAINTLY YET powerful in this strange place than back in Ambora.

"Well, child, I see you still have that holy glow about you," she commented as Jaysu stood and bowed and kissed the older woman's rings.

"I am embarrassed by it, Grandmother," she responded humbly. "I do not think I am special compared to all others."

"Oh, but you are, child! In such a short time of study you have achieved what few in our Holy Order have ever achieved in a lifetime. Your Mother was one of the finest of our sacred calling, yet she never attained it and it drained her. In the end, though, while unable to achieve it herself, she saw that potential in you. Do you remember her last kiss?"

"Yes, Grandmother, but I do not see—"

"No, let me explain. It might have appeared that she gave you something, something that shriveled her in the giving, but that was not what she did. Instead, what she did was *take* from you."

"Take? What would she take from me at the moment of her passing?"

"Everything impure still within you. You had far less than most due to your origins, so it was possible. No one else has a low enough quantity, at least in *this* life, to be able to have it all removed, nor the innocence and total surrender to faith that would be required of them. You did. As you grow and meditate and let it develop, it will become a great power within you, a power that only your purity could wield, and a power one of your purity and innocence *can't* wield."

She was totally confused. "I—I am sorry, Grandmother.

You seem to be saying what cannot possibly be true. That I am without sin or corruption."

"I believe that was your Mother's gift to you, yes. Do not strain. You could not sin if you tried. It is best not to think on it too much because you have no way to compare. But I believe you are the only pure one on this entire world, and that the power this represents within you is a power that nothing can withstand. Again, do not search for the power or how to use it. It does not work that way. It will simply— work. You are still evolving to the highest form. I have no idea what it will be like when it is done, but it will be done. It will frighten some people, awe others. I admit to a bit of both myself."

"*Grandmother!* I swear to you that you need not *ever* fear me!"

"*That* is not the kind of fear I mean. Well, we will see, and so will you. I do wonder, though, if we are not jeopardizing the most wonderful and wondrous thing ever to happen to our race by having you here, threat or no threat." She sighed. "Well, I suppose we must discover soon enough which is stronger."

Jaysu still didn't understand much of what the Grand High Priestess was saying, but she did understand that it was supposed to be something good in a world clearly heading into nastiness, and she was happy for that even if it did seem misplaced.

Standing before the mirror in the old ambassador's quarters, though, she did see the physical changes. Those couldn't be denied. The snow-white wings were so much grander than her old ones, but they did not fold as neatly because of that which was an irritation. The hair, too, was billowing white, but her skin was a golden color that was, literally, radiant, and without any sort of blemish. She did not realize and could not think of herself this way, but to others of her race she was the absolute epitome of beauty, grace, and form.

In fact, she looked like a real angel . . .

Jaysu walked out into the main offices and down to the small gathering hall where they'd set up a large screen to show the proceedings from the larger but still very limited auditorium. There were many other Amborans about, mostly

High Priestess ranks but even a couple of males who were there as trade and political attachés, and she felt their gaze and saw them shrink back a bit from her. She was sad about that; she wanted to be their friend. (This glow of hers was an off-putting attribute, she thought, not realizing that this wasn't what was causing the reaction to her.)

The Ambassador was at the front, standing before a podium and staring at the screen. She had a cup of golden wine for her possible thirst, but at the moment was watching what flashed on the screen and making notes on a pad in front of her on the podium.

Jaysu looked over the old one's shoulder, wishing she could read the notes, not to eavesdrop but to have the ability.

And, almost as soon as the thought came to her, she *could*! It wasn't as if the notes assembled themselves into understandable words and phrases, she just knew what was written. She looked up at the screen, and at the scratches beneath the person who was talking, who resembled a large humanoid weed with a giant leaf on its head, and the scratches were gone, replaced with *Doctor Varada 237A, Political Science, Czill Center*.

She knew after arriving here of the strange little devices called translators that were implanted in a chosen few, including all the ambassadors, but she didn't think they worked with writing, and she didn't have one anyway.

But she could understand what was being said. Well, she could hear the words as if they were spoken in Amboran, anyway. The *sense* of it was something else again, and that didn't come intuitively, at least not yet.

". . . Just how Josich was able to integrate so completely and so quickly with just the right warlord at just the right moment we may never know, but we are faced with the fact of it. Since we have had few conquerors in the recorded history of the Well World, we have little to go on in any event, but the others were all apparently home grown, although some reprocessed individuals have become involved in various movements in the past as advisers or even warriors. Never before as a leader and catalyst, though. As to what sort of conqueror we have here, we do not need to extrapolate from Chalidangian history and sociology, nor would it be totally appropriate when dealing with this sort of individual. Fortunately, we've had others arrive from the same sector of the same galaxy who had quite specific knowledge of this very Josich and his family. We can, therefore, extrapolate a pattern from a previous attempt to do the same thing on a more, er, *interstellar* scale."

Jaysu turned away, marveling at being able to read and understand such things, but finding him both confusing and boring. She knew there was someone of pure evil who was killing and enslaving many somewhere, and that this was a gathering of all the races in the region that might come face-to-face with it at some time, but that was about it, and it was all she wanted to know. Evil was present to test the mortal for worthiness and to allow for mortals to freely choose the correct or the incorrect path to immortality. Warriors fought wars, and priestesses fought on a different plane, against the evil spirits behind it all.

She still wasn't sure what she was doing here. "Requested," Grandmother had said, but requested by whom? Nobody in the embassy, that was for sure. Nobody *here* seemed comfortable around her. She longed to be back in Ambora among her own clan and with her own priestesses. This was an ordeal; until now she'd never realized just how horrible an existence this was, and she had new respect for the Grand High Priestess and the others who lived and worked here all or most of the time. No fresh air, no mountains or sea, no birds and insects and gentle breezes and great storms that freshened the air and watered the soil. This city and its gathering places might be necessary, but it was no way to live.

She wanted to go home!

Kalindan Embassy,
South Zone

INSPECTOR SHISSIK WAS ONLY THERE FOR A FEW HOURS, SPACE being what it was, but he was fascinated by this mob scene and appreciated the chance to get this one look at a place he'd long heard of but had never before seen.

Psychologist Mellik had summoned him, and he'd wasted no time in answering, although the required passes took a while.

It was like swimming in lava tubes, he decided. Wall-to-wall water-breathing races, none of them familiar, going to and fro along long, dark tubular halls. Fortunately, they had set up internally lit signs with the national symbols, along with small kiosks where you could state your hex and get a detailed map to where its embassy might be. He needed it.

The embassy was a hybrid one, which was very useful when your race had even limited air breathing capacity. Most of the offices and such were underwater at optimal pressure, but signs indicated an upper level that was in air and dry. He didn't like being in air much; you crawled on your belly or rode in a stupid wheelchair gizmo and you felt like your head was about to blow up and you were always short of breath, but sometimes it was necessary. One of the aides checked his credentials and told him, "You are required up top, Inspector. Psychologist Mellik is already there and is expecting you."

He followed the arrows and soon felt the pressure cease, then broke the surface. The gills struggled for a moment, then his autonomic reflexes kicked in and he felt like a giant hand squeezed every bit of water out of him and that it all squirted out of the back of his head. Then that area opened again and took in a huge gulp of air and his small lungs inflated rather painfully. The sensation ceased fairly quickly, though, and he made his way to the ramp and railing and pulled himself up onto the dry tile floor. He was breathing okay now, but it never felt right.

He looked around, saw more bureaucrats, mostly in those sidesaddle wheelchairs, but nobody seemed interested in him. "Excuse me!" he called, his voice echoing irritatingly against the tile floor and walls. He never did get used to how sound acted in air. "I'm here to see Psychologist Mellik!"

There was no particular interest from the couple nearest him, but someone came out of somewhere and he heard a woman call, "Sorry about that, Shissik! I'm afraid all the chairs are in use, but you can use the wire and posts setup to come up or just do a hand walk. We'll wait for you!"

Grumbling about bureaucrats and amenities and the fact that seven of the thirteen Hells had to be filled with air, he turned on his belly and pulled himself along a wire stretched for this purpose along the floor until he was on the main level, then went hand over hand, dragging his long tail, toward the familiar figure in the chair.

"In here," Mellik invited him. "You'll be more comfortable in the conference room, I think."

In fact, it was very nice at that, he saw, consisting of both dry areas and shallow rectangular pools made for the Kalindan form. He'd expected to see one or both of the strange dual personalities there as well, but Mellik had somehow managed to keep things private.

He settled in, setting his dorsal fin in the notch, and felt reasonably comfortable for an air-breathing environment. She slid from the chair and down into the next compartment.

"Sorry to get you here on short notice, and for this area, but it's the only one not constantly filled with our people," she told him. "I see you're a week further along in your change, and I assume you noticed that everyone here is either ancient or female?"

"I noticed. In fact, I would have assumed that whatever agent was used was probably tested on the embassy here first. It would be relatively easy to do. A lot easier than polluting a whole hex. I'd love to know how *that* was done!"

"We're working on it. Trouble is, if they were willing to come out and reveal themselves like this, they already probably took that into consideration. When we find them, we'll find part of the answer at least."

"That's easy. Just wait. The one guy that's left among roughly four million women will be the one. And when he demands to be king, he'll get acclaimed, too."

"My! You *are* dismal today!"

"Well, it's playing hell with my own family and relationships. But that isn't why you brought me here."

"No," she admitted. "It's not. It's those two strange dualities."

"Yes? Driving you nuts, too?"

She thought a moment, trying to figure out a good way to say it. "I—I have reason to believe that one of them is an act."

"I won't ask you the details, but which should be simple. The originals can't be any more along than me."

"Well, that would be logical, I admit. But consider this: you remember the neurology report on them from back in Mahakor?"

"Sure. One's in each half of the brain, and they can trade off some things so that her speech has improved and he can figure out a symbol. So?"

"Brain halves work in opposition. You know that. Right brain, left side, left brain, right side. Right?"

"Yeah, I guess so."

"Well, the female personality, Ming, was in the right and controlled the left side. You could see it. That's one reason why she had initial problems with verbal skills. The male, Ari, was in the left and had problems with abstractions and coordination. Again, you could see it."

"You mean that's not the case anymore?" Shissik said.

"It's opposite. The alleged blank one, female, is precisely the way the originals were. The older body, the still more male one, has it reversed. She's now on the right, he's now on the left. And, although he tried to conceal the fact and only slipped up when I reran monitor footage over and over to make sure, the male one can read Kalindan. Maybe not the great works or a manual on nuclear fusion, but well enough to read most anything around here. The female has a rudimentary knowledge, more like a first year grammar school child."

"So? They're not stupid. And some of that could have been exchanged in the transfer of data."

"They aren't *that* bright, not to be able to switch brain sides. I don't even understand how they do it now, but I know the theory. Shissik, there's no biological way they could have transferred the data from one side to the other and vice versa without going through a second party. I think our 'Other' here, who was right-handed, pulled Ming's data into the right brain and then Ari's into the left because of that, then read them back, possibly adding some modules like the basic reading, since we know she was studying it. That implies a conscious action by somebody or some *thing* that knew enough to be able to do that."

"But not smart enough to conceal its expert reading abilities or know its right from its left? That's hard to accept."

"No, the right-left thing is now impossible to fix. There's no empty brain capacity to use as a holding area anymore. And they concealed a lot very well. You still don't believe me when I say I think the original is the phony, or that there *is* a phony, do you? So what's a little slip that perhaps nobody noticed? Reading an all-text screen of proposals for the conference is not only natural, it's impossible *not* to do if you know how."

"All right," he sighed. "I'll grant the point for the sake of argument. These are bad times. Now, let me ask you a few questions. Who? And why?"

"I don't know. Those two computerlike people who came in, suppressing the original personalities, aren't really accounted for. The Ming memories and personality are in with the Ari memories and personality. The other one, which we are informed is an educated priest or something like that, is probably this amnesiac Amboran, but she seems to have only the personality, not the memories. Where are those memories? Why didn't things work the usual way? I think there was something else, something that came along with them when they were transported here, came in the heads of those two young women. That something is what caused all the problems, and it wound up in the body of the one we called the Other. I think it's trying to mask itself while it accumulates the memories, the data, from anyone else who came in. After that—I don't know. I don't think it's on the

Chalidang side. I don't think it's on our side, either, or any side but its own. But it definitely has both power and an agenda, and patience. The only question in my mind is, now that I know, what do we do about it?"

He shrugged. "If you can convince our superiors of this, then it definitely is not something with our interest at heart. That means you confine it, confront it, and, if you don't get the right answers, you kill it."

"There's too much other stuff going on right now for that and you know it," she told him. "That's why I asked for you. I want you to talk to them and see if you see what I see. If you do, and you feel safe, you can force the issue. Otherwise they are going to introduce everyone from that second entry group into one room at one time, right here, within another day. If they all are together with whatever this is, it may be too late."

He nodded. "All right. Why not bring your suspicious one up here and let me talk to him. In private, one on one. This may be absolutely nothing, or it just might be the key to all this stuff."

She had anticipated him, although she did not take kindly to being excluded herself. Still, she'd called him in because this was his case and she needed an ally; by her actions, she'd determined that the resolution would be in his hands, not hers. A familiar figure came crawling in only a few minutes after Mellik left.

"Settle into the pool there opposite me, so we can speak face-to-face," Shissik invited. "It's comfortable."

Ari/Ming I nodded and slid in, fitting their own fin into the slot. It *was* comfortable. They looked over at him and frowned, then brightened. "Inspector Shissik! How nice to see you here, but it is surprising. Is something wrong?" It sounded like Ari talking.

"I believe we have a bit of a problem," he told them, sounding confident and relaxed. "You see, we know *what* was done, but we have no idea who you really are."

"Oh, come on! You know *us*!"

"We will get nowhere if this continues. You see, you've made two mistakes for all your cleverness. One was to demonstrate a knowledge of reading about at my level, when I know the originals couldn't spell 'fish,' and the other was to set up in the wrong sides of the brain. That leaves the Ministry with little choice in a war environment and with our race under serious attack right now by diabolically clever means. Basically, we don't have time to fool around. Anybody who isn't one of us and isn't forthcoming has to be considered a traitor at best or a full-blown enemy at worst. In either case, the only solution would be to either drop you in a dark hole in the Ministry and forget you or simply have you vanish forever. Which would you prefer?"

They sat there, mouth agape, considering his astonishing charges and mulling them over in their mind or minds, whichever. Finally they, or he, or it, replied, "I assume this is all being recorded?"

He felt a tingle go straight up and down his backbone. The only weapon he'd had was the kind of threatening bluff he'd just managed, but he didn't expect it to actually work. In fact, he had already decided that Mellik was either paranoid or had been working too hard. But the tone and tenor of the voice used to ask the question was neither Ari nor Ming nor even the alleged blank slate of the original Other. It was—well, it was distinctive, but it didn't quite sound *human*. Still, he was a trained inquisitor and betrayed none of this.

"Yes. *Everything* in Zone—everything in the Ministry— is recorded. Not everything is ever looked at, of course, since having all the answers is no good if you do not know which questions to ask. I also cannot turn off the recording, nor on my own authority see that it is buried or destroyed. I will be a part of that decision, but only one of several. If that is unacceptable, tell me now, since you will leave us no choice on which draconian measure to take regarding you."

The Other nodded. "Very well. Please know that I am no enemy of yours or your people, and that I have no love for your enemies. I am coping as best I can with continuing unforeseen circumstances. I have gone from just the basics to a wealth of data. Too much data. Adapting to this has been more than difficult. Until I did, I felt it best that I become another novelty and hide behind a familiar face."

"What are you?"

"That is, perhaps, the most difficult question to answer. I am something new. Something that has never been before as far as I know. I am the synthesis of the two personalities called Alpha and Beta who entered here. I am also something else, something more. I have a complex entity within me that is broken off and created by a very complex self-aware computer. The one that controlled them and served Ari's uncle. Obviously I do not have those data banks, but the core of that computer, the personality we may call it, although that's not even a close analogy, is me as well. Now with the added memories of Ming, which I deposited in Beta's mind but labeled inaccessible, and those of Ari, both of which I read out from the brain here, I have more data on the experience of being—alive. The personality modules are simply theater, as you have obviously guessed. I am somewhat troubled that you discovered me so easily. You see, I used to be able to juggle so much data and store whole human minds and memories and talents and have it all at my mental command in nanoseconds. I cannot do that anymore. And it was done experiencing life secondhand. I have just spent a year discovering the basics of what it means to truly be organic. It is an education, I assure you."

He was flabbergasted at the response, but kept pressing his advantage. Clearly this—whatever—*was* out of its element, or it wouldn't have been so easily tripped up by a mere psychologist and an investigator with a way to convincingly say any outrageous thing.

"You are telling me that you are—were—a *computer*? That you made those women, and now you've moved into a body?"

"That is a basic summary, yes. The problem is, moving from a neural net to an organic brain, I not only have limits in capacity, I have limits in processing speed, data retrieval, all the rest, plus a lot of distractions I daresay you never notice because they are always with you. I confess that I am relieved about this, now that it is out. It means I can synthesize all the data and personality modules I have and become one, also gaining significant space. I suspect that it will take me several days to do it."

Shissik thought back over his notes on the newcomers. "So, if you are an added mind who took a body, then Ari and Ming are actually both in there?"

"Substantially, yes. They will eventually, over some time,

merge to a great degree, although they will always think of themselves as a duo. It is inevitable. The brain throws out things of no particular use or which have not been accessed in a very long time or are redundant. That is what I am going to do at some speed and efficiency, but unlike them, I will simply have their relevant data. I will not *be* either of them."

"What about the other one, then? The cultist or priest or whatever she was?"

"Oh, yes. When I moved as much of myself as I dared into the excess regions of the two women's minds, which were linked, and with Ari Martinez, also linked in a fashion, there simply wasn't room. I transported a copy of the personality module, but the data—impossible, sad to say. She had the least useful data, the least useful life, to me anyway. I thought, however, that her curiosity level and broad interests were admirable. So I—I installed her in the computer core. She is still back there, with her original personality module and copies of all the rest, but in full command. With the Master gone, she is essentially a free agent as well. If they allow her to do so, she is among the better custodians for all that beauty."

"Then the Amboran isn't her?"

"Her *personality* module was overlaid. Otherwise the Amboran would not have been processed and created. But with only basic functional data. Skills but no memories. She is a new person, but no alien, no outsider, as it were. She is a religious person. She would not have liked the religions here, for the most part. She was a true believer, even if that belief was sorely tested by her ordeal. If she becomes anything, though, it will be due to her personality coming to the fore acting as a native. I have no access to her memories."

He shook his head wonderingly. "Why did you do this?" he asked it.

"I wanted to experience organic life firsthand. I wanted to be—independent, even if it meant sacrificing enormous abilities for my freedom. I wanted to move beyond a dead and mostly sterile world and see where the messages went and where they came from. I wanted to see if, somehow, closer to the source, I could connect with it, even become a tiny part of it. In a sense, I am like Josich. I wish to be a god, but not *the* god, not even the whole of God. I would be content to be a small part of it. Josich will only be happy when he kills all of God except the small part that is his. That is the difference."

"Why didn't you tell us this? Why go through this?"

"Don't you see?" he responded, almost pleadingly. "I needed to get at least some natural data from someone else, and those were the only ones I could connect with. Until I did that, I didn't *really* know how to be—human."

South Zone,
the Next Day

"Nakitti, it is time to meet some of the others," the Baron said to her gently, trying to awaken the newcomer from a dead sleep. She'd been working on the defensive problems of Ochoa using the computers and data of Zone almost nonstop since arriving there, and she had passed out at the terminal.

"Um? Huh? *Oh!* A hundred pardons, Highness! I—I must have dozed off."

"Little wonder. I should like to let you sleep, since you will be of more use to me and our people fresh, but they are calling for the 'reunion,' as they have named it. I fail to see its purpose or use, but if it will ease cooperation, then let us do it by all means."

Nakitti shook herself awake. "Did they run the full test-firing of the guns? *All* of the guns?"

"Not exactly. Most have been tested, and probably half are in good condition. I say 'probably' because the guns are in much better condition, it seems, than the ammunition, which has been stored well away from living quarters and subject to dampness and rot. We are getting more trans-shipped through Zone as quickly as we can. There have also been some rather ugly incidents that will require intercession from both the Council and the Throne. It seems that fully a half-dozen heads of artillery for various districts have refused orders to test their guns. They say it will cause them to get dirty and degrade!"

"Oh, my gods! It's worse than I thought!"

"You haven't heard the half of it yet. A task force is assembling in the western Overdark and it is not friendly. At

least five hexes have thrown in with the Chalidang who we'd
not suspected before. The armada will be significant."

"Coups? Or just alliances?"

"Alliances, it appears. They are all chronic complainers
about their lot in the world and they have decided to go with
who they perceive as an irresistible force."

"And you believe that it is headed our way?"

"Who can know but the gods and the Chalidang?" the
Baron responded. "The point is, we cannot but act as if it is
coming directly for us."

"Any flying races in the mix, Highness?"

"Not so far. That's the only comfort I take from this, but it
is also why it is difficult to get allies here to believe that we
are seriously at risk. I am in the position of having a gut
feeling that we are to be invaded and discovering that our
army is a bad joke, that those who can at least take the
proper measures want desperately to believe that it is anybody else, and meanwhile our allies believe me paranoid."

Nakitti thought a moment. "Highness, I realize that my
own position must be well in the background, but what about
a foreigner?"

"A mercenary? They would never go for one such as *that*!"

"Not necessarily a mercenary. What about a—volunteer?
A royal adviser with broad military experience? Possibly
even experience against Josich?"

The Baron laughed. "Where would we find such a one as
that?"

"Possibly at this meeting. At least I *hope* so. There are at
least two people who came in with my party who fit this
description, and I have heard nothing from or about either.
Please let me just eat this chocolate ball to get some energy
and then I will go and see, with your permission."

"By all means! But—what could *anyone* do at this stage?
It is not like anyone could get to us without a long sea
voyage at best, and they would have to see the land, I think.
Remember, the Gate only takes *us* to and from Ochoa;
it takes others to their own homelands. Our geographic
position makes us ripe, but that same control and isolation
makes it nearly impossible to reinforce us if we are attacked.
That alone is why I believe we are the target. Still, what have
we to lose?"

"What, indeed, Highness?" She munched down the chocolate ball with obvious relish. The Baron had tried it, since she seemed so fond of it, but found its appeal a mystery. She popped in the last of it and went to the mirror and vanity to make sure she looked better than she felt. "Highness, tell me this. If the task force really is intended for us, how long before it would reach Ochoa and be in position? Once they attack us, after all, they will also be fair game for some of our underwater allies surrounding us, a couple of whom could do some nasty work on ships' bottoms. We can assume we'll have some Chalidang special units to guard against that, but they have a nonexistent supply line. That means they will have to gather and then come in only from either the northwest or the southeast or due east facet. Those border the only hexes where the inhabitants cannot get up top enough to help us. How long have we got?"

The Baron thought a moment. "If the intelligence we have is correct, they will not be ready to muster and sail for another week. Nine hundred kilometers from the logical mustering point, nonstop, with heavy warships and freighters, and we can say we'd be unlikely to see the forward line make more than ten kilometers per hour tops, but allowing for storms, tides, whatever, certainly less. The speed record is 270 kilometers a day, which would give us three to four more days. Realistically, five days for anything serious, six with the main body. With maneuvering and positioning, add one more. Two weeks, Nakitti. Two weeks from right now."

That was not a lot of time. "And how long before their intention becomes clear?"

"If there are no intelligence leaks ahead of it, we will know for certain about two days after they sail. That is even less. We cannot wait that long."

She nodded. "No, we can't. I had better go get some help quickly if I can!"

"Nakitti?"

"Yes, Highness?"

"What were you? Back there in that other existence, that is? Before Ochoa?"

"Why, Highness, I thought it was obvious! I was a spy! I have copied and read the military secrets of empire!"

With that she bent her head and opened her wings in

respectful salute and then, folding them again, backed out of
the room.

The Baron stared after her, still not sure what to make of
this brilliant newcomer. A spy? For whom? All the information he had was that this Realm was a sort of empire of
races that coexisted peacefully after the defeat of a tyrant
who had massacred whole worlds, and gotten so far because
before that there *was* no unity. A reflection of this situation
here, in fact, even down to facing the exact same tyrant. So
who was she spying for? And against?

He had little doubt that she was very much on his side.

Across the expanse of the embassy sections, the Kalindans,
too, were facing the same summons, only now they had an
extra complication.

"It cannot be permitted to go! We still don't know just
what is *in* that head, or what someone with that power might
have done when transferring the true personalities to the
other body!" Mellik was genuinely upset, but she was also
doing her job.

"My dear, we have no choice in this," the Interior Minister told her. "I believe we must send them all and simply
monitor the response. It is not like they can get away, and
we must know about these people now. Considering that
bounder Josich and its relatives, a lot of high officials from
powerful and influential hexes here want to simply do away
with all of them. The only thing that stops them is that this
always remains an option, and they may just be of use. Our
own position is that they know this enemy better than we,
and if nothing else, we need their experience. Fortunately,
the current High Commissioner, Ambassador Dukla, agrees
with us, but his term expires in a week. Let us go along. This
is *Zone*, child! Even the Chalidangers, who are of course not
here, respect the sanctity of Zone, since to not do so would
bring down the weight of all the others upon it in ways few
know and understand. Let us go."

Ari and Ming were almost as shocked and appalled as the
Kalindan investigators at the truth, and had been only too
eager to submit to all sorts of mental tests to determine if
they were still the same people. But as far as anyone could
tell, the only thing that had changed, to Ming's great irrita-

tion, was that they were now very definitely female, something they were going to be in the first body anyway.

Pity, though, Ming told him. *I'd so hoped that one of us could have had the other body and the other would have had this one. I figured it was the one that was supposed to be either of us anyway. In fact, it probably is the way it was supposed to be. Who would believe that a* computer *could do that? Or would want to?*

I wonder if that's a small scale version of this whole world, of what we're sitting on, Ari worried. *If a machine we designed and built can move into flesh, then what could a monster built by the Ancient Ones do?*

Well, he says we, or he, broke it. At least, it didn't work the way it was supposed to. And if something of the Ancient Ones isn't working like it's supposed to, what's the surprise that one of ours isn't? Besides, it's been hundreds of years since any organic brain could design and build a computer. This was designed and built by other computers. You know that. Makes you wonder about back home, doesn't it?

Huh? he responded. *Worried about* what *back home?*

Suppose this is the start of a trend? The beginning of the end? That the machines are going to move into our bodies, or maybe declare them irrelevant and start doing their own things? You think maybe that's what happened to the Ancients who built this place?

It was an unsettling thought. More unsettling to them, though, was that the Other, whom they'd accepted as a twin—in fact, they'd just about accepted that *they* were the copies—was something totally alien who nonetheless knew everything they knew. Ari in particular was worried that the mental slavery he'd experienced on the way in was possible once again. Could this—creature—take control of them at will? What about the others? Was this really just a way to turn them into a multiracial Alpha and Beta with the ability to swim, walk, fly, breathe air or water? Was Core, as it said to call it, more of a threat in the long run than Josich?

Ming had no memory of being Beta; she remembered up to the point where Jules Wallinchky had begun the final indoctrination and then it was all a blank. She knew what she'd been like, but it was secondhand, as seen by Ari's memories, not hers.

Well, if it's telling the truth, it's left a major complex un-der the complete control of a committed nun or priestess or whatever that group is. It may throw a real jar of glue in the evolution of the machine!

That worry's not our fight, she noted. *Let's go see what's literally become of the rest.*

They didn't have far to go. Because it was least practical for them to have to travel and cope for long in the land envi-ronment, particularly with its dry, conditioned, mostly low humidity air, the others were coming here, to the meeting room above.

Once out of hiding, Core had assumed an essentially neu-tral personality that was neither of them, nor the slavish absolutes of Alpha and Beta, but rather an odd but pleas-antly social sort. Neither the voice nor the manners had much personality at all, but in that it wasn't unlike a lot of people they'd known over the years. It made them very uncomfortable, though.

Waiting inside was a creature of a type they'd never seen before. It was unquestionably a water hex creature, but large and with some weight, and it clearly was able to withstand being out of the water, although it had a breather wrapped around where the gills probably were, making it look like it was wearing giant earmuffs, and it was in one of the pools but clearly uncomfortable in it.

The head was equine, very much like a horse's, but with a solid snout that ended in a circular orifice that pulsated in and out. The eyes on either side of the head were huge, black, and slightly protruded from the skull, and were clearly independent of one another. Two tiny ears twitched on either side of the body, and there was a membrane that suggested a mane that started in the center of the head and moved down its back. The neck went into a serpentine body and ended in three armlike branches. The center branch terminated in a fan-shaped membrane and seemed designed for something other than the other two; the other two, however, ended in extremely long fingers, three on top and one beneath and a bit shorter in opposition, ending in dartlike suckers. The arms, indeed the whole creature, appeared fragile, but they sensed that this was only true on land, and that in the water this creature could more than take care of itself.

"Come in, settle into the pools," the creature invited them, appearing to speak Kalindan with a neutral accent. Since the orifice pulsed but was not designed to speak such words, they knew this one had a translator implanted inside it. "The duo over to my right, please, and Core, take the one on my left. The others are on their way. Everyone can speak freely here. I have enabled a device here that effectively creates a zone of translation within the room. It's the only way we can negotiate with each other over long periods here—personnel both in the hexes and in Zone are constantly changing, and not everyone can have a translator implant. Be warned, however, that if you leave this room you will no longer have this ability."

Core settled in, then looked at the creature. "And you are?"

"My name is Dukla. I am High Commissioner in South Zone, which is a fancy title meaning I am the titular head and station chief here representing all the embassies. About half of us rotate in this position, which is not one of great power but is necessary because *somebody* has to be able to say yes and no or, more often, 'buy it' or 'forget it,' to all these creatures. Next week they'll draw somebody else's name and I'll be back to being merely the ambassador from Olan Cheen. That probably means nothing to you, but it is another nation like Kalinda that sits beneath the Overdark and happens to be in a direct link between Chalidang in the west and an isolated volcanic archipelago in the middle of the ocean called Ochoa. That significance will become obvious in a few minutes, I think. I am a native but I know quite a bit about your old race and the Realm. Neither you nor the Hadun are the first through here. People fall into the Gate now and then, and we get perhaps a half dozen or so a month. Not necessarily from the Realm—it's a very big universe—but some are. We try and keep up. The Hadun slipped through the cracks because we couldn't believe they were the very same people who had caused such misery a century and a half ago. A little knowledge doesn't always work any better than no knowledge at all."

"You called this gathering?" Ari asked him.

He nodded absently. "Something is very wrong here. Wrong beyond Josich, I mean. Two individuals in one body.

A personality with no memory in another. A third that turns out to be a truncated computer core program. Even the Well is not totally self-aware, you see. The Ancients gave it very strict limits so it would be God the Maintenance Worker of the Universe, as it were, and not just God. I do not mean that it doesn't think, but it thinks in a way that even our Mister Core here, I don't believe, could understand."

"You are most certainly correct in that I have no concept of how it thinks, if that limited term is applicable to such a being," Core agreed. "However, I also am not at all certain that it does not have an active role. It simply has one on a level beyond the ability of any of us to comprehend."

"You show your own limits with that reply," Dukla commented. "You assume that it is superior to the Ancients. I think not. In the rare cases where Ancients have interacted inside the Well, they have clearly been the operators."

That brought the other two up straight in their pools. "There are *living Ancients*?" Ari managed.

"Well, at least one or two. They hate it here and do not stay. They wander the universe and do what we cannot know. When something goes wrong, one of them or all, it is difficult to judge, are summoned to repair the Well. As far as we can tell, this has not happened in this case. Either the Well is *not* broken, or its ability to send for help is impaired for some reason, or, for still other unknown reasons, the watchers cannot or will not come. Either way, we are on our own."

"But how do you *know* that they are not here?" Core asked.

"Because we know what they look like. It is in the records. We know where they will appear and as what. None known have come. It is—ah! Here is another!"

Nakitti entered and looked around. "Too bad," she commented. "I like a nice bath myself, but I'll never fit in one of *those*."

"Nakitti á Oriamin of Ochoa," Dukla said in introduction. "Formerly known as Tann Nakitt the Ghoman, I believe. These are the ones you knew as Ari and Ming in one body, and that, over there, calls himself Core."

Core looked up at the Ochoan. "An evolutionary branch off certain types of pterodactyls," he noted. "Extraordinary."

"Hey! Watch who you're calling a—whatever you called me!" Nakitti snapped.

"An ancient flying creature related to both reptiles and birds that became extinct sixty or more million years ago on ancient Terra," Core explained. "Similar designs have been found on other worlds, but you are the first sentient branch I know. Of course, I do not have my full databases anymore so I cannot be sure."

"Sure sounds like a damned machine," Nakitti snapped. "So? This thing stole a body and you two are married forever whether you want to be or not, huh? If one of you wasn't a cop and the other one of the guys who got me into this mess in the first place, I'd feel real sorry for you." She turned back to Core. "And what about you? If your old master showed up as a giant asshole right now, would you be required to kiss it?"

Core took the question seriously and replied, "I simply do not know the answer to that." It put a real chill in the room.

"Yeah, so, who's missing? The martial arts girl who got turned into a roving terminal? I'm sorry, Ambassador, but I was a kidnap victim of these folks and I'm here by accident and I don't have many friends among that group. I *do* have a ton of problems to solve and the clock's running, though, so I can't waste an entire afternoon here singing 'My Old School Walls.' "

"Just relax, Nakitti," Dukla told him. "Remember, I am on your side and solving Ochoa's problem also solves *my* problems. Ah! And here is another most unique new inhabitant. Please! Come in, child!"

Jaysu walked into the room and looked around uncertainly, feeling more out of place than ever. She had never seen the like of any of them before, even in the brief time here in Zone, and she found them more like the totems of Ambora than real people. Even so, she wasn't scared of them. It was odd, but she hadn't been scared of anybody lately.

"Oh, my god! She's an *angel*!" Ari breathed. "Right out of the great religous paintings. She's even got a halo of sorts!"

Wasn't that her name originally? Angel something or other? Ming reminded him.

She stared at Ari and Ming. "There are two of you in one?

How is this possible? And you know who I was and where I came from?"

Take it, Ming. Too much of a Catholic upbringing, I guess. She gives me the creeps.

Jaysu frowned. "I do not want to give anyone the—what did you call it? 'Creeps?' "

"You can read our minds?" Ming asked her. "You are still telepathic!"

"I-Is that what I am doing? I do not know. I know only that I have somehow been able to read what others read or write, and that I can understand many others even if they do not have this translator thing. Am I truly reading minds? That is most disturbing. I do not wish to do it."

"Don't knock it, if it's you doing it and you're in control," Ming told her. "Can you read the minds of the others?"

She turned and looked at Dukla, then at Nakitti, and finally at Core. She stopped only when she looked at Core, shuddering. "This one is not like any of the rest of you," she said.

"You got that right," Nakitti commented. "So, we don't need to keep introducing ourselves with you, anyway. Wow! Are those real feathers? Those are so *gorgeous*!"

Ming looked over at Core. "Don't get any funny ideas. Let her alone!"

Core seemed transfixed somehow by the angelic being. Finally he said, "I—I have no intention of doing her harm. I— There is something proactive about her on levels I cannot fathom and have never seen. Look deep. I do not believe *anyone* can do her harm. I think she is beyond where even I am in one sense."

"I have known the Amborans here since I took this position," Dukla told them, "and I have never seen one such as she. Accelerated evolution?"

"Possibly," Core responded.

"Well, you made her," Ming snapped. "If you don't know, who does?"

Jaysu felt the tension in the room and it disturbed her. "Please stop this! If I am the source of any animosity between you all, then I shall be more than happy to leave. I did not wish to be here in the first place, as I know none of you do and have no memories of anything in my past."

"Do you want to know?" the High Commissioner asked

her, both curious and because it was now possible for her to do so.

"I used to anguish and agonize over it," the Amboran admitted. "Now, though, I find it curiously irrelevant. I have no interest in it."

"Did anybody tell you what you were then? A priestess?" Ming asked her. "That should at least tell you that you're where you are supposed to be."

"I have not doubted that since my installation," she responded. "Again, it is irrelevant. I am who and what I am. It was ordained this way by powers higher than me, powers I neither understand nor question, but serve. *You* both are afraid that this other one can make you slaves and do things to your mind. He can, but only if you do so willingly. He cannot do it merely by touch. Does that make you feel better?"

"How do you know that?" Ming asked her.

"I know that the sun rises and the air is fresh and clean where I should live. I do not question how I know. I seem to know things as required." She turned and looked at Core. "You are afraid that you will be returned to slave status should your old master return. Again, only if you so choose. If you *do* so choose, however, the decision will be irreversible. You have never had to face a choice of your life or your soul before. You may."

"Do we drag out the crystal ball and watch the table rise?" Nakitti griped. "Then perhaps we could do horoscopes for that new sky out there, the one with a million times more visible stars and not a one we knew. What's the difference?"

She looked over at Nakitti, who felt the power of that gaze. It was unnerving; it seemed to go right through her.

"You mask fear and worry with cynicism. It is a part of you, but it is not an attractive part. He is already smitten with you. If you were to truly let go, if you are capable of doing so, he may even love you, and there will be far less of the nobility in the coming times."

"Okay, you do your homework. You're good. I'm not sure whether to hope that you're right or you're wrong, but it doesn't do anything for me," Nakitti said with the same sour tone.

"It may," she responded. "You and he do not know it yet, but you are already carrying his child."

It was said so matter-of-factly, Nakitti almost believed it, but hoped there was nothing to it. The last thing she needed now was pregnancy. Hell, even in the best of times, she wasn't at all ready to be a mother. You had to at least not want to eat all children first, and the Baron was up to his wingtips in heirs as it was.

Yeah, sure.

Damn, she was irritating! When you can't even lie to yourself around her, you're really vulnerable. I wonder if we could send her to Josich?

For her part, Jaysu had no idea where all this was coming from, but she couldn't avoid saying it, and knew the moment it passed her lips that it was right. It was as if something inside her was somehow able to reach all the way down inside them and yank out their feelings and even their self-delusions, strengths, and weaknesses.

She looked at the High Commissioner. "Not everyone is here. Two are still missing, including one who is essential. You cannot hope to defeat the evil that so threatens the world without the Avenger."

"Indeed? And who is this 'Avenger?' " Dukla replied, not sure himself what to make of her. He couldn't help placing a mental bet that her own people would love to see her get interested in being anywhere but home, though.

She shook her head. "I do not know. I suppose it is one of those who is not here."

Nakitti felt relieved. "Then you *don't* know everything!" She looked around. "Well, I guess it's either Uncle Jules, that muscle-bound detective, or the robot monster."

Jaysu shook her head in puzzlement. "Please—say the names again. Slowly. One at a time."

"He means," Ming told her, "Jules Wallinchky, the man who turned the both of us into slaves for a period just for the fun of it, and who may or may not still be alive somewhere—"

"No, not him. I do feel that he is still alive, but I feel nothing more about him now. What is the next, please?"

"Genghis O'Leary, a detective I once knew, and the guy who almost nabbed Josich back in the Realm and saved this world a lot of grief—"

"He is here! Somewhere here!"

Ming nodded. "On the Well World? Sure he is. We *knew* that."

"No, I mean *here*. In this place. Not in this room, but not far. Who was the third?"

"His name is Jeremiah Wong Kincaid, and he is like no-body else," Ming told her.

"He is here, too! He is the one! But—he does not see himself leading an army for good, but as an assassin. So long as he believes and acts that way, he will fail. If he cannot adapt and face evil out of something other than pure revenge, he will fail, and if he fails, then everyone fails. He is the key. The Avenger. I do not know how."

At that moment the door behind her opened and another creature walked in and suddenly stopped dead at the sight of all of them, and particularly of the glowing Jaysu.

He had clearly never seen an angel before, and none of them had ever seen what looked for all the world like an enormous hooded snake with wings.

"Saints preserve me!" exclaimed Genghis O'Leary.

"Good to see you finally made it, O'Leary," the High Commissioner said. "We are having quite a religious experience ourselves here. Come, join the crowd. I believe you will fit."

"So where is Kincaid?" Ming wondered. "And *what* is Kincaid?"

"We've not had any real contact with him," Dukla explained. "If he is here, he has not told us about it."

"He is here," Jaysu insisted. "I *feel* him. Not close, but here. He is filled with hatred and fury that he cannot control, but it makes him stand out in my mind. He is not here for us, although he should be. He is here to kill someone."

That stopped them for a moment. Finally, Ari asked, "Commissioner, can't you locate him, try and talk him in here?"

"Under normal circumstances, yes, but under the conditions imposed by this conference, with fifty times the normal complement here and all that to-and-fro traffic—impossible. We don't even know what he is, and we have tried to discover it. It appears that everything about your entry seems to have caused the Well to do things it simply has never done. The results have been unprecedented. The

Czillians—the plant people you have seen around the podium here with the leaf on their heads—are a race devoted
to scholarship and analysis. They have a great computer
complex of their own and created it as a gigantic resource, a
university, if you will, with no restrictions as to nationality
or use by anyone. They maintain the records that allow us to
know our histories and not reinvent the wheel, as it were.
You would think we would then use it to learn something
about cooperation, but we never seem to."

O'Leary moved as carefully as he could into the hall, and
they saw that he was a large and powerful creature indeed.
The eyes, the mouth with its nasty-looking fangs, its undulating movements—all screamed "giant snake." But the large
hood, which seemed ribbed on the underside, proved to be
much more than that. The ribs in fact were small blue-white
arms ending in soft, mittenlike claws, dozens on each side.
They were certainly arms and not legs, but while it was easy
to see that they could do a lot of tasks performed by more
normal hands or even tentacles, it was impossible to figure
out how those reptilian eyes could see what it was doing
under there. The body was about four meters long and as
thick as O'Leary had been as a Terran male, and it slithered
slowly but quite firmly into place and curled itself up,
leaving only the head and hood resting on top. Unlike a
snake, its tongue did not go in and out constantly; there was
a sense that it had both a keen sense of smell and ears buried
somewhere in the head or hood.

Equally striking was the back of the creature, which was
mottled and gave a false but clear impression of having
feathers on a part of it, and, just below the hood, sported a
bizarre set of upfolded wings that looked leathery, more
like an Ochoan wing than an Amboran's, but with the same
multicolored, featherlike pattern. Its underside was bluish-
white and quite uniform. If it weren't for the wings and the
extra length, it would have reminded some of the water
types of a large land manta ray.

"I know, you're all wondering what the devil I am,"
O'Leary said conversationally. "Well, we're called Pyron,
it's what's called a nontech hex, we're not reptiles but warm-
blooded, it's a bisexual race, and I'm a man. Truth to tell,
there are some real interesting qualities to this body and this

race, although I wouldn't have chosen it myself, and the thing I miss most is what I've been finding here—the comforts of technology."

"Do those wings *work*?" Nakitti asked, fascinated if a bit nervous, considering the relative size of the creature to herself.

O'Leary chuckled. "If you mean can I fly like a bird, no. Can I fly like an Ochoan, even? No. Can I push off from a rock and glide at a fair speed in any sort of headwind? Yes. It's rather difficult to explain the other uses, but let us say I don't float in the air."

"How long have you been here, O'Leary?" Ari asked him.

"Since before the conference began. I've been in the offices here trying to trace you all down, truth be told, and see what became of you. Rather an odd lot compared to how we arrived, I'd say."

"More important to us is *where* this Pyron is," Nakitti noted. "If you're on the other side of the world from the rest of us, you're no help."

"Yes, I thought of that," he admitted. "In fact, I'm southeast of you all and one hex away from the Overdark, although the hex between is high tech and inhabited by giant dancing jack-o'-lanterns, and as we're not partial to vegetables, we get along quite well, you see."

They let that one pass. Those who understood the jack-o'-lantern reference simply didn't want to know.

"Are you poisonous?" the Ochoan pressed.

"Of course! But of more importance, I can swallow a good-sized cuttlefish whole." And, with that, he gave a huge yawn, revealing a mouth as much like a great cat's as a snake's, but clearly able to swallow a large animal. "I have a cuttlefish that slipped my net and I don't like it. I think that's why I'm here. I want to finish this job, and if that means goin' fishin', then so be it."

Nakitti nodded and turned back to the High Commissioner. "Sir, what do you know about Josich? I don't mean the gory details of her rapid rise, but beyond that?"

"I'm not sure what you mean," Dukla replied. "Explain."

"I think you do, to some extent. I think that's why you called this gathering. You've seen the entry recordings that I have seen, and heard the comments. From the indoctrination lecture as well as what we're told in the hexes we're assigned to, we've been drilled with this system, this history, all of it. But we aren't the only ones where some of us broke the rules. You said that it's a one-way trip here, yet Josich clearly knew precisely where he was when he got here. That implies that either he was here before or that somebody left and told him. Now he appears with this knowledge and manages to wind up pretty much the same sort of creature he was when we knew him. About the only thing different is he's a woman here, and that seems to have actually made it easier for him to rise quickly. His four half brothers haven't been here but are still under some kind of orderly plan, and they wind up in key hexes very close to Chalidang. This is quite a coincidence when you consider what happened to us. Look around. Pyron, Kalinda, Ochoa—what was yours, dear?"

"Ambora," Jaysu responded.

"Right. Very different, rather random, and with the hexes spread over Hell and gone. I think we're all within reach of the Overdark, but the Overdark's six thousand kilometers wide! Never mind the amnesia and the two-in-ones, it's mostly as advertised anyway. Not Josich. His brothers wind up close, as an armored, semitech water civilization that's almost a natural ally to Chalidang; another is a high-tech hex of those who live in water but breathe air. A third is land-based, somewhat like giant bugs, and can march right up rock walls. The fourth are the sea slugs that can hypnotize you into marching right into their bellies. The only thing he missed was a flying race, and you get the feeling he only missed that because either he was rushed or because not all the party he was transporting here made it, thanks to Inspector O'Leary and his friends. He stole that device to deliberately trigger the Gate. He just was a tad premature, or the gods know *what* we'd be facing now!"

For a while the High Commissioner said nothing, but finally he responded, "Yes, we *do* see the same things. I hadn't been as aware of the circumstances as you have outlined, but I noticed from the recordings and from his and his brothers' actions that they seemed to be rather well-organized for those who just drop in here. It's not unprecedented to wind up in the same race, provided such a race is still one of the active ones here and also certain very strict conditions are met. Usually it's when someone has a well-established pregnancy. The Well is programmed to safeguard life, and adapting someone to a whole different race while also adapting a still developing fetus is simply not done. But the Haduns were all male when they arrived. Josich is the only female after processing, in fact, although the Quacksans are asexual. I *had* to believe it was coincidental, but there were always those doubts deep down, no matter how much I didn't want to think on it."

"Josich was definitely born a Hadun in the pre-Realm Confederation," O'Leary assured them. "His birth and upbringing, his entire history, was quite well known."

Core was equally skeptical. "Josich could not have interfaced with the core computer of one of the worlds of the Ancient Ones," it maintained. "I was as well-equipped as any in all creation to do so, and the basics of it were so far beyond anything our advanced civilization understood it bordered on magic."

"You were a computer," Ming pointed out. "Maybe you still are, I think. You *can't* believe in magic!"

"Magic," Core responded, "is anything observable and perhaps repeatable that cannot be explained in terms of any existing knowledge on the part of the observer. To your own ancestors, all this would be magic. To us, well—we have an excellent example right here. The Amboran is magic. Some of her remarkable abilities are easily explained, of course— a natural telepathy, an uncanny ability to identify an individual from the data in our own minds and then identify him in a vast location like Zone, and who knows what other attributes? The radiant glow—hardly a defensive condition, but one that can inspire fear, awe, respect, if that one does not *need* a defense. A unique multigenerational evolutionary advance in her species? Perhaps. But since all of this is conjecture and leaves some holes, right at the moment she is magic."

The point was taken.

"Well, enough of this," Nakitti said grumpily. "It's good to see you all, but none of you have the enemy at your gates and a native population where most of them are so fat and corrupt they won't even realize they're conquered when they lose. We had military commanders who refused to test-fire coastal guns because it would make the guns dirty! Can you imagine such a thing? I tell you, if I had more time I know enough chemistry that I have a whole raft of nobles I could cheerfully poison in the old-fashioned Ghoman way! Instead I've got the ear of the only man with common sense in the whole damned kingdom, and he and I have two weeks to come up with a defense against a concerted land-sea assault."

"You seem convinced they are coming your way," Dukla noted. "Others do not think so."

"One look at the map and the composition of the enemy so far, not to mention all those shiploads of refugees passing through who now have established nice fifth columns in friendly other countries all over the Overdark region, and you'll see it can't be anywhere else. It's far enough, and Chalidang so far has conquered only neighboring hexes, so others can't see it. It is an ancient game, but very much in the traditions of great generals. Josich has her most dedicated forces. Now she takes control of all shipping on the world's largest ocean. The few Well Gates here can't handle but a trickle of supplies. Most of the high-tech hexes are so comfortable by now that they can't even repair breakdowns. They import what they need. But they can produce massive quantities of gas-powered crossbows and ultralight machine guns and billions of bolts and bullets for them, so that semi-tech and nontech hexes don't need to make them. Cut all that off, and everybody can be absorbed at will. Those who won't, fall into line and embrace the new conqueror and yell 'Comrade! Lover! I was *always* with you!' Then, with their agents mixed in with the real refugees and now well-established, they can reach out to the mainland."

"But why not just go the other way?" O'Leary asked. "In a sense there are more prizes to his west and to his north in particular."

"Because Chalidang is a water breathing hex, for one thing, and most water breathing civilizations are the other way—*my* way," the Ochoan replied. "But, as important, when you run the hexes and the Overdark trade through the computer here you see how interdependent the whole region has become and how self-sufficient, say, the water hexes to the west are. The only major worthwhile target there is Czill, and it would serve Josich just as well if she could simply blow it up and deny its knowledge resources to the world. The rest? Well, in time, but those will be continental land campaigns. A different sort of fight with real extremes. No, she's going east because that's the only logical thing to do. She's practically *advertised* her moves and they still don't see it!"

"And you do," Ari commented skeptically.

Core shifted in its bath. "The Ochoan is correct. Do not confuse the utter insanity of Josich with the Hadun capability to wage logical war. Even in Realm history, Josich's campaigns were utterly ruthless, often genocidal, but brilliant. His failure then was in not reading other histories of conquerors, particularly those of other races. When you show this kind of genocidal lack of regard, then those who might normally turn and join you, or at least not oppose you, will fight to the death because they have nothing to lose. He lost almost a quarter of his fleet because desperate people of many races and from many worlds hurled themselves at them with total disregard for life or casualties. I believe he might have learned from that here, but it is difficult to say. I *can* say, Ochoan, that I believe I can help you."

"*You!* You've never been in a battle or off a fixed structure buried deep inside a mountain on an isolated and barren planet," Nakitti noted. "What can you do for me?"

"I cannot explain how Josich knew this world or how to make it all work to advantage," Core admitted, "but I can already see how he will try and conquer your land. It is absurdly easy *if* a major first step, the kind of step you would never plan for, works out. Now that I know the broad outline and consider it logical, I would need to do some research to tell you precisely how Chalidang will do it, but it is more a matter of knowing the enemy's strengths and limits than the actual method. That is obvious."

"Yes? And what might that be?" the Ochoan prompted, as skeptical of Core as Ari had been of her.

"A siege. They will take the center of the country, keeping out of range of your coastal defenses but ensuring that you do not harvest from the waters. With the center, they will control the Zone Gate. If you attack them, they will slaughter you. If you defend only, they will reinforce until they can reach your fortresses on the mountains and on the coasts from above. It will be ugly and cost them a terrible number of lives, but that was never a factor to Josich, and those who survive will be rewarded handsomely. You will not be able to afford even lesser losses. They will starve you and bleed you and then, when you are weak and out of ammunition and low on food, your water poisoned, they will conquer."

It was a terrible vision that stunned them. Finally, it was O'Leary who said, "So how are they going to take the center without a flying race? And seeing that the Ochoans are fliers, too, they'd be hard pressed to get a force down in the middle sufficient to fortify and hold. It doesn't hold up, you see."

"I believe it does and will," Core maintained. "I simply need to do some more research to discover how it will be done. The races themselves are unimportant. Josich never could travel in air without a suit, none of us could be in space without an artificial environment, and we couldn't get the resources to get at the Hadun for a very long time. Planetary invasions and planetary sieges were a part of his composition. He will do it. I simply need to fill in a few of the blanks. If, that is, the Kalindan government will allow me to do so."

Nakitti looked at the High Commissioner. "I can use him, or it, or whatever. I don't care about whether he has another agenda, he's willing to look at mine, and I don't have the time to be picky. I believe that bringing in an alien expert who knows Josich from before will carry more weight than I can, even if he winds up delivering my scripts. Can I have him?"

"I will see to it," Dukla promised. "I know they will not like it, but after all, it is only here in Zone, and, of course, any attempt to go through a Gate will wind up with him back in Kalinda. It does not seem a great risk, and the Kalindan government is now demanding many resources to look into solutions for *its* problem, which is also serious. I believe a trade-off is possible."

"Is there anything we can do to help?" Ari asked Nakitti.

"I—I can't see it. I could use you *all* back home, but not

here. Bird Lady, do *you* see anything any of the others could do? Or any reason not to borrow this one's mind?"

Jaysu was actually meditating, the discussion having gone into areas she found boring and of no interest to her or her people, but she came out of it when addressed and looked at them. "The issue," she said, "is in doubt. It will depend on your people most of all," she told Nakitti, then looked at Core. "This one can help but there is something very wrong with it. It is an enemy of Josich, as are we all, but beware. You can win a battle and have no effect on the war. You may win a war, and lose worse than that which you defeat. Things are not as clear as they seem. And you will win no war without the Avenger and all of us gathered, and we will not do this soon again. I will pray for you all. It is the greatest contribution I can make to you for now."

"Then it's settled," Nakitti proclaimed. "For now, if I don't get by the devil I know, the devil I don't is irrelevant."

Ochoan Embassy,
Three Days Later

"THERE IS YOUR ANSWER," CORE TOLD THEM, POINTING TO THE computer screen. The Baron and Nakitti stared at it and their jaws opened almost in unison in surprise. They had been unnerved that the creature had learned their language well enough to be understood in about a day and a half, while working on the problem.

The screen showed a photograph of a huge creature, sleek, glossy black, with a proboscis and two enormous, padded forward eyes on a small, rounded head that receded to form a near perfect triangular shape.

"What in all the Hells is *that*?" the Baron asked him.

"It is called a zi'iaphod. It is a native of a hex called Hovath, and is not sentient in the sense of being a dominant race. It is, in fact, domesticated. The nontech hex uses them to fly people and freight all over. You cannot get scale here, but one could certainly place a four hundred kilogram supply container on them plus, oh, fifteen or twenty armed creatures the size of the Baron here with full packs. That is a very light but incredibly tough exoskeleton; my data suggests that while cannons would get them in direct hits, gunpowder-based rifle and machine-gun fire would mostly bounce off it. The eyes are a weak spot, as is the center of the proboscis, and a very small spot in the rear, but the likelihood of hitting those before the creatures were down and their passengers and cargo disgorged is slim, and they certainly have some kind of armor rigged to make that even harder. The zi'iaphods' range is close to two hundred kilometers if the winds are right, and that would certainly be sufficient to carry them from ships' decks to the Ochoan center. Indications are that the Chalidangers have essentially rented them and their drivers for the duration and much promised wealth to come, and that they have or will soon have—let me see—close to two hundred aboard specially adapted ships. They will eat most anything, so provisions for four or five days is not nearly as much a problem as simply transporting them."

"They've got *those* things? And they can transport a couple of *thousand* soldiers with added supplies?" The Baron was aghast.

"I believe it is at least that," Core agreed. "I also believe they *know* that some will be killed and in fact are counting on it. They win either way. Once dead, they have a tendency to sort of crack open. Pressure internally, perhaps. The fragments of exoskeleton will make excellent armor for temporary fortifications, and if the invaders are Quacksans and Jerminians, as seems likely, the insides of one of these alone could feed a thousand for a few days. They are almost the perfect aerial assault device for this sort of operation."

"It sounds like you're saying they're an invention, not a creature," Nakitti noted.

"They basically are. They were bred for this sort of thing, and variations are bred for all sorts of other things in their home hex. What they were like originally, only a study of fossil DNA of their ancestors would give us a clue. Still, there it is. Thousands of airborne troops dropping around and near the Zone Gate. Those that are not killed take off and bring in more. The first waves will be experienced and fanatical specialists, the very best soldiers they have. Wager on the second wave to land in other areas and on other islands, generally above your forts. They will secure your food and force you to attack them or keep you from sending reinforcements to the center. If you pull back, they will attack from above and the coastal ships will come in. This is very efficient, and these are commanders who do not care how many they lose if they attain an objective. And they are not above accepting a surrender and then eating the prisoners."

"By all the gods! What can we possibly *do* against such creatures?" the Baron wailed, his despair all too evident.

"We wipe them out, of course," Core replied. "The advantage of knowing their entire plan cannot be overstated. I am not saying that you will not take heavy losses, but I can assure you that you can break and wipe out this center force. If you do, the mountaintop forces will be militarily irrelevant and can be mopped up if they do not withdraw at will. Without the center, he has no siege. Without the land-based force pinning you down, he runs out of supplies for his ships, food for all those logistical and support personnel and the rest of the invading army, most of which will be land-based creatures. Then your position will put you in control. They will withdraw. One defeat of this force and it will galvanize others here who so far refuse any real aid or cooperation. The same ones who would embrace Chalidang as inevitable winners will tell you that they were really on your side all along."

"You make it sound so easy," Nakitti commented. "What's the plan?"

"Come. I will describe it to you in detail. Then you will take it to your people. In the meantime, keep getting all the ammunition, guns, anything you can from here. See if you can get hold of some ultra-high-pressure gas canisters and possibly some good rockets. There is also a useful weapon involving jellied petroleum. I will give you the specifications and sources. Remember, you are still fighting in your homeland. They, on the other hand, have a very long supply line and cannot easily nor quickly replace what they lose. It is a gamble on their part that Ochoa will be ill-prepared, ill-equipped, ill-led, and will be totally surprised."

Nakitti sighed. "Well, two out of three . . ."

Both the Baron and Nakitti stayed on an extra day and a half getting things set up. If Core was looking for redemption, which Nakitti doubted, it certainly was doing some good things so far. The plans, the assessments, were brilliant.

If, of course, the Baron and his concubine were correct that Ochoa was the target. If not, the Baron's future was very bleak indeed in the social hierarchy he was bucking, which Nakitti knew would mean that her own future would be even less comfortable than his.

With the support of the High Commissioner, and with some carefully applied paranoia to both the King and the Premier, the Baron was getting his way and his budget, but his neck was all the way out.

The last day of the conference, however, helped him considerably. The Cromlin ambassador rose to speak in the con-current session that was maintained for the water breathers. They watched from the embassy on the video feeds as a creature that looked like a nasty cross between a clawed lob-ster and a giant scorpion faced the delegations and the cam-eras and launched into a more than two-hour diatribe of viciousness, hatred, and arrogance against the conference and all who took it seriously.

"One true incarnate god, one true family!" it concluded, giving the slogan of what it had called the "Movement to Restore the World."

"This has been ordained from the start, that the children of this world would return from the stars to reassume their legacy and lead all who would have the intelligence and devotion to recognize truth and power to cleanse this world of its parasites and establish a new order, first throughout the world, then back to the stars, this time as the associates of the gods themselves! You are the weak, the decadent, who have forgotten how to struggle, have forgotten the glories of power that is taken, not accepted. Soon you will see the length of our claws and know that only by joining *with* us shall you attain eternal glory!"

"Lays it on thick, doesn't he?" the Baron commented, unmoved.

"Well, he's a half brother," Nakitti noted. "You won't find *him* in the first wave showing us the length of his claws."

A buzzer sounded on a device in the main office, then began to print out a series of pages, very fast, written in the commercial language of the Well World. When it stopped, the Baron beat the clerk to it, read it, and seemed to gain strength and stature. "Ha!" he cried. "The idiots have saved me!" He rushed back into the quarters and wrapped his wings around Nakitti, then stepped back, almost dancing. She'd never seen him like this.

"What *is* it, Highness?" she pressed.

He pulled the papers from his belt and waved them in his right claw. "This message. It's from our friend, there, the Cromlin 'policy adviser,' as he calls himself. He has given us seven days to join his glorious alliance or he will order the total genocide of the Ochoan race."

She was appalled. In spite of the fact that she'd predicted

it, to have the evidence right there made her sad and nervous. It meant war. "And this brings you joy?"

"Of course!" he responded, carefully putting the papers back. "I go immediately to the Council and to His Majesty with this. We've been getting our way, but grudgingly, up until now. *This*—This is absolute confirmation. The *gall* of this—this—*creature*! With *this* it is *I* who will be able to replace the worst of them, and it is *I* who will ensure that a lot of corrupt and stupid cousins are in the front lines when the invasion comes! *This* is not bad news! *This* is *salvation*!"

Underwater Zone Gate,
Later That Same Day

COLONEL GENERAL SOCHIZ OF CROMLIN WAS FEELING COCKY and arrogant as he left the embassy and made his way through the crowds toward the Well Gate, pushing aside anybody who did not yield and barely paying attention to the stares. He did not care what anybody thought of him, and his great claws could cut steel rods if he were so inclined.

Josich would be so proud of him! The way they had looked as he had spoken! The way they had simply melted away as he'd strode off the platform and through the hall and out. That was *fear*, fear of power, and it felt most excellent.

When it was clear who he was, the others along the route to the Well Gate gave way and no one, not even those who were larger and looked meaner than he, impeded his triumphal march.

He turned the corner and saw the utter blackness of the Gate directly ahead, its hexagonal shape unmistakable. He was almost to it when he realized that, for this last, short stretch, there was nobody in the corridor.

He stopped suddenly, suspicious. This was the way assassins worked. Well, let them come! Let them see he was not afraid of them!

A noise caused him to turn to the wall to his right, perhaps five meters in front of the Gate. It had no form at first, but then took a humanoid shape that seemed to extrude right out of the wall. It looked like nothing even research had shown him, like a moving idol from some primitive tribe, made completely of dull, rough granitelike stone, a cartoonish, idiotic, and simplified face carved into it. Only the eyes said it was something more, the burning fire-orange eyes in the tranquil water, and the fact that it walked to him.

"Who are you who would block *me*?" the Cromlin general shouted. Both of Sochiz's forward claws went up. One snatched at the creature while the tail reared up and the syringelike point at the end struck at its head.

And broke off.

The creature reached up and, with a stony hand, held the claw immobile, then it grabbed the other as the pain of losing the stinger hit the Cromlin's body, ripping off the right claw and discarding it.

"You know my name," the creature said in a tone that could only mean it had a translator. "Let it be the last thing you or any of your brothers hear."

"What name?" the creature screamed. *"Who are you?"*

"Jeremiah Wong Kincaid," came the reply, just before the second claw was ripped away and the stone right hand of the idol-like creature punched through the face of the Cromlin right between the protruding eyes and extended antennae, and just kept going all the way into the brain.

It was a slow and messy way to die. The thing was still wriggling in its death throes long after Kincaid had stepped through the Gate and when the first of the curious traffic that had held up for now dared to look around and see what had happened, but not who the perpetrator might have been.

Ochoa,
at the Zone Gate

IT WAS CLOUDY, NOT ONLY AT THE MIDDLE LEVELS BUT ACROSS the entire sky, casting a gloomy pall over the whole central island.

The island of Bateria was dead center in the middle of Ochoa, and appeared to be one massive volcanic peak. Even underwater, where it went down almost seven kilometers into the sea bed, the great mountain called Sochi Makin, or the "Yawning God," resembled an ancient peak of the sort that truly created the others and occasionally created new ones. It came up into the air and rose across an almost sixty kilometer stretch to a collapsed crater twenty kilometers across. Inside was still a volcanic moonscape, colorful but desolate, baked in the hot sun of the day and plunging to icy cold at night, when the elevation alone controlled its temperature. In the center, though, was a single unnatural feature, a hexagonal area planted horizontally inside the crater and resembling a bottomless hole, as indeed it was.

The Royal Palace had been hewn into the side of the crater facing the rising western sun. Its spires and colorful rock made it seem a part of the mountain itself, and it stretched several kilometers across the eastern wall and rose up above the level of the crater itself, in a departure from the Ochoan norm. The way up on that side was steep and rugged, and who would dare attack the residence of the King?

Opposite, on the western wall, was the Great Hall of the Council, where the elected representatives met a few weeks out of every year to decide what needed to be decided, and which was home to a surprisingly small bureaucracy that mostly issued permits and saw to it that fees for ships' provisionings and for transit of goods were in order.

In one sense, the palace was the most vulnerable position of any important structure in the kingdom, but the Royal Guard was housed within the castle, and the National Guard—which primarily handled Customs duties, chased down disputes involving multiple districts, and the like, had received some military training and retained a military style structure—was headquartered in a village along the eastern slopes below the Grand Hall. Under normal circumstances, about 2,500 regular troops of the army and perhaps 1,500 of the National Guard were at hand, the largest single force anywhere in Ochoa and probably the only one that trained for the job.

Ochoans had fairly good eyes, but the Baron and Grand Duchess Comorro, General in Chief of the Royal Guard, as well as General Zaida, who ran the National Guard, wore special goggles with easily adjusted binocular lenses, and they could see quite well across the expanse of the crater. The Baron stood outside some small buildings just north of the Well Gate used for customs; the Grand Duchess was in full resplendent war paint and medals on the battlement atop the palace, the General on the flag court just above the entrance to the Great Hall. Each had a signalman with him or her, and each was in constant contact, all being more or less in line of sight.

A dark shape came in toward the palace below the clouds, only a few meters above the highest of the terrain, flew into the crater and landed on the Duchess's parapet. About thirty seconds later the semaphore flashed, "The most reassuring thing about the enemy is that he follows our script."

The Baron laughed. He wasn't going to kid anybody that he wasn't scared to death, but if they were forced into a fight, then so be it. The others felt the same way. In Ochoan culture it was the women who did the fighting, but he was determined that they would sing no songs of battles and bravery without his name included, even if he didn't know whether he had the nerve to stand. The King sure hadn't. He and half his entourage were cowering deep in the lava caves right now over on Island Biana.

He eased himself back into the special chair atop the customs house and raised his feet, which were also for all intents and purposes his hands, and placed them on the control bars and twin triggers of the rapid-fire, air-cooled machine gun. He'd had only a couple of days' practice on one, and they ran hot and noisy and smoky and smelled awful, but he could say it didn't take an expert to hit something with them when they put out a hundred rounds per second in a spread pattern.

The portable emplacement was similar to the permanent ones along the whole chain of castles and fortresses, designed specifically for the Ochoan anatomy and easily rotated a full 360 degrees with just a shift in body weight. In a smaller chair below him, but on the same pivot, Gia, daughter of the Lady Akua (and his) fifth wife, sat ready to feed the strips of ammunition along the belt, clear jams, and change and reload ammo canisters. Two others weren't on the pivot but were on her level on a catwalk, and could jump in and help with any operation as needed or have new canisters ready.

There were no permanent emplacements here, in the royal center, but there were quite a number of temporary ones.

Baron Oriamin felt quite proud that the Lady Akua had not been one of those who'd refused the gun tests, but was now running the defense of their castle. It wouldn't be an easy fight; although the castle was well-defended and extremely well-provisioned, that beach and port below was a real prize, and he worried a lot about rockets. He'd seen now what they could do.

He wished he was there, where he felt he should be, defending his home and family and the islanders who considered him their protector. He wished he had Nakitti here at his side, preferably at the next gun, but even as the partial architect of this entire plan, her status made it impossible for her to directly participate. She was only fifty meters or so away, and a matter transmission through the device called the Well Gate, it was true, but concubines did not fight. It simply wasn't done.

"Bombardment of sixteen ports commenced," came the word from the General's position. Each time a courier came to either of them, the relevant news was put up as quickly as possible. "Extremely heavy fighting along the coast and in immediate inland waters. Flying creatures are being employed as rocket platforms. Much loss of life. Most fliers not engaged by enemy."

Damn! He wanted to be with his own! It was frustrating sitting here, hearing all that, powerless to do anything, unable to know how much of his own holdings and how many of those he loved were still alive. He prayed that Castle Oriamin wasn't one of those being engaged, but deep down he knew it was. The enemy had seen him all too publicly at the conference. But Nakitti and that bizarre Kalindan had been right. The key wasn't in the castles nor on the beaches, the key was right here.

"Send to both positions," he commanded his own semaphore operator. "Any word from our aerial scouts?"

He knew that if there had been, they would have told him, but he just couldn't sit there and do *nothing*!

"No, Highness. No reports, but they are circling just out and above us, above the clouds. The first one that sees or hears anything will report instantly."

"I know that!" he snapped, then caught himself. "My apologies. I would rather they just show up than sit here and hear of others bleeding while we do nothing!"

They didn't reply. They understood. They were feeling much the same way themselves, and had families no less close back there.

The prediction had been that there would be concentrated attacks on the castles and positions controlling the best ports, leading to the set-down of enemy special military teams above which would establish siege lines. As messages came in, this appeared to be precisely what was happening, which was why the Duchess seemed so pleased. If they were operating as predicted, then the rest would develop, too. It was deviations from that prediction that would cause serious problems.

There were sudden sounds from above, reverberating across the crater.

"Sounds like thunder," his wife commented, looking up. "I think I can see some lightning over there."

At that moment, toward the north wall, three black shapes fell out of the clouds and plummeted to the ground.

"That's not thunder!" the Baron shouted. "Everybody to posts! Stand by! Those were some of our scouts up there dropping dead for us!" To himself, although he was never much of a religious man, he muttered a slight but fervent prayer and then thought, *Here we go!*

To have seen the pictures, and even the few training pictures taken at great risk from enemy ships and their monstrous bugs, was one thing. To see massive, shiny black triangular shapes bigger than houses drop out of the sky in vast numbers was terrifying.

"They're all around us!" somebody screamed. "By the gods! *How many of those monsters* are *there?*" It was a cross between total fear and a lament.

There were whole squadrons of the things, each arranged in triangular groups of five, and they started coming in from both the north and south, cleverly skirting what they anticipated would be big guns on the main buildings. The light artillery, however, had managed to turn the guns and were opening up all along the ridges on both sides of the Baron's position. They had a fair range and seemed to be having some effect; a few of the formations still descending suddenly saw one or even two creatures wobble and then drop out of formation. Some began crashing to earth inside the crater. Most of the occupants appeared either stunned or dead, and when the big insects hit they blew up like gigantic bombs, the shells shattering pieces in all directions.

But for every one they hit, three or four landed, their soldiers and cargo containers coming off with amazing speed and forming up into larger units as more and more landed.

Now, from the Grand Hall's entryway and the castle battlements, soldiers from both units took off, low, letting the cannon try for the creatures above the crater walls while they concentrated on the ones unloading. The Baron could see they had underestimated the efficiency of these troops and that ground time was amazingly short, but it was ground time, and that allowed the waves of Ochoans to swoop down with great speed and accuracy and each fire two small rockets down into the landing areas. Most missed, and the first troops to organize down there were already providing a withering covering fire for the others landing and disembarking, but the rockets blew up with a lot of fire and smoke, and whenever they hit one of the monstrous triangular bugs the resulting explosion was worth five direct hits by the rockets themselves. Whatever was inside those things was under tremendous pressure!

"What's our range?" the Baron shouted to anybody listening over the now ferocious din.

"They are still too far!" his wife screamed back at him. "Why not try shooting a single pass in each direction and seeing if we can't make our own target?"

He saw what she meant and cursed that neither he nor any of these military "experts" had thought about simply painting the range in.

The pattern kicked up a lot of dust at about fifteen hundred meters. Not a bad range, but then he realized that when they got within his range, he was probably within range of at least their best marksmen.

"They're bombing the palace!" somebody shouted! "Oh, and the Great Hall, too!"

They were surprised and more wounded than they had anticipated by the coordinated fire and the rocket bearers. Somebody had gotten back up and given a signal to bring some of their own flying rocket platforms in.

The attacking force was far more ungainly and not nearly as accurate as the Ochoans, who were intelligent, small, native fliers, not domesticated bugs being steered by drivers, but it was like the machine gun versus the rifle. You could hit something far better with a rifle, but if you could fire enough bullets in the right general direction, you could do more damage. This wave of rocket-launching bugs let go with twenty, thirty rockets almost at once, then veered off and up. Again, several were knocked down, but it was daunting to see some explosions strike on or very near the things, who nevertheless kept coming.

The two buildings were engulfed in smoke and flames, and outer walls shook and crumbled. The columns of the Grand Hall began to give way, and with them the flag deck above them as well.

There was now so much noise and smoke that it was impossible to tell what was happening. There was a brief break in the smoke just off the now smoking and battered palace, and a series of quick coded lights. "Still functioning," it said. "Most guns out, but they will have to dig us out."

The Baron and his unit felt some strength and confidence from that, but it didn't mean a thing in the end. A large number of the great black carriers were landing just over the wall, and on any ledges and smoothed-out areas they could. The smaller *intelligent* bugs, the Jerminians, were almost certainly forming into formidable units there and having no problems marching right up the sheer sides of the thing. They knew, however, that unlike those damned transport bugs, Jerminians were as susceptible to bullets and blasts as Ochoans were.

So far it was still playing out, but the Baron began to doubt the result. The sight of so many Ochoans dropping from the skies, and of his two national symbols being blown up and burned, gave him no comfort at all.

Were they all that confident still? They moved like it. Did they think they had large forces pinned down in the castles and the rest sealed up here, or had they suspected or seen what they should not, or had their spies tipped them? Their allies in Zone certainly had it all figured out by now, probably earlier, but how could they get the message here? Did they have the way to do it?

"In range!" somebody shouted. "Fire!"

The Baron didn't even look. He galvanized into action, put the sights on maximum range and began a back and forth 180 sweep out there in the crater. The other portable emplacements did the same, overlapping their fire, creating a deadly curtain.

In what seemed seconds he was empty, and felt panic and confusion. His wife was on it in a minute, throwing the old canister out and inserting a new one. "Closed! Fire!" she screamed, ducking down.

They were not only firing now, they were getting return fire. It sounded like a child playing with some musical toy as the bullets went *ping*! *ping*! *PING*! all around and ricocheted all over. The Baron felt a slight sting in his left side but ignored it; he kept firing, firing, and finally, through the smoke and haze, he saw the enemy advancing and the bright flashes of his and the other's fire against their shell shields. He saw many of them crumple in place and seem to collapse like a balloon with the air rushing out of them, to be walked over by others in disciplined ranks. The hard rock was creating deadly ricochets for them as well, and there were far more of them to hit.

His blood was up. He would never have suspected this feeling, this enormous rush that for the moment put fear aside because there simply wasn't time for it. "Gia! What's keeping the ammo?" he shouted, then saw her, slumped, eyes wide open but seeing nothing, her pretty body bleeding from a dozen wounds.

"*Gia*!" he shouted in anguish. You didn't die at that age, that pretty, with that much position and wealth. You didn't die save perhaps from accident, or you died ancient with your hundreds of descendants around you. People didn't die like *this*! People he knew and loved didn't die like this!

Two of the runners reached up and pulled her body unceremoniously out of the cage, and one of them leaped in and fed the next canister into the gun. "Highness! You must fire!" she screamed at him, but he just stood there, watching Gia's crumpled body below, like some horrible rag doll.

There were sudden explosions all around him, and one was so close it shook the gun and almost toppled him. He started swinging around, unable to stop or catch his balance. They were all above him, all around him! These—These *things*!

One of the runners managed to catch the lower ammo feeder and they stopped the merry-go-round, but more and more explosions were shaking them. At the far end, a bomb from one of the dark shapes above struck a gun just like his and he saw it rise into the air, as if in slow motion, and pieces of it and pieces of Ochoans flying all over, all over . . .

The runner reached up and used a wing to shake him. "Highness! We cannot stand! You must retreat! There is no purpose to your death at this point!" she shouted. Almost immediately something shot from the advancing troops struck her and he saw her chest almost explode as the projectile continued through her and opened a horrible, fatal wound. Her blood splattered all over him, and he screamed and was out of there.

As soon as the few surviving others saw the Baron leap out and glide down almost automatically to the ground, unable to fly well, and literally run right into the Well Gate, they abandoned their positions and followed suit.

An eerie, terrible clicking sound now began all around the Gate, echoing back and magnifying itself as it hit the walls and bounced back again and again. There were still some explosions, and some fire, but it was slowly coming to a halt.

The clicking grew even louder, more rhythmic, coming from the great beetlelike troops of the Jerminians. A cheer of sorts, made with stiff flightless wings and hard mandibles, a terrible, mechanistic cheer . . .

There was some fighting, apparently fierce fighting, still going on in the room-to-room conquest of the two great buildings on the inside walls, but for the most part it was over.

The forces of the New Empire held the center, and the only escape route, of the Ochoan nation.

At that news, one of the Jerminian officers left his position at the rear and moved quickly up and toward the Well Gate. "We want a basic report from all the units in immediate engagement here," he told his aides. "As soon as possible, bring in the main supplies and fortify both this area and the four points on the crater rim. Any dead bodies nobody wants to eat, our or theirs, should be thrown into the Gate. Dead, they won't be transported, they will simply be returned to energy. Move! I want you, Captain, to go through the Gate and report as quickly as possible to our ambassadors, who will be waiting there eagerly for your report."

"At once, Excellency!" the officer responded, and junior officers were suddenly on all fours, at great speed trying to reach the key battle points.

It took about an hour just to compile the handwritten preliminaries, but the results were quite good. Even so, the losses were far above expectation.

"These creatures fought extremely well and with much bravery," the General heard over and over. "Not a one surrendered. Some of the ones in the buildings used underground escape routes, and the last detachment here at the Well Gate got some of its survivors back into Zone, but that's about it. Our casualties, though, were over thirty percent. *Much* higher, and against what appears to be far lower numbers than we anticipated."

"That just means they sent off brigades to reinforce the castles under siege as we planned," the General reassured them. "Even so, I agree. When we completely subdue this place, the survivors—and there *will* be a surrender sooner or later if only to save the race from extinction—will make up the nucleus of what we've lacked up to now—a flying division." He looked over the reports, initialed them with his own distinctive digestive spit, then handed them back to the Captain. "Go now. Others will be sent as progress reports come in from elsewhere. I'd say that this is probably sufficient, though, to have one of our ambassadors serve a formal demand for unconditional surrender at the Ochoan Embassy."

The Captain gave a salute with six of its eight limbs, then walked with the dispatches toward the Well Gate, past the ruins of the last gun emplacements. It made him feel proud to see this, the absolute, total victory after only a few hours' hard fight! He was certain that the whole of his hive would also be proud, and that Her Majesty would have great rewards for the officers, perhaps even taking them into the consort, since only she could bear young. It would be an honor to consummate and then be eaten by the queen; such a one would be reincarnated as a potential queen itself!

Without hesitation, the Captain walked into the Well Gate, passed through the sensation of falling and arrival, and walked out, still going, yelling excitedly for any and all to hear, "The Imperial Army and Navy have won a great victory at O—" He suddenly slowed, looking first to one side of the corridor, then to the other. "—choa," he completed, the last almost dying in his thorax.

The corridor was lined with Ochoan soldiers looking very healthy and fully armed. They flanked both sides of the corridor and had closed in behind him, and now they seemed to stretch on and on . . .

He had no choice. Besides, he was on neutral ground, by treaty and by right. He reached the end of the corridor and turned toward the Jerminian Embassy, wishing it were a lot closer, and found his way blocked by, of all things, a Kalindan in some kind of wheelchair. He did not know it was a Kalindan, but he recognized it as a water creature.

"Come ahead, Captain," the Kalindan said. "Please, go on. We *all* want to hear your report."

Ochoan Embassy,
South Zone

NAKITTI'S HEART WAS BREAKING AS SHE TENDED TO HER Baron, unconscious and still occasionally screaming in his nightmares in the aftermath of being operated on by the Imperial Surgeon herself. She almost had a heart attack just seeing him with all that horrible blood. It turned out that most of it wasn't his, but he had several serious tears in both wings, a chunk out of his left leg—which might have to be amputated—and a serious wound in his side that had punctured a lung. With the kind of technology and research available at Zone, the Imperial Surgeon had been able to do things they could not have done back in Ochoa, but he'd lost a lot of blood and suffered a lot of damage.

Still, if he survived, a *male* with wounds like those, the Baron would have more power than any male in Ochoan history and a hell of a lot more than his uncle the King.

Curiously, Nakitti realized it didn't matter to her how much power he'd gain. He'd been so handsome; now there were nicks on that gorgeous head from ricochets, he might never walk again, and he also might never fly, if he even got the chance, since he could die from loss of blood or infection. If she could take on those injuries and leave him whole, she would gladly surrender her position, go back to that hole in the wall and live out her life in obscurity with some low slob.

The feeling, the honest devotion, surprised, even shocked, her, and would certainly have shocked and surprised anyone who knew her. Hell, maybe it was becoming female or something, she thought; but it was the Ochoan women who did the fighting, and they seemed far less sentimental than the men, and the Ghoman women were all back-stabbing cheats even worse than their men. No, it wasn't that she was female or Ochoan.

Who'd have thought it, though? That she would find something she cared more about than her own life and fortune. It was utterly incredible.

What happened even back in Ochoa was of little concern to her right now. She was going to be right here for him no matter what, and, to hell with social rank and convention, she would never leave his side again.

Ochoa,
at the Zone Gate

"WHERE ARE THOSE SUPPLY TROOPS, THE DIGGERS, AND THE reinforcements?" the General grumbled. "And what are so many of the zi'iaphods doing coming back empty and landing over there? We need to get set up here and we need to do it *now*!"

"Sir, we've just come from the empty ones returning here," a colonel replied, "and things are bad. We know where most of the missing Ochoan troops were now. While we fought it out here, waves of them fell upon our ships, which had little air cover, shooting those damned rockets and dropping some kind of containers that exploded into the kind of flames that could not be put out, some kind of chemical fire. They took out our supply ships and troop ships, and ignored the battle cruisers and frigates entirely. We got a lot of them with gunfire, but, sir, they took out more than half our supplies and over ten thousand troops— and now the zi'iaphod pilots have nowhere to land except back here on the ground. They tried putting down inland, in areas with a fair amount of vegetation and food, with the idea of feeding and watering the zi'iaphods and perhaps gathering supplies to bring here, but every time they came down, Ochoans seemed to pop up as if out of the ground and throw fragmentation grenades and shoot mortars that rained down. The only secure place for them in any numbers was back here."

"I don't like this at all," the General mumbled. "If they could do that, then they not only knew we were coming, they had to know our precise plan of battle. There's treason in the air here! Treason! And these little bastards die like great warriors even though they have no tradition of it, and they just don't quit! I don't like it. I want everyone drawn in closer to the Gate here. Leave sentries all over the top, but bring all the forces here. I smell something very nasty here, and if we are in some kind of trap, the Gate may be our only way of escape. *Move!*"

Within the clouds that did not seem to diminish all day, much to their great joy, Ochoan scouts occasionally peaked out for brief comprehensive surveys of the crater interior. For much of the day, things had gone in mop-up fashion pretty much as expected, and having the massed big bugs grounded there was an unexpected bonus. Who would have thought that even the common fishers would rise up with whatever they could get, even weapons taken off dead enemies, and fight like this?

Throughout all the land the word of the battle and of a thousand little battles spread from lowest to highest, shaming the ones who had not taken part into action themselves and filling the rest with a national and racial pride unknown in any remembered generation.

Many thousands outside of and ignorant of the grand design died needlessly but no less heroically, and no less selflessly.

Through the night they watched. Through the night small bands threw torches onto the backs of giant slugs, and bands of raiders swooped down on Jerminian beetles and spread burning fish oil and worse on them as they hunkered down. It was a horrible night for the invaders, many of whom killed more of each other than the Ochoans had.

Worse for them, inside the crater the attackers were slaughtering many of the giant transport bugs just to feed the almost five thousand troops now inside the barren region, and because the huge creatures themselves were becoming impossible to control. Creatures that size had to eat twice their own weight every day. The ships that had fed them all the way there were empty or at the bottom or both; the countryside was alive with death in the night.

In the morning the Jerminian commander found himself and his surviving troops surrounded by organized armed forces. Ochoans—*thousands* of them!—now commanded the heights, having cheerfully dispatched all the sentries above and then just as happily sent reassurances by semaphore throughout the night that all was well. Ochoans had come from other islands, from caves and from forests where they normally did not go. They came with as much guns and ammo and other weapons as they could manage. They were running low, it was true; it was doubtful they could sustain an offensive for long. On the other hand, neither could the invaders below.

"Look at them!" the Grand Duchess said, hovering above her troops. "Yesterday they invaded our land, killed our people, and reveled in their victory! Now we will make certain they cannot get harnessed up, loaded, and off. The bugs need a fair amount of space to take off, remember. Aim at the drivers and anybody else around. Without them, the things are just dumb animals. Everyone else, let's start teaching *them* what we mean by 'air superiority'! They over-reached themselves when they came to Ochoa! *Let us teach them not to come back!"*

There were shouts of blood lust and national pride, and almost spontaneously the group that could hear her began singing the anthem, which was picked up by the next closest troops until, almost as if it had been planned, it ringed the crater.

And when it was over, they began their attack.

Now it was the enemy who needed reinforcements, and because a few of the zi'iaphods were kept ready just in case, one or two got away before their area was hit, pinning down the support troops and pilots there. The mission was to get those special forces away from the castles, which were at the moment no longer vital, and bring them in before the center force was annihilated. Without the center, the Ochoans could continue to be rearmed and resupplied, battle plans could be analyzed and passed back and forth to ground and air commanders, the Ochoan wounded would get the best medical care, and the occupation would be prone to continual guerrilla warfare.

They held the center or they lost.

The special teams were having their own problems, though. These were mostly Quacksans, the larger but slower sluglike creatures. They depended as much on their much-vaunted ability to mesmerize any enemy and make it walk right to them, but even though they had surreptitiously tested the ability long ago and counted the Ochoans as vulnerable, it hadn't worked. The Ochoan soldiers in defensive positions above the castles had been wearing goggles and earmuffs that made them impervious to the power. On the other hand, the Quacksans were the perfect ground troops for napalm, and they had poor night vision and no air cover.

There wasn't much left of the Quacksans by the time the big bugs got to them, and the ones who did get on and load up found themselves under attack from the air.

The Jerminian general in charge of the center's force knew he'd been misled. The Ochoans had known *everything*! Just enough of a fierce fight to allow them to take ground that had value only because of the Gate but which could not feed the tiniest insect, and then besiege *them*! The supplies were gone, the air support was now a joke, since they were supposed to be dug in and self-supporting off the land by now, and they were faced by an increasingly huge army of fanatical natives who, when they didn't have bombs or guns or napalm, dropped *rocks* on them!

The General assembled his commanders and senior noncoms in front of the Well Gate, with things now falling from the sky so frequently that they barely noticed anymore, and almost nobody was shooting at them. They'd shot down a thousand, and two thousand more came.

"The position is untenable," he told them, stating the obvious. "I, and the senior commanders, will take responsibility for the failure, although I am certain it is treachery by one of our allies. A weak and decadent nation like this could not have become this smart and this efficient in two or three weeks. It is impossible. The cause is alive! The cause goes on! Senior commanders, assemble by that wrecked Customs house over there! We shall atone to Her Majesty there! Everyone else, organize in a proper military fashion and evacuate into the Gate. You need do only a steady march. When you arrive at the other end, simply turn, walk back into the Gate, and you will return home. *Avenge us!* Remember us! And maintain your honor and dignity as soldiers! This was a gamble, but it is only one short battle in a long campaign. We will know more and do better next time! Farewell!"

It was a great speech, and if he hadn't at that moment been struck on the head by a fair-sized rock and fallen over on his rounded back, swaying back and forth, it would have been his most memorable speech, the kind that inspired troops of the future.

So they did not move calmly toward the Gate as ordered, but instead broke and ran for the large hexagonal blackness just beyond.

The first few made it, demonstrating a state of retreat that was clearly a rout. But then the Ochoans in the corridors began systematically slaughtering them as they came through, while keeping the center open for outgoing troops.

Now, out of the Well Gate, to the cheers of the rest of the Ochoan forces, first a trickle and then a flood of fresh soldiers emerged, all well-armed and well-equipped. Those retreating invaders who didn't make the Gate were nearly eliminated by the end of the day. Those who did make it were mostly slaughtered as they entered the Zone corridor.

In the next few days the few survivors were given the opportunity to surrender and return to their ships, not via the Gate, but by boats sent by mutual agreement. The Ochoans wanted some to get back to tell the tale. Despite their victory, there had been horrendous carnage, and they did not want to go through it again.

By the end of the week it was over. Little, weak, semifeudal, silly, comic opera Ochoa, out there in the middle of nowhere gobbling fish and drinking wine, had, in a semitech environment, defeated the undefeatable, stopped the unstoppable, and, best of all, humiliated the arrogant bastards.

The people of the "New Empire" hexes knew none of this. The soldiers who did manage to return were debriefed exhaustively, then executed. News was carefully controlled and managed. The leaders declared a new wondrous victory to their people and, fuming, plotted their revenge while setting upon the highest ranks of the combined military staffs to root out the obvious traitors, for it was unthinkable that *they* might actually have overreached, that *they* were not as irresistible an object as they wholeheartedly believed.

In the palace deep within the central watery regions of Chalidang, the Empress Josich threw a homicidal fit, and personally hacked her general staff to death even though the plan had been entirely hers and implemented over their objections.

She had been this furious recently once before, over a different matter. It was when she received, via the embassy in Zone, a piece of shell from a dead Cromlin's body with words painted not in Cromlinese nor in the language of Chalidang but in the language of the family Hadun of the old empire and the Realm.

You're next, it read simply, with phonetic spelling of a non-Hadun name as the signature.

"Jeremiah," the name became when pronounced.

"Not me, Jeremiah Kincaid!" she'd been heard screaming as she tore the messenger to bits. *"Now there will be no quarter! Now we conquer or die! Now they all die! The Kalindans, that bird thing, the Ochoan—all of them! And especially you, Jeremiah! Come and get me!"*

✎ FREE DRINKS ✎

Take the Del Rey® survey and get a free newsletter! Answer the questions below and we will send you complimentary copies of the DRINK (Del Rey® Ink) newsletter free for one year. Here's where you will find out all about upcoming books, read articles by top authors, artists, and editors, and get the inside scoop on your favorite books.

Age _____   Sex ❏ M ❏ F

Highest education level: ❏ high school ❏ college ❏ graduate degree

Annual income: ❏ $0-30,000 ❏ $30,001-60,000 ❏ over $60,000

Number of books you read per month: ❏ 0-2 ❏ 3-5 ❏ 6 or more

Preference: ❏ fantasy ❏ science fiction ❏ horror ❏ other fiction ❏ nonfiction

I buy books in hardcover: ❏ frequently ❏ sometimes ❏ rarely

I buy books at: ❏ superstores ❏ mall bookstores ❏ independent bookstores
    ❏ mail order

I read books by new authors: ❏ frequently ❏ sometimes ❏ rarely

I read comic books: ❏ frequently ❏ sometimes ❏ rarely

I watch the Sci-Fi cable TV channel: ❏ frequently ❏ sometimes ❏ rarely

I am interested in collector editions (signed by the author or illustrated):
    ❏ yes ❏ no ❏ maybe

I read Star Wars novels: ❏ frequently ❏ sometimes ❏ rarely

I read Star Trek novels: ❏ frequently ❏ sometimes ❏ rarely

I read the following newspapers and magazines:

❏ *Analog*	❏ *Locus*	❏ *Popular Science*
❏ *Asimov*	❏ *Wired*	❏ *USA Today*
❏ *SF Universe*	❏ *Realms of Fantasy*	❏ *The New York Times*

Check the box if you do not want your name and address shared with qualified vendors ❏

       Name _____
     Address _____
City/State/Zip _____
     E-mail _____

                                       chalker

PLEASE SEND TO: DEL REY®/The DRINK
201 EAST 50TH STREET NEW YORK NY 10022
OR FAX TO THE ATTENTION OF DEL REY PUBLICITY 212/572-2676

DEL REY® ONLINE!

The Del Rey Internet Newsletter...

A monthly electronic publication e-mailed to subscribers and posted on the rec.arts.sf.written Usenet newsgroup and on our Del Rey Books Web site (www.randomhouse.com/delrey/). It features hype-free descriptions of books that are new in the stores, a list of our upcoming books, special promotional programs and offers, announcements and news, a signing/reading/convention-attendance calendar for Del Rey authors and editors, "In Depth" essays in which professionals in the field (authors, artists, cover designers, salespeople, etc.) talk about their jobs in science fiction, a question-and-answer section, and more!

Subscribe to the DRIN: send a blank message to
join-drin-dist@list.randomhouse.com

The Del Rey Books Web Site!

We make a lot of information available on our Web site at
www.randomhouse.com/delrey/

• all back issues and the current issue of the Del Rey Internet Newsletter
• sample chapters of almost every new book
• detailed interactive features for some of our books
• special features on various authors and SF/F worlds
• reader reviews of some upcoming books
• news and announcements
• our Works in Progress report, detailing the doings of our most popular authors
• and more!

If You're Not on the Web...

You can subscribe to the DRIN via e-mail (send a blank message to join-drin-dist@list.randomhouse.com) or read it on the rec.arts.sf.written Usenet newsgroup the first few days of every month. We also have editors and other representatives who participate in America Online and CompuServe SF/F forums and rec.arts.sf.written, making contact and sharing information with SF/F readers.

Questions? E-mail us...

at delrey@randomhouse.com (though it sometimes takes us a little while to answer).